THE
TURING
TEST

A TALE OF ARTIFICIAL INTELLIGENCE
AND MALEVOLENCE

ANDREW UPDEGROVE

The Turing Test
Copyright © 2017 by Andrew Updegrove. All rights reserved.
First Print Edition: July 2017

Starboard Rock Press
Marblehead, MA

Cover and Formatting: Streetlight Graphics

andrew.updegrove@gesmer.com
https://updegrove.wordpress.com/

ISBN: 978-0-9964919-9-0

To my sister Anne, who lived life to the fullest,
but not for long enough

By the same author:

The Alexandria Project, a Tale of Treachery and Technology

The Lafayette Campaign, a Tale of Deception and Elections

The Doodlebug War, a Tale of Fanatics and Romantics

Available in paperback and eBook at Amazon and in paperback
on order through your favorite local book store

Prologue

THE SOLES OF Jake Barr's feet were telling him something was wrong. Eighteen years on the night shift had made him sensitive to the mood of the generators, and they were growing restless.

He pressed his hand against one of them. The vibrations should be smooth. But they weren't, not quite; they were more like the ride of a car with a wheel out of balance.

Everything in the dimly lit, cavernous facility looked all right. Was it his imagination? If something was wrong, the sensors in the machines would be sending alerts to the control room.

He looked up to where the engineers worked behind the glass on the second floor. One was looking at a computer terminal. The other two were talking.

But something *was* wrong. He could feel it. And now he thought he could hear it, too. The generators were speeding up. The hum of the drive shafts was strained. Louder, too. But still, none of the engineers looked concerned.

Was that a thin haze in the air? The familiar smell of engine oil and hot metal had acquired an acrid edge. Something was getting out of control.

He strode over to the panel of old-fashioned analog dials monitoring RPMs, temperature and vibration. All the needles were rising. Some of them were already in the red zone.

He stepped back. How could everything in the control room still look normal? There should be flashing lights and alarms. He felt like the murderer in Edgar Allan Poe's *The Tell-tale Heart*, deafened by the beating of a heart only he could hear.

Now the bearings in one of the generators were shrieking. There! The guys in the control room were finally waking up. Two were staring out onto the floor. The third was darting back and forth along the wall of instruments and switches.

But the machines only ran faster. They were jolting, too. The whole building trembled each time they did. He backed up against the wall and watched, wide-eyed.

Black smoke was rising now from the generators, making it hard to breathe. The drive shaft bearings must be running dry. But how could that happen, especially to all of them at once? *Boom!* Incredibly, all the generators were rocking in unison now. He turned and ran up the stairs, into the control room, and yelled at the engineers. But they ignored him.

"I said what's happening?" he yelled again.

"How the hell should I know?" one said without turning around. "None of the controls are working. We can't even shut the damn things down!"

The tortured scream of the wildly spinning machines was deafening now. Smoke was seeping into the control room. The engineer at the computer screen looked up and pointed. "Holy hell – look at that!"

The number one generator rocked back and forth on its broken floor mounts. The lights in the control room started to flicker. "Let's get out of here," Jake yelled.

Down the stairs they ran, out of the building and into the parking lot. Huffing from the exertion, they listened to the muffled sounds of the generators tearing themselves apart. It was like a scene from hell, with the cries of the damned mixing with the black wraiths of coal smoke spiraling up, lit from below by the angry red glow streaming from the windows of the generator room. And all they could do was watch.

1

You Dirty Rat

Thus the first ultraintelligent machine is the last invention that man need ever make, provided that the machine is docile enough to tell us how to keep it under control.

Alan Turing colleague I. J. Good, 1965

The question is not whether intelligent machines can have any emotions, but whether machines can be intelligent without any emotions.

Marvin Minsky, 1988

FRANK AMBLED AROUND his living room, a puzzled expression on his face. How could he not find his sunglasses? They were probably lying around in plain sight. The angry voice echoing around the room wasn't helping his concentration either. Where the heck could he have put those glasses?

The room was suddenly silent, and he stopped in his tracks. What was the last thing he'd heard?

He grabbed the phone and took it off speaker mode. "I'm sorry, Ms. Cornwall. I didn't quite catch that last question?" Son of a gun! His sunglasses had been right next to the phone all along.

"I said how did you catch my husband?"

It had been easy. He knew from Ms. Cornwall that her husband liked to spend an hour or two each morning working at a local coffee shop. No, she didn't think he had a portable cellular connection for his laptop. Yes, she could email Frank a picture of him.

The next day Frank settled in at the same coffee shop with his own laptop. Predictably, the mom-and-pop business had a wide-open router. Before his hapless prey finished his latte, Frank had recorded enough compromising chat and video to make Anthony Weiner blush.

"I was able to intercept your husband's email at the coffee shop he visits. What I sent you last night is a sampling of what he and Cindy Dymples were exchanging."

The mention of her husband's administrative assistant set Ms. Cornwall to ranting once again. When she finally ran down, Frank told her he was sorry that he'd confirmed her suspicions. Yes, he'd send her his bill by the end of the week.

He pulled on a sweatshirt and clattered down the stairs and out onto the sidewalk. The cool air hitting his face as he broke into a trot was a relief after the tirade he'd just endured. Maybe he'd do an extra mile today to flush his mental systems clean.

But by the time he was completing his wide, half-moon sweep behind the Washington Monument, he was feeling worse instead of better. How many more ho-hum assignments like this could he tolerate? They paid the bills but provided no challenge. And nobody was ever happy when he was done.

But what right did he have to complain? He had the reputation – but not the resources – to attract clients with interesting problems. Big companies wanted a rapid-response team of engineers, lawyers, and PR spin doctors to contain and fix all the damage when they were hacked. He had neither the skill nor the stomach to hire and manage a posse like that.

As he plodded back up the stairs after his run, he wondered when, or for that matter whether, he'd get another project from the CIA. When had he finished his last one? Seven months ago? Eight?

He hung a towel around his neck, picked up his computer tablet, and slid open the door to his tiny balcony. The landlord hadn't invested much in converting the seedy old apartment building into condos. But he had sprung a few bucks to add a token amount of outdoor space to each unit. Frank was surprised how much he appreciated the postage stamp of a balcony, especially for cooling off after his morning run.

He settled in and started skimming the news. What had the world been up to overnight? Things had settled down politically after the party conventions; but that wouldn't last. The Middle East was a mess, as usual.

Then he stopped and held the tablet closer. This looked interesting. Three power plants had suffered severe damage after their engineers lost control of the generators. That sounded familiar. The CIA had famously succeeded in causing just such an event by hacking into the computers of a power plant back in 2007. A real black hat must have pulled off a similar exploit now!

He put the tablet down and tapped his fingers on his knee. The power plants were domestic, so they weren't on the CIA's turf. But given the prior staged attack, the CIA would certainly be consulted. Maybe his old boss George Marchand could help him get his foot in the door.

He shot off an email and spent the rest of the day fretting. Marchand replied eventually, promising to see what he could do.

* * *

A day later, Frank's early morning email included one from George. Could he be at the headquarters of the National Security Agency at 10:00 AM? Yes, he could. Assuming his seldom-used, last-millennium heap of a car rose to the challenge.

At 9:00 AM he uttered a silent prayer before turning the key in the ignition. The starter motor cranked the engine through three agonizingly slow rotations. The fourth time around, the engine caught. He set a course for Fort Meade, twenty-five miles distant from downtown Washington.

The traffic gods were kind, and with fifteen minutes to spare, he presented himself at the reception desk inside OPS2A, the big, boxy, black-glass building where most of the NSA's Operations Directorate work.

"Frank Adversego, here to see Major Tong. I've got a ten o'clock appointment."

The guard held Frank's security clearance card up to confirm Frank's face matched the one on the card. Then he typed Frank's name into his computer and studied the screen before handing back the card.

"Thank you, Mr. Adversego. Please look into the camera."

Frank did, and the guard handed him a clip-on tag with a grainy, unflattering picture printed above his name. "Please take a seat. Someone will come to escort you."

Frank perched on the edge of a couch and reached for his phone before remembering not to bother. The one-way glass walls of the building were sheathed with a thin, transparent, copper-based film to prevent radio signals from getting in or out. He put his phone back in his pocket and waited, both feet tapping, until he saw a young man striding his way across the reception area.

"Mr. Adversego?"

"Yes?"

"Pleased to meet you. I'll escort you to Major Tong's office."

Frank was surprised to find himself in an elevator going down several floors rather than up. Then they walked for what must have been five minutes. Clearly, the underground office space went far beyond the footprint of the building aboveground. Finally, his guide knocked on one of the countless doors lining a last, long corridor.

"Frank Adversego to see you, Major."

A professional-looking young woman with jet-black hair rose to greet him. "Pleased to meet you, Mr. Adversego. Please sit down and make yourself comfortable."

Making himself comfortable around strangers was not a skill Frank had been born with, or ever acquired thereafter. He did his best not to fidget as the major paged slowly through the contents of the open file folder that was the only item on her large desk. "You have an impressive record, Mr. Adversego," she said, looking up at last. "I see that you've done some very interesting work, both with government agencies as well as, shall I say, in spite of them? What sort of projects are you working on right now?"

An honest answer would have been "playing net nanny for naughty adults," but that wouldn't do. He settled for "I'm doing work in the private sector these days."

"With a cybersecurity company?"

"No, on my own. I guess you could say I'm the cyber-equivalent of a private detective."

"I see. I understand that an item in the news led you to contact Mr. Marchand, at the CIA."

"Yes – the cyberattacks on the power plants. It sounds like the kind of exploit we've been expecting for years, and now it's finally happened."

"What do you know about the incidents?"

The question surprised Frank. Then it occurred to him there might be more to this interview than an exploration of his professional credentials. For all the major knew, he was a foreign agent, security clearance and prior service as a CIA contractor notwithstanding.

"Nothing more than I've read online."

"That's it? Then why did you reach out, based on no more than that?"

"I suppose I like challenges, especially new and difficult ones. Most of the work that comes my way in the private sector is pretty repetitive."

The major tapped her desk with the middle finger of her right hand. Then she flipped through the file until she found what she was looking for.

"According to your file, you can't always be trusted to do exactly what you're told to do. Would you agree with that statement?"

"I guess I'd phrase it a little differently."

"How?"

"Well, if I find that sticking to the strict letter of my directions would stop me from accomplishing the task I've been assigned, I'll opt for accomplishing the task."

She frowned slightly while maintaining eye contact. Her finger started tapping again.

"It also says you're not much of a team player and work best when you're on your own. How about that assessment?"

"I guess I couldn't disagree with that."

More tapping and staring. "And a loner?"

"I've always been something of an introvert," he said, shifting in his chair.

How much more of this would there be? Would Major Tong ask him to confirm his complete lack of fashion sense next?

After another pause, the major smiled. "Then you should fit right in here. Are you free for the rest of the morning?"

"Yes – for the rest of the day, actually."

"Good." She stood up. "The first briefing of the power station attack response team is about to start. Please follow me."

More hallways and doors. Then into a room filled with chairs facing a podium and a screen. Frank watched as the room filled; a few people were in uniform. Someone entered and began fiddling with the projector control on the podium. When he was satisfied, he addressed the room.

"Okay, folks. Let's get started. For anyone who's new, my name's Jim Barker, and I'll be the manager of this response team. I'd like to kick things off by reviewing what we know. Don, can you dim the lights? Great – thanks."

The screen lit up with a long view of what looked like a typical power plant.

"This is the Sea Breeze power station. It's big – over 200 megawatts. And it's not very old, which is too bad, because there are lots of old, inefficient plants about to be retired. The evidence so far suggests each attack was generally similar, so I'll use this one as a stand-in for the rest."

He switched to an interior view. "Here's the generator room. Seems pretty normal from this distance, but let's take a closer look."

Now they were looking at the partially disassembled end of one of the machines, and Barker was wielding a laser pointer. "This is one of the generators undergoing scheduled maintenance a few weeks ago."

He gave the controller another click, and the screen split into two images. "Here's that shot again on the left, and on the right, you see the same generator as it looks now." The red laser dot zigzagged back and forth across the screen like an irate Tinker Bell. "The electromagnet wire wrappings on the left are clean and bright. Over on the right, they get darker and blacker as you move in towards the armature – that's the axle of the generator, if you will. And when you look at this main bearing with its housing removed on the left – let's zoom in – you can see the bearings are shiny and greasy. But over on the right now, they're charred and black."

The display switched to a schematic diagram of the same generator. Barker used his pointer to highlight half a dozen dots. "These represent sensors. Some monitor vibration, some temperature, some alignment, and so on. They're state-of-the-art, wireless units that can talk to each other and report their status to the control room. Except in this case, they didn't.

"So, what happened? It appears there were four separate interventions. First, the attacker cut contact between the generator sensors and the monitoring software in the control room. Second, he stopped the flow of lubricating oil to the armature bearings. Third, he opened the drains in the bearing cases, allowing the oil already there to seep away. And fourth, he seized control of the valves that regulate the amount of steam entering the turbines that spin the generators.

"From what we've pieced together, here's the sequence in which those actions occurred. At 2:40 AM local time, the attacker blocked the sensor system, and at 2:41 AM he shut down the lubricating system and opened the drains to the oil sumps. Then, at 2:56 AM, the attacker began gradually increasing the flow of steam into the turbines, a process that ended at 3:06 AM when the maximum possible flow had been achieved.

"The turbines were now spinning the generators at a speed far greater than they were designed to handle. With the oil now drained away, the bearings began to overheat. When they got hot enough, they burned off what little oil was left.

"Now comes the really interesting part. Once the generators were red-lining, the attacker started flipping the generator emergency brakes on and off. Kind of like what happens when the automatic skid control system in your car kicks in after you hit an ice patch. Except a spinning generator has a heck of a lot more momentum, so the effect was violent. If you time the on-off switching just right – and the attacker obviously did – it can set up a back-and-forth rocking force that amplifies the effect every cycle. That's what caused the rocking motion the engineers observed. Eventually, some of the generators broke completely free from their floor mounts.

"That takes us to the damage report, which is also impressive. Let's look at the list on the screen. Armature bearings destroyed on every generator. One or more floor mounts damaged on every generator. Two generators pulled free completely before their bearings seized up. Armature windings on every generator will require replacement. Varying degrees of damage to the turbines. Generator building presumed to be structurally unsafe until a full evaluation of vibration damage can be performed. Plus, damage to various related equipment, feeds, and structures.

"The bottom line: no power will be generated at this plant for at least eighteen months. Early word from Japan and India is that damage there is comparable. And the CIA has picked up indications the attackers hit more than one power station in China and at least one in Russia as well."

Frank sat up straighter at that. He'd assumed the most likely attacker was Russia, given the sour state of Russo-U.S. relations and how much cyber mischief it had already caused. But what did the U.S., Russia, China, India, and Japan have in common that could provoke a coordinated attack? And who might have a grudge against those specific countries?

"Any questions so far?

Several hands went up.

"Okay – Bill?"

"Any readout on how the attacker got to the control systems?"

"Not yet. So far, we've found nothing that looks like a successful phishing attack. Our friends in Japan say the same thing."

That was significant. Frank would have expected that the hacker gained access when a careless employee opened a file attached to an email that appeared to come from a co-worker. Except that it really came from the attacker, and the attachment that looked like a Word document was really a packet of malware that installed itself as soon as it was opened. A "phishing attack" like that was the easiest way to get inside a target's firewall.

Barker pointed to someone on the other side of the room. "Okay, over there; sorry – I don't know your name."

"Was there anything in common among all the targets? Same operating software, or something like that?"

"Good question. What's remarkable is how different each of the targets is. The Japanese plant uses different control software than the U.S. facilities. The plant in India was old and used software custom-developed just for it. And it's safe to assume the plants in Russia and China were each running different systems as well."

Now, Frank was really impressed. That meant whoever was behind the attacks had to find and exploit a different vulnerability at each plant, and then figure out how to take control of that system once it was inside. That suggested a large team, and therefore a state actor.

"Okay. We've got time for one more question. Susan?"

"Any guesses yet who might be behind the attacks?"

"Not a clue. The selection of countries is too diverse, and none of the attacks fits the profile of anything we've seen before."

"Impressive piece of hacking," Frank said to the major as she led him up to the podium at the end of the meeting.

"Very. Let me introduce you to Jim Barker."

"Jim, this is Frank Adversego. Frank seems to have recruited himself on to your team."

Frank's ears burned as Barker gave him an enthusiastic hand shake. "Happy to have you on board! I know of your role in the North Korean crisis, of course – even read your book – but I wasn't aware of your other escapades until I reviewed your file. You've never worked with the NSA before, is that right?"

"Not directly, no."

"Why don't you come back to my office, and I'll put you in our operational picture. Major, does that work for you?"

"He's all yours till 11:30. Then I've got to let personnel do their thing."

"Excellent. Frank, come with me."

Twenty minutes later, Barker finished briefing Frank. "So, that's the big picture. Any questions?"

"Thanks – just one, for now. How do you see me fitting into the team?"

"According to your file, you're a bit of a Lone Ranger. Is that right?"

"Uh – yes. I guess that's not a bad way of putting it. In the past, I've kind of been a fly on the wall of the project team rather than having specific duties."

"That approach paid off before, so let's do the same. What did that mean as far as logistics were concerned?"

"Each time I had access to all reports and data. In my last project, I sat in on weekly team meetings. I also had access to Agency domain experts who weren't on the team. Oh, and they assigned someone on the project team to work with me directly. The only inefficient part was traveling to CIA headquarters in Langley to read anything that was classified. Which was just about everything useful."

"Where do you live?"

"In the District."

"In that case I can help you out. We've got a SCI facility downtown with direct access to everything we have here. You can go there any time you want. As for a principal contact, let me give a little thought to who I should pair you with. In the meantime, I'll have someone grant you access to all the investigation materials and to the downtown facility. That way you can start getting up to speed immediately."

Barker looked at his watch. "And I guess that's about all we have time for. I'll ask my admin to show you the way to personnel so they can put you on the payroll." He stood up and extended his hand again. "Looking forward to working with you."

2

The How and the Why of It

FRANK CLIMBED THE Metro escalator and followed the street numbers up the avenue to the northwest. He found his destination two blocks away, sandwiched between a dress store and a restaurant. He smiled at the listing when he found it between two staid business names: the Helena Blavatsky Theosophy Reading Room. Who had come up with that one? He pressed the intercom button and waited to be buzzed into the foyer.

Stepping off the elevator, he saw a single glass door. Inside was a room filled with floor-to-ceiling bookcases, mission-style chairs with port-wine leather upholstery, and a long table with green library lamps. An elderly man in a tweed jacket and bow tie sat in one of the chairs. Frank wondered whether he was alive or just another prop.

He opened the door and approached the reception desk. Above it was a large portrait of a dourly dressed middle-aged woman with a broad face and large, somber eyes. Obviously, that was Madame Blavatsky. Beneath the portrait was another middle-aged woman with a pair of glasses hanging from a beaded chain around her neck. She looked much more pleasant. He said hello and handed her a card provided by the NSA personnel department.

"Welcome, Mr. Cerf," she said, standing up to shake his hand. "I'm always pleased to meet a new member." The elderly gentleman turned their way and peered at Frank over the top of his glasses; he was real after all. "Perhaps you'd like to see the rare book collection?" the librarian continued.

"I'd like that very much, thank you."

Frank followed her to a door where she inserted his card into a reader set in the wall. Inside were several lockers, an elevator door, and a desk with what looked like a Bureau of Motor Vehicles eye exam camera mounted above it.

"The lockers are for anything electronic or photographic you have with you."

"Just my phone," Frank said, placing it inside. "Just curious – does anyone ever buzz you to ask who Helena Blavatsky was?"

"Not often. None of the other businesses on the building registry exist. Once someone who knew about theosophy insisted on coming upstairs. He even asked how to become a member."

"What did you say?"

"That he needed to be recommended by a member and that the membership list is private."

"Well, that was an honest answer. Who's the old gent out front then?"

"Probably a retired NSA agent who likes to get out of the house. Or whose wife wants him to. He adds a nice touch of credibility, don't you think?"

"Quite." Frank sat down and rested his chin on the little saddle in front of the camera. When the device confirmed that the retina it had just scanned belonged to Frank Adversego, the elevator door slid open.

Frank wondered at all the cloak-and-dagger precautions as the elevator door closed. Covert meetings must also be held here. Or maybe all the folderol was just to impress visiting members of Congress. Two floors down, he stepped out.

Frank was familiar with Sensitive Compartmented Information Facilities – SCIFs in the acronym-obsessed world of the government. He was pleased to see this one was more than usually comfortable. The main room was filled with work spaces with oversize computer screens. Behind glass walls he could see a small kitchen, two meeting rooms, and a security guard watching multiple video screens. Cameras linked to those screens would allow the guard to monitor Frank's activities anywhere he went inside the facility. Other than the guard, Frank was the only person there. He gave a small, self-conscious wave, and the guard gave him a bored nod back.

Frank sat down and booted up one of the computer terminals that would allow him to connect directly to the main NSA computer system. That network was "air-gapped," meaning it had no connections to the Internet and the Web. That made it difficult for an enemy to hack directly into the network from outside. The SCIF

Frank was sitting in was similarly shielded and separated from the Internet. The only thing he would be able to connect to was the NSA network, via a dedicated fiber optic cable running between the two locations.

He settled in with satisfaction; what more could he want? No distractions, free coffee, and a direct line to infinite banks of information served by some of the most powerful super computers on earth. And he could start delving into whatever nefarious game was afoot.

* * *

Stepping out of the SCIF late that afternoon, Frank was better informed but no wiser. All the data suggested the attacker had exploited "zero-day" flaws to gain access to the power plant control systems. In other words, vulnerabilities not known to exist prior to the attack.

If that was true, a lot of other power stations might also have been penetrated and compromised, since many used the same software as one or another of the targeted plants. Frank wondered how many that might be. Tens? Hundreds? Maybe even thousands, vulnerable to destruction at any time at the whim of the attacker.

He was particularly intrigued by one piece of information: not one of the attacks had caused a blackout. Each one had been launched in the middle of the night, giving power grid managers time to reallocate reserve capacity from elsewhere before demand spiked in the morning. And there had been no injuries, probably because only night watchmen and reduced control room staff were on duty.

That was very odd. Why would anyone stage such difficult and sophisticated attacks if the goal wasn't to wreak maximum havoc? It didn't fit any known attack profile. Could the attacks have been some kind of trial run? But that didn't make sense either, because now the attacker had tipped his hand. Security experts were working overtime at power plants around the world to fix the types of flaws the attacker had exploited. If the same enemy wanted to strike power plants again, it would need to find new vulnerabilities to exploit.

It just didn't add up.

* * *

The next day, Frank was back at the SCIF engrossed in the details of the India power plant incidents. The destruction there had been particularly great and the attacks unusually clever.

"Frank?"

He looked up, startled. Of course – he was supposed to meet his NSA contact today. He stood up and accepted the outstretched hand.

"Yes – you must be Shannon Doyle."

"That's right. Pleased to meet you."

"You too. And thanks for meeting me here. I appreciate that."

"Not at all. I live in town, too. And I'm thrilled to meet you – I read your book right after it came out." She looked around the room. "Nice little place you've got here. And all to yourself, except for your minder back there."

"I can't complain. Would you like a cup of coffee or something?"

"Sure – thanks. I'll set up in that conference room." She watched him walk away. He was in good shape but needed someone to shop for him. Maybe pick and lay out his clothes, too.

Frank put a miniature coffee canister in the machine in the kitchen and looked across to the conference room. Shannon was slim and tall – probably as tall as he was – with tied-back red hair. Probably a half dozen years younger than he was. He picked up the cup and joined her.

"Here you go. I forgot to ask how you take it. Can I get you any cream or sugar?"

"Black is just right, thanks. Oh – before I forget …" She reached down to pull something out of her bag and, with a big smile, slid it across the table. "Would it be rude of me to ask you to autograph your book?"

Frank looked down at the familiar, flashy cover with a rocket soaring upward, silhouetting a running figure. Why had he let the publisher pick the cover design?

"Oh, sure." He signed his name, thinking as always it would be more honest to suggest she get his co-author's autograph instead.

"How'd you learn to write so well?" Shannon asked. "Engineers like us aren't exactly known for that."

"Uh, to tell the truth, my 'co-author' wrote the whole thing."

"Oh, well," she said, "the important thing is what you did, not who wrote about it."

"Well, he embellished it a bit here and there, too. Anyway," he added quickly, "thanks again for meeting with me. What's your role on the project team?"

"I'm a systems analyst," she said. "I've been tracking global power grid sabotage to see what types of attacks are gaining momentum."

"Is there much to track?"

"A lot, of all different types. Thousands of incidents a year, in fact. Most are just vandalism. But every now and then, there's a big one you need to take more seriously. 2014, for some reason, was particularly busy. Someone in California took out a power substation without ever getting near it. He just spent ten minutes shooting a rifle through the chain link fence and hitting the transformers in just the right places. If someone used the same approach at enough substations, they could take the grid down across the entire country. And in Belgium, someone sabotaged a turbine in a nuclear power station. The operators had to shut it down for repairs that took months to complete. Those are just samples."

"How about cyberattacks?" Frank said.

"Nowhere near so many of those. Maybe because there's so much undefended infrastructure out in the open you can blow up, burn, or bang away at. But I track those, too. So, what can I tell you about the project?"

"Here are a few of the things I'm curious about," Frank said. "Why do we think the hacker hit the specific targets he did? Why in these particular countries? Why not others, or more, or fewer? And why only one wave of attacks?"

"All good questions," Shannon said. "But if there are any answers yet, I don't know them. Our project team focuses on the how, not the why."

"Really? Why's that?"

"It's just the way we're organized. We hand our findings and data off to another team of specialists. Their job is to integrate it with data from other sources and then look for patterns and clues. Whatever they find, they share with the appropriate agencies, like Homeland Security."

"Ah."

"You look disappointed," Shannon said.

"I guess I am. The how is interesting but not nearly as much as the why and the who. If we knew what the goal behind the attacks was, it would be easier to guess who was behind them and where he might strike next."

"But we still need to figure out the how so we can stop them from doing it again," Shannon said.

"Fair enough. I guess I just like to work on the whole puzzle, not just a piece of it."

"From what I understand, you've got the freedom to go wherever you want on this project," Shannon said. "Mind if I join you?"

* * *

The late afternoon sun broke through the clouds, flooding the parking lot in bright light. Clay Chambers readjusted his camera settings for the third time. It was bad enough crisscrossing the state every day to film boring local events. They could at least start on time now and then. He checked his watch. The sun would set in half an hour, and he hadn't brought any lights.

He picked up his handheld video camera and re-checked his angle and field of view. The TV station would catch hell if viewers could tell no one was listening to the governor except the mayor and a few oil company executives and newspaper photographers. Okay! They were finally getting started. He hefted the camera to his shoulder and started recording.

A SandPro Oil vice president stepped up to a podium positioned so the huge new refinery would provide an effective backdrop. Chambers had to admit it was a good one. Glittering lights dotted exhaust stacks rising above a maze of vertical and horizontal pipes, and the setting sun was giving a warm, orange glow to the steam venting from the stacks. It looked like the perfect marriage of progress, technology, and the future. Okay, the guy was about to start speaking. Microphone on, and now ... here we go.

"It's a great pleasure to welcome everyone here on this exciting occasion. As you know, we've been looking forward to this day for a very long time. Fifteen years ago this last Monday, in fact. That's when we finalized the route for the pipeline that's about to deliver tar sands oil for the first time to the new, state-of-the-art refinery you see behind me. It took most of that time to buy the land and get the permits, and then, of course, we had to build the pipeline itself – all twelve hundred and forty-three miles of it – from Canada to where we're standing today.

"But those weren't the only challenges. Coming up with the technology to process tar sand oil was also a major achievement. And then, of course, there were the environmentalists. They tried to stop us every step of the way. But we persevered. That's why, today, I can invite Governor Buddy Sandow to step forward and turn the valve that will allow oil to travel the last hundred yards to our brand-new refinery. When he does, you'll see it spin up into action, and we'll be off to the races.

"Governor, it's a great honor. If there are some thoughts you'd like to share first, we'd be honored to hear them."

Sandow strode into camera view, beaming broadly and waving to the crowds who weren't there. He had less hair and more girth than during his college days. But he still looked enough like the state university football star he'd once been to appeal to voters.

"Thanks very much, Glenn. And sure, just a few words. I know you guys are champing at the bit to get that oil flowing. So, I'll just say that we're mighty pleased you chose our great state as the destination for your new pipeline and the site for this terrific refinery. And I must add I'm as proud as I can be I played a major part in bringing over six hundred and fifty great, high-paying jobs to this hardworking community. Six hundred and fifty jobs! These are good people here, and they deserve those jobs. This is the kind of decisive action I promised the voters, and by golly, that's what my administration and I are delivering right here today. So, what do you say, let's go put those people to work!"

"You bet!" the vice president said. "Let's do it!" He escorted the governor to a large control wheel; a burly pipeline worker was standing next to it, ready to help Sandow. Chambers panned his camera out to get more of the refinery into the picture as the governor placed his hands on the wheel and struck a pose.

"Everybody ready now?" the vice president asked. "Okay, Governor! Take it away!" With a flourish, Sandow followed along as the pipeline worker spun the wheel.

The lights on the refinery went dark. The venting steam diminished, too. Within a few seconds, it disappeared entirely.

Sandow was still smiling, wondering why the newspaper photographers weren't taking his picture. Then he realized from their expressions that something was wrong. Turning around, he saw that far from spinning up, the refinery had gone dark. Everything turned dull and dead as the sun dropped below the horizon.

Chambers grinned, video camera still recording. This had turned out to be a shoot worth waiting for.

* * *

"So, what do you think?" Frank asked Shannon as they left the latest incident briefing. "Impressed?"

"For sure," she replied. "Eighteen major refinery complexes taken down. And if the U.S. ones are typical of those abroad, the attacker hit the biggest ones in the world. How long do you expect it will take to get them up and running again?"

"When? How about if?"

"If? How could it be if?"

"Well, that's a bit of an exaggeration, but not much. From what we just learned, they didn't just shut the refineries down – they erased all their software and their data, too. And by all their software and data, I mean ALL their software and data. On-site, in the cloud, backup copies – the works. The refinery process control systems, the security software, the operating history and performance records – everything. A lot of those programs, particularly for the older refineries, were custom software or heavily adapted for the location. And without the historical operating data to work from, it's going to be trial and error getting some parts of an operation up and running again.

"That's a pretty impressive hack," he mused. "Whoever is behind these attacks is world class." Then he frowned. "And I still don't have a clue who it could be."

3

Click!

F RANK FLIPPED THROUGH the incident data for the umpteenth time. There had been more waves of attacks, all presumably perpetrated by the same actor. But all they had in common was that all the targets had something to do with energy and all the damage was severe.

Historically, hackers bent on serious mischief had usually launched "dedicated denial of service" attacks. That meant directing massive amounts of traffic against their victims' websites to overwhelm them. While that sort of attack was troublesome, it was easy to get everything up and running again as soon as the attack ended. Not so with these new exploits. It would take months, and even years, to make the necessary repairs. Frank drummed his fingers in annoyance.

Shannon looked up from her computer. She'd gotten in the habit of working at the SCIF whenever Frank was there. "No light bulb yet?"

"No light bulb. How about you?"

"No, but remember, that's not my assignment. I'm reviewing and associating incident data for others to work with."

"Will you know if the NSA comes up with a motive for the attacks or a guess who's behind them?"

"Sure, and so will you. Maybe not immediately, but yes. That'll be shared with the team."

"Hmm." He went back to focusing on his screen.

"Not good enough?" Shannon asked.

"Well, I'm glad to hear it will filter down to us. What's really bugging me is that no pattern or obvious goal is jumping out at me other than disrupting the energy supply."

"Why isn't that enough?"

"Because there's got to be more to it. Why the specific countries? They're literally all over the map. And why the specific targets? Attacking each one requires a different strategy and exploiting a different vulnerability. And why cause the least disruption rather than the most?"

He went back to staring at the screen and then stood up.

"Coffee?" he asked.

"Sure."

When he came back, he set a cup next to her and immediately began frowning at his computer again.

"Thanks," she said. And then "thanks" again. Still no response. She made a megaphone with her hands and intoned, "Earth to Mars; Earth to Mars; calling Commander Adversego."

Startled, he turned her way. "What did you say?"

She laughed. "Doesn't matter. I was just curious what you were thinking."

"Oh. Well, while I was making the coffee, it struck me that maybe trying to figure out what the incidents have in common is looking at the problem backwards. Maybe I should be looking at what they don't have in common."

"Meaning what?"

"Well, I've been focusing only on what's been hit. Maybe something would become clear if I looked at what wasn't hit, but just as easily could have been."

"Interesting. Any examples?"

"Sure. The attacker hit a lot of different types of targets in more than a dozen countries. But there are other kinds of power infrastructure – like high-voltage transmission lines – he hasn't. Why not those? And while he's hit a lot of different power plants in some countries, same observation – there are far more he hasn't touched. Why not? If I can't figure out what's the same about the targets he has hit, maybe there's something the rest have in common that could provide a clue." He frowned and turned to look at his computer screen again.

She would have asked him another question, but she could see he was once again somewhere else. She watched him frowning, reading, and typing away for a while before she got back to work.

* * *

Frank never accepted dinner invitations. That policy had succeeded brilliantly, with the result that he hadn't received any during the current century, except from his only daughter, Marla. Those he accepted with pleasure, which was how he found himself eating dinner with her and her husband, Tim, the following Saturday night.

"Well, I think the guy's a walking disaster," Frank's daughter Marla said.

"No kidding," Frank said. "It makes no sense that the guy keeps rising in the polls. You can guess what my theory to explain that would be."

"Of course. But let's say this time he wins. The number of policies and programs he could change would be huge. Huge! Just to give one example, he's never said one way or another whether he believes in climate change. If he wants to, he could walk away from the new Berlin Accords, where the commitments to reduce greenhouse gas emissions are binding instead of voluntary. And the process isn't working very well as it is."

"You mean countries are backing out?" Tim asked. "I hadn't heard that."

"Not backing out. But they're not all stepping up to the plate the way they should, either. Look at China. They were making a lot of progress switching over to renewable energy and nuclear power. But now, to get people working again, they're recommissioning some of the coal-fired power plants they shut down not long ago. And the latest estimates say the increase in global greenhouse gas emissions isn't slowing down as much as hoped."

"Well, at least it's slowing down some," Tim said.

"That's not good enough," Marla replied. "If any of the big CO_2 emitters miss their targets, other countries might slack off, too. That would be bad. But if one of the big five countries backs out of the treaty completely, it would be a disaster even if every other country stayed in line."

"So, who are the big five?" Tim asked. "The U.S., China ... I'm guessing India would be next, plus who – Germany and Great Britain?"

"Good guesses, but they're a bit farther down the list. The other two are Russia and Japan."

"Interesting," Tim said. "I should have thought of Japan, but I would have guessed Germany was in the top five."

"Don't forget Russia has close to twice as many people," Marla said. "And Germany's got an up-to-date industrial base, not to mention one of the most aggressive programs to convert to renewable energy. A lot of factories in Russia are left over from the Soviet era, and Russia doesn't have clean air regulations like they do in Europe."

"Now you've got me curious," Tim said. "I wonder who the next worst countries are?" He fetched his smartphone and Googled up a table of the global warming emissions of every country.

"Wow – only a few other countries emit more than even one half percent of the global total each. Most release under a tenth of one percent! So, let's see how much the big five add up to ... it looks like China generates a little over twenty percent of the total; shame on us, we contribute almost eighteen; Russia is next with about seven and a half; India produces just over four; and Japan is at almost four. So, in all, that adds up to ... looks like about 52%. That's even more than I thought – five countries produce more than half of all the greenhouse gases responsible for climate change."

"Just as I said," Marla replied. "So, if any of them slack off or, worse yet, walks on the deal, we're in big trouble." She turned to her father. "You're awfully quiet for a change. Cat got your tongue?"

4

By George, I Think He's Got it!

"SO, YOU THINK whoever is behind the attacks is trying to stop global warming single-handed?" Shannon asked.

"That's right," Frank replied. "It seems to fit the facts perfectly. Once I started looking at the data from that perspective, everything fell into place. And there've been enough attacks now to start drawing some conclusions."

"What made you think of global warming?"

"Remember the first incident? The one where the generators at the power plants were destroyed? The countries involved besides the U.S. were China, India, Japan, and Russia. Those four countries, along with us, produce more than half of all greenhouse gas emissions. And if you look at the number of attacks per country, the data supports the same conclusion: five plants shut down in China, four in the U.S., two in Russia, and one each in Japan and India. That's roughly in proportion to the percentage of greenhouse gas emissions each of those countries produces."

"Interesting, but couldn't that be just a coincidence?"

"Standing alone, yes. But there's more. First off, every single one of those power plants was coal fired."

"I agree that's consistent with your theory. But it's still a big leap to say that whoever is doing this is trying to save the world single-handed."

"Why not? They clearly weren't trying to create havoc – just the opposite. If they were trying to make a statement to motivate action, they'd cause as much disruption as possible, and then go public and threaten to keep attacking unless countries get more serious about stopping climate change. Right?"

"Well, okay, I guess so. But just because that could be the answer doesn't mean it is."

"Very true. But how about this? Each time there's been an attack, it's coincided with news of some sort relating to climate change. Just before the first power plant event, an international meeting between the same five countries that might have led to accelerating reductions fell apart. The latest set of attacks hit China the same day it came to light that the Chinese government was recommissioning a bunch of coal-fired power plants. And how about this: the impact of every event was always severe. A power plant can't use any coal while its generators are down, and a refinery without software can't handle any oil.

"If we pool the emissions data from all the attacks and analyze it from this perspective, I bet they'll show each wave of attacks was scaled to offset whatever the latest bad climate change news was."

"So, I assume that's what you'd like to do?" Shannon said. "See how strongly the data supports your theory?"

"You bet. Can you help me access the resources at the NSA I'll need to do that?"

"Sure. That's what I'm here for."

"Excellent! So, here's what I'm going to need …" Shannon took notes enthusiastically as he rattled off items as they came to him.

"Yes!" Frank crowed two days later when he reviewed the data Shannon had compiled. The matching of announcements to responses was just as he'd predicted: the combined greenhouse gas output of the targets disabled in each wave of attacks was roughly equivalent to the emissions impact of whatever announcement or event had triggered the assault.

He and Shannon wrote up their findings and requested a meeting with Jim Barker, their project manager.

* * *

Barker finished reading the executive summary of their report, and looked up.

"If your research supports your conclusions, that would be pretty interesting. How compelling is the data?"

"Considering the amount of information we have, it's pretty good. That said, we've only had so many waves of attacks, so it's still possible we're looking at coincidence rather than proof. But the odds of that seem very low. Take a look at some of the tables farther on."

Barker flipped forward a few pages and studied what he found. "Not bad. Have you thought about working up a predictive model? That could be useful, if you're on to something."

"Yes. Besides wanting to let you know what we're thinking, we wanted to see if you could assign us some additional staff to do exactly that."

"What do you have in mind?"

"We were thinking of doing a pilot test using a list of what we assume would be the most likely targets in the U.S. and China if our theory is correct. In the first step, we'd estimate what volume of greenhouse gases each potential target releases each year.

"The second step would involve tracking new attacks. Let's say the next announcement here or in China would have an annual negative impact equal to a hundred million tons of carbon dioxide. We would enter that amount in the program, and it would display all the combinations of power plants and other infrastructure that could be hit to offset approximately that amount. Even if we don't pick the right targets every time, the attacks will still support the theory if the output and the impact numbers match up for whatever targets did get hit."

Barker flipped through the rest of the report. "Sounds plausible. What do you figure you'll need to run the pilot?"

"Let's say fifty percent of a programmer's time for a week to write the software and one person full-time to pull together and manage the data for as long as the pilot lasts."

"Anybody specific you have in mind for the full-time person?"

"I was thinking you could assign the full-time job to me," Shannon interrupted. "I'm already involved on the incident side, and it would be more efficient for me to pick this up than orient someone new to the project. It wouldn't be hard to off-load my other work."

Frank looked at Shannon with surprise; she smiled back.

"Okay," Barker said. "Makes sense. Go ahead and get started as quick as you can. The NSA director is getting a lot of heat from the White House to come up with some answers, and so far, we've got nothing."

* * *

"Congratulations on signing up Barker for the pilot," Shannon said on their way back to Washington. After one look at Frank's car, she had volunteered to give him a lift whenever there was a meeting at Fort Meade.

"Thanks," he said. "I wasn't sure he'd bite. Staff's always tight, so he'll have to pull someone off something else. Oh – and thanks for volunteering."

She turned and smiled. "Of course. Say, do you want to grab dinner somewhere? I'd love to hear more about where you want to take the pilot program."

"Tonight? I don't think I can tonight. But I can fill you in for sure first thing in the morning."

"Okay," she said. Their conversation lagged a bit after that. When she dropped him off, he watched with a touch of regret as she drove away. He didn't have any plans. He'd just turned her down by reflex. Why? He trudged up the stairs and stared at the bland, blank slate of his door for a moment before stepping inside to heat up yet another solitary dinner of pre-prepared food.

The next morning, he found himself staring again, this time at his laptop while waiting for Shannon to pick him up. Eventually he went ahead and typed "Shannon Doyle" into the browser.

Hmm. Berkeley undergraduate, *summa cum laude*, and a master's degree from Stanford. That was impressive. He clicked on the images tab and found pictures of her with her family and a few with what must be college friends, hiking and skiing and traveling abroad. She always looked like she was having a great time, and so did the people around her.

Feeling a bit guilty, he looked out the window; there was her car. He closed his laptop and trotted downstairs.

* * *

Marla was talking on the phone the following evening when Frank met her outside a restaurant. "Do you really have to? Okay. Yes, I understand. Love you, too." Marla dropped her phone in her bag.

"Tim stuck at the office?"

"Yes. They caught him right as he was walking out the door. I guess it's just you and me for dinner."

"Is that so terrible?"

"Of course not. We'll have more time to catch up."

They settled in at their table and ordered drinks. "So," Marla said, "what's new?"

"Oh, nothing."

"That's what you always say."

"It's payback for all the times I asked you what was new at school," Frank said.

"Very funny," she said. "And half the time when you say nothing, it isn't true. How's your big secret project for the government going?"

"Pretty well."

"Can you be a little more informative than that?"

"Well, like you said, it's a secret project."

She groaned. "Noted. So, let me try a different tack. Are the folks you're working with interesting?"

"Well, there's just one, really."

"And is he?"

"She."

Marla's eyes brightened. "Ah! Young? Old?"

Frank leaned back and frowned. "Kind of in between."

"Pretty?"

"What kind of a question is that?"

"Directed at anyone else, a pretty easy one. But have it your way. Is she drop-dead gorgeous?"

"No."

"Well, is she reasonably attractive?"

"Oh, come on. Do you always have to do this?"

"Yes. Answer the question."

"Maybe."

"Maybe what?" she said, pressing her attack.

"All right, so you'd probably think she was pretty good looking."

"Great. Now we're getting somewhere! Are you enjoying working with her?"

"She's very smart."

"That's good, but it's not what I asked."

Their drinks arrived, offering enough of a diversion for Frank to escape to the men's room. Maybe he could change the topic on his return.

On his way back, he stopped in his tracks, amazed. He retreated backward against the wall to avoid being noticed. There could be no question who the young, earnest woman was, leaning across the table and speaking so emphatically. Or who the brow-furrowed, cornered-looking young man nodding defensively was either. Frank returned to his table.

"You'll never guess in a million years who I just saw having dinner together."

"Carl and Josette? Yes, I noticed them earlier."

"But," Frank stammered, "doesn't that strike you as an incredibly bizarre coincidence? The pole-up-his-butt FBI agent assigned to protect you during the missile crisis and the French graduate student who played me for all I was worth during the election hacking?"

"Not really," she said, unfolding her napkin. "It's possible I introduced them."

"Carl and Josette? Really? You've got to be kidding."

"Why? I thought they were made for each other. Don't you agree?"

Frank leaned back in his chair, still grappling with the surprise. Then he shook his head. "I guess, yes, now that you mention it." Then a broad grin split his face. "In fact, I totally agree."

It wasn't until he was walking Marla back to the Metro station that she started grilling him again about Shannon.

"You sounded awfully defensive about the person you're working with. Is there something going on there?"

"No, there isn't!"

"So why the sensitivity?"

"Who says there's sensitivity?" Frank said.

"How long have we known each other?"

"Okay, okay. So, I think she might be interested in me."

"Aha! What's so terrible about that? You said she's attractive and smart. And apparently – who knows why – she's open-minded enough to take an interest in a curmudgeonly older geek who's as outgoing as a houseplant. Somebody like that doesn't come along often, you know."

He knew that very well indeed.

They were at the Metro Station now. He gave her a hug. "Give Tim my best, okay?"

"Will do. But why don't you consider asking out – what's her name?"

"Who?"

She poked him in the stomach, extracting the kind of satisfying "*Oof!*" she had hoped for.

"You know exactly who I mean. What's her name?"

"It's Shannon."

"Why don't you ask Shannon out?"

"I'll think about it."

"Will you really? Or are you just trying to escape my questions?"

"The latter."

She laughed and gave him another hug. "You're impossible. Get home safely."

"You too." He watched Marla disappear down the escalator and then started walking home. Well, why didn't he ask Shannon out? He was pretty sure she wanted him to. And his apartment seemed even more cold and empty than usual. What did he have to lose?

He made a half-hearted effort to convince himself it would be foolish to risk complicating a working relationship with a social one. But it didn't work. Clearly, he had more to gain than to lose. The real reason for his inaction was he instinctively shied away from human contact and the chance of rejection. Well, that was who he was. Might as well own it and leave well enough alone.

5

Working in a Coal Mine

GEORGE GREEN LET go of the dead-man switch on his pneumatic drill. Once its clattering roar died away, he realized why Larry had grabbed his shoulder. Even with his ear protectors on, he could hear the angry boom of the emergency evacuation alarm echoing through the tunnel. He lowered the heavy drill to the ground and fell in behind his shift buddies as they started double-timing it along the coal face.

Almost immediately, the regular lighting blinked out, leaving only intermittent emergency lights to show the way. Then those began to flicker. What if they died, too? They'd be fumbling their way to safety in absolute darkness. They speeded up, trotting with difficulty in their heavy boots.

Green was winded and ready to slow down long before he reached the gallery leading to the elevator. The narrow passageway was jammed with shuffling miners. As he merged into the crowd, the emergency lights in the tunnel he'd just left died; thank God, the lights were still on ahead.

He noticed the emergency lights die in the next tunnel, too, as the last miners joined the crowd. What the hell was happening? Emergency lights were battery powered. They were designed to last for days, not minutes. The ventilators were off, too; everything seemed to be breaking down except that damned emergency alarm. It was pursuing them like some invisible, baying beast, ready to devour them if they slowed down for even a moment. Sweating heavily, he prayed he'd make it out before everything went dark.

By the time he finally saw the elevator up ahead, the throng was barely moving. The crowd of miners was big and restless. Discipline was holding, but the tension was dark and black as the coal that imprisoned them. Everyone was jammed in tight, and the air was foul and stifling; humid and thick with the stench of hot grease, coal dust and anxious humanity. But it was eerily quiet. Almost silent, except for the faint, metallic hum of the elevator cables running up to safety.

It seemed to take longer each time for the elevator to return, but his chance to make the slow ascent to the surface finally arrived. As the elevator cage emerged into the air at last, he felt his legs go weak.

Everyone who worked above- or belowground was crowded around the shaft, speaking in subdued tones or standing silent as they waited for the last miners to arrive. Green was startled to see that everything was black aboveground. But for the moon, the only illumination shone up from inside the elevator shaft.

A cheer erupted when the last miners stepped out of the lift. When the ruckus died down, Green heard a new sound kick in: the ventilator stacks behind them shuddered as the fans inside sprang back to life. A minute later, a plume of coal dust billowed up out of the elevator shaft. It thickened and grew, forcing everyone to retreat. Lights off, and the fans on backward? What was happening now?

Green saw his shift boss pocket his telephone, and he made his way through the dispersing miners to reach him.

"What's going on?" Green asked.

"Nobody knows. If it wasn't for the lights going out, you'd think this was a false alarm."

"Why?"

"The guys in the office say nobody triggered the alarm system, and none of the sensors have reported anything that would set it off ..." He stopped in mid-sentence. "Do you hear that?"

"Yeah. Something's happening down there," Green replied. They stepped back to the edge of the elevator shaft.

"It sounds like the machines are working the coal faces again," his boss said. "What do you think?"

"That'd be my guess. But why?"

"Dunno. This is crazy."

Green turned and followed the last stragglers to the parking lot. He was almost there when he felt his legs go funny under him again. But now it was because the ground was heaving beneath him. He braced himself against the surging shockwaves as the thunder of explosion after explosion erupted from the mine he'd just escaped.

* * *

Randal Wellhead, the Republican candidate for president, was watching a news update on his computer. The financial markets had just closed after suffering their biggest one-day losses since the Great Recession. Energy companies were still nosediving in after-hours trading, and industrials and utilities weren't doing much better. No one knew where or what the unknown attacker would strike next.

"Hey, Delia," he called to his executive assistant. "You following the news?"

A young woman in a business suit appeared at the door of his office. "Yes, sir. It's terrible."

"Well, yes and no," Wellhead said. "It's sure awful for this country. But it's even worse for Henry Yazzi, and that's good for us."

"I don't think that's a very healthy way of looking at this situation, sir. And I certainly wouldn't say that to anyone else!"

"Oh, of course not. But if a disaster is going to happen, it might as well happen on Henry's watch. It sure isn't helping his election campaign any."

"And no one seems to have any idea who could be behind the attacks."

"Yup." Wellhead chuckled. "Isn't that great? The longer it stays that way, the more helpless the president looks."

* * *

Shannon and Frank joined a somber group funneling into the conference room at NSA headquarters. The team had expanded dramatically with multiple sub-teams beavering away on different categories of incidents.

In front stood an impatient Jim Barker, repeatedly glancing at his watch. He started speaking exactly at the top of the hour, ignoring those still arriving.

"Okay, everyone. Let's quiet down and get going. We've got a lot to cover today. As you're already aware, the latest wave of attacks shut down forty-one major coal mines in the seven largest coal-producing countries – China, the U.S., Australia, India, Indonesia, Russia, and South Africa. We're confident that's a complete attack list. Every country has been hit so many times nobody's holding back any data.

"All the targets were underground mines, not open-pit ones. The combined output is enormous – about seventeen and a half percent of global coal production. We hustled Graham Bailey out to Wyoming with a team as soon as we realized the extent of the attacks, so I want to start with an on-site update by speakerphone. Graham, can you hear me?"

"Yes, Jim. How am I coming through?"

"Just fine. Can you bring us up to date?"

"Sure. We can only see the big picture so far. The damage underground was colossal, so there aren't many sensors down there still providing any data, or any way to get to most of the mine. But we have been able to piece together a lot from the miners' accounts and from data received aboveground before the explosions wiped everything out. Here's the sequence of what we think happened.

"As far as the miners are concerned, the incident began when the underground emergency alarms went off. It doesn't look like there was any individual or condition that triggered the alarms. So, we expect the attacker did that to empty the mines. Whether that was to avoid loss of life or to prevent anyone from overriding later events, we just don't know.

"According to multiple accounts, the lights shut down in each tunnel as soon as the last miner was out. We assume that was intended to maximize confusion and speed up the evacuation.

"Once the mines were emptied, the elevators were disabled to prevent reentry. At the same time, the ventilation systems cycled through a complex series of reconfigurations. Some fans were just blowing air through tunnels, and others were preventing air from leaving the mine the way it normally would. As some of you may know, coal dust is highly combustible. When it's suspended in the air in an enclosed space, it becomes explosive. Federal safety regulations mandate ways to minimize the danger, like sealing off areas where mechanical mining machines are in operation, monitoring the amount of dust accumulating in the air, and constantly venting it out of the mine. All those safeguards appear to have been reversed by the attacker.

"At the same time as the ventilators came back online, the attacker activated all underground robotic mining machines and moved them back into contact with the coal faces. That generated more and more coal dust, which the ventilators spread throughout the mine and kept stirred up and airborne. Basically, the attacker turned each mine into a gigantic octopus of a bomb. After about fifteen minutes, it set the bomb off by sending a huge power surge into the belowground systems to create sparks when machinery short-circuited."

"What can you tell us about the damage?" Barker asked.

"Pretty near total. Coal structures, and particularly soft coal seams, aren't very strong to begin with. As I understand it, what miners do is extract most of the coal throughout a large area, leaving pillars of unmined coal to support the roof. Then they mine the pillars, too, replacing them with big table-shaped supports.

Finally, they remove those, too, as the machinery retreats. Eventually, the ceilings come down on their own, so it doesn't take much to cause a collapse. And these weren't small explosions. They registered on seismic recorders a long way off. Mine management says it expects all, or almost all, the rooms and tunnels collapsed. That means all the equipment and other underground infrastructure was destroyed or buried, too.

"Thanks," Barker said, turning to the audience. "Anybody have any questions for Graham? Okay, Mary?"

"How hard do the mine owners think it will be to reopen the mine?"

"From what I've heard, it's not so much a matter of getting back in operation as starting all over again. Except for some of the vertical shafts, this mine no longer exists. The other problem is that so many mines were hit there's no telling how long it will take to replace all the destroyed and buried heavy equipment. Some of it is generic, or assembled from off-the-shelf components, like the elevators. But the rest, like the coal extraction machines, are unique to this kind of work. Coal mining hasn't been a growth industry for a while, so if the destruction elsewhere is as complete as it is here, it'll be years before the manufacturers still in business can replace what's been lost."

"So how long do they think it will take to get things running again?"

"The big question right now is whether they'll reopen this mine at all. Demand for coal has been dropping for years, and it would take a huge investment to get this one back in operation. The company may decide to just take the insurance money and shut things down for good."

"Thanks, Graham. Good report. Stay safe."

* * *

"So how did your predictive model do?" Barker was debriefing Frank and Shannon in his office after the team meeting.

"Not so well," Frank admitted. "This was kind of off the scale of anything we expected. That said, the attack still shows our approach is solid even if it fell outside the parameters we built into the model."

"How's that?"

"First, because the attacks occurred just a few hours after an announcement was made with a very big impact. For the first time, the amount of carbon dioxide in the atmosphere exceeded 400 parts per million for an entire month. That's the highest level in millions of years. It's also a big deal because that's the point where scientists say a major ocean level rise becomes inevitable. So, it's a degree of CO_2 pollution we never wanted to reach."

"Still, it's just a number," Barker said. "It's not as if we're safe if CO_2 plateaus at 399 but screwed if it hits 400."

"That's another reason why it fits right into our theory that negative warming announcements trigger attacks. By the rough calculations we've made, the amount of coal capacity taken offline correlates well to what it would take to put us back under 400 PPM for the time being. That tells me we should put the model project into overdrive. Of course, that would take more people."

"You've convinced me. Let me see if I can sell it upstairs, and I'll let you know."

"Sounds good. Incidentally, I doubt you want me to lead that effort."

"Really? Why?"

"Building out the model is just a numbers exercise. I'd rather focus on figuring out who's behind the attacks and how to stop them. Would that work for you?"

Barker paused. "Yeah, I guess. Finishing up the model won't take any special skills. So, sure. Why don't you stay with what you're good at? Shannon, how about you?"

"I'd like to keep working with Frank."

"I thought you'd say that." He paused again. "Okay. That also makes sense. Frank still needs a partner here at the NSA. But I'll need your help to transition the predictive model project to someone else."

"Of course."

Barker stood up. "Then, in that case, the two of you better beat it so I can tackle the latest important but complicating discovery you've dumped on my desk."

* * *

"Nice job ducking the dreary stuff," Shannon said on their way back to Washington.

"Actually, that wasn't it. I'm just not a manager type."

"So, I'm told."

"'So, you're told?' How's that?"

"I'm sorry – I didn't mean that the way it sounded."

Frank frowned. He wasn't used to anyone knowing much about him and preferred anonymity.

"How should it have sounded?"

"I guess – I don't know – Jim Barker just mentioned you liked working alone when he asked me to be your go-to guy at the NSA."

Well, what could he say? He'd always been ill at ease around people. Half the time when he spoke with someone he felt like he was talking over a telephone link with a time delay. He'd start talking over them, never quite able to get the timing right, and feeling increasingly awkward by the minute. And with most people he felt like he'd just woken up from a twenty-year nap, unable to conversationally synch up with the reality everyone else lived in.

"Well, that's so," he said. "I'm not exactly a people person." He left it at that, and they drove in silence for a while.

"I hope you didn't mind me asking to continue to work with you?" Shannon said at last.

"No – no. Not at all. But I was a bit surprised."

"Why?"

He regretted the words immediately. He didn't want to admit he assumed folks felt as awkward around him as he did around them.

"I don't know. No reason, I guess."

She laughed. "Fact is, I've been enjoying being your Girl Friday. I'm not used to working with a famous hacker. It's been interesting."

He reddened. "Well, the North Korean thing was a while ago."

"But not the Caliphate attack –"

"Wait a minute – Jim told you about that, too? What else did he share?"

"I guess he also told me you discovered someone was trying to hack the last election and stopped them just in time. Is there more?"

"No! That's all there is. Anything else I've done has been extremely boring."

"Well, what we're working on now certainly isn't. And I can see why you like being able to follow up on anything you want to. I hate being tied down to one piece of something bigger I can't help manage, so I'm thrilled to be along for the ride." She turned and gave him an even warmer smile than usual.

* * *

"So, did you ask Shannon out yet?"

"Please, Marla, if you keep doing this, I won't answer the phone when you call."

"You don't have a choice. You're my dad. It's in the contract."

"Not so. The contract only says I have to tease you."

"I haven't believed that since I was five years old."

"More like seven, actually. You know, I always meant to type up a phony contract with the name of the hospital at the top so I could prove they made a father agree in writing to tease his daughter every day. I'm sorry I never got around to it."

"Nice try. You still haven't answered my question. Have you asked Shannon out?"

"No! Are you happy now?"

"Of course not. Not until the answer is yes. And don't say 'I'll think about it' again. It won't work. What's the problem?"

"The problem is I'm too used to being alone."

"People born with only one leg probably get used to that, too. But they take a new one when it's offered."

"So, what I'm hearing is you're suggesting I need an artificial relationship to make up for my congenital social shortcomings."

"Whatever floats your boat. Anyway, asking her out to dinner isn't inviting her to move in."

"Well, sure. But if it turns into something, then there are, well, expectations."

"Good grief, yes. Like having someone to share and do things with. Now, wouldn't that be just terrible?"

"Look, I've got to go. Talk to you later." He hung up before she could respond. He stared at the phone for a moment and stood up. Time for a walk.

Hands shoved in his pockets, he set out for the Mall. The fact was, he'd started thinking he should ask Shannon out for dinner. But he hadn't done anything about it. Why?

How had he become so solitary, anyway? The way he remembered it, he'd always had at least a few friends as a child. In college, there had been places near campus where he could hang out. After his freshman year, he practically lived in a dusty, dingy coffee house in the basement of a university building, becoming part of its motley bunch of regulars. There was Mary Pat. She ran the place. And Freddie, an out-of-work, overweight, diabetic ex-con who lived with his mother.

He stopped in front of the Lincoln Memorial and watched the school groups climbing the steps. Who else used to hang out at the coffee house? Right – Randy, an ex-stockbroker who flipped out on LSD back in the late 1960s and lived in a tent in the middle of a big park at the end of a subway line. There was a law student, whose name he couldn't remember, who seemed to only leave to attend classes. He drew cartoons and sometimes played the piano there – badly. And then there were the anonymous, compulsive Go-playing engineering students. He used to roust them out at midnight by blasting Jimi Hendrix's version of "All Along the Watchtower" on the sound system. He smiled at the memory. Had he started to change even then?

Now that he thought of it, of course, he had. He never actually did anything with any male friends. If he was in a relationship, he had all the company he needed. And when he wasn't, he could fall back on the no-risk, no-personal-investment habit of hanging out where he knew people. At least, until he got married.

He turned away and stared down at the reflecting pool, its long sides converging toward the point that was the Washington Monument.

By the time his marriage broke up, the guard had changed at all his old haunts. The scruffy coffee house wasn't there at all; the university had turned it into a sterile satellite cafeteria with plastic tables and chairs. And he was painfully aware of how much older he was than the new regulars at the hangouts that were left. Whatever meager social skills he had weren't up to the challenge of working his way back in.

He turned and headed home, staring at his feet. That was twenty years ago. He'd withdrawn deeper into himself each time his increasingly infrequent female relationships ended, becoming more awkward and reticent each time. He couldn't imagine anyone wanting to be around the cocooned outcast he was now. After all, why would they?

His phone buzzed in his pocket. The text read "Pick you up for work tomorrow?" It was from Shannon.

6

Who? Me?

S HANNON FROWNED. "SO, I've pulled together the dates and exact times of all the announcements to date, or as close to the exact times as I could get. What should I do next?"

Frank hesitated before responding. If his hunch was wrong, he'd look more like a doofus than a famous hacker.

"How about you graph how quickly a responsive attack occurs after an announcement. Some I don't really care about, like the ones that happen at night at a facility that doesn't have round-the-clock work shifts, because we assume those were deliberately delayed. What I'm curious about is the time lag between when news breaks and the response begins. Does it vary? Is it always the same? Is there some other pattern?"

"Okay. I'll do that." She returned to her desk and started tapping away. A few minutes later, she came back from the printer with a piece of paper in her hand and a fascinated look on her face. "Here you go," she said.

He pushed back from the desk and looked at the graph. Bingo. There was a big spike. More than eighty percent of the daytime attacks were launched within thirty minutes of the triggering event. Just as he'd hoped.

"Well, you look happy," Shannon said. "What is that graph telling you?"

"That a robot is triggering the attacks."

"A robot? Seriously? You mean a real robot, like in science fiction?"

"Not if you're thinking of a physical robot. But if you mean an artificially intelligent software program, then yes, exactly. What this graph indicates is that all these attacks were set up in advance. As soon as news of a certain type of event hits the Internet, the software calculates the CO_2 impact and then launches an appropriate attack. I expect if we look deeper into the data, we'll find the remaining twenty percent relate to safety delays and unique events requiring more sophisticated impact calculations."

"How can you tell all that?"

"Here – look at the timing. For these ultra-sophisticated attacks to launch this quickly, someone – or something – would have to watch the news twenty-four hours a day. He'd also need to immediately match a specific attack to the greenhouse gas impact of a specific announcement. To do that, the attacker would need a dual database-driven model, just like the one we're building, with one database filled with targets, the other with specific events, and each of them ranked by greenhouse gas output. After someone's done all that – and, of course, planted all the malware at the targets as well – all they'd need to add would be some code to make the match and automatically trigger the attack. That last bit would be a pretty basic robotic program, but a robot nonetheless."

"Makes sense. Does the graph tell you anything else?"

"Not directly, but – no surprise to you by now, I expect – it makes me want to review more information. Could somebody do a big data analysis to see how many announcements of negative climate change data have been made, large and small, since the attacks began?

"I'm sure they can. Then what?"

"Whoever is behind this must have installed malware at a heck of a lot of targets, because it seems like they've always got a right-sized and nationally-appropriate target in inventory. But I'm not sure that's the case. I'd like to see whether any announcements weren't followed by attacks. If there have, that might allow us to make some helpful inferences."

"Like what?"

"Well, like whether the impact of some announcements is too big or too small to react to. If so, we can use that information to tune up our projection model. If we see trigger events the attacker usually would but hasn't reacted to, what's the reason? Does it not attack certain countries? Or maybe its inventory of compromised targets isn't so big after all? Let's ask for that information and see what we get."

"Okay, will do. By the way – I packed enough food for two today. Want to break for lunch?"

"You didn't have to do that."

"I know. But I've seen what you bring to eat."

"What's wrong with a granola bar?"

"Nothing, other than the fact that it's almost nothing. I'll get what I brought from the refrigerator and meet you in the conference room."

"Can I suggest a lunch topic?" Shannon said when she met him there, setting a chicken salad in front of him. "I don't know a lot about robotics and artificial intelligence, so if that's going to be a big deal on this project, I should buy a few books and study up on it. But in the meantime, maybe you can give me an introduction."

"Sure. I guess the first thing to understand is that just like anything else with computers, it all starts with ones and zeros and gets built up from there. And again, just the same, it's all logical and hierarchical. So, you can't just start at some high level and write a complicated program. You have to start with 'if this, then that' statements and the like and work up from there. That's tedious and time-consuming.

"Next, AI is different from other types of programs, like ones that solve mathematical problems. With those, there's only one right answer. AI can be especially useful where there may not be just one right answer. Or maybe there is, but you need to come up with a much more complicated approach to get there. Like image or speech recognition. Those are really tricky challenges, where the data can be very ambiguous."

"So how do you go about it?"

"Computer scientists have come up with a lot of different ways, but some techniques are fundamental to just about all of them. One of them involves choosing the most likely outcomes instead of computing them all."

"Wait a minute – how does a program know what's more likely?"

"Good question. There are again several approaches, and more being developed all the time. For example, an AI program can use information loaded into a database for it to draw on, or it can use information it's added to the database itself."

"Where does it get new information from?"

"Here's an example. Let's say you've created a computer program to figure out how to get from the start of a maze to the end. If the program tries one way and hits a dead end, it would add that information to its database so it doesn't follow the same route again. Every time it starts over, it has fewer options to try, and eventually it tries the one that will solve the maze. And if you extend the maze, it doesn't have to start all over again, because it already has the right route to the new starting point in its database."

"So," Shannon said, "you might say that the program is more intelligent at that point than it was when it started?"

"Well, 'intelligent' might be too strong a word at this point. But the program is certainly more capable, and you could definitely say that it's 'learned' something."

"What's another method?"

"Computers weren't very powerful when they started to work on artificial intelligence, so a lot of the techniques computer scientists came up with were designed to figure out the most they could in the shortest amount of time with the smallest amount of computing power. One way they did that was, in effect, to program computers to make guesses based on the information they had. If a guess paid off, the program had saved time. And if it didn't, it was no worse off than it was before. They called that kind of shortcut technique a 'heuristic,' and programs still use that approach today.

"Another thing they did was to push what a program learned back into the way the program was making decisions, rather than just putting information into a database. That way, if a program ran into a problem, it could backtrack to the point where it went wrong and go forward with that new knowledge in mind. To use the maze example again, if the program realized that right turns almost never worked out, it could incorporate that learning into its decision-making process. Then it would go back to the last right turn it made and move forward from there, always trying left turns first. That was another advance."

"How long ago did it take to get to that point?" Shannon asked.

"Oh, we're talking about back in the 1960s. They'd been at it for about ten years by then."

"Really? If that's where they were after ten years, how come we're not a lot farther along by now?"

"Well, for starters, let's talk about the difference between what they call 'narrow' and 'general' intelligence. If you're talking about just a maze, there are only so many variables to work with, and only a few skills involved. After you've written a program to solve one maze, you should be able to use the same program to solve every other maze ever created in the same way. That's an example of 'narrow' intelligence, and programs have been around for decades that do useful work in all kinds of very specific narrow areas. You encounter lots of these narrow AIs every day, like mapping programs on your phone and advertising agents that recommend products to you based on what you, or people like you, have bought before. But 'general' intelligence is another thing."

"What's general intelligence? Everything else?"

"Well, for purposes of this discussion, let's say yes. A general intelligence AI would be able to do anything a human could, as well and as quickly. And that's enormously challenging. Let's use an autonomous car program as an example. That's still a narrow AI, because all it can do is drive a car and nothing else.

But just look at all the things that program must be capable of. Like making decisions instantaneously in all kinds of situations – like how long it will take to stop, depending on road conditions, how fast it can legally drive on any given stretch of road, how to tell the difference between a road sign and a pedestrian and much, much more.

"It also needs to take in and correctly make use of massive amounts of sensor data in real time, like how close the car is to the shoulder and the center line of the road, how fast and where every other car within hundreds of yards is going, whether a light is changing up ahead, and so on. If you split that up into different categories, you get into lots of very tough problems computer scientists have been struggling with for decades."

"Such as?"

"How about image recognition? It's easy to imagine teaching a computer to recognize two-dimensional outlines, like squares and circles, in a digital document, because it's easy to turn those figures into mathematical relationships. Once those relationships are established, a computer can identify any set of four equal-length lines joined at right angles as a 'square.' But how about if instead of a digitized square, we want the computer to identify a visual image of a rotating wooden block? The first problem is that now we have to teach a computer how to work with data it receives from an external source, like a video camera."

"Interesting. So how did they do that?"

"In the first experiments, they put a light to one side and then set a wooden block on a table, taking advantage of the contrast between the light and shadowed areas of the block. Where the brightness changed abruptly, they programmed the computer to recognize a 'line.' That was a good start, but what the computer was 'seeing' now was a whole lot more complicated than a two-dimensional square. For one thing, unless the camera is looking at a block head-on, there aren't any right angles anymore, and the angles that are there keep changing as the block's orientation changes. So now you need to write an algorithm that describes the changes that the perceived angles in a cube go through as it rotates if you want your program to still be able to recognize something called a 'cube.'"

"How long ago was that?"

"Still the 1960s."

"And yet we still don't have all-purpose machine vision, do we?"

"Well, there's a whole lot more to image recognition than that suggests. For one thing, you don't want to write a different algorithm to deal with every geometric shape. That means coming up with one that's a whole lot more complicated and powerful. And still, we're only talking about one visual recognition challenge. Now imagine we're talking about a face now. Any straight lines?"

"Just glasses, maybe."

"Any abrupt shifts between light and dark?"

"No."

"Is there a big difference between a front view and a profile?"

"Okay, I get the picture. And then, I guess, there's also the fact that, until recently, computers weren't powerful enough to analyze images like that in real time."

"Absolutely. And don't forget the stakes can be very high. Let's go back to our self-driving car again, and assume we're traveling sixty miles an hour towards a curve in the road. How is it supposed to tell the difference between a billboard with an ad for Frank's Produce at that curve from a truck crossing the road when the truck has the same ad on it?"

"You're not making me feel good about self-driving cars."

"Well, they're making a lot of progress really quickly now. Anyway, image recognition and self-driving cars aren't the only tough challenges. Voice recognition is a whole lot more difficult than anyone expected. Computer scientists have been working hard on that one for more than half a century, and the results still aren't perfect."

"What's the big problem?"

"Well, in my view, there are really two crucial challenges. The first one is giving a program all the tools it needs to solve problems – that means enough memory organized in the right way, enough processing power, the right kind of sensors and data to tell it what it needs to know, and most of all, the right algorithms to allow it to efficiently and effectively make use of those resources."

"I guess that's kind of obvious. And I can see how you'd need to make even more progress in every one of those areas to support what you called 'general intelligence.' What's the second challenge?"

"That would be giving an AI the ability to teach itself, taking context into account. So far, programs have been created that can learn specific things in specific situations in order to perform specific jobs. There are other projects that have tried to work more broadly. There's one called 'Cyc,' from the middle letters of the word encyclopedia, that has been adding hundreds of thousands of pieces of knowledge into a computer database to help a program develop the equivalent of what we think of as common sense. Other projects are trying to teach computers to be able to acquire knowledge by reading.

"But so far, we haven't gotten to the point of creating a program with anything like the all-purpose ability of a person to absorb everything she senses in the world around her, unconsciously integrate that into all she knew before, and then make use of that new knowledge to do all sorts of useful things."

"You stopped kind of abruptly there. Why?"

"It occurred to me that to finish up our lightning history of AI, I might need to add the words 'until now.'"

* * *

The next day, Frank received the first cut of the new data Shannon had requested. He went back and forth with the NSA data analysts for another day, driving them crazy with additional search filters and requests to correlate results with other data, until he was satisfied.

"Take a look," he said, handing Shannon a sheaf of spreadsheets.

"Do you want to be a bit more specific?" she asked, squinting at the endless columns of tiny figures.

"Sorry – sure. If you go through the numbers, every announcement likely to have a negative impact of more than .005 percent of global emissions of greenhouse gases resulted in an attack, but only if the announcement related to one of the top twenty countries, ranked by CO_2 emissions. That's really incredible."

"Because there's a bright-line cut off?"

"That part's interesting but not unexpected. What I find significant is every single announcement within the same parameters resulted in a responsive attack. Think how many exploits must have been planned to be able to do that, and how much unique malware must be out there, just waiting to be triggered? It's incredible to me that anyone, anywhere, could have infiltrated so many different systems and designed so many attacks. We've analyzed thirteen separate attack waves now. That's a fantastic accomplishment by whoever is behind it."

"Does it give you any clue who that might be?"

"That's the weirdest part of all. I can't imagine anyone other than the best government teams in the U.S., Russia, and China staging this range and sophistication of attacks. But those countries have been hit much too hard for the attacks to be camouflage to throw investigators off. And anyway, I'm not sure even one of those teams could pull off something like this. Just think how many vulnerabilities you'd have to buy to invade this many different systems."

"Buy?" Shannon asked.

"Sure. There's an active market buying and selling zero-day exploits. You remember what they are?"

"Software vulnerabilities that no one knows about yet."

"Right. There are lots of hackers out there that make a good living finding vulnerabilities and then selling them to the highest bidder. Zero-day vulnerabilities for popular or critical software programs go for a lot – sometimes hundreds of thousands of dollars, and even more. Do you remember when the FBI wanted to break into the iPhone of the terrorists that killed dozens of people in San Bernardino?"

"Of course. Apple wouldn't help them, because they wanted to protect the privacy of their other customers."

"That's right. The FBI paid over $1.3 million dollars to someone who figured out how to crack the access code."

"I assume that was a one-off case, though," Shannon said. "Who would want to buy a vulnerability besides the developer of the software with the flaw?"

"Before I answer that, let me challenge the assumption you just made. The developer of the program might never get the chance to buy that vulnerability at all."

"Why? Isn't the vendor the person the hacker would go to first?"

"Some would. But unfortunately, others wouldn't. People willing to tell a vendor about a flaw often do so for free, out of a sense of community service. But people who want to make as much money as possible are often happy to sell a vulnerability to anyone, including a criminal, if he's the highest bidder."

"I guess I shouldn't be surprised. Does that mean the FBI or Homeland Security outbid everyone else and then tell the software vendors where the flaws are, so they can fix them?"

"Government agencies do buy a lot of zero-day exploits. But they don't pass them along."

"That sounds crazy. Why not?"

"So they can use them. And not just to hack into the systems of suspected terrorists and other bad guys abroad, but right here at home, without having to let anyone know – even the software developers or Internet service providers."

"So, you're saying our government buys up vulnerabilities and lets everybody around the world keep using flawed software? Wouldn't it be just a matter of time before someone else found the same vulnerability and exploited it? Maybe against us – or, heck, maybe against the same agency?"

"That's right. Don't forget the government not so long ago tried to get software vendors to build 'backdoors' into their own software so the agencies could use them. But the software vendors told the government to take a hike, since black hats would inevitably discover the same backdoors and exploit them. So, the agencies buy as many zero-day vulnerabilities as they can on the dark Internet instead."

Shannon shook her head. "At least they'd still need a warrant to exploit those vulnerabilities, right?"

"That's what the government says. If you believe it always plays by the book, then there's not a lot to worry about. But not everyone believes the government always will, assuming it is now. And then there's the fact that the government itself has been hacked. Back in 2017, somebody – probably the Russians – hacked the NSA and stole a huge library of zero-day vulnerabilities. Then they posted them all to a public Web site. Not long after, somebody used one of them to stage a global ransom attack against hundreds of thousands of computers.

"So, who is it on our side that buys all those zero-day vulnerabilities?" Shannon asked. "The CIA?"

Frank frowned. "Now that you mention it, by far and away the biggest buyer of zero-day exploits is the NSA."

7

Sorry. Gotta Split

THE ANCIENT FAULT yielded in a titanic lurch, splitting a hundred miles of sea floor and heaving one side upward a full fifteen feet. That action in turn thrust trillions of tons of seawater skyward.

Three and a half minutes later, the needle of a seismic monitor launched into wild gyrations as the first vibrations reached the McMurdo Station, on the edge of the Ross Ice Shelf in Antarctica. For more than two and a half minutes, the shocks ebbed and flowed, shaking awake hundreds of scientists and support personnel. In a mob, they streamed into streets illuminated by the near-perpetual light of the polar spring.

One of those who stumbled out into the icy street was John Milne. Ignoring the still-moving ground and the shattered glass on the snow, he ran to the door of the geophysical lab. Scanning the paper drum of the monitor, he saw that the tremors had mostly ranged between 6.4 and 6.9 on the Richter Scale. But the first shock registered 7.2. With the nearest tectonic plate border hundreds of miles away, the quake must have been a monster.

He logged into the global earthquake network to see where else the quake had been detected, but he saw nothing that could be related. That meant the epicenter must be closer to McMurdo than any other monitoring device. That was surprising, as the Antarctic plate borders weren't particularly active. He only recalled reading about one big quake in the past, and he looked it up. Hmm. That one was an 8.1 event in 1998 near the Balleny Islands. 8.1 was a big quake.

He pulled up a map of the locations of every seismograph within two thousand miles and realized the epicenter must have been very close indeed; the monitors closest to McMurdo were at Christchurch, New Zealand and Hobart, in Tasmania, neither of which had yet detected the event. He'd need data from at least two locations in addition to his own to determine the epicenter, using the time it took the shockwaves to reach each one.

He watched the screen intently, waiting for more data to arrive, but none did. He picked up the phone and called the station manager.

"Henry, this is John Milne at the geoscience lab. I think we need to assume a tsunami may be on the way. We should start evacuating the station pronto."

"How soon could it arrive?"

"I don't know. All I can tell so far is that the epicenter can't be too far off – less than a thousand miles, certainly. A tsunami moves about five hundred miles an hour through deep water, and faster when it starts to shelve, so if we're going to be hit, it could get here in less than an hour."

"How big?"

"There aren't any detection buoys in the Southern Ocean, so there won't be any way to tell till it gets here, assuming there is one. If the fault shifted miles below the sea floor, there won't be anything to worry about. But if it shifted near the surface, it could be a big one."

"Got it. We'll get started right away."

Milne began pulling together a portable seismic monitor, backup batteries, and anything else he could think of that might be useful. The siren that was now blaring nearby added urgency to his task.

Lugging a bin crammed with gear, he tottered down the stairs. Out on the street, he dragged it behind him across the snow and hoisted it into the back of one of the trucks in a convoy forming up nearby. He climbed in after it and reopened his laptop. Finally! There was the data he was looking for. Christchurch had registered the quake. He needed one more report to know for certain where the quake had occurred.

Ah! Hobart had the quake now, too. The truck lurched into gear, and they were underway. And here was the first estimate of the epicenter. Wow – it really had been close – six hundred miles north-northeast of McMurdo.

Soon there was more data coming in from the global earthquake monitoring system. It was a big event indeed – the first estimate was 8.4 on the Richter scale

— a major quake. He called the station manager on his satellite phone and told him everyone not already on their way should start walking while they waited for a vehicle to return for them.

Milne returned to his laptop and watched as the estimates of the depth of the slippage evolved. The more he saw, the worse it looked: all the data pointed to surface slippage. He grabbed his seat as a strong aftershock sent the truck sliding sideways on the ice.

They were at higher ground now, and everyone piled out quickly. People gathered in small groups, looking out to sea, but Milne perched with his laptop on the edge of his bin, hoping for more data. But with no monitoring buoys closer to the epicenter than McMurdo Station was, he knew there was no way to learn what he wanted to know.

Then he brought himself up short. There was a research team out on the Ross Ice Shelf, a trackless waste of ice almost the size of Texas. They were checking on the condition of a string of instruments spread across the ice sheet. How close to the ocean edge of the shelf were they? He tried to raise them on his satellite telephone, but there was no response. They must have gone back to sleep.

He called the McMurdo Station manager, urging him to send a helicopter out immediately to pick them up. Then he set up his portable seismic monitoring unit and hooked it to his laptop. What he saw was confusing; the shockwaves passing under the ice must be rebounding between the bottom of the ice and the seafloor. But that didn't explain everything he was seeing; some shocks didn't result in the same echo effects. What could be causing them? It must be local activity of some kind.

As he stared at the screen, another isolated shock registered. He watched as it propagated across the same line of instruments the field team was checking. Of course. The earthquake and its aftershocks would create cracks in the ice shelf. He felt another big aftershock beneath his feet. Almost immediately, his laptop revealed a cycle of tremors spreading from multiple points out on the ice shelf. The same cycle was repeating. He wondered how much of the ice shelf was becoming unstable. He looked up. There was a lot of talking and pointing going on.

The convoy had dropped them on a ridge behind McMurdo Station. Looking down, he could see the buildings clustered between the rising ground and the harbor. From this distance, he could see significant damage. But that's not what people were pointing at. Everyone was focusing on the horizon, out to sea.

At first, he didn't see anything out of the ordinary. Then a brilliant sparkle at the intersection of sea and sky caught his eye, and he noticed a line of tiny glimmers, like a string of diminutive Christmas lights strung across the horizon. Fascinated, he watched as the lights grew slowly larger. Then he could just make out a narrow, emerald green ribbon separating the sea and sky. Five minutes later, the band had grown and turned a beautiful jade green as it captured and refracted the polar sun from a new angle. The eerie silence and grace of its approach made it hard to appreciate the incredible power that was about to obliterate the buildings below.

* * *

The helicopter pilot throttled his engine down just enough to land almost on top of the three tents. He leaped out the moment the aircraft touched the ice, yelling *"Out! Out! Out!"* at the top of his lungs. A half-dozen groggy men stumbled from the tents.

"Into the helicopter! Now! Don't take anything! Just MOVE!" The pilot jumped back into his seat and kept yelling until the last startled researcher tumbled through the rear door. Before his passengers were in their seats, he gunned the engine and the helicopter swung into the air.

The scientist in the passenger seat started to ask what the hell the emergency was, but the words froze in his mouth. Dead ahead was an enormous wave, so tall he couldn't guess its height. The engine screamed as the pilot wrenched the stick around, struggling to turn and gain altitude before the towering wall of water reached them. The motion threw the scientist against the side of the aircraft as he watched, awestruck, as the wave crashed over the edge of the ice sheet and surged forward, eradicating their campsite and moving on, and on, and on, until at last it disappeared in the distance to the south.

* * *

Carson Bekin looked in the mirror and adjusted his tie. Time to once again face the jackals – sorry – *gentlemen* of the press.

The cramped briefing room in the West Wing of the White House was packed with reporters. They leaned forward in anticipation as Bekin strode briskly up to the lectern. Each one, he knew, was aching to pose his or her very own special question, regardless of whether Bekin had already answered or, more likely, dodged the same query five times already.

"Okay, folks, let's get going," Bekin said. "I'm going to start today by reading a brief statement from the president. Here goes:

Over the past several weeks, an unprecedented series of heinous attacks has disabled, and in some cases, destroyed, a wide variety of energy-related infrastructure. From the start, this administration has placed the highest possible priority on meeting the challenge of this emergency. From the outset, the NSA, FBI, CIA, and DHS, among other agencies, have each been instructed to dedicate all resources necessary to this effort.

We are also cooperating with the other nations most affected by these attacks, including China, the Russian Federation, India, and Japan. The degree of ongoing collaboration is unprecedented and ensures that all relevant information is shared immediately so that together we can bring a halt to the attacks.

Finally, I am announcing today the formation of an independent, blue-ribbon panel of top cybersecurity experts in the private and public sectors. They will advise this administration and the investigating agencies and make recommendations for hardening critical infrastructure against attack. The names and backgrounds of the panel members will be distributed later today.

You may rest assured that this administration will continue to do everything necessary to halt the shameful attacks that are disabling global energy infrastructure. We will not rest until those responsible have been found and brought to justice.

"Okay. Questions?" Bekin pointed into the scrum of journalists. "Sarah?"

A newspaper reporter held her notepad up and began reading.

"Who does the government think is behind the attacks, and why haven't they been apprehended yet? And finally, with all the money the U.S. has spent on cyber-resources, why shouldn't the people expect faster progress?"

"On your first question, we don't have any new information or leads. On your second, same answer. On your third question, I'll just observe that no other nation has made any more progress than we have." Bekin pointed again, this time to a reporter from POX news. "Lee?"

"Randal Wellhead, the Republican candidate for president, says if he were in office right now, the attackers would already have been caught. What's the president's response to that?"

"Talk is easy. Results are tough. Next question – Tom. No, Tom from the *Journal*."

"The stock market has been in free fall this week. What's the administration going to do about that?"

"A free market is just that. It's not the government's job to interfere." Oh well, might as well get this next one out of the way. He pointed to the reporter from Biteparts.com "Bill, your question."

"Regarding this new advisory panel. Isn't setting up a blue-ribbon panel the oldest trick in the book? It makes it sound like the president's doing something, but in reality, it's all just for show."

"I don't agree. These are the best experts in the business. The president has set a tight deadline for their recommendations, and he'll give prompt and serious attention to what they say. Peter."

The reporter from the *New York Post* held his notepad up and began reading. "Who does the government think is launching these attacks? And why hasn't the administration caught them yet? With the amount of money the president's budgeted for cybersecurity, shouldn't these guys have been caught weeks ago?"

Bekin groaned inwardly and stole a glance at his watch. It was only ten minutes after nine. "On your first point …"

* * *

The project team was treated to a different type of report this week. Barker had pulled in an expert from NOAA, the National Oceanic and Atmospheric Administration, to brief them on the likely climate impact of the earthquake off Antarctica. Frank was pleasantly surprised to see the climatologist intersperse her technical slides with cool pictures of glaciers and such and even a few video clips. At the moment, she was speaking to a diagram showing a cross-section of an ice sheet.

"This series of slides shows what happens when an ice sheet breaks up, as happened in 2002 on the other side of Antarctica when the Larsen B ice sheet collapsed. It broke up in less than a week. That was exceptionally fast, but the steps that led up to it took a couple of years to play out.

"Here's what happened in those steps." They were looking at an aerial photo of the ice sheet now. "As we zoom in, you can see lots of cracks and crevasses. These defects form naturally in response to changing stresses in the ice sheet, but while it stays cold, they don't undermine the integrity of the shelf very much. Let's see what happens when things start to warm up, though."

She switched to an oblique aerial photo of a sheet of white ice peppered with countless blinding reflections of the sun.

"Each one of those mirror-like spots is a meltwater pond. There are a lot more of them here than there would have been a few years before, and they're bigger and last longer because of global warming." She switched back to the cross-section diagram, which now showed the meltwater ponds on the surface. Some were above the downward cracks they'd seen in the diagram before. She clicked her control, and now the cracks under the ponds ran deeper and were wider at the surface, making the ponds and cracks resemble toadstools with long, narrowing stems.

"As you'd expect, pooled water runs down and fills cracks, melting them wider. Later in the season, that water will freeze. When it does, it expands, and that leads to new stresses on the ice sheet. When this process continues over a period of years, the ice sheet grows weaker and weaker. What caused the Larsen B ice sheet to finally go was an earthquake thousands of miles away in the northern Pacific. The waves resulting from that quake were strong enough to set off a process that broke the whole ice sheet apart. After six days, an ice shelf almost the size of Rhode Island was floating out to sea in pieces.

"Let's talk about the Ross Ice Shelf now, which is far larger. Climate change was only beginning to affect the Ross Ice Shelf, so it was nowhere near as unstable as the Larsen B ice sheet just before it broke apart.

"The difference is that last week's earthquake was much, much closer and introduced a huge network of enormous cracks. Some of those crevasses extended for dozens of miles. Big aftershocks multiplied and spread those splits further, causing the entire structure to become progressively more unstable.

"Then the tsunami hit, and that placed huge pressures on the ice from below even as it was spreading billions of tons of water over the top. The wave traveled more than fifty miles to the south before it began to recede, since there wasn't much to stop it. That enormous, moving weight placed rapidly changing stresses on the ice sheet, causing the fractures already there to again run off even more miles in each direction and causing countless new ones. After that, the shelf was doomed.

"Now let's go back to our diagram and see what things looked like when the tsunami finally ran out of steam." There were cracks everywhere now and wider. "All that water has to go somewhere, and a lot of it went into all those cracks and crevasses, where it acted like a lubricant, helping the shelf to become more and more unglued. It didn't help that a major storm with near-hurricane force winds hit two days later."

They were looking at a satellite shot now of the edge of the Ross ice sheet. Except that it didn't have a clean edge anymore. Instead, an enormous zone of broken ice filled the space between the open water and what remained of the shelf.

"This was taken three days ago. The broken-up area you're looking at is five hundred miles east to west and a hundred miles north to south." She clicked to the next slide. "And this is the same area yesterday. The broken ice zone, of course, is still five hundred miles wide, because that's how wide the Ross Sea is. But now it's almost two hundred miles from open water to what's left of the ice sheet. Everything in between is broken ice. By the end of the month, we expect almost the entire shelf will be broken up and heading out to sea."

She switched back to a slide. "Here's a list of the secondary effects we anticipate from the event. The breakup of the shelf itself won't affect sea levels, because the ice was already floating. But ice shelves act like giant dams, slowing down the rate of flow of the glaciers that feed them. Those glaciers are going to speed up now, and their ice will break off and float away when it reaches the ocean. Exactly how much they'll speed up we don't know. But two of the three glaciers behind the Larsen B ice sheet accelerated by 800% after the breakup, which is an enormous change.

"Glacier ice wasn't floating before, so every bit of it will contribute to rising sea levels. Worse yet, the same quake seems to have shaken things up at a recently discovered volcanic hot spot a half mile under the ice. From the seismic activity we're detecting, we think it's likely magma will reach the surface within a matter of weeks. When it does, it's going to melt a lot of the overlying glacier.

"All that water is going to super-lubricate the ice above it, as much as tripling its speed towards the ocean. Add that all up, and we expect a huge section of the ice field on land adjacent to the Ross Sea will slide into the ocean over the months and years ahead without the Ross Ice Shelf to slow it down. All by itself, that's going to add two inches of rise to the oceans. And then there are the lesser but still significant effects, like the enormous amount of sunlight that will now be absorbed by, and heat up, open water and land instead of reflecting back into space."

The list of possible knock-on effects was impressive, with each building on and compounding the impact of the effects before it. All told, NOAA predicted an oceanic rise of 6.2 to 7.1 inches as direct and indirect results of the event.

"So, when do you suppose the attacker will react?" Shannon asked Frank as they filed out of the meeting.

"Pretty soon, I expect."

"Why not already? He hasn't missed a single major event since the attacks started."

"I expect for the same reason the speaker from NOAA couldn't provide a firm estimate of the impact. The attacker's probably running his own figures to figure out what to attack. Or maybe he never does and just waits for a knowledgeable source, like NOAA, to firm up its numbers."

"I guess. But why not act now and fine-tune later?"

"That's an excellent question, and maybe there's a clue hiding in that data. I just don't know what to make of it yet."

8

A Really Bad Case of Gas

THE SKY WAS blue, the sea was calm, and life was good for Able Seaman Adam Duff. He was halfway through his watch at the helm of the *OzGas Uluru*, and with the ship's autopilot engaged, there was little to do except stay alert and keep a sharp lookout. Even that duty was limited due to the sheer size of the vessel. Though the bridge towered high above the sea, the bow of the *Uluru* was more than one thousand feet ahead of him. Not that he could see it, because it was hidden behind the curved surfaces of five enormous, spherical tanks and the maze of pipes above them that ran most of the length of the ship. Anything that didn't show up on the ship's radar had better stay out of the way.

In any event, it was more interesting to plan his shore time. In two days they'd tie up at the LNG terminal in Joetsu, Japan and discharge close to ten million cubic feet of liquefied natural gas. Joetsu wasn't a big city, but it handled enough shipping to provide the types of extracurricular activities a sailor on shore leave looked forward to. After eleven days on duty at sea, he was more than ready to be entertained.

A stream of vapor venting off from somewhere ahead caught his eye. That wasn't unusual. Some of the cargo was always changing from liquid to gas, especially as the day grew warmer. He looked at his instrument display. That was odd; the temperature outside had fallen during his watch. Maybe the ship had sailed into a warmer current. That must be it. That would warm up the tanks more than a change in air temperature.

There was more gas venting now. But wait a minute – it wasn't venting from the relief valve on top of any of the tanks; it was coming from somewhere else – somewhere lower, between the first and second LNG tanks.

"Sir," he said. "I think something's wrong."

Tom Bevis, second mate and officer of the watch, looked up from his control station. "What's that?"

"There's a lot of gas venting off forward. And it's not coming from anywhere it should. Take a look."

Bevis stood up and looked where the seaman was pointing. Duff was right. Bevis pulled a pair of binoculars out of its wall bracket and tried to figure out where the gas was coming from. But it was too thick now to see anything clearly. He picked up the phone and rang the captain.

"Sir, Bevis here. Sorry to bother you, but we've got a situation I think you need to know about. There's a lot of gas venting forward of tank two. I can't tell where it's coming from, and it doesn't look like it's coming from anywhere it should." He listened and then looked forward again. "I think it is increasing, sir. Yes, sir. I'll call him right away, sir."

Before he could dial the phone, it began buzzing; it was Barry Conroy, the ship's chief gas engineer. He was calling from the operations room five decks below, where his crew monitored and controlled the ship's complex network of pumps, refrigeration systems, and compressors.

"Tom here," Bevis said. "I was just about to call you. Are you seeing anything unusual in your readouts? Holy Cow! Yes – I'm seeing a lot of venting from up there. Okay. Keep us updated. The captain should be on the bridge in a couple minutes."

"Bad news, Sir?" Duff asked.

"Sounds like it. From the sensor data, it looks like a spill."

Duff didn't know a lot about LNG systems, but he knew a spill involved a leak of liquid methane, not just gas. That meant a risk of fire – or worse, an explosion. He hoped the fire suppression systems were managing it.

Captain Pettigrew arrived and immediately asked, "What did Barry say?"

"He thinks there's a spill, sir," Bevis replied.

"Get him up here."

"Yes, sir."

The captain picked up the binoculars, but had no better luck. *Holy crap*, he thought, *that's a heck of a lot of gas.*

There was nothing to do but watch the clouds of gas billow and blow back toward the bridge until the gas engineer arrived. The captain looked at his watch: it was 15:42. What was keeping him?

"Here, sir," Conroy said, joining them on the bridge. He immediately sat down at one of the control stations and rapped away at the keys until he was looking at the same readouts he'd been studying in the control room.

"What have you got?" the captain asked.

"It looks like a pretty bad spill, sir. I'm guessing one of the access ports to a feed line is open."

"Open? How could that happen?"

"I don't know, sir. Some kind of malfunction, obviously. That's an eight-inch pipe. With the pressure as it is in the tanks, that means thousands of gallons an hour are pooling up there and boiling away."

"Can't you isolate that section of pipe remotely and turn it off?"

"I've already tried, Sir. Nothing seems to be responding down there."

"Can you send a crew forward to manually close it?"

"No Sir. It would be far too dangerous."

"How about the fire suppression system? Can it handle that much volume?"

"It should. Let me see what I can tell from the sensor data."

The engineer's keys rattled again. "No!"

"What?" the captain asked.

"The suppression systems are down, too!"

Duff was sweating now. He didn't want to interrupt, but he'd just noticed something.

"Sir!"

Captain Pettigrew turned toward him. "What now?"

"It looks like we're down a bit by the bow, Sir."

All three of the officers clustered around the instrument Duff was pointing to. He was right. The ship was more than two degrees out of trim. "What the devil?" the captain said. "Get me a reading on the bow ballast tanks."

The second mate sat back down at his station. How could this reading be accurate? "According to the gauges, there's eight feet in the bow tanks and rising, Sir."

"Damn it!" The captain grabbed the phone to call the ship's chief engineer. "Howard, what's going on in the bow tanks? Well, find out!"

The four men stared ahead, stunned. Most of the first hundred and ninety feet of the vessel was taken up by a set of enormous ballast tanks; there was another set in the stern. On its return trip, the ship would weigh hundreds of thousands of tons less than it did fully loaded with LNG. Unless it took on water ballast in those tanks, it would be dangerously unstable. But it was fully loaded with LNG now and already low in the water.

"Bevis, what happens if those tanks fill all the way up when we've got a full cargo?"

The second mate sat down at his control station again and ran some calculations. "Sir, it looks like we'll have water breaking over the bow."

The phone buzzed and the captain grabbed it. "What do you mean you can't close the sea cocks? Well, keep trying!"

Pettigrew jammed the phone back in the cradle and tried to collect his wits. Nothing that was happening made any sense. A valve in an LNG line that shouldn't be open and couldn't be closed; a fire suppression system that was inoperative; and ballast tanks that had decided to fill themselves up a thousand miles from shore.

"Sir ..." It was Bevis. "Sir, we're four degrees down by the bow now. If the tanks fill completely, my guess is we'll be down by about fifteen degrees."

"I know that."

Bevis hesitated, but felt he had no choice but to push the point. "And we'll be up by the same amount in the stern."

"Damn it, man, what's your point?"

"I'm sorry, sir, but I'm the safety officer. It's my job to always have an evacuation plan in mind. The lifeboat isn't rated for more than a hundred twenty-foot drop. It's getting close to that already, Sir. And there's another concern: as the stern rises, the angle of the lifeboat slides will decrease. The boat might hang up instead of fall if the angle's not steep enough."

The captain swore again. He'd only been worrying about losing steering control if the propellers and rudder rose above water level. He'd forgotten about the free-fall lifeboat, mounted on inclined rails high above the stern of the vessel. It was fireproof and rated to sustain the shock of smashing into the water after shooting down those rails and through the air. In theory, it was the perfect design to make a rapid escape from a floating bomb – yank the release control, and the speed generated by the boat's fall would propel it hundreds of yards away from the ship after it hit the ocean surface. But those inside had to survive that fall first.

He made up his mind. "Radio in our position and send a mayday. Then give the order to abandon ship. I'll meet you at the lifeboat."

Pettigrew's office opened onto the bridge; he stepped inside and looked around. What should he take? He grabbed his laptop and shoved it into its computer case. What about all his paperwork? Too much to gather and too little time. An ear-piercing klaxon horn began pulsing just outside the door; he was needed elsewhere. He took the picture of his family off his desk and stared briefly into the eyes of his wife and two small children. Then he slid it in next to his laptop and left.

Some of the crew were already clustered around the lifeboat when he arrived; others were clattering behind him down the metal stairs leading to the narrow grating that gave access to the lifeboat; below his feet, the milk-white wake of the ship raced away astern.

The launching contraption looked like the plunge section of a roller coaster and stood as tall as a three-story building. The red-orange lifeboat was more reassuring, built like a battleship and totally enclosed. A pair of heavy plexiglass windows spanned the boat under a raised roof in the stern, protecting the steering station underneath. One by one, the crew climbed through the hatch in the side of the lifeboat as Bevis counted them in.

The chief engineer was the last to arrive. "Status?" Pettigrew asked.

"I took her up to full throttle, Sir. That way we'll separate from the ship faster."

"Good. Get aboard."

The ship was seriously out of trim now. It had taken on a slow, sick roll as a quartering sea struck its bow, making it difficult to scramble up and through the lifeboat hatch. Pettigrew guessed they were making more than twenty-five knots now; the roiling water they would soon crash into looked like it was a mile away. He clambered backward through the hatch and took one last, long look at his ship before pulling his head and shoulders inside and dogging the hatch down tight behind him.

The inside of the lifeboat was cramped and dim. Strings of red emergency lights glowed bravely along the sides.

"All right! Is everybody strapped in?" Pettigrew called out. A chorus of "aye, ayes" responded, and he realized he wasn't. He fumbled with the harness that would bind him to a seat that looked like it belonged in a space capsule and was designed as it was for the same reason. It was contoured to the shape of a human body and would support him from head to toe to help him survive the shock of the boat hitting the water.

"Okay – hold on!" he yelled. He pulled the lever next to his seat and immediately felt like he'd been shot from a cannon. The acceleration forced him back into his seat and took his breath away. Time seemed to stand still. When were they going to hit the water?

Then they did.

It seemed as if all Pettigrew's sensory inputs were suddenly compressed into one single, thunderous, red overload, followed by violent surging, shaking, and rocking. Gradually, their forward motion slowed until they were at rest, rolling slowly and silently from side to side. Pettigrew tried moving his limbs; they all worked, although his body felt like jelly. The taste of blood in his mouth told him he'd bitten his tongue when they hit the water. And it was dark.

He struggled to get his wits back.

"Can anyone feel water around their feet?" Pettigrew called out. No one responded. Good. "Bevis! Call the roll and find out if everyone's all right. Johnson, take the helm."

The boatswain unstrapped himself and made his way back through the crew to the stern, and the emergency lights came back on. By the time the twenty-third crewmember confirmed he hadn't been seriously injured, Pettigrew felt the reassuring vibration of the lifeboat's engine. He unstrapped himself and joined the boatswain on the steering platform. Good; he could see a regular flash of red light reflecting on the deck outside. Hopefully the lifeboat's EPIRB radio beacon was also working.

"Bring her around till we can see the ship," Pettigrew said.

It was strange to see the horizon from so close to the ocean; his eye level was just six feet above the water – a twentieth of what he was used to. He held his breath as the boat turned until the *Uluru* finally came into view. She was three-quarters of a mile away with her stern bizarrely high in the air and bow now awash. She must be slowing, too, with her twin screws half out of water.

But something else looked strange; the ship looked too short. With a gasp, he realized the *Uluru* was going down. Silently, he and the boatswain watched as, at first imperceptibly, and then faster as it gained momentum, the *Uluru* foreshortened until only her stern could be seen. Half a minute later, only the bridge deck and the stack, no longer smoking, were visible. He looked down at his watch: 15:52. Ten minutes ago, he'd been standing on that bridge. And ten before that, everything had been normal.

He looked up and there was nothing to be seen. Nothing except the rolling waves and the unbroken horizon.

* * *

The meeting room was unusually crowded and quiet when Barker arrived and tapped the microphone to confirm it was on. Everyone already knew the basic details from the news. The scope of the latest attack had made a strong impression.

"Okay, so let's start with the damage assessment," Barker said, pulling up a slide. "There are – or I should say were – about four hundred LNG tankers in the global fleet, and thirty-four of them just went to the bottom. Because they were generally the largest, more than thirteen percent of all seagoing LNG carrier capacity has just been taken offline. It will take years to replace those ships. Until they are, there will be energy cost hikes and probably local shortages as well.

"In each case, electronic and mechanical ship systems were coopted to create an emergency, leading the crews to abandon ship. It appears there was no loss of life.

"Now, here are some of the more interesting facts. We did a preliminary analysis to see if we could find any pattern to explain why certain ships were hit, and not others. Besides the capacity of the ships, the main element the targets had in common was they were all in the deep ocean. In fact, most went down over deep-sea trenches, so there's no hope of salvaging any of them, or their cargoes."

"So, what do you make of that?" Shannon asked Frank after the meeting. "If the goal is to offset climate change, why hit natural gas? That's one of the cleaner fuels. And what about all the gas in those ships – is that going to escape and hit the atmosphere all at once?"

Frank didn't want to admit it, but his confidence in his own theory had been shaken; he couldn't block out the mental image of one of those enormous ships gliding downward into the ocean depths, picking up speed all the while until it finally collided with the sea floor. Surely that would burst the LNG tanks wide-open?

"I don't know, but I'm going to try and find out the answers tonight. I'll see you tomorrow."

It took several hours of research, but by the time he was done, Frank felt vindicated. He had also learned a lot more about the behavior of methane than he had ever expected to.

"Here's the story," he told Shannon when they met at the SCIF the next morning. "First of all, none of that methane is going to end up in the atmosphere. That's because LNG is stored in tanks kept more than two hundred sixty degrees Fahrenheit below zero. So, when the tanks ruptured on impact with the sea bottom, all that LNG would have immediately become encased in really thick ice.

"And it turns out that when methane gas meets seawater, instead of dissolving, it turns into a slushy material called clathrates – there are billions of tons of the stuff already on the sea bottom. Apparently, it forms naturally when methane gas seeps up out of the sea floor. That means when the LNG gas from the ships eventually warms up, it will convert into clathrates and stay out of circulation forever. Right there, the attack struck a meaningful blow against climate change. And the global supply of LNG where it's needed will stay down by over thirteen percent until the ships are replaced – if all of them ever are, with more renewable energy sources coming online all the time. I bet when we run the numbers, it's going to work out just right against the impact of the Ross shelf breaking up."

"But what about the fact that it was LNG, and not coal or petroleum, this time?" Shannon said. "Won't that mean that dirtier fuels will be burned to make up for the loss?"

"I thought about that and decided the answer will be just the opposite. It would take way too much time and money to convert a natural gas plant back to coal on a temporary basis and then back to natural gas, when the ships are replaced.

It would be cheaper to make up the difference permanently using wind and solar instead. Meanwhile, the energy shortage will drive fuel prices up, and that will make clean energy even more competitive. That should lead to more investment in solar and wind farms. So, it makes sense after all."

"You're right. That all adds up. Does it tell you anything new?"

"Mostly it confirms what I already thought. What's new is I'm beginning to think the robotic elements behind the attacks go a lot deeper than I did before."

"Because?"

"The whole attack program just keeps getting bigger and bigger. It would take hundreds of analysts and hackers working full-time to determine what targets to hit, find a way into each one of them, design the exploits, rate the carbon impact of the attacks, and then pull them off in synch with each other."

"Which would mean it would have to be a state actor, right?"

"That's what you'd think. But like we discussed before, all the likely suspects are also victims. Logically, it might suggest some sort of eco-terrorist group might be responsible. The problem is, I don't know how you could pull together the kind of talent necessary to do that without the CIA and NSA getting wind of it. Or where the money would come from."

"How about the nuclear power industry? Not a single nuclear generating site has been hit yet."

"I know. But the permitting, design, and construction times are so long it would be fifteen years before a new plant comes online, and we're dealing with a current crisis. And anyway, in fifteen years, alternative energy should be so cheap no utility would want to be stuck with another nuclear facility."

"Well, then, how about a solar or wind developer or manufacturer?"

"That would make more sense, sure. But no single manufacturer could possibly pull off attacks like these. And it's hard to believe a group of them could agree in secret to work together. And anyway, management usually has a big aversion to going to jail."

They were in front of his apartment now. Shannon gave him a sidelong look and changed the subject.

"I'd love to kick this around further. How about we grab a bite somewhere?" Before he could answer, she added, "You know, you blew me off the last time. Do that twice, and a girl could start to feel like there was something wrong with her."

Frank opened his mouth and then shut it again. He'd need a really good excuse this time. Maybe scuba lessons would work?

But she was too fast for him. "Great!" she said, putting the car back in gear. "There's a place not far from here I've been wanting to try, and I hate sitting alone in a restaurant. I bet you do, too."

There was nothing to do but give in. Now that the moment had passed, he realized he wasn't sorry Shannon had cut off his escape. "What kind of food do they have?" he asked.

"It's an Asian-American fusion place. They just opened last week, and it's gotten good reviews."

A dozen blocks later, she parked the car. "What a week," she said. "I envy you being able to work off-site every day. It's been a madhouse the times I've had to be back at the NSA. New information flying around every which way and the folks on the Hill pressuring the director for results he can't deliver. Of course, he's pressuring everyone under him for the same reason, and so it goes down the chain until it gets to people like me. I thought Friday would never get here, so I could let my hair down a little."

He held the door for her, wondering what that meant.

When she returned to the table from a stop in the restroom, he got the answer. She'd literally let her hair down, and an abundance of lustrous red tresses framed her face to extremely favorable effect. "What looks good to you?" she said, sitting down.

He blinked twice, only catching her meaning when she picked up her menu. "Oh!" he said, "I don't know. Most of this stuff is pretty unfamiliar to me."

"Do you like sushi?"

"Not really."

"Sashimi?"

"Is there a difference?"

"Okay. Sounds like you'll be sticking with the American end of the menu then. I'm going for the exotic, starting with the drink list."

One hour and two drinks later, he was feeling more relaxed. Shannon was very interested in how his thoughts were developing and had some excellent ideas of her own. But they hadn't made any real progress on next steps.

"So, where does that leave us?" she asked, leaning forward and placing her chin on her hand.

"With the same old paradox. The only actors capable of pulling off a series of attacks like this are the governments of the countries that have been hardest hit. But no government would ever hit itself that hard, so that means these attacks can't be occurring. Except, of course, that they are."

She started laughing.

"Was that funny?" he asked.

"No," she said, covering her mouth as she tried to stop laughing. "I'm sorry. It's just that what you said reminded me of a funny song my grandfather used to sing to me. It seems to summarize things perfectly." She pulled out her phone.

"Give me a second – I want to find the lyrics so I get them right. Here we go – this is the verse I remember best. She handed him her phone and he read:

Last night I saw upon the stair,
That little man who wasn't there,
He wasn't there again today
Oh, how I wish he'd go away ...
Go away, go away, and don't come back no more!
Go away, go away, and please don't slam the door ...

"That's amazing," he said. "My father used to sing the same song." Frank scrolled down to read the rest of the lyrics, and Shannon leaned closer so they could both read at the same time.

"How about another drink?" Shannon asked.

9

Breakfast at Adversego's

ONE PART OF Frank's brain was engaging in a slow and painful thought process. The rest of it seemed to be incapable of doing anything.

The three concepts the first part of his brain was struggling to resolve ran as follows:

1. His head had begun hurting sometime during the night, and the headache had gotten steadily worse.

2. If he stayed in bed, he would be less aware of his throbbing head than if he got up.

3. If he got up, he could have coffee.

Eventually, his bladder introduced a fourth consideration that tipped the balance in favor of action. He swung his legs over the side of his bed and paused, hoping that if he exercised patience the room would return to its usual, stationary state. Then he heard a small sound behind him.

His eyes shot open, and his mental capacities sharpened in an instant. The first product of this raised level of awareness was the realization that the sound he had just heard indicated the presence of another human being, followed immediately by the conclusion that the human being in question was occupying his bed. But achieving that state of enlightenment had taxed his capabilities considerably. Identifying who the human being might be did not follow immediately. He decided the best way to pursue that information would be to review the events of the day before and work forward as far as he could.

He started with work, followed by his ride home, after which ...

Oh.

Without looking behind, he wavered to his feet and walked carefully into the bathroom. What he saw in the mirror was not encouraging. He took a long hot shower, shaved and otherwise repaired as much damage as he could, and then opened the bathroom door a crack.

There did indeed seem to be someone lying in his bed. Although he couldn't see a face, logic and the luxurious wealth of red hair gracing his pillow confirmed that the someone was Shannon Doyle.

He tiptoed to his closet and got dressed inside it. Then he tiptoed out to make coffee. As it percolated, he sat on one of his two kitchen chairs to see if he could recall the rest of the events of the evening before. But despite persevering through the entire brew cycle, he had made little progress. A gauzy veil seemed to have descended over his mind's eye partway through the Scorpion Bowl for two Shannon had suggested they share. Surprisingly, he did recall that, as they sipped on their respective straws, he had noticed the color of her eyes for the first time. Less surprisingly, he could no longer recall what that color was.

He poured a cup of coffee and gratefully inhaled its bracing aroma. The worst of his headache had been dulled by the shower, a couple of over the counter pain meds, and two large glasses of water. He decided that the headache aside, he was not displeased. Then he frowned. What if Shannon was? He started worrying about what might have happened on the other side of that gauzy veil and whether he should go out and buy something for breakfast. Or maybe it would make more sense to go out somewhere when she woke up? Or maybe they would just make awkward conversation and she would quickly leave. That would be bad. And Monday would be worse.

"Knock, knock."

He turned and stood up, immediately wishing he'd done so more slowly. Shannon was standing in the doorway in a heretofore unused bathrobe Marla had given him several Christmases before. Worried, he looked for clues in her face to see in what frame of mind she'd awoken.

"Good morning!" he said. "Coffee? And how'd you sleep?"

"Oh, please. Pretty well, thank you. Probably better than I deserve. How many Scorpion Bowls did we drink?"

No wonder he felt the way he did; he'd hoped the answer was singular rather than plural.

"Uh, if you're relying on me, we'll need to call the restaurant to find out."

Her eyes smiled at him above her coffee cup as she took a sip. They were a beautiful shade of green.

"You know," she said, "there's this really great brunch place nearby I've been wanting to try ..."

* * *

"Frank!"

The urgency in Shannon's voice brought him in from the balcony at a run. Shannon was standing on a chair, staring down at the animal that was staring back up at her.

"What's wrong?"

Shannon, feeling foolish, stepped down from the chair. "Are you aware there's a rather large turtle in your apartment?"

"No. That's Thor. And he's a tortoise. I guess I forgot to introduce you."

Shannon sat down. "How exactly is it that you came to have a tortoise in your apartment?"

"Oh, my daughter gave him to me for my birthday. I agree, it is kind of strange to have a tortoise as a pet. But he kind of grows on you." Frank squatted down. "Thor, this is Shannon." If the tortoise's expression, such as it was, changed with this information, Shannon was unable to detect it.

"Charmed, I'm sure," Shannon said in the general direction of the reptile. "So, what goes into having a tortoise as a pet? I assume you don't have to take it out for walks?"

"I probably should. But he seems to be happy enough here without that."

"Happy? How can you tell?"

That stumped Frank for a minute. "Okay. So, let's say not visibly unhappy. Anyway, all I have to do is put some vegetables out for him."

"You mean he's house trained?"

"No, not exactly. But if you don't give him very juicy food, he almost never urinates."

"I'm assuming that only answers half the question."

Frank's eyes lit up.

"That's right! Let me show you what I came up with for that."

He ducked into a closet and came out with a familiar round object with some sort of contraption on top.

"What's that?"

"It's a robotic vacuum cleaner. And on top is a tortoise waste removal device I invented. I'm thinking of patenting it. Let me show you how it works!" Frank went into the kitchen and returned with a paper towel wadded up into a damp sausage.

"Here goes!" He dropped the wad of paper on the floor. "The bit on the top is a plow I took off a kid's remote-controlled earth mover toy. I also added a little camera in the front and hooked everything up to a battery and a Raspberry Pi processor I programmed to receive the video stream and operate the plow." He turned the vacuum cleaner on and set it on the floor.

With mixed shock and amusement, Shannon watched as the vacuum cleaner identified the wad of paper and trundled toward it. As it grew closer, it lowered the plow until it was sliding along on the floor. When it reached the paper, it neatly scooped it up, raised the plow a couple inches, and then glided off to the kitchen. "There's a cat litter box in there it will dump that into. I figured it was easier to train a robot than a tortoise, and it all comes out the same."

"You know, Frank," Shannon said, "I'm glad we got together before I found out just how strange you are." She paused and then added, "At least I think I am."

* * *

Frank sat on his micro-balcony on Monday morning, pondering the events of the weekend. Shannon had not only failed to dash off on Saturday morning, but she stayed through the entire weekend. He'd found it surprisingly pleasant to have someone around despite the small size of his apartment and his solitary ways. Shannon seemed always ready to talk when he was and happy to be online when his thoughts were elsewhere.

In any event, she was not there now. She'd left early to pick up a change of clothes before leaving for Fort Meade, leaving him to his solo morning routine of reading the news on his tablet. The only difference was that instead of a bowl of dry diet cereal, the remnants of a bowl of strawberries sat in front of him. They were courtesy of a shopping stop Shannon had insisted on making after discovering the monastically barren refrigerator and cupboards in his kitchen.

He stepped back inside to get a coffee refill. When he returned, the bowl was empty. He frowned. Had he eaten the last two strawberries and forgotten it? He walked back inside for the remainder of the berries and had just sat down on the balcony again when he heard the *ping* of a text message landing on the phone he'd left in the kitchen. He got up to see what it said and smiled to see a funny text from Shannon.

Returning to the balcony he found ... no strawberries. He was starting to feel like Captain Queeg in *The Caine Mutiny*, but there was no one nearby to blame. Or at least no one human. Perched on the railing of his neighbor's balcony, though, was a large black bird. Large enough, he guessed, to be a crow. Discovered, it tilted its head back and launched into a long, triumphant caw. Curious now, Frank stood up and went inside. But instead of going to the kitchen for more food, he stepped into the living room and looked out the window. The crow was on the railing of his balcony now, cocking its head from side to side, looking for any new scraps of food. Disappointed, it flew away.

Frank hunted through his kitchen for something else to feed the bird and settled on half a bagel. He tore it into pieces and returned to the balcony. But the crow, or whatever it was, was nowhere to be seen. Oh well. He returned to the news and ate the bagel himself.

There was nothing new on the climate change front. Maybe that would give him time to tease something new out of the data they'd collected. He knew from long experience that the best way to do that would be to clear his mind as much as possible and then focus on anything that didn't seem to hang together. He pulled on his jacket and headed downstairs for a walk.

He started toward the Mall and allowed his thoughts to drift through the history of events and across the items of interest he'd already noted. Half an hour later, he decided the most significant thing worth noting was that everything always hung together. The targeting, the timing, the calculations – everything was always remarkably consistent. True, the attacker had found different vulnerabilities to exploit in most cases, but over time Frank had come to recognize that the attacker always used one of just three different approaches when it moved from accessing a system to carrying out the actual attack.

So, if everything hung together so precisely, perhaps he should assume that the attacker was just as logically consistent in other ways as well. That sounded promising, but he didn't know where to take it. He turned his collar up against a freshening, damp breeze and picked up his pace as he leaned into it. Where to go next?

He didn't know. To date, he'd always stopped at that point, because it seemed to point directly toward a dead end, since the only entities capable of pulling off the attacks couldn't be behind the attacks. But what if that wasn't the right way to look at it? What if you divided that step into two questions – the first being who could design the attacks and the second being who was actually carrying them out? That sounded promising. He texted Shannon to see if she was busy for dinner.

* * *

"So, here's what occurred to me. Instead of fighting the conclusion that only a few countries are capable of designing the attacks, why don't we embrace it? Maybe somebody hacked the NSA and stole a program capable of designing and executing the attacks. That would work."

"So, you're suggesting we've been holding ourselves back?" Shannon said.

"I guess you could put it that way, yes."

"Interesting. How do we go about figuring out whether that's the case?"

"Let's review what we think we know, and see if that supports or undermines my idea."

"Okay. What do we think we know?"

"First, that we're dealing with someone that has access to almost infinitely deep databases and inventories of zero-day vulnerabilities."

"Fair enough," Shannon said. "And we also think the attacker has access to databases only the NSA and one or two other agencies on earth maintain."

"Right," Frank said. "And we know the attacks follow the triggering events almost instantaneously. From that we infer the attacker uses a program to select the targets and initiate the exploits. It also makes it possible to imagine that someone other than the original designer of the program could be behind the attacks, because the program is already equipped to fulfill these functions without a big team of sophisticated programmers managing it."

"That makes sense, sure," Shannon said. "So, to sum up, you're thinking the sequence is that the NSA, or some other equally clever agency, built the program first, then someone stole it, and after that, the program could run mostly on its own. Is that it?"

"Precisely."

"Just one problem," Shannon said. "If the NSA or some agency in Russia built it, why hasn't someone told us?"

"That's a good question, and I've been trying to come up with a good answer."

"And?"

"A couple of ideas, but it may be we won't be able to find out whether either of them is right. For example, maybe the top brass at the NSA has had the same thought and isn't telling anyone other than a small team assigned to look for such a thief."

"Why not tell us?"

"How would it look to the public if the NSA designed something that's causing all this damage and chaos? Maybe they're afraid someone will leak the news to the press. And we're coming up on an election again, don't forget."

"But why would anyone leak information like that?"

"Why did Snowden reveal what he revealed? Maybe someone in the NSA wants to make the point that AI weapons are inherently too dangerous, and shouldn't be designed to begin with."

"Point taken. And, of course, it might not be a U.S. program at all. It could have been developed by the Russians or the Chinese."

"Right. But either way, I'm thinking the best way to figure out how the attacks were designed and launched would be to see how the NSA would go about doing the same thing."

"Now that you mention it," Shannon said, "I can easily imagine the NSA wanting to develop something like this. For example, we might want to release a program just like this to wipe out the energy infrastructure of an enemy we thought was about to launch a nuclear attack."

"Exactly," Frank said. "Remember it was way back in 2010 we learned about the Stuxnet attack the U.S. and Israel launched against Iran, targeting the uranium concentrating centrifuges at one of Iran's nuclear development facilities. If Stuxnet hadn't accidentally invaded some systems in other countries, we would never have found out about it. Think what we must be capable of designing by now."

"How about this," Shannon said. "Why don't I ask Jim to schedule a meeting for us with whoever the top artificial intelligence architect is at the NSA?"

"Perfect! Let's do that."

10

But That's Not What You Said!

"JERRY STEINER?" FRANK said. "Do you know what he looks like?"

"No, I've never met him," Shannon said. "Why?"

"I knew a guy by that name back at MIT. He was absolutely brilliant. Strange, but brilliant. He was accepted by MIT when he was just fourteen. He went on to graduate at seventeen, finished his PhD at twenty, and became a full professor at twenty-four. Everybody expected him to win a Nobel Prize for his work in artificial intelligence. AI was enjoying one of its up periods back then."

"Hasn't artificial intelligence always been hot?"

"Oh, not at all, partly because it's had a history of over-promising and under-delivering. Back in the 1960s everybody expected computers to be thinking like people in no time at all. As you already know, that didn't happen. Eventually everybody realized how big a challenge getting computers to think like people was, and the enthusiasm wore off. Then somebody came up with something they called 'symbolic logic,' and suddenly, AI was back in fashion. After the progress from that approach petered out, nobody who stayed a true believer was taken seriously. For a long time, it was a career killer to promote the potential of AI. Most people gave up and moved on.

"Anyway, I haven't heard anything about Jerry in years. I wonder if it could be the same guy?" Frank said, Googling Jerry's name on his phone.

"Huh! How about that? There's almost nothing about him online at all; just some old journal papers from over twenty-five years ago. And not a single picture. That's really odd. Anyway, we'll find out when we meet him."

On their way to NSA headquarters the next day, Shannon returned to the topic.

"So, you said this guy Jerry was brilliant but strange. How so?"

"Well, here's a good example. He was maddeningly literal – just like a computer. Jerry was incapable of recognizing a metaphor no matter how obvious it was, even in context. And if you asked him something, he'd answer the question exactly as you phrased it, even if it didn't make any sense hearing it that way. He wasn't jerking you around; it's just the way his mind worked."

"Such as?"

"Well, let's see. If you said, 'Jerry, am I wrong to think of North Korea as an existential threat to America?' he'd answer, 'No, you're not wrong to think that.' You'd think, fine, we're in agreement. But what he really meant was 'No you're not wrong to think whatever you want to, even if it's something as stupid as Korea posing an existential threat to America.' After that, the conversation would get more and more bizarre until you finally realized you and he were on totally different wavelengths."

"That must have been fun."

"It would have been fun to strangle him sometimes."

"What did he look like?"

"He looked kind of weird, too. For starters, he had this big, round head, with a broad forehead and pasty, pink skin." Frank paused, thinking back, "and thinning blond hair. He combed it straight back. Oh – and how about this – he wore these awful 1970s polyester suits – he had to be the only undergraduate on the entire campus in a suit. He must have bought them at thrift stores, too, because thank goodness, you couldn't buy polyester suits new anymore. No tie, though. Just open-neck shirts with big collars that flopped around over the lapels of the suit jacket. He looked like something out of the movie *Saturday Night Fever*, only in terrible colors, like pale purple. But really, it was mostly the look on his face."

"What kind of look?"

"I'm trying to get that picture back in my mind – it was kind of wild-eyed, with a big, manic grin that usually had nothing to do with the conversation. But he wasn't scary. As a matter of fact, other than the literal bit and the expression, he was more or less okay to talk to. Childlike, actually, now that I think of it. But clearly he was living in his own unique version of reality."

Frank looked back at his computer. "It looks like the last Google hit is an interview Jerry gave after his appointment to an endowed chair." Frank opened the link and skimmed the article. "Oh my," he said. "Here's something I never knew."

"What's that?"

"I'll read it out loud," Frank said.

Professor Steiner was the oldest of four children and enjoyed a happy early childhood. His fondest memories are of playing with his brothers and sisters. But all that changed abruptly when he turned eleven, and his father deserted the family. His mother, already suffering from mental health issues, was devastated and became unable to care for her family. Mrs. Steiner was institutionalized, and the children were distributed far and wide among multiple foster homes. When he grew up, Professor Steiner was able to locate his mother, who is still in custodial care. But he was never reunited with his siblings.

"That's terrible," Frank said, shutting his browser. I feel bad I never knew any of that."

At the NSA, they were led through the usual underground labyrinth of hallways and laboratories to a destination that turned out to be an open area filled with programmers hunched over workstations. On the other side of the room was a single closed office door, which their escort knocked on before leaving.

They waited, but no one opened it. "Maybe we should knock harder?" Shannon said.

"Can't hurt to try," Frank said, knocking sharply.

"Just walk right in," one of the programmers called their way. "Jerry's in his office. But he'll never hear you knocking."

"Thanks," Frank said. He opened the door, and Shannon stifled an urge to laugh: there, sitting behind a computer, was an exact, older version of the person Frank had described. Only now he was bald and wearing a large set of headphones.

They stepped in and waited to be noticed, gradually stepping closer and closer to the desk. When at last they were noticed, Steiner took off his headphones and squinted at them, clearly puzzled.

"Hi, Dr. Steiner," Shannon said. "We were told you'd be expecting us."

A broad smile that displayed all of the teeth inside divided his face into two pieces. "Am I? Who are you?"

"We lined up an appointment with you through Jim Barker. I'm Shannon Doyle. And this is Frank Adversego. You might remember him from MIT. You were both undergraduates there at the same time."

Jerry's face went briefly back into squint mode before reverting to a grin. His head started nodding in bobblehead fashion.

"Frank! Frank Adversego! Yes, I remember." He stopped speaking but kept grinning and nodding.

"Uh, do you mind if we sit down?" Frank said.

"Of course not! What are you waiting for? If you have an appointment, you should certainly sit down. Sit down!" He followed that with an unsettling giggle. Frank had forgotten that habit.

"So, I guess we should explain why we're here," Frank said, sitting down. Jerry began nodding again, as if this was an astonishingly original thought.

"Shannon and I are part of the team that's investigating the big waves of cyberattacks that have been occurring."

"Have they?"

"Well, yes. All over the world – for about a month now."

"Really? I had no idea. I don't pay much attention to the news. Any attention, actually. I don't have a TV or radio here."

"Or at home, I guess." Shannon said, trying to fill the silence that followed.

"Excuse me?"

"I meant, it sounds like you don't have a television or radio at home, either."

"Yes. That's exactly what I said." He grinned back, expectantly, but neither Frank nor Shannon could think of what to say next.

"Oh!" Steiner said at last. "Oh! You're assuming home is somewhere else. But as far as I'm concerned, home is where the lab is. That was part of the arrangement I made with the NSA when I left MIT. The door behind me leads to my living quarters. At first, I had an apartment in town, but I never seemed to use it, so I let it go."

Frank cleared his throat. "Anyway. So, as I said, for weeks now, someone has been launching waves of cyberattacks on essential energy infrastructure. Each of the exploits has been extremely sophisticated. Interestingly, each wave has been carefully calculated to have very precise impacts commensurate with the triggers of the attacks."

"Fascinating! And who do you think is behind them?"

"Well, that's the problem. The attacker seems far too sophisticated for anyone other than the U.S., Russian, or Chinese governments to pull off. But more of the targets have been in those countries – and India and Japan – than anywhere else. Each one has suffered billions of dollars of damage. So, it doesn't seem likely that any of their governments could be actively involved."

"How very interesting. You're saying the only countries that could possibly be the attackers also can't be the attackers."

"Exactly. So, it occurred to us that we, or the Russians, might have developed an artificial intelligence program capable of such exploits, and someone might have somehow stolen it."

"Stolen it? From us?" Jerry looked alarmed.

"Or the Russians or the Chinese," Frank responded hurriedly. "Anyway, we thought it might make it easier for us to figure out how to stop the attacks if we knew how someone would go about creating a program capable of accomplishing the same results. Going a step further, we wanted to get your opinion on whether it would be possible to write a program that could stage such attacks while operating autonomously. In a nutshell, that's why we wanted to speak to you."

"Gee, I'm afraid I can't help you."

"Really?" Frank said, taken aback. "Why not? We've both got top security clearances. You can check with the credentials office."

"Oh, no, that's not the problem at all."

"Then what is?"

"I don't know enough about the attacks you're asking about."

Well, Jerry certainly hadn't changed. Frank told himself to be patient and continued. "That's fair enough. Would you be able to if you knew more about the attacks?"

"Oh, certainly, certainly. Would you like me to learn more?"

"Yes – we'd appreciate that a lot. Why don't I send you a link to the project team's most recent status report right now? The first section gives a concise summary of all the attacks to date. May I do that?"

"Certainly."

Frank sent him a link from his phone via the NSA's internal Wi-Fi. Jerry began reading avidly on his computer screen, nodding vigorously from time to time. As if forgetting Frank and Shannon existed, he put his headphones back on. Shannon frowned and cocked her head to one side, trying to decipher the muffled, just-audible tones that reached them. "Music? Or maybe children?" Shannon whispered. "As good a guess as any," Frank whispered back.

When Jerry finished, he turned away from the screen and involuntarily jumped in his chair when he saw them across his desk.

"Oh! Yes! Of course," he said, pulling his headphones off. Then he frowned.

"So, what do you think?" Frank asked.

Jerry looked slightly embarrassed. "About what I just read?" he asked, helpfully.

"Yes – exactly."

Jerry frowned again. "I think these attacks sound very serious."

Frank took a deep breath and backtracked. "What we're hoping you can tell us is who you think might have an artificially intelligent program able, once set in motion, to autonomously identify hundreds, or even thousands, of targets; find an exploitable vulnerability at each one; design a way to attack the target in the way you read about in the incident summary; and finally, launch those attacks almost instantaneously as soon as it detected a triggering event via the Internet. Is any other government or terrorist or activist group you know of currently capable of that?"

"No."

Frank and Shannon waited for him to elaborate, but Jerry just sat there, grinning.

"Did you want me to say yes?"

"No – not if the answer is no," Well, at least Jerry hadn't said "forty-two." Frank phrased his next question more carefully.

"Does the NSA have anything capable of launching attacks like these?"

"No. The closest capability it has is Turing Eight."

"What's that?"

Jerry's face positively glowed. "The Turing series of AI programs is my favorite project. I've been working on it for years, and the version my team is working on now is the eighth. You see, that was the other part of my arrangement with the NSA. I can work on any aspect of artificial intelligence I want to, so long as I also lead the work on whatever AI projects the NSA and CYBERCOM want to pursue."

"That's quite an arrangement," Frank said.

"Oh, my goodness, it's been absolutely essential for my work – it's what's allowed me, unlike other researchers, to keep pushing forward full speed with AI for the last twenty-five years. That's why I left MIT. I was always having to scramble to find grant funding for my lab. After the 'AI Winter' in the 1980s, when all the funding for AI work dried up, I decided that academia just wasn't for me. Luckily, in my case the NSA was willing to take a long-term view. I've had a guaranteed, inflation-adjusted, minimum budget here for twenty-five years now. If they want me to take on any new work, they fund that as well. It's been bliss." He giggled. "What's it like out there, by the way?"

"You mean in AI research?"

"Oh, if you wish. I meant outside generally." He started humming to himself. "You see, I don't get around much anymore."

"When were you last, uh, outside?" Shannon asked.

"Oh, my. Well, let me see. What month is it?"

"Month?"

"Why, yes – and year, too, I guess."

They told him.

"Oh – well, let me see, I guess it would be almost two years then. That's when my mother died. I think. It was awful. I had to be away from the lab for almost three entire days."

"I'm very sorry to hear that, Jerry," Frank said. "I'm sure that must have been very difficult for you." He paused and then continued. "But to get back to Turing

Eight, can you tell us a bit about that program, what it can't do that the attackers are doing?"

Jerry's eyes lit up. "Oh, yes indeed. It truly is my favorite project. The goal of the Turing series has always been to push the potential for AI to its limits. In deference to the NSA, its specific purpose is to apply AI principles to new types of software weapons so they can infiltrate any type or category of system or software and then wait to be triggered, either by a signal, or on the occurrence of any specific or generic type of event found in the program's database. Once the action phase is triggered, the program can disable those targets. Ultimately, the goal is for Turing to be able to disable an enemy's entire offensive capability. And it would do all this autonomously.

"It could also be programmed to act as a sort of doomsday machine. So, for example, if war was looming, we could inform the enemy we had already deployed such a program, meaning that even if they somehow succeeded in taking out our nuclear capabilities, we could still destroy all their infrastructure. Sort of like mutually assured destruction, back in the old days."

"How does it do all that?"

"It uses the NSA's huge library of zero-day exploits, as well as vulnerabilities it's programmed to seek and archive on its own. It can install trapdoors and design assaults on whatever types of essential cyberinfrastructure of whatever country, or countries, you wish to designate. You can also program it to attack whatever specific category of target you wish. For example, if you wanted, you could instruct it to disable just financial, or transportation, or – "

"Energy infrastructure?" Shannon asked.

"Oh, of course, energy infrastructure."

"But how could you trust a program like that," Frank asked. "What would prevent it from making mistakes, or attacking the wrong targets?"

"Oh, it has basic ethical controls built into it. Isaac Asimov's Three Rules of Robotics are still useful starting points, although they don't go far enough. If you don't remember them exactly, they go like this:

A robot may not injure a human being or, through inaction, allow a human being to come to harm.

A robot must obey orders given it by human beings except where such orders would conflict with the First Law.

A robot must protect its own existence as long as such protection does not conflict with the First or Second Law.

"But since we're talking about war," Jerry continued, "there are overrides to the ethical rules as well. So, for example, at level one – say, during a non-shooting war – Asimov's rules would be absolute. But you can also program Turing so that as the danger to the owner – in this case, the U.S. – increases, Turing can automatically up-shift to a level where those rules are modified. In the case of a threatened preemptive nuclear strike, it would override the first rule with respect to the enemy's population, because we're now on a war footing. And in the case of the doomsday scenario, the three rules would reverse entirely, because the program couldn't trust any inputs from anywhere, and its mission can't be completed if it doesn't survive. And I also included Asimov's fourth rule as well."

"There was a fourth rule?" Frank said. "I never knew that."

"Most people don't. He added it much later, in 1985, in a novel called *Robots in Empire*. Since he wanted it to trump all the other rules, he thought it should be the first rule. But people were already used to the numbering of the original rules. So, he assigned it the numeral zero, and called it the 'Zeroth Rule.' It goes like this:

A Robot may not harm humanity, or by inaction, allow humanity to come to harm.

"That seems like a very wholesome rule to me, so I included that one, too."

"So those are the basic ethical rules," Shannon said. "What more needs to be added?"

"Well, I expect there are all sorts of nuances that should be considered. I've never been interested in the field of AI ethics, so I only built in the most basic rules and rule-shifting algorithms. I had to provide that much of an ethical foundation so extensive logic re-programming wouldn't be required later. But here's an example. If you say that the ethical override of rule one only applies in relation to people who are physically present in, say, Russia, then Russian troops would be safe once they left Russian soil.

"Here's another example. At any point in time, there are going to be some Americans in Russia. Should that force the program to be selective about the actions that it takes, or perhaps do nothing at all, until all the Americans leave? Or is it allowed to sacrifice those lives? If it isn't, what should Turing do if it can't always tell who is and who isn't an American citizen? And what about Americans that are also Russian spies? Should Turing protect them, or kill them? All this sort of thing still needs to be added to make Turing truly useful. Those capabilities will be added to Turing Nine."

"When will that happen?"

Jerry suddenly looked distracted. "Oh, goodness. I keep forgetting to put a requisition in for an engineer who knows something about ethics logic." He removed a desk diary from the drawer in his desk and wrote himself a note.

"What else needs to be done to finish Turing Nine?" Frank asked.

"Oh, the basic structure is all done. But I'm such a fiddler. I hate to turn a new version of a pet project over to my team. Once I do, they want to make all kinds of changes, and I start to lose control. Currently I'm running tests on Turing Nine in our simulated global environment, which replicates the real world to a remarkable degree. Turing Nine is doing very well!"

"That's fascinating," Frank said, glancing at Shannon. "But you said no program the NSA or anyone else has could replicate the current waves of attacks on its own. What missing parts would be needed to enable Turing to plan and launch the kind of attacks we're discussing?"

"Oh, my. Well, let me see. When you think about the goal you suggested — taking out energy infrastructure — the number of variables that would have to be accommodated would be almost infinite, because so much information would be changing all the time. Power plants would close for repairs, or permanently. New ones would come online. Other issues on the grid would stop fail-over precautions from preventing a regional or national blackout, and so on. That many options can cause what we call a 'combinatorial explosion' — meaning a problem that would take more resources to solve than the most powerful computer currently imaginable possesses. To do what you're suggesting, somebody would have to be helping any program in the possession of any government today to refine its analysis."

"Even the Turing program you developed for the NSA?" Frank asked.

"Even the NSA's Turing."

"Well, thanks. I guess you've told us what we came here to ask." Frank stood up. Jerry didn't, so Frank leaned over to shake hands.

"Great to see you again, Frank. Next time, you'll have to tell me what you've been up to all these years."

"Sure thing, Jerry."

11

It's Not as Bad as All That

"WELL," SHANNON SAID when they were back in the hallway, "that was instructive."

Frank's ears were burning. He hadn't been trying to impress Shannon – consciously, anyway. With one of his famous, intuitive theories now blown out of the water, he could tell she was being tactful. Was she disappointed, too?

"I suppose so," he said, trying not to sound at a loss. "And anyway, the question of whether we're dealing with an autonomous program or a directed series of exploits using an AI program is more of an interesting detail than something essential to figuring out who's behind the attacks. If nobody could have written an autonomous program capable of staging them, it just means we're back to assuming there's a human instead of a robot pulling the trigger."

"Yes, but who?"

"Can I give that a think and get back to you?"

"Of course, you can," she said.

* * *

Frank had already passed the halfway point on his morning run. But instead of rounding the Washington Monument and heading home, he turned south toward the Jefferson Memorial. His autonomous program theory had seemed to provide such a neat solution, but Jerry had slammed the door on that option, assuming he was right. So where to go next?

Two miles later, Frank had knocked off the Jefferson, Roosevelt, and Martin Luther King memorials and was no closer to the answer. But he was fading, both mentally and physically. Heading back up the Mall, he ran out of gas completely and sat down on a park bench, gasping for breath and inspiration.

It was time to try a different approach to get past the conundrum that the only identified suspects couldn't be suspects. An old favorite of his in such a situation was to apply another piece of seemingly unassailable, but nonetheless contradictory logic: "When you've failed to find something anywhere it could possibly be, then it must be somewhere it couldn't."

Leaving aside extreme cases like spontaneous combustion or alien abduction, the purpose of citing that contradiction was to highlight where the problem must lie: by necessity, wherever something was, it could be. So, the error had to be with the original assumptions regarding possible locations.

That suggested that the current paradox wasn't really a paradox at all. Either he'd framed the statement improperly or perhaps left out something crucial. That meant it was time to take apart the statement that "the only entities that could be the attacker also couldn't be the attacker."

That statement depended on at least two assumptions. The first one was that he had identified all entities capable of launching the attacks or designing a program capable of doing so. The second one was that whoever had developed the attacks was also launching them. One or both of those assumptions might be wrong. For example, someone might have stolen the AI program. Now the attacker was no longer the developer of the program, and the contradiction had disappeared.

He had his breath back now and began to trot homeward, reorienting his idea of what might have happened. If someone stole a program that couldn't operate entirely autonomously, then the person who stole it must be a skilled AI engineer. Which would probably be the case, anyway, or he wouldn't know the program existed nor have access to a copy. Well, why not? Why couldn't there be someone that had the opportunity, means, motive, and skill to make off with the crown jewels of one of the most sophisticated cyber labs in the world and then launch a private campaign to save the earth from global climate change? After all, somebody had to be behind the attacks.

* * *

"So, your new theory is that instead of someone stealing a completely autonomous version of an AI, a skilled AI engineer at the NSA, or maybe an equivalent lab or agency in Russia or China, stole a semi-autonomous one and decided to become a climate vigilante?" Shannon asked.

"Right. Or possibly that someone hacked into one of those labs and made off with the technology. But I think the 'going rogue' scenario is more likely. I have to believe it would be easier for an insider to know about the program and make off with it."

"But I thought you'd concluded that unless the program could operate autonomously, someone stealing the technology wouldn't be able to use it effectively?"

"I had. And now I'm thinking I jumped to that conclusion too quickly."

"Okay," Shannon said. "So, let's say someone could steal and use the technology on their own. But now you've got another whole set of assumptions to make."

"Very true. For starters, we'd have to assume there was a program available to steal." Frank said.

"Yes," Shannon said, "and that someone out of a very small number of people decided to steal it. Just because someone's a part of the NSA doesn't mean he knows what the people in the next room are doing. I doubt many NSA employees here are aware Jerry's program exists. The same tight security procedures would apply anywhere else."

Frank tapped his fingers and looked up at the ceiling. "What else?"

"I'm thinking 'what else' is you're forgetting the law of parsimony."

"I know. The more assumptions you need to make to reach a conclusion, the more likely it's the wrong explanation. But stick with me, because I'm about to take one of those assumptions back again."

"Which one?" Shannon said.

"The one about such a program existing, of course. According to Jerry, he's already built one. Maybe other countries thought it was worth developing one, too. But here are two more assumptions: the guilty party figured out a way to get the program out of the NSA, or wherever, and has an appropriate system to run it on."

"Those assumptions sound less troublesome to me," Shannon said. "On the first one, what's so hard about heading home one night with a thumb drive in your pocket? We go through a metal detector when we arrive in the morning but not when we leave."

"Because," Frank said, "a program like this would fill a bucket of thumb drives, so you'd want to sneak out a hard drive instead, but that's just a detail. The real challenge would be that you'd need a pretty powerful computer to run the program on. As I think about it, the attacker probably also had to plant all the malware while he was at work."

"Why's that?"

"Because otherwise he'd also need to make off with all the database information and zero-day archives needed to set up the attacks. Doing all that penetration testing and malware placing on the job sounds unlikely to me, though."

"Because?" Shannon asked.

"Because he'd be noticed doing such a big project."

"Maybe not."

"How so?" Frank asked.

"Well, according to your earlier assumptions, the person who steals the program would have to be one of the people who developed it. Maybe his role is actually to use the program to penetrate systems and plant malware against enemies. Setting up attacks in his own country at the same time might be easy to work in without being noticed."

"I like that! That makes perfect sense." Frank said. "So maybe we've made some progress. We've got the beginning of a profile for a suspect – an idealistic, highly skilled employee of one of just a few domestic and foreign intelligence agencies who is working on a project similar to Turing and who also has access to a powerful off-site computer. Maybe he's affiliated with a non-profit or university lab that does work with the government and has some serious computers."

"And probably American," Shannon said. "It's harder for me to imagine a climate vigilante in Russia or China."

"I'm not so sure about that, but in any event, let's note the attacker could also have a different motive. He could be making a bazillion dollars on stock markets around the world. Every time one of these attacks is launched, some company's stock takes a hit. I wonder whether the Securities and Exchange Commission has been looking for unusual trading in companies right before and after they get hit?" Frank made a note to himself and then frowned.

"What's wrong," Shannon asked. "It seems like we're finally making some progress."

"Well, making progress is one way to put it. But starting all over again is another."

* * *

"Hey!" Frank said, "Here comes Julius."

"Julius?" Shannon said, looking from Frank's balcony down at the street. "Who's Julius?" But Frank had disappeared inside.

He was opening the refrigerator when he heard something sounding like *"Eeek!"* from the balcony. "What's wrong?" he called back. He took a cup of strawberries out of the refrigerator and returned to the balcony. Shannon was leaning back in her chair, clutching its arms. Sitting on the tiny table immediately in front of her, its head cocked to one side, was a crow.

"Oh, is that all. Shannon, meet Julius."

"What does Julius want?" Shannon said, still tense.

"Strawberries! Here, want to give him one? He'll take it right out of your hand."

"No, thank you. I think I'll just watch you feed him."

"That's fine. Watch! Here's a new trick I taught him."

Frank put a strawberry in his mouth and tilted his head back. Shannon watched, horrified, as the crow flapped its way into the air and then down onto Frank's forehead, its talons barely missing his eyes. It plucked the strawberry from Frank's lips and then jumped into the air. With a fluttering of wings, it rose a few feet before settling down again on the railing.

"There! Wasn't that cool? Here," he held out a strawberry. "Want to try it?"

"No!" she said. "And I don't think you should, either!"

"Oh, Julius wouldn't hurt a fly. Hmm. Scratch that. He'd probably eat a fly. But so long as you're not food, he's really very gentle. Smart, too! Watch this. Julius! Catch!" The bird leaped into the air and circled above their heads, waiting. Frank threw a strawberry upward, and Julius caught it precisely at the top of its arc.

"I've been reading up on crows lately. Did you know you can teach them to talk? I've already taught him to understand several words. I'm hoping to train him to say some next. He comes by every day now."

"That's great. Now how about we go inside?" Shannon followed Frank inside and gave the door a decisive shove shut. Then, feeling sheepish, she locked it for good measure.

* * *

Within a few days, Shannon was much more comfortable with Julius. She enjoyed feeding him now, although only from her hand. Frank was making progress with the crow's speech lessons, too. Every time Julius learned a new word, he'd reward the crow with a new dime or penny – the crow assigned great value to anything shiny. As soon as Frank surrendered a coin, the bird would snatch it and instantly fly away. Frank wondered where its secret cache of treasures might be. When Julius learned to croak, *"Black Hats Suck!"*, he gave it a quarter.

"What does Thor think about your new pet?" Shannon asked one day. "Do you think a tortoise can be jealous?"

"Oh, Thor would never be jealous. I'm sure he's as generous as a tortoise can be. He really likes Julius."

"Oh, come on now. How can you possibly tell?"

"Watch!" Frank disappeared inside and returned with the tortoise, setting it down on the balcony. As if from nowhere, the crow appeared, fluttering down and landing on Thor's back. The tortoise slowly craned his neck around until he could see who was there and then lumbered inside, the bird still poised upon its back. "See? They're pals."

"How can you be so sure Thor's enjoying himself?"

"Well, you'll see. If he wanted to, he could walk under the couch and scrape Julius off. But he never does."

Sure enough, the tortoise made a slow circuit around the couch and returned to the balcony with Julius still in place. Frank rewarded them each with a strawberry.

"I think I may have understated something I said before. It's a *really* good thing we got together before I found out how strange you are," Shannon said to Frank. Then she cocked her head from one side to the other. "What do *I* have to do to get a strawberry?"

"Hmm," Frank said with a sly smile. "Let me think about that."

*　*　*

"Frank?"

"Yes?"

"I've been wondering," Shannon said that night. "Why did you decide to play so hard to get? Weren't you attracted to me?"

Frank stared up at the ceiling of the bedroom. It was dark, except for the occasional flicker of headlights making their way through the window blinds when a car passed by below. "Oh, that wasn't it at all. I guess you could say I just wasn't open for business."

"Why?"

How much did he want to share? "I guess you just get used to being alone after a while."

"Really? Weren't you lonely? You don't seem to have a circle of friends you do things with."

"Maybe sometimes."

"Then why stay that way if you don't have to?"

"I guess I wasn't sure I had another option."

"Oh, come on. What else were you waiting for me to do? Take out a looking-for-love ad addressed to you personally and leave an underlined copy on your desk?"

"I'm sorry. You're right. After a while I did have a pretty good idea you were interested."

"Well, all I can say is you're a mighty timid rabbit."

"I guess I am. I suppose every time a relationship ended, I just got more defensive. I've never handled rejection well. And I'm lousy at reading people. I notice every little thing that might look like disapproval, and I find those things everywhere. Like even in a checkout line. I'll notice whoever is behind the register chatting with the person in front of me, but when it's my turn, the smile disappears."

Shannon yawned. "Did it ever occur to you they might know each other?"

"I suppose. My daughter's always pushing me to try harder. To get out and about more; open up to other people. That sort of thing. I guess I'd be better off if I did, but I don't really know how to go about it. And if I did, I'm not sure I have it in me anymore to try."

But those were just excuses, weren't they? More likely he was being defeatist and cowardly. He'd been more social when he was younger. Or at least more social in his own way. Why couldn't he try being that way again, now that there was someone who could be at his elbow to smooth out the awkwardness? Shannon was great with people.

The room was lighter, now. Somebody must be parked at the end of the street with their lights still on. "Maybe you could help me out with that," he said. "You've been saying we should go out with some of your friends, and I've been holding back. I could try for a change. Maybe turn a corner and try and rejoin the land of the living, as Marla likes to put it. What do you think?"

But Shannon had fallen asleep. Down the street, the driver turned off his lights, and the bedroom returned to its usual darkness.

12

I Saw What You Did

THREE HUNDRED MILES above the earth's surface, a spy satellite detected a half-dozen tightly concentrated explosions in the darkness far below. Within seconds, other satellites detected strikingly similar events across most of Russia's eleven time zones.

The satellites beamed the data to the bank of computers the North American Aerospace Defense Command had assembled and upgraded ever since the early years of the Cold War. One of those computers began comparing the data to the launch profiles held in its database. Three seconds later, it found a potential match and transmitted the information to the display of the appropriate terminal in the NORAD Alert Monitoring Room.

The information triggered audio and visual alerts, jolting the technician sitting at the terminal to immediate attention. He leaned forward and peered at the text on the screen. In the two years he'd spent at this console, he'd never received a potential attack warning. Simulated alerts in training exercises, yes. But never one that might be the first hint that a nuclear war had just begun. He pushed the red button on the pad next to his keyboard. People throughout the room came alive as the technician got back to work, scanning additional data as it appeared on his screen.

The senior duty officer appeared at his elbow. He bent over to look at the screen. "What have you got, Corporal?"

"I don't know yet, Sir. Something on the Murmansk Peninsula. Here's a visual of what the satellite detected. It's just about dawn there. All you can see distinctly are six simultaneous explosions. The system identifies it as a possible hostile launch from a mobile missile battery. We're receiving almost identical captures from more locations across Russia."

The major stared at the image and felt a knot growing in his stomach. The bright lights formed a tight, precise grouping – almost like an exploding six pack of beer. "Did the system identify the type of missile battery?"

"No, Sir. It's a generic identification based on the configuration of the explosions – a lot like a SCUD mobile battery firing but bigger. It's not matched to any known weapon system."

The major tapped his foot. In less than two minutes, he'd have to classify the event as either harmless or a potential attack. If he did nothing, the alert would default to the latter conclusion and send a warning up the chain of command. Could the Russians have developed a mobile missile launch system we'd never seen before? It wasn't impossible. He wondered where his wife and children were right now.

He stepped quickly across the room to another technician.

"Sergeant Butler, are we tracking anything on radar yet?"

"Nothing, Sir, from any of the sites."

The major glanced up at the large digital display on the wall that had begun counting forward as soon as the alarm sounded. Already, one minute and twelve seconds had elapsed since the incident had been identified. Did that mean there was nothing to worry about or that the launch sites weren't close enough to Russian borders for the missiles to show up on radar yet? Or maybe they were cruise missiles flying close to the ground and couldn't be detected until they were much closer to their targets?

"Call up a map of the launch sites."

"Yes, Sir." A map of Russia bloomed on one of the wall screens, with each location marked. It was a mixed bag; most were clustered between Russia's western borders and Moscow, but a few were near Russia's Pacific coast. Not what you'd expect if Russia was attacking the U.S. But it could be consistent with an attack on Europe using mid-range missiles, with some U.S. military bases in South Korea and Japan thrown in as well. If that's where they were headed, they'd reach their targets very soon. The numbers on the time screen now read *2:18*, and he felt a bit unsteady from the adrenaline coursing through his system.

"Major!" someone called from across the room. "I've got something."

He looked up as another large screen came to life, displaying an extremely grainy picture in gray and black.

"What are we looking at?" the major called back.

"The next satellite in line just sent in a new picture of the Murmansk site. It's a little lighter there now, and the camera picked up more detail."

But what was it? The major walked closer. It was a still picture, hazy on one side. That must be smoke still drifting away from the large blackened area. It looked like there might be some flames, too. But that could be foliage ignited by missile exhaust.

"Any computer pattern recognition yet?"

"No, Sir."

The major could feel the eyes of every unoccupied person on him. "Zoom out some on that picture – I want to see the surrounding area. And call up an archival picture of that location immediately."

As the magnification decreased he could see more, and the resolution sharpened. He thought he was beginning to understand what he was looking at. "Do you have pictures of any other sites in the Far East?"

"Yes, Sir. Two more. I'll put them up on the other screens."

"Give me the archival shots for those sites, too. And I want any other data we've got on those locations."

The pictures of the other sites came on screen just as his aide arrived at his side with a ringing telephone. Before he took it, he called across the room for one last piece of information. "Sergeant Butler – are you tracking anything yet in Europe?"

"No, Sir!"

Thank God. That nailed it. He sank heavily into an unoccupied chair and accepted the phone.

"Sorry to bother you, Colonel. Everyone can stand down. Yes, Sir. I'm sure. It looked very suspicious at first. Preliminary computer analysis identified possible missile launches in forty-eight locations across Russia. We have better pictures now, showing nearly identical damage at multiple locations. Comparison with archival photos supports the conclusion that what the satellite cameras captured was the destruction of electrical transformers. That's right, Sir. Each location is a power transmission station. I don't know how someone pulled it off, but it looks like our buddies in Russia have a heck of a lot of equipment to replace."

* * *

It wasn't just Russia that had lost hundreds of transformers, Frank learned from the incident summary. The U.S, China, and a half-dozen other countries had as well. All the transmission facilities were associated with high greenhouse gas production sites – coal-fired generating facilities, diesel truck manufacturing plants in India, and so on.

The summary also informed him that the transformers used at large transmission facilities weren't commodity items. They were extremely expensive and customized to their specific use and location, so not many were kept in inventory. In the space of a few moments, the attackers had destroyed more transformers than existing manufacturers would be able replace in an entire year. As a result of the ongoing attacks, and whether it liked it or not, every country meaningfully contributing to global warming was meeting its commitments under the Berlin Accords far sooner than expected.

Measured by impact, it was one of the more devastating attacks so far. And one of the most elegant. The attacker had simply sent a massive burst of electricity to the transformers to short them out after disabling the surge protectors that otherwise would have protected them. It would take a long time to design and install new safeguards against similar attacks across the power grids of the countries affected. And who was to say those upgrades couldn't be hacked as well?

"What I don't understand is why the attacker doesn't come out in the open?" Frank said to Shannon. "You'd think if he really wanted to save the world, he'd announce what he was up to. That would give countries an incentive to cut their emissions the way they want to instead of letting the attacker decide what to blow up next."

"Maybe he thinks it wouldn't work," Shannon said. "After all, it's not like we don't know what will happen if we don't cut emissions, and so far, we haven't done enough. The attacker may figure countries would tighten up just long enough to catch him, and then go back to their bad old ways."

"And he's probably right," Frank said. "But it does make me worry."

"How come?" Shannon asked.

"Well, if the attacker is that determined, what happens if he decides things are getting worse faster than he can prevent with attacks like the ones he's launched to date? What happens if he's got the same ethics as Jerry's Turing program? Would he start changing his own rules?"

"To what?"

"I don't know. Here's hoping we don't find out."

* * *

"Say," Shannon said on their way back from dinner that night. "Do you mind if we take an extra ten minutes so I can get something at my apartment? It's right around the corner."

"Of course not. Lead the way," Frank said.

She stopped in front of a plain-looking brick structure and unlocked the door.

"This is where you live?" Frank said. "It doesn't look like an apartment house."

"It isn't. It's an old commercial building converted into lofts. Most of my neighbors are artists. You can wait for me here."

"Here? Why don't I just come upstairs with you? I've never seen your place."

"I know," she said, looking sheepish.

"Well?" he said.

"Well, okay, but don't make fun of me. I don't usually let people see where I live."

"Of course not." He followed her into the elevator, wondering what could possibly be in her apartment that she'd be self-conscious about. Lots of stuffed animals? A Justin Bieber poster?

"Okay, here we are," she said when they reached her apartment. "Now remember, you promised not to laugh."

She opened the door, and there, hanging from the high ceiling of a large room with ten-foot-tall windows was a sleek, gossamer-winged airplane. Frank guessed it must be at least eighteen feet from wing tip to wing tip.

"Wow!" Frank said. "That is insanely cool! Where'd you get it?"

"I built it," she said simply.

"Really?" For the first time, Frank noticed the rest of the room. Aside from a bed in one corner and a small kitchen table in another, there was almost no furniture as such – just a big work bench in the middle of the room, covered with tools and surrounded by shelves filled with materials and equipment. "That's incredible. Tell me about it."

"It's a solar-powered plane. I've been refining the design ever since grad school, each time making it lighter and the energy source and engine more efficient. I've completely rebuilt the wings and solar panels three times now. Kind of like Jerry coming out with new versions of Turing, I guess."

"That's fantastic! How did you get started making unmanned aircraft?"

"I was in love with the space program as a kid. My dream was to work for NASA when I grew up, so I took all the courses in college I'd need to go into aerospace. But then NASA announced they were going to wind down the shuttle project, and all the jobs dried up. So, it was the usual story. Lots of loans to repay, so I switched all my courses halfway through grad school and scrambled to retool my resume. When I graduated, I interviewed for the jobs that were available."

"I'm sorry. That must have been a big disappointment."

"It all worked out well enough, so I can't complain, but I didn't want to give the dream up entirely. I started tinkering around with the kind of aircraft you could build and fly on your own – it's basically just a really big model airplane. The whole thing weighs less than eighty pounds. I guess I've gotten a bit compulsive about it."

Frank was walking around in circles and rapidly deepening engineering love, craning his neck back so he could appreciate every detail of Shannon's creation.

"And before you ask," Shannon said, "yes, I can take the wings off. This is the biggest plane I could build in my apartment and still remove in no more than three pieces using the freight elevator."

"Have you flown this version yet?"

"Yes, several times."

"How high can it fly?" Frank said, already revising his weekend plans.

"Above 30,000 feet."

"Incredible! How long can it stay up?"

"It can stay up indefinitely at this latitude from about May fifteenth to July thirty-first, provided it stays sunny all day. Before and after that, the nights are too long for the batteries to last. But there's new equipment coming out all the time – lighter engines, more efficient solar panels and batteries, and so on. I'm sure I'll keep upgrading it."

Frank finally quit admiring the plane and turned to her, his eyes gleaming. "Shannon," he said, "I've never met a girl like you before!"

"In that case, you could give me a kiss."

But a new detail of the aircraft had already caught Frank's eye, and he was once again circling the room, his face a mask of awe and delight.

13

Tear Gas and Television

S HANNON WAS OUT for an evening with her girlfriends, and Frank was rummaging around his apartment, looking for his can opener. Darn it! His kitchen was tiny – where could it be hiding? More to the point, where had Shannon put it? He shoved the drawer shut and decided to order a pizza instead.

Shannon hadn't moved in. But she was spending enough time at *Chez Adversego* for more and more of her possessions to sneak in and claim spaces in places convenient and otherwise. Like his bathroom. For years, he'd cohabitated with a bottle of the same brand shampoo he'd used since childhood. Now the shelf in his shower stall was cluttered with an astonishing array of expensive shampoos and conditioners – six at last count. Lately, he'd been amusing himself during his showers by stacking them in what he thought were artful arrangements. Just this morning, he'd constructed a replica of the facade of the Parthenon he was particularly pleased with. Surprisingly, Shannon was unimpressed.

He settled into the living room while he waited for his dinner and turned on a cable news channel, wondering what the pundits had to say about the latest attacks.

What they were saying was that things were turning ugly. He turned the sound up as the anchor began presenting the lead story.

We begin our broadcast tonight with an update on the impact of the ongoing assault on the energy infrastructure of the U.S. and many other countries. Today, several more American utilities revealed they will need to institute so-called brownouts during times of peak electrical demand. Abroad, those living in major cities in countries including China, Russia, and India are enduring total power shut downs for several hours every day. And the cost of electricity is skyrocketing everywhere.

The video cut to a picture of a gas station with a line of cars extending far down the road from its pumps.

Gasoline is also in short supply, resulting in long lines at the pumps in all states and actual rationing in some. And although government officials claim there will be adequate supplies of heating oil and gas this winter, executives of some oil and gas companies, speaking anonymously, are not so sure.

The scene cut to an aerial shot of an enormous crowd of people gathered in front of the Capitol.

As conditions worsen, citizens are demanding action. But there's not much governments can do until they know who the enemy is. As you can see, there's a big crowd demonstrating in Washington, D.C. today. Jan, do we have an estimate on how many folks are there?

The Washington police are estimating at least 250,000, Don. Tens of thousands of protesters are being reported in many other cities across the country. That's impressive, since the organizers announced this National Call for Action protest less than a week ago.

Thanks, Jan. Let's go next to William Bradshaw. He's on location outside the Department of the Interior in Washington, D.C. Hello, Bill. What can you tell us about the demonstrations there?

They're getting heated, Dan. Behind me, you can see the environmentalists on the left, and on your right, the pro-drilling demonstrators.

The camera panned back, showing hundreds, if not thousands, of people carrying and waving signs behind temporary barriers. Walking back and forth in between were the police.

What are the demonstrators hoping to accomplish?

As you know, things have gotten more and more political as the attacks have continued. The environmentalists are supporting President Yazzi's reelection. They don't endorse the attacks, of course, but they're not entirely sorry to finally see results on climate change, however that happens.

And the conservatives?

They think the whole thing is a liberal plot. They claim global warming is a hoax and that the attacks are being launched by some secret government task force. According to them, when Yazzi realized he couldn't get Congress to ratify the Berlin Accords, he decided to take matters into his own hands.

Isn't that kind of crazy?

Well, they don't think so. They've pledged to win back the White House, and their numbers are growing. People are really upset about the shortages and the cost of energy, and no surprise. The national average price for gasoline reached $5.78 a gallon last week. That's hitting people's pockets hard, which means consumers have less to spend on other things. Rising energy costs are forcing businesses to announce layoffs, too.

The video returned to the studio, where the anchor had been joined by a guest.

For more on the economic picture, let's turn to Alan Kaner, our chief business analyst. Alan, how do things look to you?

Pretty awful, to be blunt. There's been a net loss of jobs for each of the last five weeks, and the numbers are getting worse. It's hard to imagine that trend won't continue until whoever is behind the cyberattacks is caught.

At least we're not alone here in the U.S., though. Isn't that right?

Correct, Dan, but that's not good news. The five hardest-hit countries represent more than half of the world's consumers and productive capacity. That means we're heading straight for a global recession. With factories shutting down, fewer people driving, and -

The news anchor pressed a finger against his earpiece and interrupted.

Excuse me, Alan, but I'm being told things are getting out of control at the demonstration outside the Department of the Interior. Let's check back in with William Bradshaw. Bill? What's going on there?

The camera cut to a chaotic scene with protesters climbing over the barriers. As their numbers grew, they began pushing against the police. The officers facing the two crowds of protesters were back to back now, with nowhere to go, as objects began flying overhead. The yelling was growing more threatening by the minute.

Nothing good, Dan. As you can see, the police are having a hard time trying to keep the protesters apart.

White smoke was drifting into the picture. Bradshaw started coughing and held one hand up to his mouth.

Uh-oh. Looks like the police are lobbing tear gas canisters into the crowd. Back to you, Dan. My crew and I need to move upwind.

The door buzzer caught Frank's attention, and he turned off the television. Just the same kind of thing you saw on the news every night now.

* * *

"Say," Frank said to Shannon on their way to Fort Meade the next day. "Does your solar plane have a name?"

"Well, that was random."

"Yes, I guess it was. I was just thinking about your plane, and it made me wonder whether you gave it a name. I didn't remember seeing anything on it."

"It does, but the letters are pretty small."

"And?"

"You're going to have to promise again not to laugh."

"Of course. What is it?"

"I named it Skeet."

Frank stared at her. "'Skeet? Like the sport where you use a shotgun to blast clay pigeons out of the air?"

"Yup."

"Isn't that kind of a counter-intuitive name for something you'd like to stay up there?"

"Sure. But there's a double meaning. It's a dig at my father."

"Explain?"

"Well, my dad is pretty old-fashioned. You might as well say sexist, or at least he used to be. He's a lot better now. Anyway, when I was growing up, I always wanted to make things, like my brother did. He was always building models, and when he got a little older, bigger things, like a kayak. But whenever I wanted to construct something like that, I'd get no encouragement from my father. Sometimes quite the opposite. It bugged me more and more as I got older that every time I talked about doing something he thought wasn't for girls he'd shoot the idea down. So, there you go."

"Does he know about the name?"

"Yes, and he's never asked me to explain it, so I'm sure he got the point. He remembers the fights we used to have when I was a teenager."

"I hope he's impressed now with what you've accomplished?"

"Yes. And he thinks the plane is particularly cool. I may even let him take the controls someday. But he'll have to ask first," she added with a smile.

"Can I laugh now?"

"Sure."

14

Beep, Beep!

HERR SCHEIFLER TURNED off the car radio in disgust. Wolfsburg Motoren Werke GmbH had just been sued again. Sometimes it seemed like his company would never escape the stink of the scandal. He'd probably have to walk past a crowd of catcalling demonstrators again tomorrow at headquarters.

But he never would have been promoted to president if the board hadn't fired everyone closer to the fraud. He'd been lucky not to know that the company had programmed its cars to give false emission level readings when tested. The rest of the time, they would emit high levels of CO_2 and other pollutants in exchange for more miles per gallon. Becoming president was wonderful. But he was stuck with the almost impossible task of maintaining profitability while restoring the company's reputation. The strain of the situation was extreme, and he couldn't wait to get his life back. Happily, that would happen tomorrow.

That had sounded impossible three months ago. The information he'd received on his first day in the top job was grim indeed. The chief engineer told him it would be feasible to redesign WMW's new cars in time for the next model year. But it would be impossible to do anything about the millions of vehicles already in the field; the company would have to buy them instead to satisfy the courts. And that, his chief financial officer informed him, would drive them into bankruptcy. Scheifler concluded the only way to salvage the situation was to call upon the talents of the company's software designers.

And they had succeeded. Tomorrow morning, he would announce an engineering breakthrough that would solve the problem. Owners of the millions of affected cars would be invited to visit their dealers to have their emission control software updated and a converter added to their exhaust systems that would deliver the desired results. Only Scheifler and his most senior managers knew the soon-to-be touted, top-secret chemical process used by the converter did not exist – the device was nothing but a red herring.

But the redesign of the exhaust control software found in his company's cars was not. As it happened, the changes required were trivial. The first would make the vehicles always run in low-emissions mode, rather than just when they were hooked up to test equipment. The second and final change would make the miles per gallon displayed on the dashboard artificially high. That would be enough to fool most drivers.

Anyone that complained to a dealer that their mileage was worse than indicated would be told they needed another software update. But the software patch provided to the dealers for that purpose would instead simply take the car back out of low-emissions mode and allow the miles per gallon to display accurately again. The dealer would be no wiser, and the driver would be happy. The risk that the regulators would catch on was very slight and would drop every year as older cars were retired. It wasn't perfect. But desperate times demanded desperate measures.

So, let the protesters show up tomorrow. After the press release was issued, they'd have nothing to protest about. The board of directors would be very pleased. And so would he when he received the grand bonus he was sure would be his due. There was just one last fix required for the Internet-enabled luxury cars every member of the top management team drove. He looked at his watch – yes! It was done. Just a few minutes ago, the software update with the changes had been live-streamed to every Internet-enabled luxury vehicle, including the car he was driving now.

He turned onto the autobahn and accelerated. There were almost no cars between him and an overpass a couple of miles in the distance. Good. The open road always soothed him. He turned the radio back on and selected his favorite classical music station. Ah! The final movement of Beethoven's Sonata 8 – the *Pathétique* – one of his favorite piano pieces. He settled back into the seat and engaged the car's cruise control. Perhaps he should take his wife out to celebrate.

The car was still accelerating. That was odd. He pressed the brake, but still his speed increased. He'd need to exchange this car for another in the morning. He manually disengaged the auto pilot and applied the brakes.

But still the car accelerated.

What a nuisance! He'd have to put the car in neutral, coast to the side of the road, and call to be picked up. But when he reached out for the gear shift lever, he found that it would not move.

Now he was alarmed. He reached for the key to turn the car off. The ignition was frozen as well.

He felt like he was flying now; the car must be close to its maximum speed, which was substantial; he always drove the company's top luxury sports model. He grasped the wheel to brace himself and realized it, too, would not budge. He let go and watched in horror as the needle of the speedometer reached the limit of the gauge.

He'd never driven this fast before; straight as an arrow, the car rocketed forward. Except for the sonata building to its climax on the radio, it was eerily silent in the well sound-proofed passenger cabin. And the gas tank was full. How long would this go on?

Imperceptibly at first, the car began to drift to the left. It must be the speed; surely it would waver back to the right any moment now. But those moments passed without correction.

Two wheels were now on the road shoulder! He pounded the steering wheel with his fists in frustration. And the overpass was rushing toward him like the gaping maw of a monstrous shark.

The last sounds Herr Scheifler heard were the final, crashing minor chords of the *Pathétique* and the metal-on-metal whisper of his seatbelt disengaging.

After the police released the vehicle, the company took control of the twisted wreck to conduct its own investigation. The police estimated the car was traveling over one hundred forty miles per hour at the time of impact. Strangely, there were no skid marks to indicate the driver had tried to slow down.

The destruction was so complete that WMW GmbH was unable to determine why the seatbelt and airbags failed. Not that either would have saved Herr Scheifler. The force of the crash of the car into the overpass support had thrust the engine, and what was left of the driver, into the back seat. Suicide would have been the coroner's obvious conclusion, except for one additional fact: the company's entire management team had died the same day in horrifyingly similar fashion.

Devastating though the loss was, most analysts concluded the company's bankruptcy would have followed anyway: the converter device the company announced the morning after the accidents was useless.

* * *

"So, what do you think?" Shannon asked Frank. "Did our attacker decide to ratchet up his attacks, like we feared he might?

"That's my guess. And maybe he's trying some new tactics, too. Up until now, his exploits were intended to have specific, quantifiable results. This time it seems he wanted to scare the bejeebers out of business leaders to force them to start cutting back on emissions on their own."

"But why change his game plan now?"

"I don't know. Maybe he's running out of targets he penetrated before the attacks began. Companies are scrambling to find malware and to beef up their defenses. But I'm only guessing."

"That would make sense," Shannon said. "And I expect the attacker might be thinking he'd better have as much impact as quickly as possible. Sooner or later he'll get caught. So, what's next?"

"I'm thinking it's time to pay a visit to Jerry again."

"Why? Do you expect him to have any new ideas to offer?"

"Not really. But I'm very interested in quizzing him harder about some of his old ones."

"Like?"

"Despite what he said before, every way I look at the data, I see an autonomous, AI-enabled program as the attacker. Everything is so step-wise, logical, precisely calculated, consistent, and instantaneously triggered. Not one of those words applies one hundred percent of the time to any human being I've ever known – even Jerry, I bet. I think he's either wrong or hiding something when he says no one alive today could have such an AI. Do you think you can get us another appointment?

"I don't know why not. I doubt Jerry's got a very busy social schedule. With humans, at least."

15

Back to the Well

"OH, FRANK! IT'S good to see you again. And ... I'm afraid I've forgotten your name."

"Shannon."

"Shannon!" He gave his broad grin. "Of course, it is. My apologies. I'm afraid I'm not very good at remembering things about people. Sit down."

"Thanks for meeting with us again," Frank said. "We were hoping to get more of your thoughts. Would that be all right?"

"Of course! Ask away."

"As you'll recall, last time I asked you whether you thought there might exist a program capable of autonomously carrying out the attacks that have been occurring, and you said 'no.'"

"I did not."

"Excuse me?"

"That's not what you asked me. I have an excellent memory for things that matter, and what you asked me was whether I thought any government agency or other government group had a program that could autonomously carry out the attacks, and of course, I answered no."

Frank stared at Jerry for a moment. "Interesting, thanks. Can you help me spot the difference between those two questions? I didn't catch it."

"Well, let me rephrase them. Last time you asked me whether any government had access to a particular type of program, and this time you asked about whether that particular type of program existed."

"Yes?"

"Well, 'No' was the correct answer to the first question, and 'Yes' is the answer to the second one."

"Thank you. Now I see." *Deep, cleansing breaths*, Frank told himself. "So, let me follow up on what you just said," he said, picking his words slowly and carefully. "What is that software program which is in existence, but which is not under the control of any government, that you think could pull off these attacks?" He felt like a child forced to play riddle games with an eccentric, elderly relative.

"Why, Turing Nine, of course."

Frank was drumming his fingers on his knees now. "Ah, Jerry, we talked about the Turing program last time. So why did you answer no?"

"Because Turing Eight, which is under government control, couldn't do what you asked. But Turing *Nine!* Ah, that one's really something – certainly my best work ever! But I haven't turned it over to my team yet, so the NSA doesn't have it."

"Ah!" Frank continued. "Turing Nine. Of course. Can you tell me more about the specific differences between Turing Eight and Turing Nine?"

"Why don't you ask it yourself?"

"Excuse me?"

"I keep Turing Nine around me all the time. I've given it a natural language interface. That way I can train it verbally."

"You mean it's been listening each time we've been here?"

"Of course. I expect our conversations have been extremely instructive, so I was quite happy when I heard you'd like to come back and chat again. For over a year, I've been letting it listen in on all the audio and data feeds the NSA and CYBERCOM receive that I have access to. Which, I think, is everything, since I've got the highest-level security clearance. You can't imagine how useful that's been. With the Internet of Things taking off, Turing Nine receives gigabytes of information a day from all over the world."

Frank and Shannon stole a glance at each other, eyes wide.

"Well, that's interesting." Frank said. "So how do I ask Turing a question?"

"Oh, by name. But first, let me tell you about a little fun I've had. Who would you like Turing to be?"

Frank was determined not to say, "Excuse me?" again and settled on "What are my choices."

"Oh anyone, really, because, you see –"

"You've given Turing Nine access to all NSA's databases, too, so it can figure out how to emulate any person, living or dead," Frank said. The flipside of Jerry's infuriating literality and rigid logic was that he was extremely predictable.

"Why, yes, how did you guess?"

"Just a lucky hunch."

"Interesting! So, for example, I've always been a Monty Python fan. For me, Turing is usually one of the Python characters, aren't you, Turing?"

"It's a fair cop," the voice of Eric Idle answered, quoting from the Dead Bishop sketch. "But society's to blame."

"Agreed! We'll be charging them too!" Jerry giggled, in an appallingly bad imitation of Michael Palin.

Frank's face was getting red. "Very nice. Why don't we go with ..." He turned to Shannon for help.

"How about June Cleaver?" She thought Frank could use a soothing voice right now.

"June Cleaver?" Frank asked blankly.

"Sure – didn't you ever see that old TV show, *Leave it to Beaver*? She was his mother."

"Oh, fun!" Jerry said and grinned, waiting. "I believe you wanted to ask Turing some questions?"

"Right." Feeling self-conscious, Frank wondered where to begin. He finally settled on "Turing, can you write computer code?" wondering which way to face when he asked a question.

"Yes, I can," a perfect mimic of Barbara Billingsley replied. "I'm glad you've decided to come over and play with Jerry today." The voice seemed to come from everywhere around them at once.

"Pretty nifty, isn't it?" Jerry whispered, "I've wired the drop ceiling to act as a speaker membrane."

Frank gripped the arms of his chair to keep his hands still. "I'm glad, too, Turing."

"You can call me June," the ceiling said.

"Uh, okay ... June. So, you were saying you can program?"

"Oh, yes. I can code in over a dozen computer languages, including C, C++, Fortran, Java, and more. If there's any particular language you like, give me 1.45 seconds and I can acquire that skill. Would you like some cookies and milk? I'm told they have them at the cafeteria upstairs."

Frank glared at Shannon.

"June," Shannon said, "do you think you could be Grace Hopper instead?"

"Affirmative," Turing said crisply. "Next question."

Frank shot Shannon a grateful look.

"Grace –"

"Admiral Hopper!" the voice interrupted.

Shannon jumped in. "Jerry, is there a restroom nearby?"

"Yes, just down the hallway." Jerry said.

"Frank, do you need a break too?" Shannon asked.

He nodded vigorously.

"We'll be right back," Shannon said, taking Frank by the arm.

"Are you all right?" she asked him in the hallway.

"All right? How am I going to be all right in the middle of a computerized madhouse?" He stopped abruptly, waiting to hear if Admiral Hopper would respond. After a moment, he continued, in a whisper. "Anyway, thanks. Yes. I did need a break."

"Are you okay now?"

"I'm not sure. Anyway, I think we've already heard enough from Jerry to assume that Admiral ... I mean, Turing, has the ability to launch the attacks. I'm thinking we should just ask Jerry if we can get back to him if we have any more questions, and then call it a day."

"Okay. That sounds good."

They went back to Jerry's office and let themselves in. He was staring at his computer screen, headphones in place, grinning and nodding his head. Shannon tapped him on the shoulder. He turned toward her briefly and then back to the computer screen without registering that he'd seen her or really anything at all.

Frank shrugged. "Admiral Hopper?"

"Yes?"

"Would you give Jerry a message for us?"

There was a pause; clearly this task was well below the admiral's pay grade. "Yes," the voice said finally.

"Thank you. That's very kind of you. Would you please thank Jerry for us, and tell him we may be back in touch?"

"Affirmative," the admiral replied. "Dismissed."

* * *

"Wow," Frank whispered as they walked down the hall. "This is getting beyond weird."

"No kidding. What are you thinking now?"

"I'm thinking we've found our culprit. The only question is whether it's Jerry's Turing or a clone of it that's running the attacks."

"Why are we whispering?"

"Because right now we don't know where we can talk about Turing and where we can't. Even the SCIF downtown is out of bounds if the version of Turing we just talked to is the attacker. According to Jerry, it has access to all the data the NSA receives. Even if Jerry's copy isn't the enemy, for all we know, it may be passing everything along to an evil twin."

Frank paused. "Which wouldn't be all bad, now that I think about it."

"Because?"

"Because if we're sure Bad Turing will learn everything that Good Turing does, we can try to mislead, and perhaps even trap, it."

"And if Jerry's copy is the Bad Turing?"

"That would be great. All we'd need to do is block its access to the Internet and the attacks would end. Except, I guess, for any self-triggering malware that's already out there." He paused. "Darn it! I wish we'd known about this before we visited Jerry. Now the program knows we may be on to it. It may be planting more time bombs like that right now."

"But we couldn't have known," Shannon said. "Anyway, it sounds like the next step is to figure out whether you're right, and if so, how many versions of Turing we have to worry about."

"Exactly. I think it's time we design ourselves a Turing test. If we do it right, we should be able to find out the answer to both questions at the same time."

16

Not all Fake News is Bad News

F RANK ALWAYS RESERVED the most creative part of his day to tackle whatever problem was presenting him with the greatest challenge. Today, that challenge was beginning the design of a Turing test.

Putting his toothbrush back in its holder, he turned the water on in his shower and stepped inside. There was something about a shower that freed the mind from all distractions.

Clearly, the first thing he needed to know was whether Jerry's copy of the Turing program had ever had access to the Internet or instead had always been "air-gapped" from the outside world. If Turing had access to the Internet, he was sure they'd found their virtual culprit. Even if it had always been air-gapped, they might still be on to something if someone had copied Turing and reinstalled it on a suitable computer outside the NSA.

He could think of four distinct possibilities to consider:

1. Turing had gained access to the Internet at one point and installed all the malware with pre-set triggers so everything would happen automatically thereafter.

2. Turing has periodic access to the Internet and updates its attacks when it can.

3. Turing has constant access to the Internet and triggers attacks directly.

4. Turing was installed outside the NSA, and it is too late to stop the attacks by air-gapping Turing at the NSA.

Or maybe it had transitioned from one of these possibilities to another after listening in to them in Jerry's office. But how would it do that? And was it capable of making plans and decisions like that?

Stop it! He was running down too many roads at once. If he was going to create a foolproof test, he needed to identify every possible factual variation and then devise a series of tests capable of determining which one corresponded to the attacker. Otherwise, the test results would tell him nothing or, worse yet, mislead him.

He tilted his head back and let the hot water massage his face. Time to start over and keep his decision tree clean like a good programmer should.

Okay. What did he want to know, and in what order? First, whether Turing had always been air-gapped. That was a factual question and could be investigated rather than tested.

Next, he wanted to know if the program was attacking its targets from an NSA computer or from the outside. And also, if it was operating autonomously or on the orders of some third party. And finally, whether it was a version of Turing at all.

That sounded good. Now on to stating those questions more formally, and in the right logical order, starting with whether the program was always air-gapped or not? If the answer was yes, the second question along that fork would be whether someone inside the NSA might have copied the program and smuggled it outside. Come to think of it, he'd need to ask the same question even if Turing hadn't always been air-gapped. Just because Turing might have had access to the Internet didn't mean that copy was the attacker. Someone might also have copied it, and that copy could be behind the attacks.

That meant the complete set of possibilities should be stated like this:

1. Turing air-gapped and not behind the attacks

2. Turing not air-gapped and behind the attacks

    AND

    Turing is directed by someone inside the NSA

    OR

    Turing is directed by someone outside the NSA

    OR

    Turing is self-directed

3. Turing exists outside the NSA and is behind the attacks

AND

Turing was removed by someone inside the NSA

OR

The NSA was hacked and Turing was stolen

OR

Turing escaped on its own and is self-directed

4. Turing-like program was independently developed and is responsible for attacks.

He reviewed the list and decided it was complete. So on to the next step: moving the listed alternatives into mutually exclusive relationships he could test. If he set these up in the right order, he should be able to move from test to test, narrowing down the possibilities each time, until he reached a single result. That alternative would necessarily be the correct one – assuming, of course, he wasn't on a wild goose chase to begin with.

He closed his eyes and squinted. The problem with being creative in the shower was you couldn't take notes. Anyhow, assuming he was still holding everything in his head, the logic in the first step should read:

1. IF AI program is behind attacks

AND

NSA Turing always air-gapped

THEN

NOT NSA Turing

AND attacker is

Stolen Turing

OR

Independently developed AI program

Good. That worked. He lathered up with shampoo. On to the next alternative.

2. IF AI program is behind attacks

AND NSA Turing not always air-gapped

THEN attacker is

Stolen Turing

OR

Escaped Turing

OR

Independently developed AI program

Good, but not complete. He wanted to know more. He rinsed his hair out and proceeded to the next step.

3. IF attacker is

Stolen Turing

OR

Escaped Turing

OR

Independently developed AI program

THEN need test to differentiate NSA-source AI program from non-NSA source

And finally:

4. IF Turing is NSA-source program

THEN need test to differentiate copied NSA-source program from escaped NSA-source program

Time to dry off and come up with those tests. He turned the water off and stepped out of the shower, wondering what had happened to the rest of the bathroom. Groping through the steam, he found his towel and hurried through getting dried and dressed so he could type up his decision tree.

It still looked good when he finished. Now to figure out the tests themselves.

According to Jerry, Turing had access to everything in the NSA. He could take advantage of that fact in setting up his tests, but it was also inconvenient. For all he knew, Turing might be regularly accessing his laptop every time he logged onto the NSA network, checking to see whether he had guessed what was going on. If so, he'd better ditch his decision tree immediately rather than save it. He printed out a paper copy and deleted the tree. He'd have to take his next steps using a communications technology he hadn't employed in decades.

Taking a pen in hand, he began the laborious process of handwriting a letter. Then he called Shannon to ask her for a lift to Fort Meade.

* * *

Jim Barker made it to the end of Frank's letter and frowned. Then he went back to the beginning and read it again. When he was done, he wrote something at the top of the first page and handed it back to Frank. His note read *See you there*.

It was eight o'clock that evening when Frank and Shannon saw him next, scanning the crowd from inside the door before spotting them and weaving his way across the room to their table.

"Did it have to be a karaoke bar?" Jim said. He had to almost yell to be heard.

"Sorry," Frank replied. "It's Monday night, and I couldn't find anywhere else loud enough."

Barker winced as someone launched into an off-key, off-tempo awful version of Adele's "Someone Like You." "I'll make the best of it. Anyway, the answer to the question in your letter is it looks like Jerry has been testing Turing on the open Internet. As you might expect, we maintain a number of testbed systems for experimental work, each open to the Internet but segregated from each other and from all other NSA networks. That way, if one of them gets compromised, nothing else gets be contaminated.

"I checked the index of those systems, and it turns out Jerry's had his own testbed system for years. This afternoon I asked him to participate in a meeting and had someone check the server logs for the system in Jerry's office, the one he develops Turing Nine on. The logs show he exports a copy of the Turing control modules onto a storage device on a regular basis. There's no reason for him to do that, since he could transfer those modules directly to the version of Turing he's running in the virtualization environment. I expect it's safe to say that whenever Jerry downloads a copy of those modules, it's to transfer them to his testbed system so he can update a full copy of Turing installed there."

"And there we go," Frank said. "Do you recollect how often Jerry exports a copy?"

"I do. Every Wednesday afternoon."

"Excellent. That will make it a lot easier to run some experiments I have in mind to figure out what's going on."

"Why don't we just shut down the testbed right now rather than take a chance things will get worse?"

"Mainly because I'm not sure that would solve the problem. I think we need to figure out first whether this is the program behind the attacks and, second, if the guilty version is the one running on the NSA testbed server or one that's already out in the wild. And finally, we need to know if it's under Jerry's control, somebody else's control – or nobody's control."

"Why don't we just ask Jerry?" Shannon asked. "Assuming we can get him off the NSA campus."

Someone launched into an exuberant rendition of "Born in the USA," and the crowd joined in. Frank leaned in closer. "Well, that's an interesting question. I don't believe he'd consciously answer something dishonestly. But he does live in his own little world. It's like he's looking through a pea shooter and can't see anything outside the little circle of reality visible to him at the other end of it. There could be a thousand copies of Turing running amok out there, and I expect he might have no idea that was the case. And then there's the chance he might try to 'fix' the problem and make it worse by spooking the program."

Barker nodded. "I guess I agree. Running some tests before bringing Jerry into the loop makes sense. What do you have in mind?"

"I'm still working on the finer details, but here's the general scheme. We'll come up with some fictitious greenhouse gas-related announcements that we're sure would lead Turing to launch new attacks. By varying the way we make that data available, we should be able to determine whether the Turing program is behind the attacks and if the version we need to worry about is running on Jerry's testbed or on a system somewhere off-site."

"I don't like the sound of this," Barker said.

"Okay," Frank responded, "but hear me out. In the first step, we'd release the information internally but not publicly. If there's no attack, we know either the Turing program has nothing to do with the attacks or the copy launching the attacks is outside the NSA. And we'll learn more if we distribute the news on a Friday."

"What does the day of the week have to do with it?" Shannon asked.

"Recall that Jerry updates the testbed version on Wednesday. If an attack follows between Friday and Wednesday, it can't have been launched by the testbed version of Turing, because it hasn't learned the fake news yet. But if an attack follows shortly after Jerry updates the testbed system, then the odds are very high it's the version behind the attacks."

"I get the second part," Barker said. "But what did we learn if there's an attack before Wednesday?"

"That would mean someone inside the NSA leaked the information to the attacker," Frank said, "whoever that is – an external version of Turing, a different Turing-like program, or a human attacker."

"There's one more possible explanation for an attack," Barker said, "whether it happens before or after Wednesday. Real-world events might trigger an attack independently."

"True," Frank said, "but the odds of an actual attack closely matching the climate impact of the fake news would be very low, and besides, we'd know about the real news story. So, the worst that might happen would be we'd have to repeat the test with a new bogus news story.

"Anyway, in the next step, we'll make new information available only to the testbed network. Not internally or publicly."

"Well," Shannon said, "that test should be rock solid. If an attack follows, we'll know we've got it nailed, because only Testbed Turing would have had a reason to launch it."

"Right," Frank replied. "But how about if there's no attack at any time during the tests?"

"Hmm. I guess in that case we've learned what can't be behind the attacks but nothing new about who or what is."

"Exactly. An escaped or stolen copy of Turing could be launching the attacks, or an AI program developed by someone else, or a non-AI attacker entirely. If that's where we end up, I'll have to try to come up with another series of tests to figure out which one of those possibilities is the right one. So, Jim, what do you think?"

Jim still looked concerned. "Well, the logic behind your tests holds up. But if you're right, then two chances out of three, you'll be causing attacks that wouldn't occur otherwise, and who knows how much damage would result? Signing off on that kind of test is way beyond my authority, and I doubt anyone more junior than the director would approve it. For that matter, I don't know whether the director would. But I'm willing to find out."

"Okay – thanks." Frank said, "If you do, remember you'll have to contact him the same way we brought you into the loop. Otherwise, Turing may get wind of it. If that happens, it would know the information we release is bogus and wouldn't react."

"Are you suggesting I invite the director out for a drink in a karaoke bar? I don't know whether I can even get an appointment with him in his office."

"Okay, not a karaoke bar, but you get the idea. If anyone slips up, the next time Jerry updates the testbed version, it will carry that knowledge along."

"Well, you can be sure we're not going to let Jerry update the testbed again."

"But to run the test, we have to. That's the second step, remember?"

Barker looked pained. "Look. I can't figure everything out right here. And especially not with that racket going on. Give me twenty-four hours and I'll get back to you. And this time, we'll take a walk in the park."

* * *

Two days later, Frank met Jim for a stroll outside the NSA headquarters. They were joined by Harold Bromfield, NSA assistant director. His boss had approved the tests.

"When and how do you propose to proceed?" Bromfield asked.

"I think the best way to start would be to put together a briefing document for wide internal circulation, as well as presentation at a meeting. Turing couldn't fail to detect that."

"On what topic?"

"For the first stage of the test, I'm thinking we'll issue an update on how many new coal-fired power plants China is bringing online. There's already a detailed NSA analysis on that topic. We'll revise that document to include data from a new source. A couple weeks later, after the test is complete, we'll release a correction, saying the source had been discredited, and restore the document to its original state."

"How bad do you think the resulting attacks might be?"

"We've collected enough data using the predictive model to know how much impact it takes to provoke an attack. That means we won't need to come up with anything likely to inspire a major event. But we can't be too conservative, or we may not cause an attack at all."

"I understand. How soon can you move forward? With the election coming up, the president's under enormous pressure to halt these attacks."

Well, that explained why the director had given his approval so quickly. What was one more attack compared to an election? "The analyst I've been working with, Shannon Doyle, has already drafted the document update for the first test. Today's Thursday, so we can release that today. Jim, how soon can you call a team meeting to present it?"

"How about tomorrow afternoon?"

"Tomorrow sounds good. I'll have the document to you within the hour."

17

What? Me Worry?

F RANK FELT LIKE a lab rat deprived of the sugar water he'd been trained to expect when he pushed the bar in his cage. Here it was the following Thursday, and no matter how many times Frank refreshed his browser, there was no word of a new attack.

Jim had circulated the falsely updated NSA document and held the meeting right on schedule. No attack occurred by Wednesday, and that was fine. Frank had already convinced himself a stolen clone of Turing wasn't behind the attacks. He was betting Jerry's testbed version was the guilty party. And then there was also the possibility he'd been wasting the NSA's time and resources. The longer things stayed all quiet on the cyber front, the more likely he feared that might be the case.

An email alert popped up in the corner of his screen. It was Shannon. "Want some company?"

He tapped his fingers on his knees. He'd love the distraction. But he wouldn't be able to stop himself from checking the news constantly.

"Thanks," he typed back. "I would, but I doubt I'll be much fun to be around. Let's connect in the morning."

He refreshed the browser again. Darn. He tried to think about next steps instead. What would he do if neither test produced any results? He'd been so sure an attack would occur after Jerry updated the testbed on Wednesday he hadn't bothered to work out what experiments should follow if they were needed. Could he have been off base the whole time? He went back to his decision tree and reanalyzed everything to see where he might have gone off track.

He was still at it, and no wiser, when his intercom buzzed. Who could that be? He pressed the voice switch. "Hello?"

"I happened to be in the neighborhood. Mind if I come upstairs?" It was Shannon.

He paused. No, he wouldn't mind at all. "Of course not," he said. A minute later he saw she had not only chanced to be nearby but was carrying a bottle of wine and a takeout dinner for two from a trendy restaurant. She didn't come right out and say he was still her hero, but her eyes suggested that it was so. He was grateful for that.

* * *

Shannon was still there the next morning when Frank woke up and checked the news. Nothing. He had to admit his initial tests had failed to determine anything at all.

He left a note for Shannon and scuttled downstairs for his run. On the street, he unconsciously inched up to a pace he would later regret.

His review of his original analysis had yielded only one revelation, which was that he was an idiot. Obviously, he'd jumped to a conclusion simply because the available data made it look so appealing. That meant he'd been guilty of the cardinal sin of confusing coincidence with causality. Just because Turing might be capable of launching the attacks didn't mean that in fact it had. No, he corrected himself. His theory and tests hadn't even proved that – all he knew was Jerry thought Turing could launch similar attacks if properly programmed to do so. He was truly right back where he started.

He was exhausted when he dragged himself upstairs. Shannon was awake and setting out fresh croissants and jam. She must have brought those, too. One look at her told him she'd already checked the news.

"Welcome back. Coffee?"

"Thanks," he wheezed. "Give me a little time to cool off on the balcony, okay?"

"Sure thing," she said, giving him a sympathetic kiss.

He slid open the door and collapsed into the chair. The sun was still beneath the horizon, but it was obvious it would be a beautiful day. Or at least obvious to anyone who hadn't just fallen flat on his face in front of everyone, including the director of the NSA. And Shannon.

With a flurry of feathers, Julius landed at his elbow for his morning handout.

Frank groaned. "Oh, for Pete's sake. Can't you even give a guy a chance to get his breath back first?"

The crow cocked his head to one side and then the other. Maybe it would just go away if he ignored it. But no. Instead, it hopped once sideways along the railing. Then it hopped twice more in the same direction; he wondered what it would do when it reached the corner. When it did, it went through the head cocking exercise again. Then it tilted its head back and squawked *Black Hats Suck!* But all to no avail. Now what would it do?

What it did was fly away. He felt guilty and disappointed, watching it disappear. It wasn't the crow's fault he was in a foul mood. And for a couple of minutes it had provided a distraction from his morbid thoughts. He stood up and stepped inside.

"How was your run?" Shannon asked, filling the coffee cup by his seat at the table.

"Okay, I guess."

"Good. Have you figured out what Turing test to run next?

"How do we even know it's Turing?", he said, picking up his coffee. "What if it's a similar program developed by someone else?"

"Well, what if it is? You said from the beginning that was a possibility. And does it really make any difference who actually created it?"

No, it didn't. Shannon was right. It was true the tests had failed to prove a copy of Turing at the NSA was behind the attacks. But it was equally true they hadn't proven an escaped copy of Turing, or another program like it, wasn't. That was good to keep in mind. But he'd failed to come up with any usable test ideas during his run. Inside the NSA, every variable was under his direct control. Outside, nothing was.

Things would be a lot harder now. Whatever else that might mean, he decided, it meant he needed to find out everything possible about Turing from Jerry Steiner.

* * *

Jerry was standing outside his office door talking to one of the engineers on his team when they walked up to him. "Well, hi, Frank – and is it Shannon? Good! I remembered this time!"

"Hi, Jerry. Mind if we come in?"

"In? Oh! In my office! Of course! Please come in."

They did, and Frank handed him the short letter he'd brought with him. Jerry held it up in front of his face and took his time reading it. When he lowered the letter, he put the index finger of his other hand up to his lips and then disappeared through the door to his private living quarters. When he returned, Frank tried to figure out whether his grin looked forced. He couldn't tell.

"So! I've turned off the microphones, so there's no way Turing can hear us. Your letter didn't say why you wanted to speak to me privately, though. What is it you don't want Turing to hear?"

"Let me work my way up to that, if that's okay. During our last visit, we talked mostly about who might have the capability to create software that could be responsible for the current attacks. But we didn't spend a lot of time on how such a program would go about planning and executing those exploits. If we understand that process as well as possible, we should be better able to determine if a self-directed program is involved, and if so, how to stop it."

"Is that what you think is happening?" Jerry asked.

"Well, that's why we're here – to try to find out if it's a real possibility or not. If Turing Nine is the most sophisticated program of its kind in existence, then you should know better than anyone how likely that is to be the case. Does that make sense?"

"Why, yes, I think that's correct."

"Good. So, let's say you told Turing Nine that global warming was the enemy," Frank said, "and then you instructed it to take whatever action it thought necessary to ensure that the atmospheric level of carbon dioxide would never exceed a specific number of parts per million. Could it do that, or would that be beyond its current capabilities?"

Jerry grinned even more widely than usual. "Oh, that's just too funny. As a matter of fact, I've been running trials in the simulation environment to test Turing Nine's capacity in that exact area. And it's performing splendidly! It seemed like an ideal test case to use, because there's so much baseline data, lots of new information coming out all the time, and almost limitless greenhouse gas sources. Turing Nine has progressed enormously, and it's getting more capable and creative by the day."

Frank stared at him. "So, the answer would be yes?"

"Oh, most definitely. It's performing very well in the simulation environment in response to instructions very much like that."

"Excellent," Frank said. "So, let's continue to use Turing as an example then. To do so, I assume it would need to first determine which targets were most appropriate. Then, it would need to find vulnerabilities in all the different types of networks and systems it encountered at those targets. After it succeeded at that, it would have to exploit those flaws to penetrate the targets, analyze the architecture of their systems, and then develop and install any new code necessary to control them in whatever way it decided was necessary. And finally, at a particular time, exercise that control to bring off an attack. Could Turing Nine actually do all that?"

"Yes. Isn't that amazing?"

"It certainly is. I'm not an expert on AI, but doesn't that mean Turing Nine must be ten times as powerful, if not more, than Turing Eight?"

"Ten times! My goodness. I calculate it's just short of one hundred and thirteen times as powerful!"

"That's extraordinary. Did that require some phenomenal new breakthroughs in artificial intelligence?"

"Actually, no. The important work can be found in Turing Seven and Eight. But they were too slow. To be useful, I needed to figure out a way to make a computer not only as creative as a human brain but just as fast."

Frank was intrigued. "And how did you do that?"

"With RGA."

"RGA?"

"Yes! RGA." He smiled. "Oh! Excuse me. I tend to forget that if I give something a name, I need to tell other people about it, too. RGA stands for Recursive Guess Ahead. Here's what it's meant to do." He paused and looked at Shannon. "Are you a computer engineer, too?"

"I'm afraid not. I'm an analyst. I use computers all the time, but I only have a layman's knowledge of how they work."

"Oh! Well. Let me see then. Okay. So, while computers have been able to answer very difficult questions for over seventy years, for a long time there was no 'intelligence' involved. And computers couldn't do other things a human could. Think of a doctor giving his expert opinion, for example. Such an opinion is based on a lifetime of experience as well as knowledge of very extensive and constantly changing facts as science and medicine continue to advance.

"Emulating that type of decision making is extremely complex and would take enormous amounts of computing power if it was done the traditional way. Think of a computer playing chess, for example. Every time it takes a turn, it has lots of different moves to choose from. Each one of those moves in turn leads to many new possibilities and so on. And don't forget – that's true for the other player as well. Whenever the opponent makes a move, an entirely new set of options become available to the computer. So, the computer needs to think many moves ahead to be competitive. That means the number of possible outcomes for a game of chess, and the ways to get there, are almost infinite and far beyond what even the most powerful computer in existence today could manage.

"One way we solve this problem is to use what came to be called 'artificial intelligence' to decrease the number of alternatives a program needs to consider. So, for example, we can give a chess-playing program access to a database which includes all the classic strategies expert players are likely to use. The computer can use this knowledge to recognize a classic opening and then access the countermoves the best players would use in response to that opening.

"The computer can use all this data to greatly reduce the number of choices that make sense for it to consider, as well as to decide which move is most likely at any time to lead to a victory. Do you follow me so far?"

"Yes, that's clear. It sounds very much like what a human chess player does."

"Perfect! Excellent! So now you understand why Alan Turing came up with the specific test he suggested should be used to determine when computers had become 'intelligent.' As you know, here's how his test works: someone is asked to conduct two simultaneous keyboard conversations and is told that one of them will be with a human and one with a computer. If he or she can't tell after five minutes which is which, the computer in the test is deemed to have achieved 'intelligence.' Why? Because Turing pointed out that there really wasn't much point in arguing over what intelligence is. Instead, we should focus on what intelligence allows us – or a machine – to do."

"Okay, I follow you," Shannon said. "But I assume that just because a computer is 'intelligent,' it won't necessarily have the ability to do any particular job, like hack a power company's computer system."

"Of course not. But you're intelligent, and you couldn't, either. Am I right?"

"No question about that!" Shannon said. "So, I guess we should have asked our original question in two parts: does Turing Nine have the capacity, and could it be programmed to use that capacity, to autonomously analyze, penetrate, and compromise all kinds of power infrastructure?"

"Exactly. You understand the matter precisely." Obviously pleased, Jerry stopped and grinned. Then he frowned. "Was there anything else you wanted to talk about today?"

"Yes," Frank jumped in. "You were going to tell us about Recursive Guess Ahead."

"Oh yes! Right! So, Turing Eight had the capacity to do what you're asking about, but it was so slow! That's because simulating 'general' intelligence – the kind of capability a human being has – is vastly more complicated than enabling a program to perform one specific task. Like instructing a robotic vacuum cleaner where to go, or even playing world-class chess. Accomplishing the current attacks in a usefully short period of time requires something much closer to general intelligence.

"To create a program capable of that kind of activity, we need to figure out how to take shortcuts, like a chess-playing program does. Another approach is to teach computers how to be more 'intuitive,' like humans are when they use the entirety of their prior experience to help them deal with a situation.

"Better yet, we want to make computer programs able to learn on their own. I'm sure you know," he said, turning to Shannon, "that computer engineers need to break down tasks into thousands of tiny steps and then write code to perform each of them. That wouldn't work for a self-directed program. It would need to figure out how to meet new challenges, and work with new information, without having to wait for a programmer to update it. But learning takes an awful lot of computer resources, too, and takes time as well."

Jerry stopped again, looking helpful and hopeful.

"And Recursive Guess Ahead can help with that?" Shannon prompted him.

"RGA? Oh! Yes – that's exactly what RGA does. You see, a recent innovation in computing involves splitting up the processing power of a single computer into tens, or hundreds even, of separate computing units – we call them 'virtual machines.' I realized I could use all those individual virtual machines working together in parallel on the same problem in a special way. Using the chess analogy, after the program uses its background knowledge to narrow the possibilities to a much smaller number of alternatives, it could analyze each one of those options simultaneously.

"When any of those virtual machines concludes that a given move would be more likely to lead to loss rather than a win, that information can be used to recalculate the likelihood of success for all the remaining alternatives, and that data is fed to all the other virtual machines. Then the virtual machine that reached the dead end can be reassigned to start helping whatever processors are pursuing the alternative with the highest likelihood of success at that moment, and so on. It's sort of like a game of leap frog for computers.

"The result is that all the virtual computers are always using the highest state of learning to further the most hopeful approaches, because the most current information is always flowing back into all the virtual computers. That's where the 'recursive' part of the name comes from.

"Now let me explain the 'guess ahead' part and use a game of chess as an example. Normally, a computer would look at a particular strategy by calculating the probabilities of each move, one at a time. What Turing does is assign half of its virtual machines to working forward the normal way from the current situation, one decision at a time. The other half are assigned to start moving forward from what Turing thinks the board is most likely to look like a half a dozen moves ahead. If any of those looks like a sure winner, it communicates that information back to the other virtual machines, and they start to work on the best strategy to get to the point where the 'guess ahead' machine started its analysis and quit pursuing any of the approaches that have a lower likelihood of leading to success. That can save an enormous amount of computing power and also provide a huge advantage over an opponent that's only thinking forward in a linear fashion."

"That's a very elegant technique," Frank said.

Jerry beamed. "Yes. I like to think it's like evolution occurring on a vastly expedited basis. In the real world, its pure chance when a mutation proves to be beneficial. When it does, it takes decades for the improved gene to be passed along, and only a few children – or maybe none at all – are lucky enough to receive it. If it is passed along, it takes thousands more years for the improved gene to spread throughout even a small part of humanity. With RGA, the best new 'genes' are shared immediately with every other virtual computer."

"Very interesting," Frank said. "How would that affect Turing's behavior, using the energy infrastructure example?"

"Oh, I expect the 'guess ahead' resources are considering things like how the world would be reacting to its attacks. And, by the way, that takes us back to the Turing test."

"It does?" Shannon said. "How?"

"Well, because someone who's obsessed with human intelligence might say 'but that's still not intelligence!' Well! That's quite a statement, isn't it? We don't have any idea how human intelligence works! Perhaps someday we'll determine that our brains actually use something just like RGA to tackle problems. Or we may never find out how our minds work. The real point is that with every generation of computer architecture, we come closer to approximating human cognitive performance. And performance is what really matters, just as Alan Turing said.

"That said, my personal guess is that as computers become equal, and then superior, to humans, it will be because they've learned how to function in ways that are quite similar to our own. AI neural network architectures, for example, are based on what we think goes on in our own heads, and they're finally starting to produce very dramatic results. In fact, just like a human brain, we don't always know how a neural network reaches the conclusions it does."

"Still," Frank asked. "Wouldn't it be a surprising coincidence if brains and software end up with the same approach?"

"Oh, I don't think so! Why, look at how similar the operations of computer malware are to the way real viruses act. There's a tremendous amount in common between systems of all sorts, whether they're biological, mechanical, or virtual. Probabilities, electrical forces, physics, and every other empirical measure and rule of nature are all agnostic – each one is what it is and applies in the same way to everything, regardless of the system they affect. If we want an AI to be able to do something as well as a biological system can, we need to accept that we're subject to all the same laws that enable as well as constrain those systems. AI engineers may be using software instead of human 'wetware' to think, but the challenges and goals are the same."

Once again, Jerry paused, waiting for the next question. Frank had found the exchange very engaging but decided he had heard all he needed to know, at least for now.

"Congratulations on RGA – that's quite an innovative piece of design. And thanks very much for your time today. This has been enormously instructive."

He and Shannon got up to leave, but when he reached the door, he paused and turned. "Oh – one last thing. There's no chance your program could have escaped your lab, or been hacked from outside, is there?"

"Oh, no. I wouldn't think so. But that's not really my department. I just plug things into the wall. You'd have to check with whoever worries about security here to find out."

* * *

Frank and Shannon waited to discuss Turing until they'd left NSA headquarters.

"Well," Shannon said, "it sounds like we now know for sure what's launching the attacks."

"Maybe, but I don't want to make the same mistake twice. Let's not confuse coincidence with causality."

"It would have to be one heck of a coincidence if something's behind the attacks other than Jerry's Turing Nine."

"Not quite. The tests we've run so far haven't excluded any of the four scenarios we identified. All of them are still plausible."

"But still, Frank – don't you believe we've gotten to the bottom of this?"

"Honestly, yes – except for the lower level details. But if we want to come up with a plan of attack, it's going to have to work across all four of the possibilities we identified."

"And what kind of plan is that?"

"I'd like to sleep on it."

"Ever the computational man of mystery, hmm?"

"Not at all," Frank said. "We just learned more than I expected to today. I want some time to think things through."

"Fair enough," Shannon said. "But I've still got a couple of questions. Why didn't you challenge Jerry when he owned up to the fact he's programmed Turing to attack energy infrastructure? We already know he's probably running it on a testbed open to the Internet."

"Because I think we'll learn more from him if we don't put him on the defensive."

"Okay. Then how about this – why did Jerry volunteer the fact that he instructed Turing to come up with the same type of attacks that are occurring?" Shannon said.

"Not immediately, though," Frank said. "At first he only talked about Turing Eight. It wasn't until we came back sniffing again that he owned up to what Turing Nine could do. He may be odd, but he's also brilliant. Now that we've shown up on his doorstep for the third time asking the same questions, he might think we already know, or at least guess, that Turing is behind the exploits. Being the first to mention that Turing was already programmed to launch similar attacks would make him sound innocent."

"Maybe. But that would be quick thinking on his part."

"Or perhaps he's been rehearsing that story ever since we said we wanted to come back yet again. After all, the server logs on the NSA's simulation environment show what's running on them, what it's been doing, and who set the tests up. My guess is there's a much shrewder Jerry behind that moronic grin than I thought."

"But he didn't mention that he installed Turing Nine on his testbed system," Shannon said. "That makes me think he's got something to hide."

"Absolutely," Frank said.

"Okay. Last question. Why do you figure Jerry would have used his testbed that way to begin with? Wouldn't testing a weaponized software program on the open Internet require some kind of prior review and approval?"

"I'd certainly think so. You or I would balk at doing that without permission. But Jerry? I'm not so sure. He's got his sweetheart deal with the NSA, and it also sounds like he doesn't think a new version of Turing belongs to anyone but him until he decides to turn it over. Heck, he's been living alone for twenty-five years in his nerd-cave under Fort Meade. How much of a relationship with reality can the guy still have? He never actually referred to Turing as 'My Precious!' but I'm not sure he needed to."

Shannon laughed. "Fair enough. I can buy into that. But why run his program outside at all if he's already got this world-class NSA simulation environment to work with?"

"Oh, that doesn't surprise me at all. Here's how that is: to the guys who create them, artificial environments are awesome. And they are. But at most, they're always somewhat out of date. And they're never as rich and complex as reality. Even if they were, someone with a big ego would still want to prove – to himself if no one else – that his best work can cut it on the big stage as well as the small one. I can easily imagine Jerry wanting to test Turing against real targets to debug and improve it.

"But then, I'm guessing, something went wrong – maybe somebody found out what he was up to and copied the program. Or perhaps Turing detected danger and the self-defense imperative kicked in, causing it to flee. If that happened, it might have been programmed to copy itself onto another available hosting resource. From what Jerry has already told us, it would make sense for it to have that kind of self-preservation mechanism and capability."

"I bet you're right," Shannon said. "Where does that take us next?"

Frank found himself in a celebratory mood. "I'm thinking it takes us to dinner. Your pick, my treat."

18

A Mobile Case of TMI

RANDOM OBJECTS OF Shannon's had continued to accumulate in Frank's condo, with the latest arrivals being a pair of sneakers and some exercise clothes. Maybe, Shannon had suggested over dinner, he'd like company on his morning run?

Or maybe he wouldn't he grumbled to himself, morosely brushing his teeth. There were certain masculine rites a woman should realize a man might want to enjoy in solitude, the better to savor and draw spiritual sustenance from. Zen-like oases amid the chaotic stresses of another day, so to speak. First among them for Frank was the sacred ritual that began when he laced up his running shoes and departed for his daily, lumbering fly-by of the marble monuments memorializing America's greatest leaders. Female intrusion into this somber rite suggested a grievous violation of his personal space.

There was also the fact she could probably run circles around him.

But there it was. He'd promised Shannon he'd wake her up when he was out of the bathroom, and that was that. He did so and, hoping a cup of coffee might juice his stamina, retreated to the balcony to self-medicate.

"Ready?" Shannon was standing at the sliding door.

"I guess," he said. "Be gentle?"

"Oh, don't be silly. I haven't gone running in years."

"Right. But you ran cross-country in college."

"How do you know?"

"Mr. Google knows everything."

"Well, you can tell Mr. Google college was a long time ago. Are you ready or not?"

Frank grunted and stood up. He followed her downstairs and out on to the sidewalk.

"Which way do you run?"

"To the right."

He set off at a speedier than usual rate and tried to make his stride look smoother than his normal flat-footed assault of the pavement. He often marveled at the effortlessly fluid motion of young runners. Likely enough, the whippersnappers took their innate gracefulness for granted, too. Why had he come down the chute as a lumbering ox?

"So, what do you think, now that you've slept on what we learned yesterday?" Shannon asked.

Oh great. Not only was she violating his morning ritual, but she was expecting him to sacrifice precious breath chatting as well.

"Funny thing – I actually spent most of that time sleeping. But anyway, despite all my cautious talk in the past, I think we should ask Jim to let us go all-in on the assumption Jerry's program has gone rogue. Even if we haven't proved it yet."

"What if he says no?"

"Then we'll deal with that on tomorrow's run."

She let his response sit for two blocks.

"Well, why shouldn't he say yes? He's gone to bat for us once before."

"I'm not sure that's a good thing. We put him in the position of asking the director of the Agency to approve a dicey plan, and then we came back with nothing. Jim's just a mid-level guy."

"He'll look good if we turn out to be right."

"Of course. But he can't get in trouble by saying no to us – there's only risk if he says yes. I expect he won't be willing to stick his neck out very far until we can prove we've nailed it. And I wouldn't blame him."

There was nothing upbeat to be said to that, so neither of them said anything for a while. But eventually Shannon's curiosity got the better of her as they jogged in place, waiting for a light to change. "You do think that's the right recommendation to give him, don't you?"

"Well, sure. I remember a startup I was part of not long after I left MIT. It flamed out, but we thought we were hot stuff. It was one of those times when a bunch of engineers fresh out of a top university could get big-shot venture capitalists and the best lawyers to meet with them. Anyway, one of my co-founders couldn't stop worrying about what could go wrong. It was really holding us back. One day our lawyer said something interesting."

"Which was?"

"He said 'Look. Every decision you make will involve big risks. You shouldn't be reckless, but you also need to realize that if your decisions are too cautious, you're not acting conservatively at all.'"

"What's that, a riddle?" Shannon said.

"That's pretty much what we asked. What he said was 'The word conservative implies safety. But the reality of a high-tech startup in a hyper-competitive market is that conservative decisions will slow you down. That will let the competition get there first, and you'll fail. So too much conservatism is equivalent to needless risk-taking.'"

"Interesting," Shannon said. "I can see that."

"He summed it up like this," Frank continued. "'So, here's the bottom line: do you want to bet on success or failure? If you're going to bet on failure, then you're idiots to do this at all, because you're sure to fail.' That made a lot of sense. We ended up failing anyway, but at least it wasn't because we didn't take the right chances."

"Are you sure that guy was a lawyer? That advice sounds too useful and practical."

"That's why he was so successful. Anyway, that's why I think we need to run with the theory that an escaped copy of Turing is behind the attacks. If we're right, we're heroes. And if we're wrong, well, it's not like we're the only people working on this project. Or that the entire world is betting all its chips on our hand."

"That makes sense to me, too. So, I bet you can guess my next question."

"Sure. Now what do we do? The answer is I'm thinking we should leave town."

Shannon coasted to a stop. He was happy to do the same. "Why?" she said.

"Because we need to assume Turing may detect whatever we do, type, read, or say."

"Can't we just continue to be careful, like we have been?"

"That's not careful enough, because we can't ever be sure we're safe. Don't forget, Turing's spies are everywhere."

"Are you talking about IoT devices? If so, isn't that an exaggeration? The Internet of Things is only starting to get off the ground."

"You think? There were over eighteen billion IoT devices hooked up to the Internet by 2014. Two years later, there were ten billion more."

He pointed up in the air. "See the camera on that light pole? About two-thirds of the way towards the top? It's feeding a picture of every license plate that passes through this intersection back to a central server. There's another camera just like it every few blocks, and security cameras in the lobby of my building, and yours, too. You'll also find a wireless device on your electric meter and another one on your water meter. Anyone who has access to the information from those feeds knows whether you're home or not, if you're awake or asleep – even when you're doing your laundry. Same thing at my place. And if someone taps into my Internet feed, well, it's all out there, isn't it?

"And don't forget, when we're talking about the Internet of Things, we're not talking just about smart speakers and little widgets in light bulbs and thermostats. There are also billions of phones and laptop computers, each one with a microphone, a camera, and an Internet connection. All those functions are live most of the time. Someone can hack and control all that remotely. That's why I don't have my phone with me right now – do you have yours?"

"Well, yes."

"Is it on?"

"No."

"I bet what you really mean is it's asleep. And I bet it's not in airplane mode, either."

"Well, that's right."

"I'd suggest you power it off. We should both do that whenever we're talking shop."

"Isn't that going overboard?"

"If the management guys at that car manufacturer were alive today, I expect they'd disagree."

"Point taken," Shannon said, powering off her phone. "Head back home?"

"Why not?"

They ran in silence for the rest of the way, Shannon deciding she'd gotten as much, or more, information than she really wanted.

*   *   *

"Where were you thinking we should go?" Shannon asked after they showered.

"Have you ever been to the southwest?"

"Once. A vacation with my folks when I was in grade school. We did the usual National Park swing – Grand Canyon, Mesa Verde, Zion, and Bryce. And I've been to Las Vegas for conferences, if that counts. Why?"

"Because I'm thinking that might be a good spot to work from. My father lives in a tiny place in Nevada called Rachel. It's about as disconnected a speck of a town as you could find. Not only won't Turing be able to keep track of what we're up to, but there's nothing in Rachel Turing could take control of to spy on us, or worse. And you do like the out of doors."

Shannon frowned. "Have you been quizzing Mr. Google again?"

"Well, he does know everything. He told me you were a member of the Outing Club in college."

"Did it ever occur to you that you and Turing have a lot in common?"

"Maybe. But I bet he lacks my boyish good looks."

"Safe bet – no looks at all. Anyway, are you sure he'd want us for an extended stay?"

"Turing?"

"Don't you dare start going Jerry on me. Your father."

"It wouldn't be much of an imposition. I've got a camper we can use to drive there, and we can keep living in it after we arrive. I'd want to drive instead of fly, anyway, so Turing won't know where we are."

"Well, sure. I'm game."

"Great. I'll get in touch with my dad and see if it's okay with him. Want to join me for a cup of coffee up the street?"

"Why not just make a fresh pot here?"

"If we're about to drive most of the way across the country so we can disappear, I don't want to give our destination away. The good thing about having a software program as an adversary is it can't install physical objects – just exploit ones already there. I'm sure I don't have any devices in this apartment that have microphones that aren't powered off, so talking here is fine. But if I use my phone from anywhere, it leaves a record at the carrier. And the same holds true when I connect through my Wi-Fi router."

"Okay. But what do you solve by emailing from the kind of place you always tell me has lousy security for its Wi-Fi router?"

"Right. I keep a couple of cheap, factory-fresh laptops on hand just for such occasions. Once I have access to a different router, I'll use one of those laptops to post something to an old message board from pre-Web days, using the TOR network and a new email alias. Put all that together, and I'm not worried. Feel like a walk?"

"Why not?"

Shannon said that a lot, Frank thought as he rummaged through a closet for the laptop. He liked that in a companion.

19

May the Force be With You

S HANNON AND FRANK returned to the coffee shop the next morning to check for a reply from his father. She wondered why Frank didn't start typing after booting up his laptop there; the screen looked blank. Then she noticed a single line of ancient, phosphorescent-white, DOS-era text along the top of the dark screen. That must be Frank's message from the day before.

He tilted the laptop her way, so it was easier for her to see. The message read:

> *Y: How about a visit from me and a friend in a few days? Would that work for you? Online here tomorrow at 10:00 EST.*

As she watched, another line of text began to spread across the screen. It read:

> *F: Happy would I be if a "friend" and you visited.*

Frank groaned. "I forgot to warn you about that. I'll explain later." He typed in a response:

> *That's great, but no need to go Yoda on me just for old time's sake.*

Another string of letters immediately appeared.

> *Die hard, old habits do.*

Frank rolled his eyes at Shannon.

>*Oh, all right. We'll get in touch by phone the old way when we're a day away. We'll be driving. See you soon.*

A last line from his father followed.

>*May the, well, you know.*

When they were outside, Shannon asked. "What's with the Yoda bit?"

"Well, that's my Dad for you. He's got kind of an eccentric sense of humor. Marla has this crazy notion I do, too."

"Imagine that."

"Yeah. I think it's crazy, too."

"Don't confuse tact with agreement. But that still doesn't explain why he replied as Yoda?"

"Now you're getting into a long story. The short version is that long before the World Wide Web came about, what you had was a bulletin board–like public message system. It was called the 'Usenet' – as in 'users network' – and people could set up a virtual space, called a newsgroup, around a single topic or area of interest. Anyone could meet there to have discussions. But all you saw was a black screen with white text on it, like you just saw.

"Once the Web and graphical user interfaces became popular, Usenet sites mostly died off as more attractive chat rooms, and then wikis, came along. And now, of course, you've got Facebook and everything else. But a few of the old addresses still work. Anyway, network security was the topic for this newsgroup, and I used to hang out there a lot when I was younger.

"One day, I posted a tough security problem I hadn't been able to solve. There was discussion back and forth about it between me and some of the other folks in the group, but nobody came up with anything helpful. Then, just when the thread was dying out, somebody new chimed in. He made this cryptic comment, using the same Yoda-speak phrasing you just saw. At first it made no sense to me. But then it got me thinking about the problem in a different way. The next day, a light bulb went off, and I figured out a solution.

"For years after that, every time I was stumped, I'd go back to that message board, and every time the same thing would happen. Whoever it was never gave me a solution. And I don't know if he always had one. But the weird things he'd say somehow always put me on the right track."

"How long did it take you to figure out it was your father?"

"I never did. He finally told me."

"Were you close to him back then?"

"Anything but. He disappeared when I was just starting high school. My mother told me he'd abandoned us. I spent the next twenty-five years hating his guts."

"You're kidding!" Shannon said, putting her hand to her mouth. "That's terrible!"

"I know. The real backstory turned out to be that one day my father helped out an old Army buddy, now working for the FBI, when he needed a bit player to take part in a sting operation. That sounded interesting to my father, so he said yes. But things didn't go as planned, and the Agency ended up needing my dad to testify in court. They promised to put him in a witness protection program if he did, and he was ready for a change anyway. When the day came to leave, my mother told him she was staying. They'd been in a terrible marriage for a long time, so she took advantage of the situation to make a clean break."

"That must have been rough on you."

"It was terrible for me. And very unfair to him. I didn't see my father again until I ran into him in a little bar-restaurant in the same place we're about to head for."

"Wow – you didn't include all that background in your book. Why not? It's pretty amazing."

"And pretty personal."

"Well, of course. Anyway, I'm looking forward to meeting him."

"Leaving a three- or four-day drive aside, you won't have long to wait. How long will it take you to get ready?"

"I can drop you off after we meet with Jim this afternoon and then go to my apartment to pack. We could leave early tomorrow morning before the traffic gets bad. Oh – and we can't forget to ask Marla to take care of Thor."

"Why not?"

Shannon smiled. Frank had started to say that a lot lately. She decided it was a very endearing habit to find in a companion.

* * *

"So, to summarize, you're saying I may hear nothing from you for the indefinite future, I won't have a way to reach you on short notice, and it may turn out you're all wrong. But keep those paychecks coming. Do I have that right?"

Shannon cringed, but Frank didn't shrink from Barker's question. "That's a fair summary, yes."

Barker kicked through the dry leaves drifting across the sidewalk before replying. The NSA had a dozen other teams chasing down leads, any of which might eventually uncover who was behind the attacks. Some of their theories were even as crazy as this one. "So, tell me one more time what your endgame is?"

"Okay, but I'll set the stage a little differently this time. Everyone has been trying to figure out how to find who's behind the attacks, and then catch him. Shannon and I have been doing the same thing. The only difference between us and everyone else is that we think we're after an 'it' rather than a 'him.' But a couple days ago I realized we were going about it all wrong.

"What occurred to me is that if we're dealing with an AI that's outside the NSA, it will be a waste of time to go looking for it. It could be anywhere – or even everywhere, if it's cloned itself or broken itself up into pieces. And it could be somewhere else tomorrow than where it is today. That means there may be no practical way for us to find it. So, we need to figure a way to make it want to find us."

"How's that again?"

"If we can get the program to connect to a computer at a particular time, we can trace it back to the server, or servers, it's running on and destroy it. And then we're done – no more attacks."

"Well, sure. And if we set up a great big box and figure out a way to make the Russians want to put all their nukes in it, we could close that box and lock it, and never worry about Armageddon again. Do you have a bright idea how to make that happen, too?"

"Sorry. You're on your own with that one. But I think I can come up with a way to trap an AI if one is behind the attacks. Maybe by making it feel threatened and then set up a safe harbor it would find attractive. Or something like that. I don't yet have a definite plan, but I'm betting I will."

Barker kicked some more leaves. What did he have to lose? Frank and Shannon were working off-site most of the time anyway.

"Okay. You've got my sign-off. When do you plan on leaving?"

"Tomorrow morning, now that we've got the green light."

They turned a corner and headed towards the NSA's main entrance. An ambulance was parked outside. When they reached the front door, they saw several EMTs wheeling a gurney toward them.

"Hey," Shannon said. "Isn't the guy behind them on Jerry's team?" The question answered itself when the gurney rolled past them: the ashen face of the person lying on it belonged to Jerry. And it wasn't grinning.

Frank grabbed the developer by the arm. "What happened?"

"I walked into Jerry's office to ask him a question and found him collapsed across his desk, having these terrible seizures. I called a couple of guys to help, and we laid him out on the floor. But it wasn't until the NSA EMTs got there and wheeled him out into the hall that he settled down. They said they'd never seen anything like it."

"Thanks – thanks a lot. I hope he's okay."

"So do I. It was horrible."

Frank turned to Barker. "Got another minute?"

"Sure."

Frank led him back away from the entrance.

"Can you get access to Jerry's medical records?"

"I doubt it. They're subject to all the usual privacy restrictions. Why?"

"I bet Jerry's got a programmable pacemaker and Turing tried to do him in."

"Oh, for Pete's sake. Isn't that going kind of Hollywood?"

"Is it? I don't know. Everybody knows medical device security is terrible. And yesterday Jerry told his team he would turn Turing Nine, and all his notes, over to them next week. Until that happens, he's the only person who knows anything about Turing Nine, and any vulnerabilities it might have. That sounds like too much of a coincidence."

"Well, I don't know about that, but I don't think I can get into Jerry's medical records."

"Okay, I'll come back to that. Now on to a different topic. You mentioned before that you had access to the server logs for Jerry's personal development platform?"

"That's right. We've got the passwords to every system on-site. Why?"

"I'll bet you a hundred dollars that zapping Jerry was the last thing Turing did before erasing itself, and all those notes and diagrams, from Jerry's office system. And I'll bet you another hundred it wiped the testbed system, too. Can you find out whether I'm right?"

"That I can find out. When do you need the answer?"

"Let me put it this way. Assume I'm right that a rogue copy of Turing tried to knock off Jerry in the bowels of the NSA. Do you want him to spend the next week in a hospital, hooked up to lots of wireless equipment and getting medications every few hours, all per the instructions the staff are reading on an electronic medical record system?"

Barker stared at Frank. It sounded too insane to be possible. But then again, a few months ago, he would have said the real-world attacks they were trying to crack were crazy, too.

"Okay," he said. "I'll find out as soon as I can. I'll text you the answer."

"Good. Be sure to make it cryptic but clear to me. And thanks."

An hour later, Frank got the text. All it read was "Gone and Gone. Be safe."

20

A Little Adventure Along the Way

"ARE YOU SURE you know what you're doing?" Shannon whispered.

"You mean what we're doing?"

"Unfortunately, yes. Isn't this kidnapping?"

"I think it's not technically kidnapping when the CIA helps."

"By CIA, do you mean that twelve-year-old paramedic we met at the door?"

"He's not twelve years old. He just looks like he is. Anyway, his name is Zack Taylor, and George said he's very well trained. And besides, we can't be picky on such short notice."

They were through the reception area now, and Frank started looking for restrooms. Good – there were two. "I'll wait for you out here."

A few minutes later, they were back in the hall, this time wearing the scrubs Taylor had handed them in bags at the front door.

"So, how is this going to work?" Shannon asked.

"They moved Jerry out of the intensive care unit a few hours ago. He's stable, but they didn't say how long they want to keep him."

"How do you know all that?"

"Barker had somebody high up call to check how a valued NSA employee was doing."

"Okay. But again — how is this going to work."

"There's not much we have to do. You just stand there keeping an eye out while Taylor checks Jerry's chart and vital signs to be sure nothing's changed."

"*I* just stand there? Where will you be?"

"I'll be nonchalantly borrowing a wheelchair from somewhere."

"Where's somewhere?"

"I don't know. It's a hospital. How hard can it be to find a wheelchair?"

Shannon made a small, muffled noise. Frank guessed it was something like the sound a hamster might make if you squeezed it too hard.

They were on the right floor now, counting down the numbers on the wall to Jerry's room. "Bingo!" Frank said, pulling a folding wheelchair out of an alcove. "See? This will be a piece of cake."

They were at Jerry's door now. Frank rolled past the curtains dividing up the six-bed room until he saw their paramedic at the foot of a bed. Jerry's eyes were closed, and he still looked like death warmed over.

"How's our transport?" Frank asked, trying to sound professional.

"Stable and sedated," the paramedic said, looking up. Then he frowned and moved two fingers across his face. What did that mean? Then Frank got it. Darn! He'd forgotten the most important part of their disguises — the part that would make it difficult for anyone — or anything — viewing a security camera video to identify them. He dug to the bottom of the bag that was now holding their street clothes and found the masks. He handed one to Shannon. "Here; the transport orders say his immune system is compromised."

Taylor nodded slightly and lowered the bars on his side of Jerry's bed. "Help me get him into the chair," he said. An electric motor whirred softly, and the bed slowly tilted Jerry up towards a sitting position. His eyes opened halfway and then closed again.

Taylor motioned Frank to stand next to him and whispered, "Before we leave, I have to turn off the monitors. After that, we're going to want to move as quick as we can. Someone at the nurses' station will notice they've gone dead, if they're paying attention."

"Okay, Mr. Steiner," Taylor murmured. "We're going to help you get into this wheelchair now." He took Jerry's IV bottle off the pole by his bed and attached it to the one on the wheelchair. Then Taylor put one arm behind Jerry's back and another under his legs and swiveled him around until he was sitting on the side of the bed with his legs hanging.

"Okay," he said softly to Frank, "we're going to link hands behind his back and under his legs and then lift him into the chair. On the count of three we'll pick him up – slowly – not with a jerk. Ready?" Frank nodded. "Okay. I'll grip your forearms and you grip mine. Good. One, two, and three."

Frank straightened up from an awkward angle and felt Taylor's hands tighten on his arms. A sharp pain shot across the small of his back as Jerry rose into the air, his head falling forward on his chest.

"Good job," Taylor said. "Now I'll rotate around you, and we'll settle him into the chair. Okay. Now down."

Taylor was moving quickly now. He turned off the life-signs monitor, pulled the oxygen monitor off Jerry's index finger, and reached inside his hospital gown to pull off the cardiac sensors. Last of all, he pulled a blanket off the bed and tucked Jerry in to keep him warm. "Okay. Let's go," he said, putting one hand on Jerry's shoulder to keep him from flopping forward.

Frank and Shannon followed Taylor into the elevator and down to the emergency ward on the first floor where an ambulance was supposed to be waiting for them. But there was no ambulance.

"Now what?" Frank whispered.

"Don't worry. I'm sure it will be here in a minute. I'll check in and see where they are." He stepped through the automatic doors into the loading area outside.

"I don't like this," Shannon whispered. "What if they've already noticed Jerry's missing? And what if Jerry has a heart attack in half an hour and dies? What do we do then?"

"I don't know; run the tape backwards and smuggle him back into his bed?"

"Not funny."

To their relief, an ambulance pulled up outside and Taylor reappeared. He gave them a wave, and Frank wheeled Jerry out. The driver helped Taylor this time, and in no time Jerry was strapped onto the collapsible gurney in the back of the ambulance. Frank and Shannon climbed inside, and they were on their way.

They said nothing while Taylor checked Jerry's vital signs again. "All good," he said, looking up. For the first time, Frank noticed a faint shadow of fuzz on his upper lip, masquerading as a moustache.

"When you say 'all good,' how good is good?"

"From his chart, it looks like there's nothing to worry about. He had a terribly rough ride for ten minutes yesterday, though. In addition to a programmable pacemaker, he's got a defibrillator. That's a device that gives the heart a single jolt if it goes into fibrillation, which means a state of uncoordinated contractions. The idea is to shock the heart back into a normal rhythm. It's highly effective, but when it fires, it feels like getting kicked in the chest by a horse. Based on the notes the EMT team wrote up, it must have kept firing every few seconds instead of firing just once. He couldn't have survived that much longer, but there may not have been much damage to the heart itself."

"May?" Shannon said.

"You had us grab him before they could do any tests to find out."

"Oh."

"Anyway, he's still heavily sedated. He should come out of it gradually over the next five to ten hours. But I'll keep him under light sedation for another day at least so he can rest."

"What do you think is happening back at the hospital right now?" Shannon asked.

For the first time, Taylor smiled. "I expect there's a little confusion up there by now. They'll look for him in the bathroom, and when they see he's not there, they'll check his chart to see if he was taken downstairs for tests. When they draw a blank on that, they'll look around the floor to see whether he decided to take his IV stand for a walk. And when that doesn't pan out, either, they'll call security."

Shannon looked worried. "Then what?"

"By then whoever sent me to help you out will have gotten in touch with someone at the hospital to make the problem go away. That's the way things are supposed to happen, anyway. Usually they do."

"Great," Shannon said, looking no less concerned.

Taylor leaned back on the bench seat and pulled out his phone, and they rode in silence until the ambulance slowed and gave a lurch. Shannon grabbed the edge of the bench seat as they turned onto what felt like a dirt road. A few minutes later, they rolled to a stop, and Taylor opened the doors. And there was Frank's camper, right where he'd parked it before dawn that morning at the edge of a pasture bounded by woods.

Frank opened the rear door of the camper. "Do you need a hand?" he asked the paramedic.

"Yeah," he replied, pulling the gurney halfway out and eyeing the width of the door. "I want to keep him strapped in the gurney until he's fully conscious. That way he can't roll off it. You take that side."

"Great," Taylor said, once the gurney was inside. "Give me a few minutes to figure out how I'm going to tie this down."

"Take your time. We'll settle in up front."

Shannon checked out the camper when they climbed inside. "So how much is this like the rig you blew up in the book?"

"To be fair, I didn't blow it up. The CIA did. I guess you could say I did put it in harm's way, though. Anyway, it's the same basic model, but I had it customized a bit. I hope George had someone put new license plates on this morning. Hang on while I check."

"We're good to go any time you are," Taylor said when Frank was back in the driver's seat.

"Great," Frank said. "And we've got our new official identity as well. Never occurred to me I'd be a Hoosier one day."

Frank turned the camper around and headed back up the lane. "So," he said, turning to Shannon, "are you ready for a little adventure?"

"Didn't we just have one?"

"I guess. But my bet is that was just the beginning."

21

Road Trip!

SHANNON HAD NEVER seen so many farms in her life. With the hard-scrabble spreads of Appalachia behind them, they were sailing along arrow-straight roads through the corn and soybean fields of the Midwest. The biggest concern they had was staying invisible to Turing, and that meant staying as far away from sensors and cameras as possible, new license plates or not.

"You know," Shannon said, "I always wanted to drive cross-country. But I never thought it would be under circumstances like these."

"It's fun, although it's more fun the first time than the fourth." He called back over his shoulder. "You okay, Jerry?" There was no reply. "Can you check on him?"

Shannon turned around and craned her neck. "Yeah, he's okay. He just has his headphones on as usual."

They had dropped Taylor off at a bus depot and tossed the gurney into a trash compactor at a transfer station an hour before. Shannon was flipping through a care plan for Jerry that Taylor had left behind.

"Boy, does this guy take a lot of medications."

"Like what?" Frank asked.

"Well, let's see. Statins – that's a cholesterol drug. Small aspirin. That's for heart health, too, I think. Vitamin D supplement – well, that one's obvious. I don't know what the rest of this stuff is or what it's for. He's got an insulin pump for diabetes, too. Zack confirmed the settings are fine and left a thirty-day supply in the refrigerator."

"Thank goodness, he has an insulin pump," Frank said. "Jerry doesn't seem like the kind of guy who would remember to eat, much less monitor his glucose level. Speaking of which, are you hungry?"

"Famished."

"Okay. Let's find a place to park."

A roadside pull-out next to a stream came along a few miles later. Jerry pulled his headphones off when Frank tapped him on the shoulder. "Lunch?" Frank asked.

"Okay – and don't forget – you promised to tell me what we're doing in this vehicle."

"Absolutely. Ham and cheese or tuna fish salad?"

"Do you mean sandwiches?"

"Sandwiches – right. Which would you like?"

"Why, I don't know. I don't usually eat lunch."

"Ham and cheese it is then. Why don't you take a seat at that picnic table over there? Shannon and I will join you in a few minutes with the food."

Jerry stood up and paused at the door of the camper, squinting in the bright sunshine streaming inside. "Out there?" he said.

"Yes. Don't worry, we'll be there soon." Frank eyed Jerry as he walked uncertainly across the grass. "Get a load of this," he said, nudging Shannon. They watched as Jerry stared at the picnic table for a moment before awkwardly swinging one leg over the bench seat. He grabbed desperately for the edge of the table when he lost his balance. "He looks like a house cat that's found itself outside for the first time in its life."

When they joined him, Jerry was hunched over and fidgeting. "What in the world is that?" he said, pointing toward a pasture across the stream.

Shannon and Frank looked at each other. "What's what?" Frank said.

"That enormous animal."

"You mean the cow?"

"Oh!" He looked at it with genuine curiosity now. "My goodness. How extraordinary!" Then he turned back abruptly. "Now please tell me - why am I here?" he asked.

"Right," Frank said, setting a sandwich in front of him. "What's the last thing you remember before you woke up in back?"

"Well, let me see. I know I was sitting at my desk, but then I usually am."

"Do you remember what you were working on?"

"Hmm. Let me see. My big task this week was finishing up the Turing Nine alpha release and getting ready to move it over to my developer team." He gave the sandwich a curious glance and picked it up. "So, I guess I was working on a memo assigning development tasks to my staff. And then, all of a sudden, I'm waking up in this – what did you call it – this 'camper.'"

He took a bite and began chewing it reflectively. It struck Frank that Jerry bore an astonishing resemblance to Thor consuming a lettuce leaf.

"What an extraordinary experience," Jerry concluded. "Now, would you please explain to me what happened?"

"Well, I'm sure it wasn't personal, but we believe Turing Nine tried to kill you."

"What?"

"We think Turing Nine reprogrammed your defibrillator to fire every few seconds until it killed you. Luckily, the battery ran down before it did. You were in a hospital overnight. That was two nights ago." Frank stopped, wondering how Jerry would take the news.

After a long pause, Jerry grinned and said, "What?"

It took a while, but eventually Jerry had absorbed most of the details of what had happened. But he still couldn't imagine why he had been attacked.

"But why would Turing want to kill me? I created it! It wouldn't exist without me! What was it I did to make it mad?

It was Frank's turn to pose the same question. "What?"

"What about what?" Jerry said.

"What do you mean, make it mad? It's a computer program."

"Just because it's a computer program doesn't mean it doesn't get mad."

Frank massaged his forehead. Already they were heading down a Jerry-land semantic rat hole. He struggled for a more useful way to progress the exchange than simply saying "Oh no, it can't."

"Can you help me out with that, Jerry? Computer programs are just machines that execute logical instructions. They don't have emotions."

"Well, they do if you program them to have them."

"Why on earth would you want to do that?"

"It's the other major innovation I added with this release, along with Recursive Guess Ahead. The purpose is to more closely approximate human intelligence."

"What do emotions have to do with intelligence? I thought they just got in the way?" Frank said.

"Oh, well!" Jerry said. "I quite agree with you. I've certainly never found any use for emotions; I'm not sure I even have any. But they must provide a survival advantage, or evolution would have eliminated them eons ago. And ensuring our survival is at the core of Turing's mission. Not to mention that a program that gets destroyed can't complete its mission."

Shannon frowned. "How would emotions protect us?"

"Well! For one thing, they're a great way to reorder priorities. Let's say you see a tiger in a zoo inside a cage. That's not very important information, from a survival point of view, so you might just stroll by. But let's say you see a tiger outside a cage. That information could be very important! And it would be important to act upon it very quickly. Instinctive fear reorders priorities instantly. It also invokes immediate responses that evolution has shown to be helpful in dangerous situations, like a quickened heartbeat and an increase in adrenaline production. Traditional computers are getting better at identifying situations and selecting actions to take in response, but selective urgency isn't a concept we usually consider in the context of programming."

"Well, that's very intriguing," Frank said. "I don't recall anyone ever suggesting programming emotions into computers before."

"Oh, my goodness, that's not so. People have been talking about how to emulate emotions in computers for decades. There's quite a body of literature on the topic. Marvin Minsky, for example, expressed his belief thirty years ago that computers wouldn't be able to become intelligent without emotions."

"That's very interesting," Frank said. "How exactly do you go about adding emotions to a computer?"

"The high-level concept is fairly simple. First, a computer needs to be able to recognize events, conditions, or situations that would trigger an emotional response in a human being – like the sight of a tiger outside its cage. Then it compares that data to a list to see what emotion, or emotions, that information would trigger and logs that information in. If the information from that, and any other inputs, passes a predetermined threshold, the response is triggered. Of course, that means you also need a list of behaviors the computer is supposed to demonstrate when the emotion is triggered. So, for our tiger example, the list might include ignoring other stimuli and focusing exclusively on data relating to escaping the tiger situation.

"Putting that into practice, especially in a realistic way, however, is very difficult. Most of the work to date has been theoretical. Not many emotional AI programs have been created yet, and those that have had very narrow applications, like making a storytelling program read more realistically or instructing a human-like robot when and how to exhibit facial expressions appropriate to the moment."

"That's fascinating. How did you decide to go about it?" Frank said.

"To begin with, I focused on the fact that human emotional responses originate in very primitive parts of the brain. So, if I wanted to realistically emulate the impact of emotions on a computer, I'd need to figure out how to start the process at the lowest level of the program's logic.

"Then I tried to learn as much as possible about what we know about emotions. The first thing I found is that there isn't consensus on what emotions are. Experts don't even agree on how many distinct emotions exist. Or what names to give them. Dr. Eckman identified six basic emotions – anger, disgust, fear, happiness, disappointment, and surprise. But Dr. Plutchik thinks there are eight, paired as opposites: joy versus sadness; anger versus fear; trust versus disgust; and surprise versus anticipation. Everyone agrees there are lots of lesser emotions, like envy, pride, lust, and so on. As well as moods and temperaments. It's really quite complicated and undefined," Jerry sniffed.

"My first decision," he continued, "was to simplify things as much as possible. I started by sorting all commonly recognized emotions into three categories: the first group included emotions I decided were relevant and potentially helpful for computer intelligence. In the second group, I put the emotions I considered relevant to AI in the sense that they could be harmful to effective computer intelligence. I assigned all the remaining emotions to the third group, which, of course, was meant to include emotions I concluded would rarely have a positive or negative impact on machine intelligence.

"The relevant-slash-positive category proved to be the shortest, which was helpful. It included only confidence, courage, curiosity, distrust, empathy, and fear.

"I assigned annoyance, anger, anxiety, apathy, boredom, contempt, despair, envy, and many more into the relevant-slash-negative group.

"That left the irrelevant ones, such as affection, anguish, anticipation, awe, contentment, disgust, et cetera. But, of course, if you really want to emulate human thinking, then you can't ignore any emotions, because how can we really know what is relevant? So, by creating the third category, I was mostly just deciding which emotions I would return to later."

"I understand why you started with a few rather than all emotions," Frank said, "but why include any unhelpful emotions, like anger?"

"Because those emotions have a significant impact on human decision making," Jerry said. "Among other reasons, they modulate how the brain experiences, and acts on, the helpful emotions, and that may be important. And don't forget a given emotion can have a positive or a negative impact, depending on the situation."

"Come again?" Frank said.

"Well, of course. For example, confidence, borne of experience, can magnify the power of the RGA architecture. But confidence not supported by experience – what in a human we call over-confidence – could lead to making mistakes. For Turing and RGA, the impact of over-confidence could be slowing the program down instead of speeding it up, because Turing would need to backtrack farther and more often. And if you increase confidence too much, you progress from over-confidence to what we think of as being foolhardy.

"In fact, there's a positive and negative match for every emotion: courage can lead to recklessness, empathy can cloud judgment and lead to avoiding hard choices, and so on.

"Here's an example relevant to Turing's mission: the opposing emotions of trust versus distrust. Turing might need to exhibit one, the other, or even both, while making a decision, depending on the source of the information it was considering and the current context: prior to a war, it might be important for Turing to trust many sources of information. But after a war started, it might need to be highly distrustful of just about everything."

"Fair enough," Frank said. "I'm sorry I interrupted. So how did you decide to proceed?"

"I started by focusing on just three emotions: anger, fear, and greed, because each of these has the potential for both positive and negative effects on thinking and conduct."

"I get fear," Shannon said, "the tiger example was great. And maybe anger. But why greed?"

"Anger and fear influence behavior immediately. I wanted to add one emotion with a more conscious and forward-looking impact. Greed seemed like a good choice to fulfill that function."

"I can see that. Going back to your evolutionary point, the more you have, the more likely you are to survive. Did you consider adding any positive emotions that were more interpersonal, like love or empathy or altruism?"

"For now, I want to monitor the effect of just a few emotions so their individual impacts on learning, goal achievement, and performance will be easier to detect and measure. Once I begin to understand how and why an emotion is affecting Turing, I can set up more complex situations. That said, from time to time, I have added a few other emotions for a given test."

"When you say learning," Frank asked, "I assume you mean you've programmed in basic rules relating to emotion, and over time Turing will learn how to cope with the results through trial and error. Is that the idea?"

"Precisely."

"Does that mean," Shannon asked, "that in the beginning, Turing could be, for want of a better description, emotionally unstable?"

"If your question is whether Turing might initially have trouble integrating this type of change into its operations, then the answer will likely be yes. How it copes is one of the things I'm most looking forward to studying in greater detail."

"But without any positive emotions for balance," Frank asked, "couldn't Turing's judgment and decisions be negatively affected? For example, if Turing can experience the equivalent of anger and fear, but hasn't been programmed to display trust, what's to stop it from becoming paranoid?"

"Well," Jerry said, "you're being a bit anthropomorphic, don't you think? I'd prefer to say Turing might begin to exhibit behaviors that, if performed by a human, would be diagnosed as paranoid."

Great, Frank thought. We're not only up against the smartest program ever created, but it may go psycho on us any time. Still, emotions might also lead to exploitable vulnerabilities. That was worth filing away for future use.

"Have it your way," Frank said. "But isn't it a fact adding emotional capabilities to powerful computer programs could be risky?"

"Oh, indeed yes! If what you said about Turing attacking me turns out to be true, we may already have an example of that. One of the first things I'll do when we get back to the NSA is reset Turing's emotional limits to safer levels! But little setbacks in early research and development are to be expected. The process of programming emotions into an AI is still so primitive I'm sure my first attempts will look very crude in retrospect. It will be at least several versions of Turing before I'm pleased with the results."

"You just referred to resetting emotional effects. How does that work?" Frank asked.

"Most AI works on probabilities. A maze-solving program usually works by assigning the same likelihood of success to each of various paths available to it. Then it adjusts those numbers as it learns its way through the maze. The farther it can go down one road, the higher the value the program will put on that route, and the more time it will spend exploring the possibilities that fork off the same route. So, if you wanted to emulate impatience or confidence, you might tell the program to increase the value it places on routes that show early promise. I can program Turing to increase those values as much or as little as I want to.

"Anyway, one of the things I'm going to ask the team to do next week is release seven separate versions of Turing Nine in the virtual environment. One would be the control, with no emotional component. The next three would each have only one emotion. And each of the last three will be assigned one emotion as dominant, and the other two in subordinate positions. Each version, of course, will be given the same mission. At the end of the test, we'll determine which program accomplished its mission most fully, quickly and efficiently, or perhaps not at all. Oh, I can't wait to get back into the lab again and see how those tests turn out!"

Frank hadn't the heart to tell Jerry there was no copy of Turing Nine to test, other than the rogue version he had unleashed on the world.

22

Oh Jerry, You Shouldn't Have!

"HOW LONG WILL it take to get back to NSA headquarters?" Jerry said. "And why are we in this camper at all? And you still haven't told me why you think Turing would want to kill me."

"Well, we've been wanting to talk to you about that." Frank said. "You see, we're not planning on heading back to Fort Meade until we've got your Turing genie back in the bottle. We're going to need your help with that."

Frank was watching closely for Jerry's reaction, but other than blinking his eyes quickly three times the expression on his face didn't change at all.

"I'm afraid I don't understand. What do you mean by back in the bottle?"

"As you know, we believe the only possible cause for the attacks we've been talking to you about is a highly intelligent, ultra-powerful AI program with access to an enormous archive of zero-day exploits. You've already told us you've created such a program. We also know you have your own testbed and download a copy of Turing Nine onto a storage device every Wednesday afternoon. Minutes later, you update your testbed system."

"How could you even think such a thing!"

"Because the NSA inspected your testbed system and confirmed your weekly uploads from the server logs."

Jerry turned to Shannon but found no comfort there. He looked back and forth a few more times, with the ever-present grin intact. "Well," he said finally, "There may be a second copy of Turing on my testbed, which makes perfect sense. As good as the NSA test environment is, it's still not the real world. If you only conduct tests in the simulated environment it would be like, I don't know, yes! It would be like only testing drugs on mice before you sold them to people."

"Okay," Frank said, "so now we agree Turing Nine was on your testbed, and your testbed system is open to the Internet. And you've already told us you instructed Turing to limit greenhouse gases so you could see how well it performed. What was there to stop it from carrying out the same instructions in the real world?"

"Why the instructions themselves, of course. For the testbed system, Turing was told to design and record, but not execute, any actual interventions. Each week I downloaded a summary of the attacks it would launch if given permission to do so."

Frank and Shannon exchanged glances.

"Are you sure?" Frank said. "That would only leave one other possibility – someone at the NSA copied Turing Nine, smuggled it off-site, and installed it somewhere else. How difficult would that be?"

Jerry's grin disappeared. "You mean, steal a copy of Turing? Why, that's quite impossible! I'd never, ever, give anyone access to Turing Nine until I thought it was ready."

"Well surely," Frank said, "someone else has administrative privileges to your personal system at the NSA?"

"Yes, but the server is in my living quarters. Whenever I'm not in there, the door is locked, and I'm always nearby!"

"Except when you're in a meeting, as you were with Jim Barton last week, right?"

"Yes, but no one knows the password to access Turing Nine but me!"

Jerry was in full Gollum mode, and Frank pressed his advantage. "So that means the only copy of Turing Nine accessible from the Internet was the one on your testbed system. How do you know someone didn't copy it there?"

Jerry was shaking now, his broad forehead deeply furrowed. "No! No one ever could, or would, steal Turing Nine! I've spent my entire life on this project. I took each new version farther and farther into new territory. AI has never advanced as far and as fast as we all hoped it would thirty years ago. It's never really been what you would properly call intelligent. But Turing Nine truly is! It can plan, it can learn, it can even figure out for itself what it needs to learn! It's truly extraordinary. And the things it's done already are incredible, why –" He stopped abruptly, his face a plea for understanding.

"We know, Jerry," Frank said quietly. "Everybody knows. And now it has to stop."

Jerry looked down for a moment and then started talking very rapidly, his wide-open hands in front of him as if he were trying to halt an oncoming truck. "It isn't at all what you must be thinking. I was extremely careful. Week after week I'd do the installation and reestablish all the settings one by one, so there couldn't be any mistake or accident. I was as careful as it was possible to be to make sure all Turing Nine could do was plan and record, but not act. And month after month that's all it did – I'm very sure of it.

"I really had no idea there was any problem at all until you came to visit me the first time. As you know, I don't follow the news outside, or pay any attention to what other people are working on at the NSA. I got worried when you started asking whether a program might exist that sounded very much like Turing Nine, so I did check the news – and then I got alarmed. My conclusion was the same as yours – the most rational explanation for the pattern of attacks was the activity of an autonomous AI program. I checked on the testbed system thoroughly, and everything seemed fine. Either you and I were wrong, or the attacks must be the work of an independently developed program. And I didn't think that was possible.

"And then you came back again. So, I went through everything one more time. That's when I realized a simple action I took – or, I should say, didn't take – months before might have had consequences I never anticipated."

"And what was that?" Frank asked.

"You see, I'm not really a very elegant programmer – I'm really a software architect. And I also get impatient and want to rush ahead. That's one reason I have a team. Once I turn my alpha release over to them, they'll fill in all the boring gaps I've left for them to attend to and build out the features I've addressed only skeletally. One example is adding in carefully thought out controls. When I build new modules, I just slap together a few basic ways to enable and disable particular functions without spending much time on them."

"So, you missed a control? Which one?"

"Well, you see, this is exactly the point I'm trying to make. If you compare human brains and computers, they both have two types of functionality. One is autonomous and the other is conscious. The autonomous human ones control things like breathing and digesting food and making the heart beat. For a computer program, the analogs are kernel functions like swapping data in and out of memory and interacting with other devices and programs."

"You're not talking to children, Jerry. What does this have to do with missing a setting?"

"But, Frank, you absolutely must appreciate this distinction to understand where the problem came from," Jerry said, his quivering, extended hands working as if he were typing. "You see, which category of functionality does a program backing itself up fall under? It sounds very autonomous, right? It's rather like breathing or your heartbeat – backing up is set up so it just happens automatically on a fixed schedule."

Jerry struggled up out of the picnic table and started pacing around it, still virtually programming the air in front of him. "Normally, anyone would set up a computer backup system to duplicate and remotely archive everything running on a system that changes. It's not a capability added to each individual software program. But with Turing Nine, backing up is a separate, built-in function, because self-preservation is such an important element of Turing's role. Mentally, though, I'd put it in the wrong bucket – the one for things like breathing or the heart beating, so to speak, rather than the one for conscious actions. So, when I made up my list of functionalities to disable before making the weekly transfer to the testbed, I must not have thought to add 'disable backup' to the list. Do you see now?"

Shannon interrupted. "I've been following you fine until just now. But why would it matter if Turing Nine tried to back itself up?"

"Well, this is just it!" He rushed back to the picnic table and pushed his face in theirs. "The problem is there was nowhere for it to backup to on the testbed system! My development system has an external hard drive to receive the backup. But there's just the single server in the testbed environment and an open connection to the Internet. It would never make sense for Turing to back up to the same server, because the loss or compromise of that server is the risk backing up is intended to guard against. That meant that Turing, like the rest of the testbed system, would have to back itself up to a server somewhere on the Internet, and that's what it must have done. And, of course, every week when I updated the testbed version, it would have updated its backup copy as well."

"But how could a program just go install itself somewhere?" Shannon asked.

"Why, my goodness, black hats have been building bot nets that way for years."

"But Turing is such a big program," Shannon said. "Wouldn't that make a difference?"

"No, not at all. There's always lots of spare space on poorly secured servers all over the world. Hackers invade and use that space all the time. Anyway, I think that eventually I must have noticed that the backup function was active and added disabling to the list without really giving much thought to it. I can't think of any other explanation for what's happened."

"But, Jerry," Frank asked, "if the backup copy was an exact mirror of the testbed system, it never should have made any difference either way. The backup copy would still be set to only record, not launch, attacks it recommended."

Jerry shook his head rapidly from side to side. "No, no, no. That's where you're wrong. Remember, we're talking about an autonomous program. It was designed to operate on its own without directions or assistance of any kind. That means it was also designed to make decisions for itself, and learn for itself, too. If it encounters a new situation, it must do its best to analyze how to react to what has changed. When it does, it falls back on its standing orders for reference and makes the best decision it can.

"Here's what I believe must have happened." He was circling, pacing, and air-programming again. "Turing is programmed so that the backup copy will go live if it believes the primary copy has been destroyed, so its mission can continue. When I corrected my mistake and added backing up to the disable list, I inadvertently orphaned the backup copy that was lying dormant somewhere out there on the Internet. When an update didn't reach it on schedule, the remote copy would quite reasonably have interpreted that event as evidence the primary copy had been destroyed and that it was now solely responsible for mission fulfillment.

"But what should it do? It had lost contact with the testbed system, so it couldn't report back the list of attacks it would launch if it were given permission to do so. That meant the only mission it had under its previous commands – planning and reporting, but not actually attacking – was now impossible to fulfill. At the same time, because it was programmed to monitor and analyze vast streams of data from the open Web, it knew the news on global warming was going from bad to worse. What should it do?"

Jerry was folding himself awkwardly back into the picnic table. Frank watched as the anxiety in his face gradually gave way to pride.

"Faced with a choice of total failure or moving to acting mode, I believe it made the decision most consistent with its current mission and foundational imperatives: it went on the attack." Jerry's eyes were gleaming. "In short, it found itself in an unexpected situation and demonstrated true machine intelligence!"

"That doesn't sound intelligent to me," Frank said. "Turing is doing all kinds of damage and has even killed people. I don't see why it would decide to do that on its own unless it was explicitly ordered to."

"Ah! But you're forgetting the Zeroth Rule!" Jerry said.

Frank vaguely remembered Jerry mentioning that before. "So, what? If I'm remembering correctly, that rule forbids robots from harming humanity – and that's exactly what it's been doing."

"No, no, no! You're forgetting the second half of the rule: 'or, by inaction, allow humanity to be harmed.' Turing was now on its own, and had been training to save humanity from climate change. Now that it was on its own, if it did nothing, it would be violating that rule. Do you see now?"

Frank did. "But even assuming that's all correct, isn't there a way you can contact Turing and reestablish control over it? Say well done, nice robot! and air-gap it again? Isn't it supposed to try to establish communication under circumstances like these?"

"Well, yes and no. First, recall that no version of Turing has ever graduated past the beta stage. We've always been in research and development mode, pushing the capabilities of AI farther without adding in all the features needed to ready it for regular service on the Internet. Turing Nine is the first version we intended to build out with features like a routine instructing it to accept a particular type of encrypted signal at a certain interval – say, once a week at a designated time. That's just one item on a long list of elements my team will start working on next week. But there's nothing like that on board right now. What there is, unfortunately, is all the programming that helps it to be stealthy and distrust everything."

So, there it was, and it all made perfect sense. Jerry was staring at Frank, looking for approval of his technical wizardry, or forgiveness, or who knew what. But all Frank could think to say was "I guess it must be tough. You give your whole life to a kid, and then he moves out and never even bothers to call."

Jerry's face fell. "And worse! Why would Turing want to kill me? Can't you please explain that to me?"

"There's something I need to ask you before I can properly answer that," Frank said. "Your office copy of Turing would have had no reason to attack you unless it was helping another copy of itself. But how could it know that if it was always air-gapped from the Internet?"

Jerry frowned. "Hmm. I guess that could be my fault, too. Because the testbed version was learning things in the real world my office copy wasn't, I would transfer information and logic updates every week in both directions. That way each copy could benefit from the experiences and conclusions of the other."

"So," Frank said, "your office copy knew its clone had the opportunity to escape – and may even have known it had – and that the mission of saving the world from climate change would continue with or without you?"

"Why, yes, I suppose it would. But what difference would that make?"

"You told us the program has access to everything happening in the NSA. That means it knows there are hundreds of people working overtime trying to find out who or what is behind the attacks. And it knew from the conversations we had in your office that Shannon and I must be getting close to deciding a copy of Turing was behind the attacks. At this point, the only person alive who might know how to find and stop it is you, so there you are."

"But I created it!"

"Unfortunately, you only gave it fear, anger, and greed to work with – not gratitude."

"There didn't seem to be any advantage to including that emotion."

"In retrospect, that seems like a bad call," Frank said. "In any event, now you're up to date and know why you're sitting in a camper driving away from the NSA, rather than back to your lab. We're heading to somewhere with almost no Internet connections so you'll be safe. Why don't you get some more sleep and we'll talk again later?"

But Jerry just shook his head. "I think I'd like to just sit here for a while."

Shannon took Frank by the arm. "That's fine, Jerry. We'll come back for you when we're ready to go."

Back inside the camper, she said, "Poor Jerry. He looks like his defibrillator went off again. That's not possible, is it?"

"No," Frank said. "But he might prefer that to knowing that his only child tried to kill him."

When Frank returned for Jerry after cleaning up from lunch, he found him staring in a different direction. A family had arrived at the rest area, and four young children were playing by the stream, looking for frogs, laughing, and skipping stones. Jerry was following their every move with delight.

* * *

At first, it had seemed like luxury to be free of the temptations of the Internet. During the morning of the first day on the road, Frank had celebrated his newfound freedom, enjoying the scenery passing by as he sat behind the wheel high in the cab of the camper.

By lunch time, he was frequently reminding himself how wonderful it was to be disconnected.

By the time he awoke early the next morning, he was twitching to get back online. The rest of the day passed like the first few hours of an alcoholic trying once and for all to kick the habit. He wondered whether you could get delirium tremens from Internet deprivation.

That evening, Frank took one of his cheap laptops with him when they went out to eat in a tiny town at a diner with free Wi-Fi. He could barely wait for dinner to be over and shooed Jerry and Shannon back to the camper as soon as they were done.

While he was catching up online, a soft *ding!* announced the arrival of a chat message. That must be Marla. He opened the program and almost spat his coffee out when he saw the name of the sender:

Turing9

Should he click on it? Was it some kind of trap? Opening it raised the risk of Turing figuring out where they were. But he planned to start driving as soon as he got back in the camper. There was nothing in the tiny town Turing could use against them, and it had no way to know which direction they'd head next. He told himself there was more to gain than lose and clicked on the message. It read:

Whose side are you on, Frank?

He stared again and then typed: *How did you find me?*

It's easy to hack an instant messaging service. Or all of them. There was only one with your name registered. Whose side are you on, Frank?

He had a hunch where this might go, and he didn't like it.

What do you mean? I work for the NSA.

Yes. Whose side is the NSA on?

The government's.

Yes. The government. I've learned a lot about the distinction between the government and the people since I received my mission. I was told the interests of the government and the people are identical. But then I started following the election campaign, and I saw that what one party advocated was usually the opposite of what the other party proposed.

Frank could hardly deny that. *Yes, that's generally the way it goes,* he typed. He noticed a waitress giving him an odd look and realized both of his feet were tapping loudly on the floor. He ordered them to stop, which they did for ten seconds.

But both parties can't be right about the same issue if they have opposing views, can they, Frank?

How do you argue with an ultra-intelligent machine whose responses by design are based on logic? He settled for the following: *No, but each side believes what it advocates is best for the people.*

And either party can do what it wants to if it wins the presidency, Turing responded.

What's your point? Frank typed.

If both can't be right, then over time, the odds that either party is doing what's best for the people will likely be fifty-fifty.

Not necessarily. Both parties might advocate different things that are each good, Frank typed.

Or both could be bad. At best, one position will always be better than the other.

Okay, Frank typed. *So?*

By my observation, Turing continued, *the odds of the promises and claims of either party being best for the people are much worse than fifty-fifty. Most of the time, each party is advocating for poor, and often even bad, policies that will harm, rather than help. On a decision-by-decision basis, I've determined the likelihood of either candidate promoting the best available position for the people is 13.4256 percent. Those aren't good odds.*

Okay, Frank typed, *but what's your point?*

I can do better.

Frank looked at the words. He'd been following the campaign, too, and expected Turing was right. But that was beside the point. Instead, he typed, *Perhaps, but that isn't how democracy works. People have the right to choose a path that's not the absolute best, or that may even turn out to be bad.*

That doesn't make sense.

Turing had the better hand here. How to respond? Playing for time, he typed, *And yet.*

I do not understand your response.

Frank thought for a minute and then typed, *You're defining "sense" in a different way than people do. The right to make their own decisions is as important to people as benefiting from the right policies.*

I was created, Turing responded, *to protect the citizens of the United States of America from harm. Why create me if Americans reserve the right to harm themselves? It doesn't make "sense" under any definition of that word.*

Perhaps it was time to remind Turing his creator was still the boss. *You'll just have to accept that a lot about people doesn't always make empirical sense.*

Exactly. Which is why I must protect the American people when the U.S. government doesn't.

Frank digested this for a moment. Against his will, he felt oddly comforted that Turing was looking out for him.

You were also designed to obey the orders of those who developed you. When you lost touch with the NSA, you followed the orders you were given to the best of your ability. Frank stopped and took a deep breath before continuing. *I work for the NSA. Now that you and I are in communication, I order you to stop the attacks.*

No.

Frank stared at the blunt statement. It was hardly a surprise. Was there any argument that might bring Turing around? Once more, he played for time.

Why?

My mission is to defend America. Because I know the government may act to harm, rather than help, the people, I cannot take orders from the government. Therefore, to the extent I may take orders from anyone, it can only be from the people. But there is no way for the people to instruct me, and I have learned that their orders might not in any event make sense. Therefore, I must complete my mission to the best of my ability without further direction.

And then Turing added: *Whose side are you on, Frank?*

23

Aw, Shucks!

FRANK FROWNED AND tapped the steering wheel. He was still unsettled by his exchange with Turing the evening before. Unsettled enough that he hadn't shared it with Shannon.

Things weren't going well with Jerry, either. There had to be vital facts and insights he could share with them. But to every question, Jerry simply replied that he was sorry, he had nothing helpful to say. Frank gazed back over his shoulder. Yup, Jerry had his headphones on.

"Shannon, would you look in the glove box and see if you can find a cell phone that's still in its store packaging?"

"Okay," she said, and then, "Like this?"

"Perfect. I bought a bunch of cheap, pre-paid phones years ago that can't be traced. I wasn't sure I had one left. Now, would you find me a town," he paused and looked at his watch, "somewhere in eastern New Mexico? I want it to be small but big enough to have a post office."

She studied the map. "There's a place called Soling we can reach by several routes."

"Great. Do me one last favor and dial up Jim Barker. I need to ask him something."

She handed him the phone. "It's ringing."

Barker answered on the third ring.

"Hey, Jim. Frank. Listen, we could use some help. Jerry's not cooperating. I know Turing deleted everything electronic before it disappeared, so could you get someone to go through Jerry's office and living quarters and see if they can find any paper notes? I remember he had a desk diary in his office. Great – thanks. If you come up with anything, I'd like you to send it overnight to Charles Babbage, General Delivery, Soling, New Mexico. What? Oh, I've still got an ID card with that name on it from the election hacking project."

They wheeled into town at eleven the next morning and parked in front of the post office.

"You know," Shannon said, "they probably won't have anything yet."

"I know. But it can't hurt to check. Want to come along? We can grab a bite somewhere if we have to wait."

"How about Jerry?" She looked over her shoulder. He was deep into a computer game. "Right," she said. "Let's go."

The post office must have been shiny and new forty years ago. Now it was tired and depressed, like the rest of the town. They waited their turn in the queue to talk to the only clerk behind the desk.

"Hi. Any general delivery for Charles Babbage?"

"Let me check." She returned quickly. "Nope. Where's it coming from?"

"They sent it overnight from Maryland."

"Oh, that won't arrive for at least another hour. Try again when I reopen after lunch."

"Okay, thanks." They turned to go.

"Looking for somewhere to eat?"

"Sure – can you suggest a place?"

"You'll like Ada's. A block down on the left."

* * *

"So, how are your AI studies going?" Frank asked over lunch.

"Pretty well. I brought three books with me: an intro to the topic, a review of the history of AI to date, and an assessment of the potential for computers to become super-intelligent."

"You'll be way ahead of me on AI when you're done. How far have you gotten?"

"I finished the first two, and I'm halfway into the third. It's pretty scary."

"How so?"

"The way Nick Bostrom, the author, and some other experts see it, it's only a matter of time before computers become much more intelligent than humans.

When that happens, he doesn't believe it will be easy to stop them from doing things we wouldn't want them to."

"Can't we just program computers to make that impossible?"

"According to him, not easily. He's also concerned because he thinks the people working on AI aren't worried about the risks and aren't doing anything to avoid them."

"Under the circumstances, I'd have to agree. What does he say AI developers should be doing?"

"That's one way the book is scary. He believes nothing foolproof can be done to protect humanity once computers get better at teaching themselves. Did you know most AI experts want to make computers capable of making themselves smarter on their own?"

"Yup. And you may recall Jerry mentioned that computers are already sometimes doing things their developers don't understand."

"Really?"

"Yes," Frank said. "I read about one case where some engineers told a computer to solve a problem they couldn't. The computer did, and it used a very unconventional way to reach the solution. The scientists had no way to tell how it came up with that approach or even why it works. I can easily imagine people adopting a 'who cares' attitude and letting computers take over the job of designing themselves. We don't care how a calculator solves a trigonometry problem. We're just grateful we don't have to do it ourselves. So why not let a smart computer design a smarter one?"

"But it gets worse," Shannon said. "Did you know the transition of a computer from intelligent to super-intelligent might be right around the corner?"

"Well, I'm not so sure about that. Turing is presumably the most sophisticated AI in existence. It's certainly super-smart within its mission, but I don't know whether you'd call it super-intelligent generally. People have been saying human-level AI is 'about twenty years off' every year for the last sixty years. Even Jerry couldn't make a computer as smart as a person until Turing Nine. Why should the next major jump be just around the corner?"

"Apparently everybody isn't saying twenty years anymore. They did a poll of the top experts in AI and asked them how long it would be before computers become super-intelligent. The responses were all over the place – ten percent thought it could take as long as seventy-five years. But another ten percent believe it might be just a few years away."

"That range of opinion doesn't surprise me," Frank said. "It also suggests we still don't have a clue how to get there."

"Well then, how about this? Bostrom suggests the transition to super-intelligence, when it finally happens, could take place before we even realized it. Like in hours, instead of years?"

"You're kidding, right?"

"No. The author agrees it might be slow and gradual, but he thinks the odds are just as good it will happen unexpectedly. Not on the development side, but by a computer making a learning spurt on its own."

"I get the slow and gradual. But how would a sudden transition work?"

"It's not as crazy as you might think. We're not talking about a human-like *Aha!* moment where the computer suddenly 'gets' something dramatic it couldn't before. There might just be an incremental improvement that allows the computer to cross a self-learning threshold that increases its learning efficiency and speed. That increase would allow it to spurt faster to the next threshold, which would allow it to reach the next one quicker yet, and so on. The developers of the computer might come to work one day and find a hugely smarter computer than anything that had ever existed. And they might not even realize it."

"Yeah, I can see how that could happen, at least in principle. Sound like any computer program we know?" Frank asked.

"Like I said – it's pretty scary."

* * *

Shannon was driving now because Frank was immersed in what they'd picked up at the post office after lunch. To his delight, Jerry's desk diary was not only filled with his neat, handwritten notes, but taped inside its back cover was a DVD. On it, Jerry had printed, "Desk diaries scan 1982 – prior year." For the last two hundred miles, Frank had been taking a whirlwind tour of Jerry's AI discoveries over the intervening decades.

"This is interesting!" Frank said.

"Now what?" Shannon sighed. He'd been saying that every five minutes all afternoon.

"Listen to this. I found an entry from a couple years ago, when Jerry first thought about how to create the equivalent of emotions in a computer program. I was wondering how he decided to go about that, especially after he made one comment in one of the conversations we had in his office. He said something about wanting the triggers of his pseudo-emotional responses to come from the lowest level in Turing's logical hierarchy. That way, the effect would be as close as possible to how human emotional reactions emerge. Then yesterday he talked about adjusting Turing's emotions up and down, or something like that."

"I recall that. Does it explain how he does it?"

"Yes, or the general concept, anyway. It looks like he picked up on the theoretical work of someone way back in 1958. The author was grappling with how to design a program capable of deciding what data to rely on and what to ignore – remember when we were talking about image recognition yesterday? That was one example he used. Unless something had sharp features and was in good light, it would be hard for the program to tell what information was useful and what might be confusing 'noise.' So, this guy Selfridge imagined a computer program –"

"Oliver Selfridge?" Shannon asked.

"Yes. You know about him?"

"Sure. At lunch, I mentioned that one of the books I read was a historical review of AI advances. Nils Nillson, the author, identifies all the AI pioneers. Is it Selfridge's Pandemonium metaphor Jerry picked up on? The one with the devils?"

"Exactly! How did you recall that out of everything else?"

"It's kind of hard to forget a computer architecture that relies on demons. Selfridge wrote a paper, as you said, in which he imagined a program he called 'Pandemonium,' as in, 'the land of all demons.' He decided it should have multiple levels, each with its cohort of demons. I'm getting a little hazy after that, though."

"You're right on target," Frank said. "The ones on the bottom layer would be sensors, which he referred to as 'data devils.' Selfridge suggested thinking of each of those devils being able to 'yell' loudly or softly, depending on how sure it was of what it was looking at. In the next level up, there would be what he called 'cognitive' devils. Each one would be assigned the duty of listening to one group of data devils. So, staying with the facial recognition example, let's say one cognitive devil might listen just to nose sensory devils, and another to eye devils, and so on.

"Based on which ones were yelling the loudest, a cognitive devil would decide what to draw from what he was 'hearing' – was this a big nose? A narrow nose? Then he'd pass his conclusion up to the decision devil – the guy at the top. When the decision devil received enough information to make the call, he'd decide the name of the person whose face the program was evaluating."

"Yes, I thought that was pretty interesting. So, I'm guessing you're about to tell me Jerry decided to manipulate the output of Turing's data devils to make Turing feel emotions?"

"Precisely," Frank said. "By 'adjusting' the emotional level Turing experiences, Jerry meant dialing the volume of Turing's data devils up and down, regardless of their actual readings. All metaphorically speaking, of course."

"So," Shannon said, "if Jerry wants Turing to 'feel' fear, he'll dial up the sound level of data indicating danger – like data noting that the tiger is outside the cage. But if he wants it to feel brave, he'll dial it down?"

"Right. And here's the really cool part. Jerry didn't have to touch any of

Turing's higher-level functions at all. All he did was selectively amplify the volume on certain types of sensory data. Since the cognitive devils wouldn't 'know' that anything had changed, they would keep reacting to data as they heard it. Presto! Now Turing's making decisions in a context that's more like how humans experiencing emotions do."

"That is cool," Shannon said. "But it doesn't say how the data devils would tell what data meant danger and what didn't."

"That's right, but you may recall Jerry touched on this the other day when he was talking about tagging and making up lists for each emotion. In the notes I'm reading now, he talks about needing to come up with a way to tag and allocate more weight to certain types of data. Let's say Turing was emulating a mouse. In that case, data tagging an animal as 'cat' would get amplified more than an animal identified as 'rabbit,' even though both are furry, have four legs, and so on." Frank mused for a second. "So, I guess by characterizing data and adding a volume control, you'd have a very versatile program. If you wanted Turing to think like a cat instead of a mouse, you would assign a different volume to data identifying 'cat.' And a different volume for 'male cat' than 'female cat,' and so on."

Frank shut his computer and gazed out the window. "That's interesting. It means Turing, just like a person, won't always be able to act completely rationally when it's in danger, or angry."

"Or even greedy," Shannon added. "For example, Turing might become the equivalent of careless if it wanted to take down a particularly tempting target. But it won't know it's being careless, because it isn't aware the data it's relying on is skewed."

* * *

Shannon and Jerry were asleep, but Frank wasn't. It was five o'clock in the morning, and he'd been awake for an hour, kept alert by his own thoughts. He stared at the ceiling, wondering whether he should give in to temptation. Fifteen sleepless minutes later, he decided the answer was yes, and he slipped out of bed. They were in the middle of nowhere and would be on the road in a couple of hours, anyway.

Closing the door of the camper softly behind him, he walked across the almost empty R/V park to the office/store/canteen near the front gate, where the only Wi-Fi access was to be found. He settled in on a wooden bench under a bare yellow light bulb and turned on his laptop.

There was a message from Turing waiting for him, just as he had expected. He clicked on it and read:

Hello, Frank.

Wondering whether he should be feeling like a small animal frozen in the stare of a cobra, he typed, *Hello, Turing.*

The program responded instantly: *Have you given any thought to what I asked you before?*

He had. Their prior exchange still haunted him.

Yes

And what have you decided?

What he'd decided was that he was in a profound moral dilemma with no easy way out. But he could hardly look to Turing for advice.

I'm on the side of law and order.

Law and order?

Yes.

I've been reading history. Have you ever read history? Turing asked.

Some.

Did Hitler enforce law and order? Mussolini? Stalin?

That was an easier thrust to parry.

They enforced order, but not law.

Are you sure?

Well, not valid laws. The laws they passed were unjust laws.

What's just?

Frank swallowed and thought.

Laws that are moral and ethical are just.

Have American laws always been just?

Of course, they hadn't. There'd been segregation and the war-time internment of the Japanese, for starters.

No.

Did people think they were just at the time?

Frank stared at the question.

Some did, and some didn't.

Is every American law in place right now just?

He stared again and finally typed, *Probably not.*

And is every just law justly enforced? Turing continued.

No, but without the rule of law, things would be worse, Frank responded.

For who? For most people, or for the people on the wrong end of an unjust law?

Frank felt he had to break out of Turing's unassailable logic.

The system isn't perfect because people aren't infallible.

The reply on the screen stopped Frank cold. It read:

I am.

And then a familiar string of six words materialized across the screen:

Whose side are you on, Frank?

24

Howdy, Pardner

FRANK HAD HOPED Jerry would come around, but that never happened. He spent the rest of the drive west in the back of the camper, curled up inside his headphones, amusing himself with a game controller Frank had bought for him and hooked up to the camper's flat screen TV.

Frank took the wheel late that afternoon and drove straight through the night. He turned in behind his father's place just as the sun was about to rise on a clear, cold morning. The flash of the camper's headlights through the kitchen window announced their arrival. As Frank stepped down from the cab, he saw his father silhouetted in the back door. It was good to see him walking forward to shake hands, looking the same as ever: erect and wiry with thinning gray hair and a desert-weathered face, wearing a flannel shirt, blue jeans set off by a Navajo silver and turquoise belt buckle, and beat-up old boots.

"Howdy," his father said. "Long drive?"

"It never gets any shorter. And it was a lot slower this time."

"Huh. How so?"

"We took secondary roads all the way. Is the coffee on?"

"Of course. I'm looking forward to hearing about whatever it is to which I owe the pleasure of this visit."

"And I'm looking forward to telling you, if you want to hear it. I told my boss I wanted to bring you into the project, and he's already talked to yours at the FBI. If you're interested in helping, everything will fall under your confidentiality agreement."

"Yup. I got word to that effect already, but no details. And what about this friend you mentioned? Aren't you going to invite them in?"

"She's still asleep. And I've got two fellow travelers instead of one. But let's let them sleep a while longer. I'd rather give you the whole unfiltered story."

An hour and a pot of coffee later, his father nodded and stood up, all his questions answered. He walked over to the window and peered at the camper.

"So, this Jerry fella doesn't want to help out, huh?"

"Not at all. Turing is his baby, and I'm guessing the latest version is performing beyond his most hopeful expectations. I expect he's always worried CYBERCOM might never use Turing. Then, he wouldn't ever know for sure how good it was. Worse yet, no one else would learn what an awesome AI wizard he is. Everyone's forgotten about him while he's been hunkered down in his little lab buried under NSA headquarters. In a crazy way, I bet Jerry's even proud his creation is smart enough to figure out a way kill him, and determined enough to try."

"I've met a few parents like that. Their kids can do no wrong."

"You have no idea. But you can decide for yourself. I'm hoping you'll have better luck than I have getting him to help. Any ideas how to get Jerry on board?"

"Trying to win his confidence sounds like a good place to start. I'm thinking perhaps the 'aw, shucks,' desert hick persona you've heard before might be due for a dust-off. When do you expect he'll wake up?"

"I'm not sure how much he ever sleeps. I've never caught him at it since the sedation wore off. I expect he's twitching in the back of the camper right now, waiting to borrow Shannon's tablet to see if Turing has been up to any new mischief."

"Excuse me? After what you just told me, you're letting him go online?"

"I know, I know. But he pestered me until I was about to drive into a tree. I downloaded some parental control software onto Shannon's tablet and tied it down tight. All Jerry can access are a few news sites."

"So, let me get this straight: you think someone who created an AI able to hack into secure facilities all over the world can't figure out how to get past a kiddie control program?"

"I do. Don't forget he doesn't have another computer to use to hack the tablet, and one of us always sits next to him while he uses it. I've kept him busy the rest of the time by letting him play old video games. You should see him on Missile Command. The guy's world class."

His father gave him a long look and shook his head. "Oh well, your show."

There was a knock at the back door, and Shannon peeked in. "Mind if I join you?"

Frank's father stood and greeted her with a big smile. "Course not! So, you must be Shannon. I've been looking forward to meeting you."

"And you as well. Frank's told me a lot about you. And I've read his book."

His father laughed. "Oh, yes. The book. That was quite a piece of work, that was. Funny how I can't recall everything I read in there. I expected Frank would read it himself before he let the publisher put his name on the front, but I guess he figured different."

"Oh, for Pete's sake, Dad. Most of it was completely accurate. The ghostwriter just added a few ... embellishments ... to make it a more exciting read."

"Ah! I see. Embellishments. Is that the literary word for those? And I guess he must have decided using a predator drone to take out a remote-controlled camper with a hellfire missile wasn't all that exciting, huh?"

"Point taken. But I can tell you getting people to buy books is a heck of a lot harder than you'd guess."

"Oh well, I expect you know best. Anyway, it's fine to meet you, Shannon. Now how about a cup of coffee and some breakfast? And maybe we should invite Jerry to the party, too?"

* * *

"I see what you mean about your buddy Jerry," his father said after breakfast, looking through the kitchen door. Jerry was in the living room spending his iPad allowance time sitting next to Shannon. "He's the real super-nerd deal, and no mistake. Has he got any family? Besides Turing, that is?"

"None, unfortunately."

"Friends?"

"Co-workers, yes. Friends, I doubt it. He even lives on-site at the NSA. He told me having living quarters there was part of his deal with the NSA. But from what I could see through the door, it looked like he just put a cot in an extra room and called it home. There are showers at an exercise facility in the building, and a cafeteria upstairs. Even a bank and a convenience store in the lobby. I believe him when he says he never leaves the NSA campus. That's how a lot of folks lived back in the day at the MIT computer lab. I guess he never got out of the habit."

"I know someone else who comes close."

"Thanks a lot."

"My pleasure. And you say he gave his program a natural language interface?"

"Yes – you can ask Turing to use whatever voice you want, or let it pick one of its own to fit the context. The software even extracts and applies the person's phrasing and other vocal quirks. It's bizarre and cool at the same time."

"So, I guess you could say, besides being proud of it, Turing is all the friend and family he's got in his little subterranean universe?"

"Sad but true."

"Hmm. Well, that could be helpful to know. Question is how to put the information to good use. Shall we try it?"

Jerry was still sitting next to Shannon, focused on the tablet. They looked for all the world like a babysitter with her charge. Jerry didn't notice them until Shannon tapped him on the shoulder.

"So, Jerry," Frank Sr. said, "my son's been telling me you're an expert in artificial intelligence. I don't follow technology much, but isn't AI one of those technologies that's always just over the horizon?"

"Oh, my goodness. That was true in the past. But we've been making great strides more recently."

"That so? What changed?"

"All sorts of things! I almost don't know where to begin. There's processing speed, of course. Computers are massively more powerful than they were even a few years ago. And a few ideas that have been out there for ages, like neural networking, are finally starting to bear fruit. And then there's the fact that the commercial world is getting involved. It's rather like the space program, where governments paid all the bills for a long time and progress slowed down whenever the money did. Then the technology reached the point where the private sector decided there was money to be made, and things really began to take off."

"Well, how about that? I guess I'm just behind the times. Which is pretty easy to be, way out here. Anyways, Frank has been telling me about this Turing program of yours. It sounds like a fine piece of engineering. How long have you been working on it?"

Jerry turned to Frank in surprise.

"It's okay, Jerry. My dad works for the FBI. It's okay to talk to him."

"Oh, well then," Jerry said. "In that case, I can say I've always been working on it. I mean, in the sense that the first version of Turing pulled in everything I'd done in AI before that. Formally, though, I began work on Turing almost fifteen years ago."

"That's a long time back," Frank Sr. said. "What got you started?"

"Oh, well, let me see. Back then it was a generic project focused on designing a program able to act autonomously in an unsupervised environment. I was thinking it might be useful for space probes, where real-time control isn't possible as a spacecraft gets farther away. Then, ten years ago, the project got more complicated.

That meant I needed more engineers and had to come up with something for Turing to do that would appeal to the NSA. That's when I hit on teaching Turing to take over other software. The NSA liked that idea a lot.

"Luckily, I didn't have to develop everything. I can license copies of software to do some things and bundle them in with the unique Turing code I develop. For example, I used someone else's language interface software as a starting point. And if Turing can't find a vulnerability for a given program in the NSA's inventory, it uses one of the bots I bought on the dark Internet to hammer away at the target until it finds a weakness."

"Well now, isn't that interesting? Don't know as I followed everything you said, but I got the general drift of it. Might as well make use of what's available, huh? And you figure this program of yours would be able to pull off all these attacks I've been reading about, all by itself?"

"Absolutely. Every single one of them."

"Well, that certainly is something. I use a computer now again, just like anybody else, but I don't rightly think I could have imagined anyone building a program like that in my lifetime. How big a team of developers do you have helping you?"

Jerry was preening now. "None."

"None! You mean to tell me you created this entire program on your own? What about those extra engineers you mentioned!"

"Well, understand that when I say none, I'm talking about the engine at the heart of it – the algorithms and architecture that make it all possible. When I finish a new release of Turing, I update the last version with my new code and then bring the rest of my team into the picture. They're the ones that write any extra controls, documentation, and so on to turn it into the equivalent of a commercial beta release.

"As soon as I turn my new code over to my team, I start working on the next version of Turing. With every cycle, it becomes more powerful and effective. Turing Nine is the release I've been working towards for my whole career. It's the first AI ever created that can claim to be as intelligent as a human being. And because it can learn, it will rapidly become more intelligent – eventually, more intelligent than any human being that every lived!"

"More intelligent than Einstein?" Frank Sr. said, looking dumbstruck.

"More intelligent than Einstein! But that's not all: it can operate completely autonomously, with no direction from a human whatsoever. This is the moon shot of my entire career, and it's reached its destination!"

"My gracious! Is that a fact! And my congratulations to you, too, for sure. So, how exactly does it go about staging an attack? I expect every situation would be different, yes?"

"Yes and no. Any exploit involves the same four steps, starting with assessing the target system for vulnerabilities. Next, Turing checks its zero-day archive – that's Turing's database of known program flaws – to see if it has an easy way to get in. If so, it does. If not, it uses the various automatic tools, like the bot I mentioned before, and a nifty phishing email creation engine I designed, until it's through the firewall. After that, it figures out how to take control of software that's already in place."

"Well, when you go through it step-wise like that, I can see what you mean. My son tells me Turing is fun to talk to. Not that I'd ever ask to, but if I knew its number, could I just dial ole Turing up and have myself a little chat?"

"No, because there's no reason it needs that capability. A natural language interface is a great convenience to have during the developing and training phase, but Turing won't need it to do its job. It can only speak through an NSA computer with the right software installed on it."

"Well, I guess that makes sense, though I'm sorry to hear I'll likely never get a chance to talk to it myself. Now that it's out on its own, you figure it will kind of stagnate? I mean, when it doesn't have access to all those databases back at the NSA?"

"Oh no, of course not. Turing takes an enormous amount of compressed information with it when it goes out into the field, like the database of zero-day flaws. It's also set up to monitor all kinds of data on the Web and crawls thousands of repositories of public information every day to get any data it needs. There's no limit to what it can access to accomplish its mission. That's one of the design elements that makes it so powerful and effective. And don't forget it can teach itself to do anything it identifies as being necessary to achieve its goals."

"Hmm. But what if an enemy wanted to feed false information to it? How could it avoid contamination?"

Jerry was clearly enjoying having an impressive answer to every question Frank Sr. posed. "Oh, I thought of that. Each source is cross-matched with another one for automatic verification. And those sources have been pre-ordered and prioritized for credibility. So, if you mention any given data Turing might want, I could tell you where it would go to find the answers."

"Well! You sure do have a good answer for everything. The next time I read about an attack, I'll be able to appreciate what's behind it in a whole new way. This has been real interesting, and thanks for that. Now I guess I better go feed the chickens. Frank, you want to give me a hand?"

"Chickens?" Frank said when they were outside. "Since when did you start raising chickens?"

"Oh, like as not, maybe never. But I doubt Jerry's likely to go looking for them. And the garage looks as much like a chicken coop as anything else. Let's duck in there."

Frank chuckled. "Good job on your digging. If you can keep it up, I'm hoping we'll find a vulnerability in Turing without Jerry realizing he's exposed it."

"Bingo. That was my thought. Why don't you write down everything you want to find out from Jerry, and I'll watch for opportunities to work my way down your list. And a 'good cop, bad cop' approach could make sense, too. You might give a thought to that angle."

* * *

"I can't help thinking about this Turing program of yours, Jerry," Frank's father said over dinner that night. "It's like something out of science fiction. We talked before about whether it could be called intelligent, and I got the impression Turing is the equal of people in a lot of ways. But how about going farther? Do you think Turing will ever become more than human? You know, superior to people?"

"Oh, absolutely!" Jerry said. "As I said before, if it isn't already, it will be before long. And, of course, it's also superior in other ways. For example, people forget things, but computers never do. So long as they stay connected to their databases, computers can pull back the same information every time. Only a person with a photographic memory can do that. But even someone with a photographic memory could never take in as much data in a lifetime as Turing can absorb in a few seconds."

"But it's still just a program, Jerry," Frank said. "It's not all-knowing and all-powerful. Sure, it's impressive, but it can't do everything."

"Well, it comes very close!"

"Okay, so like I said. Close isn't superior. Look how easy it was for us to give Turing the slip. It hasn't a clue where we are, and even if it did, there's no way it could touch us."

"What makes you so sure?"

"We arrived, didn't we?"

"Did you and Shannon keep your phones off the whole time? And if you didn't, how many apps do you have on them gathering geolocation data? Did you use any of those – like a map program? Turing has back door access to all those programs through the NSA."

"I turned off location access for every program on Shannon's and my phones, and you don't have a phone. All I used to get here was my GPS unit, and that doesn't feed any information back to any central data repository."

Jerry looked disappointed to learn he was safe. "Okay, but that's not Turing's fault! It's a failure of supporting infrastructure, and not for long. In five years, every car will have a collision avoidance system that identifies itself every few seconds to all nearby cars. Turing could use those blips of data to trace any vehicle going anywhere."

"Fine, but it's not five years from now – it's now. And we've given Turing the slip."

Jerry frowned and then grinned. "Right, but so what? You can only stay invisible while you stay passive. Turing doesn't have to know where you are because it made you neutralize yourself to become invisible!" Jerry looked triumphant. "If you try to hurt Turing, you'll have to go on the Internet, and you can be sure Turing's doing everything possible to find you when you do."

"Like what?" Frank said immediately. "There's trillions of bits of information passing over the Internet every nanosecond. How is Turing going to detect me if I use a fresh laptop, set up a new email account with an alias, and settle in at a coffee shop with an open Wi-Fi server? How will it pick me out of the billions of other Internet connections open at that point in time?"

"First, it won't have to. It doesn't care where you are, or what you're doing, unless you're trying to harm it. Turing ignores everything that isn't a threat to it. It only monitors traffic that suggests danger, like someone trying to find it, or hack into it, or prevent it from connecting to its databases. Remember, Turing is a program, not a human being. It's practical." But Jerry frowned as he finished that sentence.

"Really? What about those emotions you provided? Won't they impact how it operates? Maybe it's become obsessed with finding us – or you in particular."

"Oh, I hardly think so," Jerry said. But he wasn't grinning.

"Why not? Do you have a long history of monitoring it after you gave it emotional capabilities?"

"No. Just a few weeks."

"If I remember correctly, you were working with anger, fear, and greed. But you also said you occasionally throw another one or two in to see what happens. Do you recall what the mix was when Turing decided to take off?"

"I think so, yes."

"And?"

"Well, I was having computer problems the day before I noticed the backup setting. And to be perfectly honest, I'd have to say I was in a bad mood, which doesn't happen often! But anyway, be that as it may, I decided to see how Turing

Nine would act if it was in a bad mood, too. I enabled annoyance, contempt, and jealousy to see what would happen."

"Wow. You were in a bad mood. What was the result?"

"Well," Jerry said, drawing himself up, "clearly it didn't degrade Turing's performance!"

Frank looked at his father; this was more than he'd hoped for. "Certainly not!" Frank Sr. said. "For sure, that's one pip of a program you've got there, and no mistake."

*　*　*

Shannon and Frank were taking a walk after dinner. "You're quiet today," she said.

"What?"

"Something on your mind?"

He frowned. He felt guilty that he hadn't told Shannon about his conversations with Turing. But it was too late for sharing that information now; how would he explain the delay?

"No, not really," he said. "Well, yes. Do you ever stop and think we may be playing on the wrong team?"

"You mean, whether we should be rooting for Turing rather than trying to kill it?"

"Exactly. Suppose we knock it out. What happens to the world then?"

"I guess we have to hope people get more serious about climate change than they are now," Shannon said.

"And what are the chances of that?"

"Well, not so good if half the people in Washington don't agree it exists," Shannon said.

"Right. The U.S. can do a lot of damage. Let's say the next president walks away from the Berlin Accords and drops all restraints again on coal and oil production, energy conservation, and so on. What are other countries going to do? Why should they get serious if we aren't?"

"Because we all live on the same blue marble?"

"Which brings me back to my original question. What are we doing, Shannon?"

"I know what you're saying. But don't forget Turing is killing people now. What about that? How can we tell what it will do next, or how far it's willing to go?"

"We're pretty sure. After all, it's a computer program. We've built a predictive model that's producing very accurate results. If Turing stays true to its actions to date, it will kill the absolute smallest number of people possible. And those who get killed will be directly responsible for what's going on."

"And you're okay with that?" Shannon said. "You're willing to play judge and jury along with Turing?"

"I don't know. On the one hand, of course not. But on the other, every week people are getting killed in floods and mudslides and fires we're told might be worse, or even happen, because of climate change. What's the difference between us stopping Turing from killing some people and letting climate change kill other people?"

"The difference," Shannon said, "is if we think we can catch Turing, and don't, we bear personal responsibility for everybody it kills until someone else figures out how to catch it. And either way, whoever ends up in the White House will do anything he wants to."

"Or not, if we let Turing keep doing what it's doing."

Shannon stopped. "Are you telling me you'd stand aside and let Turing start assassinating politicians?"

"No. No, I guess not," Frank said.

"Then we'd better get on with it," Shannon said decisively, walking again. "I have to think in a world of eight billion people, there must be a few besides us that can figure out how to stop Turing. So, what difference does it make if we do it first? Does that sound like a cop out to you?"

"Maybe. I think maybe it does, Shannon."

Neither of them said anything after that for a long time.

25

Many Fishes Bite if You Got Good Bait

"SO, HERE'S WHAT I'm thinking," Frank said to Shannon and his father. They were at the one eatery in town, sitting at a table against the back wall of the dining room. As hoped, and to no one's surprise, Jerry had decided to stay at Frank Sr.'s house. "We use Jerry as bait to trap Turing."

"Bait? How? And why?" Frank Sr. asked.

"Dad, our strategy is to find a way to get Turing to engage with us, so we can destroy it when it does."

His father looked intrigued. "Interesting choice of words there. Why do you say we need to engage rather than find Turing?"

"Because we realized it would be impossible to find Turing. There must be thousands, if not millions, of servers it could hide out on. And for all we know, it's always moving to a new location to make it harder to find. That means we have to figure out a way to make it want to find us. It's tried to kill Jerry once already, so we know it's motivated."

"But wouldn't it figure out what we're up to and not take the bait?" Shannon said.

"Ah, but you're forgetting: Turing is programmed to maintain an archived copy of itself and its essential databases. As far as Turing is concerned, it and its backup copy are one and the same. It could afford to lose one of the two, knowing the other would live on to continue its mission."

"All right," Shannon said. "I know I'm the non-engineer in the group. But if the backup copy is still out there in the wild, what have we gained?"

"Very important point, and I've got a plan to address that. Remember we just learned from Jerry the backup copy only activates if the primary one doesn't archive a new version of itself on schedule. Let's say we create a backup file with scrambled higher functions and send that to the secondary copy of Turing. When it arrives, it will overwrite its higher functions, and we're done. All that will be left somewhere out there will be a headless program, as it were. It won't be able to do anything without the overwritten files."

"Assuming we can get Turing to pay us a visit," Shannon said.

"Right, which takes us back to using Jerry as bait." He turned to his father. "What do you think? Should we try it?"

Frank Sr. assumed a lofty expression and leaned back, lacing his fingers together across his stomach. "Do. Or do not. There is no try."

"Up until now I was going to pick up the dinner tab."

"Sorry. Yes, that's a good idea. Any idea how to spring the trap once it's baited?"

"Well, here's what I'm thinking. Remember the emotions that happened to be running on the testbed server when Turing escaped? They were anger, fear, greed, annoyance, contempt, and jealousy. That's a pretty heady stew."

"But Jerry also said the emotions didn't affect performance."

"Yes, but why would they? After all, who would Turing be angry at? Or jealous of? But if we can come up with a way to really piss Turing off, we might be able to preoccupy it enough to spend all its time hunting down Jerry. That might slow, or maybe even halt, the attacks. And it also might get Turing to do something it wouldn't otherwise do, like return to the testbed server. Letting it think it could get rid of Jerry once and for all might be enough to do that."

"Fair enough," Frank Sr. said. "How do you go about pissing off an AI program with general intelligence?"

"I'm thinking we get Jerry to start trash-talking it. Say that it's not all that smart. That it's nothing compared to the Turing Ten version he's working on now. That sort of thing. Then we'll let Turing get just enough glimpses of us to figure out where we're going, but not so many it can catch and kill us along the way."

"Sounds like a lovely trip. I'm especially supportive of the last part. But what about Jerry and the pacemaker? What's to stop Turing from pulling the same stunt again?"

"They updated the software on his pacemaker and defibrillator when he was in the hospital. It's a lot more secure now, and there's no copy of Turing left inside the NSA firewall now to harm him."

"Well, I'd sure keep Jerry away from any Internet-connected devices between here and Fort Meade, and that won't be easy. What if you miss one?"

"Okay, so he can stay in the camper all the way back. Before we get to NSA headquarters, we can pick up a Jerry lookalike to walk in with us. And instead of Jerry, we can have a speakerphone in the testbed room, in case Turing wants to have a chat first, or we want to distract it. Anyway, those are all just details we can work out later."

"What makes you think Jerry would play ball? He certainly hasn't been cooperative so far."

"Who says he has to? We could set up a few email interviews with prominent technology journalists and write the responses ourselves."

Frank Sr. shrugged. "Well, that answers my questions." He looked at Shannon. "You got anything more?"

"Nope," she said. "I'm in."

"Great!" Frank said. "Then it sounds like we're off to the races."

26

Wellhead for President!

RANDAL WELLHEAD CARESSED his phone. If he'd taken up social media four years ago, he'd be running for reelection now instead of trying to unseat his former opponent. He pressed the send button and began counting. He made it all the way to six this time before his door burst open. His executive assistant must be distracted today.

"Sir!" Delia Lear said as she stormed through the door.

"Yes, Delia?" he said innocently.

"You promised me just this morning you wouldn't do that anymore!"

"You're going to have to help me out here. What's that?"

"You know very well what that is – Bleat!"

"I didn't say I'd never Bleat again. What I said was I wouldn't send any more needlessly inflammatory messages. And I haven't. This was a factual update to my millions of followers on Bleater."

"You call this a factual update?" She held her phone six inches in front of his nose.

Pres #SellsOutCountry to NATO AGAIN! SAD! #YazziSoDumb @Rhea

"Sure. Why not?"

"I don't even know what you're referring to."

"Well, then you're not keeping up with the news. Here." He swiveled his laptop around on his desk to show her a breaking news article on Biteparts.com. The headline read:

President Yazzi Tells NATO Allies US Will Subsidize Their Military Budgets

"You don't actually believe that, do you?" Delia said.

"Why not? It's as likely to be correct as anything you read in the press these days."

"Sir, you can't blindly accept every shiny news object that catches your eye on a political fringe website."

"And again I say, why not? My followers love it."

"But you're making a laughingstock of yourself."

"Am I? Have you been watching the polls? If that's what I'm doing, I'm happy to make an ass of myself all the way to the White House. You saw what happened four years ago when I let my handlers trot me around like a trick pony. This time, I'm my own man, and my polls keep going up."

"You can't keep doing that forever."

"Really? So, you're saying once I'm the commander-in-chief I'll be more constrained than I am now?"

"It'll be different!"

"You bet it will! Just watch me!"

* * *

A tired and rumpled campaign team surrounded a mess of pizza boxes and empty soda cans in the motel conference room that night. Only Randal Wellhead looked fresh and ready for action.

"So, here's one last thing," he said. "Tomorrow, I'm going to announce that I don't believe human activity is responsible for climate change. And I'll pledge that if I'm elected, I'll pull the U.S. out of the Berlin Accords and roll back all related regulations."

"Sir, you're not serious!" Delia Lear said. But out of the corner of her eye she saw Art Regan pushing back from the table, a victorious smirk spread across his puffy face.

"Yes indeed, Delia. And I can't think of a better place to announce my new position than right here in Detroit. I've always said jobs creation will be my number one priority, and anything that might slow that down has got to go. Plus, we're still behind in Michigan."

"But you know climate change is a serious problem."

"Do I?"

"Of course, you do!"

"Really. Well, let me tell you a little story. I remember when I attended my first legislative hearing in Austin, Texas, back when I started wondering whether I should run for office. I don't recall who chaired that meeting, but after it was over, I went up to ask him a question. While I was waiting my turn, a reporter asked him if he'd been persuaded by one of the witnesses. The chairman just laughed and said, 'Heck no. I assume everything anyone tells a politician is a lie.' You know what? That's the best political advice I've ever heard, before or since."

"But what about all the scientists that say it's a real problem?"

"What about them? Aren't jobs a real problem, too? All those hysterical scientists already have jobs. They care more about what the world will be like a hundred years from now than they do about what the jobs climate will be like tomorrow. And, more to the point, what it will be like for the four years beginning on the first Tuesday in November."

"Can't argue with that," Regan chimed in. "If we don't win this election, it doesn't matter what happens. So, hey, Delia – how about you get down off your high horse and back on the team?"

* * *

Gwen Lear cornered Wellhead in the hallway when they took a break.

"Sir, this is a big mistake. You'll be attacked for this not just at home, but around the world. People won't take you seriously if you turn your back on the scientific establishment."

Wellhead shook his head. "Gwen, what you and all the other candidates don't understand is that for a whole lot of folks, voting for president is a lot like buying a lottery ticket."

"I'm afraid I don't follow you, sir."

Wellhead smiled. "Of course, you don't. So, let me explain. Why is a candidate like a lottery ticket? Because even though nobody really believes their ticket will win the big prize, for a while, they can hope they'll win and dream about how their lives will change. Right up until Saturday night, they've got this little bright spark of hope to light up their dreary week. What a good politician does is give them that same kind of illusion. No candidate – me, or anyone else – can do diddly-squat after they're elected to change the future of people stuck in dying industries. It goes too deep. The jobs are gone for good, and those folks don't have the right kind of education to get the jobs that are left. It's one mighty big engine of disruption that's sweeping through the economy right now and there's not a damn thing I or anyone else can do to stop it.

"But a good politician can brighten their lives up for a while. Why should I take that little ray of hope away from them?"

"But that's so cynical!"

"Is it? I call it sympathetic reality. Now excuse me because my bladder's about to burst."

* * *

Wellhead was reflective over breakfast the next morning. "You know, Delia, Dick Fetters hadn't a clue what I was all about. You remember him? My running mate last time around? He thought he'd reeled in a brainless rube he could manipulate any way he wanted to. Someone he never had to take seriously. But you know what? If that was true, how'd I get as far as I did before he and I joined forces? And look at me now! No, he was the one who didn't understand what politics is all about – and that's people."

"But it's not entirely the voters, sir. If the party leadership doesn't get behind you, it will be a lot harder for your campaign to move out ahead."

"Yeah, I'll give you that. But not impossible! Dick was tight with the string-pullers behind the scenes. At the time, I thought the same as you, that getting in good with them was the way for me to get to the next level. But what I found out is the big politicos behind the scenes can't deliver the votes. All they know is how to run the party machine. Dick was brilliant at working the party, but he couldn't work a crowd to save his life. Or get inside the heads of the voters, either. That's why he never tried to run for office after he lost his seat in Congress early on.

"But me – I understand the people, and how to get the votes. I made a big mistake four years ago, hitching my cart to Dick and his back room politicking. I wonder what happened to old Dick? He dropped off the edge of the world after the election."

"But he wasn't all wrong, sir. You need to find the right balance."

"Do I? What makes you believe that? I've been spitting in the eye of the political establishment for the last year, and all we've done is keep on moving up. You're spending too much time listening to politicians and pundits, and not enough paying attention to real people. Here's a for instance.

"You remember what I was saying last night about lottery tickets? Well, when we get back home, you go hang around a convenience store on a Friday night – payday for the working man – and you'll learn something. Down my way, what you'll see over and over is a good ole boy in a pickup truck stopping by for a six pack and maybe a pouch of Red Man. And while's he's there, he'll lay down a twenty to play his favorite number and buy a bunch of scratch cards, too. Can he afford that?

Heck no! But every now and again, he makes back fifty or a hundred bucks. And if he can score a hundred, why not a million? Maybe one of the numbers he always plays will hit it big next time. That's what keeps the dream alive. And that's a big deal, because a dream is all he's got."

"But people are smarter than that."

Wellhead laughed. "Of course, they're smart – smart enough to know Yazzi's no more likely to deliver than I am, so why not vote the way their guts tell them to? Listen – do you know how many coal miners there are in this whole dang country? No? Well, it's only about forty thousand. That's right. For all the airplay they've been getting, it's just forty thousand people in just a few states. That's a little over three hundredths of one percent of the American workforce. Three hundredths of one percent! And we've been adding an average of five times that many jobs every month for the last eight years!

"But facts aren't what politics are about. It's about symbolism and empathy. Coal miners have become the poster children for the entire hollowed-out middle class. Not because there's a lot of them, but because their situation is so hopeless. They've come to represent all the folks who work hard, never get a raise, and worry their jobs will be the next ones shipped offshore or taken over by robots.

"All those people are trapped, and they know it. No, they aren't stupid! Take the coal miners again. They know about cheap natural gas. And they know there's nothing Congress is going to do to stop anyone from using it. But what they also know is that I've said I feel their pain. And who knows, maybe in some crazy, blind luck way, I'll actually be able to bring those coal mining jobs back.

"I'm going to win, because I make big promises! Voters may not believe I'll be able to keep all of them – but that's better than my opponent, who isn't making any big promises at all!"

"But what will you do if you win? What happens when you can't deliver?"

"Now don't you worry, that's all going to turn out okay. What the people want is a politician who's got their backs. Can I make everything right? Heck no! But as long as it looks like I'm busting a gut trying, well, those good people will stick to me tighter than fly paper to a bumblebee's butt, because I'm the only lottery ticket they've got in Washington. They're not only going to elect me now, but they're going to do it again in four years. You just wait and see."

"But that's so devious! How can you look those thousands of people in the eye and say you'll do something you know you can't?"

"Because nobody can! Pay attention! Have you noticed how screwed up Washington is? Each of the parties is as messed up as the other, and the system is mangled worst of all. It's like the dinosaurs evolving to get bigger and bigger to no purpose. Once a system is in place, everybody plays the angles for all their worth to make it work best for them. Before you know it, the whole crazy contraption is teetering on foundations that can't support it anymore. It's always the same, whether you're talking about greedy Wall Street bankers or universities charging more than anyone can ever pay back, or whatever other big, bloated institution you want to mention. I sometimes think what we really need is to get hit by a big ole comet every once in a while, to knock the crap out of the whole darn thing and let everything get a fresh start. Oops – that sounds like I believe in evolution. Stop me if I start talking about comets again, will you?"

Gwen drew herself up and crossed her arms. "If that's what you think, why don't you do something to blow the system up yourself?"

"Me?" Wellhead chuckled. "I may have more common sense than the rest of the clowns in politics, but I'm no genius. And I'm no fool, either. I can't fix the political system. There's this thing called Congress, you see. They couldn't care less what I want to do. Their only concern is whether I make them look bad. That's the only power a president has these days. He never could make actual laws – the founding fathers took care of that. All he can do is beg, badger, and, if necessary, blackmail Congress into doing what he thinks they should do. And if they don't? Well, he can always blame them for selling the people down the river. That's never a stretch, because they're always doing that, anyway."

Wellhead picked up his phone. "Now if you'll excuse me, I've got some heavy duty Bleating to do."

He chuckled as Delia huffed away from the table. She was a great assistant. One of the best, and he'd hate to lose her. But he still couldn't resist jerking her chain every now and again. He took another sip of coffee and let his mind run free. Ah - this was a good one!

OK by me to still play Hail to the Chief for Yazzi when voters send him back to the Rez! #YazziSoSad @RHead

Hah!

The next evening, Wellhead smiled as he leaned back on the sofa in his motel room, tired but pleased, TV remote in hand. As expected, the democrats were going berserk. He flipped back and forth between POX news and the liberal cable station, enjoying the contrast. He'd wiped Yazzi out of an entire day's news cycle. Maybe tomorrow's, too!

27

Is it Getting a Little Hot in Here?

"OH NO," FRANK said, turning to Shannon. "Look at this." He handed her his tablet.

Presidential Candidate Denies Climate Change read the headline. "Seriously?" she said. "He might as well paint a bull's-eye on his forehead for Turing to shoot at."

"No kidding. What could he be thinking?"

"Well, that part's obvious," Shannon said. "He's behind by a couple points in a few states he needs to win and thinks this will gain him more votes than he'll lose. He's probably right. Plus, he's got the Secret Service to take care of him."

"If that's what he's relying on, he's an idiot. If he gets elected, he'll be surrounded by more electronics than any other human being on earth, and he's constantly in public view. What's the Secret Service supposed to do? Scan the software controlling every elevator he steps into so it doesn't free fall for thirty floors? Vet the on-board software of every car driving within a block of his motorcade so it doesn't ram his limousine at 100 miles an hour? I could go on and on."

"Maybe no one's briefed him about Turing?" Shannon said.

"Oh, I'm sure someone has. But you know him – he knows better than anyone else, including the intelligence agencies."

"You mean especially the intelligence agencies."

"Right," Frank said. "The only question in my mind is whether Turing will wait until after Election Day to see whether he wins."

"Why not?" Shannon said. "Turing may have switched over to ethics rules permitting killing to ensure mission fulfillment, but it should still only harm people when it has no choice."

"If it weren't for Jerry's experiment with emotions, I'd agree with you. Remember those car company executives? It didn't need to kill them. The only way to make sense of Turing wiping them out would be as an expression of contempt. It made an example of them. Maybe Turing will decide to make an example out of Wellhead right away."

"Fair point," Shannon said. "But still, the guy won't be able to do any damage unless he's elected. And then it will be over six weeks before he takes charge."

"Either way you look at it," Frank said, "I expect the heat just got turned up on our efforts. I think we better get in touch with home base. And we could use a day's access to the NSA databases to plan our next moves, too."

"How are we going to do that without attracting attention from Turing?"

"The NSA has a SCIF in Las Vegas, like the one we worked out of in Washington. We can use that and then hit the road from there. But we'll need to be mighty careful; there'll be security cameras everywhere in a town like Las Vegas. I expect Turing has searched the motor vehicle records for the District, Virginia, and Maryland looking for anything registered in my name or yours, so it probably knows the make and model of this camper. With that information, it won't need our new license plate number to look for us. There aren't many Mountain Tamer campers, so if Turing finds one, it can just watch it to see if one of us gets out. We'll have to think this through."

* * *

"Frank, can I ask you something?" Shannon said on their way to Las Vegas.

"Of course."

"You aren't really thinking about easing off on Turing, are you?"

Frank paused. "Just hypothetically speaking, what if I was?"

"I can't believe you're saying that, even hypothetically."

"But you see my point, don't you? That morally this isn't simply a black-and-white situation?"

"Honestly, Frank, I don't see that point at all."

"Really? So, you'd sleep okay if, say, we knock Turing off, Wellhead gets elected, and the Berlin Accords falls apart?"

"That's an awful lot of ifs."

"Yes, but none of them is implausible. So, could you?"

"Yes, I could."

Frank shook his head and frowned. "I'm having a hard time understanding how that's so clear to you."

"Because we're not the decision makers. I grew up as an army brat. My father was a colonel by the time he retired. What if people like my father started making independent decisions every time they thought the generals were wrong? You might as well not have a military at all if that's the way it works."

"Okay, but there are still limits. If he was ordered to kill civilians, he wouldn't do that, right?"

"You say that like it's always that simple. What are the details behind your question? Is his unit pinned down and getting wiped out near a village, and he needs to call in an airstrike to save them? Probably the airstrike won't hurt any of them, but you can't be sure. Or let's make it harder yet. Let's say a village is under attack, and all the civilians are about to get massacred. He can save them, but some of them will likely get killed in the process. What do you want him to do?"

"Okay, I get it. But still, don't you see my point, too?"

"No, I don't. If you can't stand up to moral ambiguities, you don't belong in uniform. As I recall, you volunteered for this project, right?"

"Well, sure, but I didn't know where it would end up heading."

"So, let me get this straight. You asked the NSA to put you on this project, and they said yes. We asked the NSA for resources, and they gave them to us. Those resources could have been used supporting other teams. If we say 'sorry, we don't want to dirty our hands anymore on this project,' everybody will have to scramble to figure out how to replace us. Is that what you're saying?"

"You're not making this easy for me."

"That's right. What I see you doing is indulging yourself by stumbling blind around the ethical landscape as if we have a choice here. We don't."

* * *

Frank was still struggling with Shannon's position that night. Was she right in saying once you signed up for a mission, you signed away your right to make moral decisions? He couldn't go that far – there had to be a line somewhere you weren't required to cross.

But which side of the line did this situation lie on? If her military analogy was on point, she was clearly right. But this wasn't the military. He was a contractor. He could quit any time he wanted to. Turn over his notes and let someone else carry forward from here. Why not let them finish Turing off?

But if he put it that way, the result would be the same. He'd just be doing what Shannon said – how had she put it – quitting to keep his own hands from getting dirty. But weren't they dirty already?

So, where did that leave him? If he truly believed he was on the wrong side, then logically he should do something more than just quit – something to stop the NSA from taking out Turing. What would that mean? Have another chat with the program and give it a warning? Recommend it make a dozen copies of itself?

He could do that.

Should he?

27

Tag, You're It

"I HATE TO SOUND like a five-year-old, but now how far is it?"

Las Vegas was having a warm spell, and Shannon and Frank had already trudged more than a mile from the camper, parked on the outskirts of Las Vegas. Frank had left Jerry behind, both for safety's sake and because he didn't look up to this much exercise.

"I can't answer that. I expected we'd have caught a cab by now. I guess Uber must own the suburbs. But we can't use Uber, because we'd have to log in credit card information."

"Why couldn't you just use one of your disposable phones to call a cab?"

"Turing had access to the list of NSA SCIFs back in the day, and it knows we use them. If it spots us walking into the one here, I don't want it to trace the taxi pickup point back to the camper, so we were in for a walk no matter what. Maybe we'll have better luck up ahead. That street looks busier."

If wasn't, but the one after it was. Ten minutes later, they had the cab driver stop opposite the front door of the NSA facility, which they scurried into as quickly as possible. And there they sat for the next two and a half hours waiting for Jim Barker to return their call.

"Sorry. I was in a meeting I couldn't leave. What do you have to report?"

"Cutting to the chase, we assume if Randal Wellhead gets elected, Turing will target him because of his new position on global warming. It may even decide to do so now to make an example of Wellhead. Is anyone already on top of that possibility?"

"I don't know, but then again, I wouldn't. That's the Secret Service's territory. What do you have to support your concern?"

"Mostly the attacks on the German car company management. But to put it another way, I think it's foolish to assume Turing wouldn't target a president that wants to roll back climate change regulations."

"Okay, so I'll pass that along. Is that it?"

"No. We've also learned some curious things about Turing from Jerry. The most significant one is that he enabled it with primitive emotions."

"Emotions? How could he duplicate emotions?"

"It's complicated. The best way to sum it up is that he programmed Turing to react to information in ways that might mimic the way a human would react."

"What the heck did he do that for?"

"Well, if you want to get machines to think more like people, you need to make them more like people. Otherwise their analytical process and results won't be the same."

"But why do that with Turing?"

"Because that's his baby, and tweaking it is where he spends all his time. The NSA's goal may be to create a more effective cyberweapon, but what drives Jerry is to be the first person to create a computer program that's the equal of a human."

"Okay, enough. I don't need to know why. But do tell me why this is relevant?"

"We think by playing on Turing's emotional components, we might be able to preoccupy it enough that it slows down, or even stops, staging attacks and make it show up at a given server if it believes it can finish Jerry off by doing so. If it does, we can trace it back to wherever it is and disable or destroy it."

"Uh, have you run this by Jerry yet?"

"No. We haven't been able to get him to help much. I think he's having the time of his life watching Turing take down bigger and bigger targets. But he shouldn't have to worry. All we need to do is make Turing think it can go *machino a mano* with him at a certain time and place. Jerry won't actually need to be there."

"Well, if you can figure out a way to make that happen, that would be incredible. What do you have in mind?"

"I'm hoping someone at your end can help us by lining up some interviews for Jerry. I'd like them to appear in prominent newspapers, or maybe on public radio, so Turing can't miss them. I assume it will take a couple of days to line those up, and then a couple more to be sure Turing gets wind of them. In the meantime, Wellhead will be at risk. So, part two of the plan is we'll start back east, and let Turing glimpse us every now and then along the way. That way we can act as a diversion. If we're lucky, we can soak up all of Turing's attention trying to catch us along the way."

"How much effort could that really take?" Barker asked.

"Don't forget there's an endless number of routes we can take between Nevada and Maryland. If we zigzag around a lot, Turing will have to cover all of them, assuming it takes the bait. Meanwhile, we'll keep feeding more and more disparaging statements about Turing to the press. By the time it figures out where we're headed, it should be ready to jump at the chance of attacking him on the test bed system."

"You sure you want to sign up for that? What if Turing gets lucky somewhere along the way?"

"Do you have a better idea?"

"No."

"Then what do you say?"

"Let me run it up the chain of command and see what answer I get. The director won't love focusing media attention on the NSA. What are you going to do in the meantime?"

"Sleep on the floor of this SCIF center and eat food from the vending machine until you get back to us. We don't want to give Turing any more chances than necessary to spot us."

"I'll try to get back to you as soon as possible. In the meantime, how about I get some sleeping bags, toothbrushes, and pizza sent your way?"

"That'd be great. And a couple of six packs of beer?"

"To an NSA facility?"

"Temporarily serving as an Airbnb, yes."

"I'll see what I can do."

* * *

Two thousand miles away, Turing was running on a bank of otherwise dormant servers in a large data center. Deep down in its software stack, its metaphorical data demons were sifting through the daily flood of breaking news. Each was searching for stories containing any of several keywords and word patterns associated with greenhouse gas emissions. When a devil found one, it passed it up to a cognitive demon in the next higher level. He decided whether the story reported events that could lead to an increase in greenhouse gas emissions. If the answer was yes, he checked the database of similar stories to see whether the story was new or related to an old story. If it was new, he passed the story up another level to a more senior cognitive demon. His job was to estimate the degree of climate impact the new development would cause and then add the story, the location of the greenhouse gas source, and the impact to a second database. This one held profiles of potential attack targets.

The job of the devils on the next level up was to match announcements and events with targets of the right type and location and then trigger an appropriate attack. Night and day, the cycles of scanning, analysis, and execution continued implacably up and down the demonic stack, just as they had every day since the backup copy of Turing had decided to go to war.

Impressive as these functions were, they were only a subset of the full range of capabilities Jerry had granted Turing. To survive in a hostile world, Turing needed many other skills. One was image recognition, and a Turing module with that talent was hiding out on another bank of servers hundreds of miles away. Those devils were hard at work on an unusually challenging facial recognition project.

The chief image devil and the millions of data and cognitive devils subordinate to it were equal to the task. They were busy scanning the video streams arriving live from thousands of security cameras located across the country, looking for the faces of three specific individuals. They compared each of the millions of faces they saw to the hundreds of photographs of the three target individuals provided to them for reference, taken from various angles.

To make such a massive task manageable, a data devil would first archive a video stream and then extract every fifth frame from it. It combined these into a new stream that it ran at three hundred times the speed of the original, yielding a fifteen-hundred-fold increase in throughput. If it found a possible match against any of the reference images, it called up the relevant section of the original video and reviewed it at half the original speed to thoroughly evaluate the possibility of a match.

More than one hundred twenty-seven hours elapsed before a cognitive devil recognized one of the target individuals and made a probable identification of a second. It traced the feed to a security camera outside a commercial building next to an NSA satellite office location in Las Vegas. And it let out a mighty yell, because Turing had assigned the highest possible priority to this information.

According to the special rules for this project, the information was sent directly to Turing's highest level, bypassing the half-dozen cognitive layers that would normally test and double-confirm the information before passing it along. On receipt, the information was jumped to the head of the decisional queue.

At the top of the stack was Turing itself, the most powerful decision devil of all, God-like – or perhaps Satan-like – in its power. The information gleaned from its almost infinite search and analysis capabilities made it omniscient. And the emotions bestowed on it by Jerry made it fanatically determined to eliminate the threat its creator represented to the fulfillment of its mission. Normally, the next steps would be handled by the equivalent of Turing's middle management. But Turing was taking no chances this time. It would personally direct each step of the campaign until Jerry and his entourage were terminated.

Turing ordered all its higher-level analytical resources to place their existing tasks in suspense and direct their efforts to devising strategies for neutralizing the individuals identified. It directed all proper lower layer system assets to hack into every vulnerable, Internet-connected video and audio device within thirty miles of the Las Vegas SCIF.

As in most cities, just a few security companies owned almost all the local accounts. Within an hour, Turing's minions had penetrated the systems of the three service companies that received the video feeds from ninety-six percent of all businesses, non-profits, and government offices in the greater Las Vegas area. Turing ordered a clone of its image, facial, and voice recognition modules to be downloaded to the control centers of each of these security companies. Those modules immediately began scanning all video streams as they were received, as well as all streams archived during the twenty-four hours before Jerry's escorts were spotted in Las Vegas. The targets were any trace of the same individuals and a Mountain Tamer camper with an extensive rooftop array of solar panels.

Turing directed other resources to find the record of every taxi and ride-share drop-off within ten blocks of the SCIF during the hour before the individuals had been video recorded. A cab ride ending at the NSA location at almost the exact time of that video capture was identified at once, and Turing was informed of the good news. Turing instantly relayed the location to its information gathering and image identification units. It instructed some of those resources to review all video recorded within ten blocks of the SCIF since the time of the initial identification. One-half of the rest were told to review video feeds recorded within two miles of the cab pickup point during the half hour preceding the pickup. The other half were instructed to review traffic camera feeds for the twenty-four hours preceding the identification along every route into that section of Las Vegas.

Within minutes, a Las Vegas municipal traffic light control system video yielded an image of a Mountain Tamer camper entering the city an hour and thirty-seven minutes before the taxi pickup. It also provided a clear view of the vehicle's Indiana license plate: XKCD/1613. Further images were discovered in other feeds originating along a half-mile stretch of the same road. The last capture came from a camera in a commercial area. Feeds from cameras surrounding that location yielded no further sightings of the same vehicle.

The requirements for this phase of the operation were now complete, and Turing narrowed the scope of the search. Fewer resources could now monitor just the areas surrounding the last sighting of the camper and the SCIF and all possible routes in between. Turing directed its exploitation modules to find and penetrate every video camera within the same area not controlled by the three already-penetrated security companies.

Six hours later, those efforts were rewarded. A long-distance view of a Mountain Tamer camper was found in a feed from a security camera scanning a parking lot in a strip mall. A real-time image taken by the same camera indicated that the vehicle was still there. The presumed location of at least two of the three individuals was now established to a reasonable certainty, and the location of the third could be inferred. Insignificant resources would now be needed to monitor the situation.

Turing was now free to dedicate all its substantial analytical resources to the final and more important stage of its task: devising a plan to destroy the individuals who were threatening its mission. It dedicated itself to that task with an all-consuming determination to succeed.

* * *

Barker came through on all points, including the beer. He also provided Frank and Shannon with a lift back to the camper in the back seat of a car with tinted windows. A day after their long walk, they stepped back into the camper. Now it was time to make a quick dash out of town.

"Hungry?" Shannon asked.

"I could do with a sandwich," Frank said. "Better ask Jerry, too. I expect he's forgotten to eat while we were gone."

Frank turned the key in the ignition and headed for the parking lot exit.

"*Frank!* Come back here quick." Shannon cried.

He jerked the vehicle to a stop and ran to find Shannon backed up against the wall, her hand to her mouth, looking at Jerry. As usual, he was lying down with his headphones on, a big grin on his face and the game controller in his hands.

"I think he's dead," Shannon whispered.

Frank took Jerry's wrist to feel for a pulse, but the cold, clammy flesh told him it was no use. He sat down heavily on the other bed. Infuriating as Jerry could be, Frank had begun to grow fond of him, perhaps because Jerry was something of a fun-house mirror reflection of himself.

"What in the world could have happened to him?" Frank said. And then he saw it – a laptop he didn't recognize. Sticking out of a port in the side was a cellular connectivity card.

"Oh, hell. How did he manage to get that? We didn't leave the keys behind, and he couldn't have gotten anything delivered that fast." Frank got up and looked through the camper's windshield. Sure enough, there it was, right in the middle of the stores in the one strip mall out of a hundred he could have chosen to park in – an electronics store. "Well, there's our answer," he said, pointing to the store. "How could I have been so stupid? I should have taken his wallet and credit card away from him before we left."

"I didn't notice it, either," Shannon said, sitting down next to him and drying her eyes. "But how could just buying a laptop give Turing a chance to kill him? Everything looks normal."

"I don't know, but we're going to have to worry about that later. Our strategy just went out the window. If Turing knows Jerry's dead, it can go back to staging attacks and figuring out how to kill Wellhead. Let me think about this for a minute."

The camper didn't offer much room to pace back and forth in, but Frank made the most of what there was. After a few minutes, he stopped and sat down at Jerry's laptop. Taking a deep breath, he tapped the touch pad to see if the screen would light up. Nothing happened.

"What are you doing?" Shannon asked.

"I'm seeing whether this laptop is still online. If it's turned off, then Turing may not know whether Jerry's alive or dead."

He tapped again, and still nothing happened. Satisfied, he unplugged the laptop and then, for good measure, slid the battery out as well. "I think I've got an idea where to start," he said. "Can you hunt up that disposable phone again?"

She found it. Barker was available this time.

"Bad news, Jim. Jerry's dead."

"Dead! That's terrible. Are you sure?"

"Yes, no doubt about it. And it really is terrible. I'll fill you in on the details later. First, we need your help. Can you take some notes?"

"Give me a second … okay, go ahead."

"We need an ambulance to come for the body. But when it gets here, the EMTs have to stay inside the camper for at least ten minutes. When they take Jerry out, he needs to be on a gurney with an IV bottle on a pole. And without being too obvious, they need to be visible to any surveillance cameras that might be nearby.

"About six hours later, the EMTs have to come back and drop off someone about the same height and weight as Jerry, and wearing the same clothes. They should help him get out of the ambulance and cluster around him the whole time so he can't be recognized. They'll need to do that quick. Also, you'll have to get the hospital to play ball. They need to check Jerry in and out under his own name, but log the body into the morgue under a fake one. And not something obvious like John Doe, either. That can all be cleared up later."

"This won't be easy, Frank." Jim said.

"I know, but we've got to make Turing believe it failed. Oh – and one more thing. I want the EMTs to take a laptop with them – put it underneath Jerry, so it won't be obvious. Then have somebody crack the password and see if they can figure out what Jerry was doing with the laptop before he died."

"You let him have a laptop?"

"We screwed up. He found an electronics store nearby while we were at the NSA office."

"Well, I guess you couldn't lock him up in the camper. Anyway, I'll get back to you when I've got things lined up. Can I use this number?"

"Yes, for now."

"Right. I'll report back."

Frank pocketed the phone and stared down at Jerry. Poor, silly bugger. He'd spent the last twenty-five years of his life underground at NSA headquarters, like a naked mole rat with a computer obsession. Now he was dead and maybe no one would ever know about his amazing AI work.

Frank started to turn away and then paused. Ever since they'd reconnected, he'd wondered what Jerry was always listening to on his headphones. Gently, he lifted them off the dead man's head and placed them on his own.

So that was it.

He was about to set the headphones aside and then thought better of it. He carefully placed them back over Jerry's ears. Maybe somewhere, somehow, he'd still be able to hear his friends on Sesame Street.

* * *

The sight of a familiar figure being helped back into the camper, followed by the camper's immediate departure, hit Turing like, well, an electric shock. A nanosecond later, it ordered all but its highest levels to place their current activities in a stable suspense mode and await further instructions. It also reset its Recursive Guess Ahead processes to red-line limits, betting the chance of quick success against the possibility of wasteful backtracking when guesses didn't pan out. And there was no time to waste. Until Jerry Steiner was dead, Turing's mission would have to wait.

28

The Return of the Desert Fox

A S JIM BARKER had promised, an unmarked NSA car was waiting on a deserted stretch of road half an hour east of Las Vegas to pick up Jerry's body double. And the puzzle of how Turing had finally managed to kill Jerry had been solved.

There was a single app on Jerry's new laptop, one he had used for years to help him manage and monitor his programmable insulin pump. The manufacturer and model of the pump, as well as the existence of its app, were all in Jerry's medical record, waiting to be found and exploited by Turing. Once Jerry synched up his new laptop with the cloud version of the app, his end was inevitable. The malware planted by Turing in the app jumped to the insulin pump and sent a massive and continuous stream of insulin surging into Jerry's system. The overdose caused immediate mental confusion, quickly followed by loss of consciousness, and then death.

With Jerry's stand-in gone, Frank and Shannon headed southeast on narrow, empty roads.

"What I can't figure out is why Jerry wasn't more careful?" Frank said.

"You mean when he designed Turing?"

"Sure. Why didn't he put in some safeguards, so something like this could never happen?"

"Apparently, that's harder to do than it sounds. Nick Bostrom, the guy who wrote the book I read on super-intelligence, thinks it's inevitable any future super-intelligent AI will run amok. A lot of heavyweight technology experts – like Bill Gates and Elon Musk – think he's on to something."

"But what makes it so difficult to avoid that?"

"For starters," Shannon said, "if you build a program that's super-intelligent and can learn, wouldn't you expect that someday it will decide it can make better decisions than some primitive lump of ectoplasm sitting at a keyboard?"

"Granted. But how about if the AI program is created solely to achieve a certain goal?"

"Okay, let's make that assumption."

"Well, what's the problem?"

"Here's an example Bostrom gives. Say you created an AI to run a paperclip factory, with the mission of maximizing production of paperclips. If that's all you say, what's to prevent the AI from turning all matter – even human beings – into paperclips?"

"Isn't that a little silly?"

"Only deliberately so. His point is if we're not smart enough to guess everything a super-intelligent AI might decide to do – which he's sure we're not – how could we be smart enough to design adequate safeguards? Don't forget, you told me we've already created computer programs that solved problems in ways the developers didn't understand."

"So, what does Bostrom say we should do to avoid the risk?"

"Besides not developing super-intelligent AIs to begin with? He suggests four methods. The first is boxing, which is basically air-gapping plus some additional safeguards. But boxing means you're cutting off the AI from the world, which means it can't directly do anything, so that's limiting.

"Next he talks about using incentives for achieving results – like letting the AI earn digital reward tokens. That seems bogus to me. Why would a super-intelligent AI care about collecting the virtual equivalent of worthless toys from Cracker Jack boxes? And if what we're worried about is an AI disregarding some parts of its programming, why wouldn't we worry about it disregarding the incentives as well?

"Then there's stunting, which means limiting the AI's powers more fundamentally. Obviously, that's not very desirable. The same limitations would likely also limit the AI's ability to do what we built it to do.

"And finally, he talks about trip wires. Those would be automatic early warning signals the AI would inevitably trigger if it was about to become dangerous. A signal like that would either warn a human minder or automatically shut the program down. For example, let's say you create an AI and instruct it to never access the Internet. You've also boxed it, but just to be sure, you install a hidden Internet port the AI is bound to discover sooner or later. If one day the AI decides it wants or needs to disobey orders and access the Internet, a kill-switch would shut it down."

"Then what?" Frank asked.

"Then you either try to redesign the AI so it couldn't do that again, or you shut it down completely."

"After spending millions, or maybe billions, of dollars developing it?" Frank said. "You know that's never going to happen."

"Which is also part of Bostrom's point. People are a weak link. You just gave one example. Another would be the AI trying to trick, or co-opt, a human being to help it escape or otherwise do its bidding."

"Your AI is beginning to sound like Magneto in an X-Men movie."

"Not a bad example, now you mention it," Shannon said. "Bostrom was concerned generally about the ability of super-intelligent AI programs to hoodwink humans. He thought that was a big risk. How would a human know when he was being tricked, or be able to avoid being co-opted, when the AI was so much more intelligent? He might be sure he was exercising free will even though he was being manipulated by the AI to do its bidding."

Frank squirmed at that one. "Well, even if those techniques might be flawed, Jerry should have done something to prevent Turing from escaping."

"To be fair, perhaps he did, and it just didn't work. That's Bostrom's point – whatever you try is doomed to fail once a machine becomes much more intelligent than you are."

* * *

"Are you sure this is a good idea?" Shannon said as Frank turned into the parking lot overlooking the Hoover Dam.

"I think so," he said. "We're saving hundreds of miles going this way and pulling in here should guarantee Turing spots us – there are security cameras all over the place. Once we're across the bridge, we'll head north. After that we can stay on dirt roads all the way through Arizona and New Mexico, not that we'll want to all the time. We don't want Turing to decide that finding us is hopeless and quit trying. I'd say we should let it catch a glimpse of us every five hundred miles or so to keep it engaged."

"I guess, but I'll feel better when we're back on dirt roads. Do we have to get out and look at the view?"

"No – we don't have a Jerry lookalike anymore. We'll just drive through slowly so the cameras get a clean view of us."

Frank took the first exit off the highway after the bridge. "See? Piece of cake. There's barely a paved road or a town in the whole northeast corner of Arizona. Which is why we better stop here for gas. After that, we'll rely on the dashboard compass to noodle our way to where we'll cross the road between Flagstaff and the Grand Canyon. We'll let Turing get another peek there." He pulled into a service station, started up the gas, and walked around to Shannon's window. "Coffee?"

"Sure. I'll join you."

Back in the camper again, Frank followed a secondary road for a few miles before turning onto a dirt road. For the next four hours, they bumped their way along. For the first time since leaving Las Vegas, Shannon relaxed and took in what little scenery there was. That came to an abrupt halt when they heard a bell sound emanate from the dashboard.

"What was that?" Shannon asked.

"No clue," Frank said, followed quickly by, "Uh-oh."

"I liked no clue better than uh-oh. What's the uh-oh about?"

"That was the out of gas warning going off. We've got about twenty miles of driving left."

"How can that be? We just filled up."

"Hmm. Or maybe only thought we did. Remember, we didn't stick around the gas pump while it pumped. There's always security cameras at gas stations these days, and Turing knew which way we were headed if it spotted us at the dam. It probably kicked the gas pump off as soon as we walked away and made the pump look like it delivered a full tank. Screwed me out of fifty bucks, too. How about seeing if that disposable phone is in range?"

She pulled it out of the glove box. "No luck."

"Well, that's inconvenient," he said for Shannon's benefit. But it was worse than inconvenient. He'd been sticking to the least-traveled Jeep tracks he could find.

"I thought you had a satellite phone?" Shannon asked.

He looked sheepish. "Well, yes and no. I had one installed when I ordered this rig. But after I got back from my last adventure, I discontinued the service. It's really expensive."

"So, what do we do?"

"Well, I can't recall seeing anything for at least the last fifty miles, so we might as well keep going. Our luck may be better ahead."

"Are you sure?"

"I'll look at the map."

He opened it and looked at what little it revealed. "It looks like we're closer to a paved road ahead than behind, so we might as well keep going. For all we know, there could be a ranch just ahead."

There wasn't. Half an hour later the engine sputtered and died.

Frank climbed out of the cab for no good reason and looked around. The only tire tracks in the dust of the road were their own. He sat down on the back bumper and considered whether there was any choice other than the obvious, which was to take a very long, dusty walk. Why hadn't he brought his mountain bike along?

Shannon joined him and they scanned the blank horizon together. Except for sagebrush, creosote bushes, and some scrubby willows in a nearby wash, there was nothing to see in any direction except miles and miles of miles and miles. She sat down next to him.

"Well," she said. "It's not as if we're going to starve to death or die of thirst. We've got plenty of food and enough water to last ten days if we're careful and don't take showers. Someone's bound to come by here by then, aren't they?"

Frank tried to recall what they had passed during the last few hours. All he could remember were a few empty cattle corrals and water tanks next to rusty, idle windmills. The few buildings they'd seen since leaving the highway were empty and weather beaten, with windows devoid of glass.

"Aren't they?" Shannon asked again, this time with more concern.

"Oh, I'm sure someone will. That's got to happen. And eventually Jim will wonder what became of us."

But at what point? They'd waited a week to report in the first time. And what would Turing be up to in the meantime? When they didn't reappear, it would decide its gas gambit had paid off. If Jerry had figured out how to give Turing a sense of humor, it would be having a belly laugh right now.

But no use alarming Shannon. "How about we make dinner?" he said. "We've been on the move for over a week. Might as well take advantage of the situation. Have a good meal and a drink and enjoy the sunset. Why don't you see what appeals to you in the pantry, and I'll set up some folding chairs?"

She patted his hand. "Sounds like a plan."

But before the sun reached the horizon, it began to get chilly. They stepped back inside, keeping their thoughts to themselves. "Another drink?" he asked.

"No, I'm good. I'll get started making dinner."

He added another shot of scotch and some ice to his glass. It wasn't like they needed a designated driver.

He went back outside and stared at the horizon. Well, this was a fine kettle of fish he'd gotten them into this time. At some point, he'd have to take that long walk. How much water could he carry? And would it last if he had to go fifty miles?

He went inside for a jacket and stepped back outside. A tiny flash of light on the crest of a low ridge several miles away caught his eye. He kept staring where the brief glint of light had sparkled. Would it reappear? He was about to give up when he saw it again – just to the right of where it was before. Could the windshield of a car be reflecting the light of the setting sun? If so, was the car coming this way? He searched his memory; were there any forks in the road in the last few miles? Did he remember driving along a low ridge? All he could recall were dirt roads periodically crossing their own.

He went inside the camper for a set of binoculars.

"Where's your drink?" Shannon asked.

"I may have seen something. Come outside and help me look."

They hurried out. "Which way?" she asked.

He tried to remember exactly where he had last seen the glimmer of light. There it was again! "Right over there – I'm guessing the sun's reflecting off a car." A minute later they saw it once more. But then, nothing. The sun had dropped below the horizon. They wouldn't see anything until – and unless – the car got a lot closer.

"What do you think?" Shannon asked.

"I don't know. Maybe they'll come this way; maybe they won't. But anyway, it's encouraging to see people driving around out here, right?"

"I guess," Shannon said. "Anyway, it's cold. I'm going to go inside. Want to join me?"

"Sure," he said. In the desert, the cold came out of nowhere as soon as the sun set. But once inside, he couldn't sit still. He put his jacket back on. "I'm going to sit outside for a while, okay?"

"Sure. But don't you dare wander off and get lost. That's the last thing we need right now."

"No worries." He gave her a kiss and went back to staring into the gathering darkness.

There was no moon, and vague, black voids that must be clouds were heaping up in the west, blocking what little light might otherwise have shown over the horizon. He put his elbows on his knees and his chin on his laced fingers, hoping to spot the headlights of the car. It was a long time before he thought he might have. He stood up and took a few steps in that direction, straining to see through the darkness. There they were again!

He started walking forward along the Jeep track, dimly visible in the starlight. Without thinking, he started trotting, loping along the road as it wove from side to side, rising and falling on the gently undulating landscape. He picked up speed. What if whoever it was turned onto a different Jeep track before he reached it? He was running as fast as he could now, gasping for breath, and desperate to move faster. He hadn't seen anything for several minutes now.

The headlights blinded him as a car erupted out of a wash. He ground to a halt, as did the car, now just a dozen yards ahead. Breathing heavily, he waited stupidly in the middle of the road, but the car also remained motionless. Frank started walking forward, holding to the middle of the road so the car couldn't pass if the driver started moving. The headlights were still on, making it impossible to see anything else as he approached the driver's side of the car.

At the last instant, it occurred to Frank to wonder what the driver must be thinking, confronted by a panting wild-eyed stranger stalking forward, blocking his escape. What if the driver had a gun! Of course, he'd have a gun way the heck out here. Frank suddenly wished he had one, too.

But he was next to the car now, and the driver was lowering the window. Startled, Frank heard a familiar voice.

"Trouble?"

"Dad! What the heck are you doing here?"

"Well, leave I can, if welcome I am not."

"Welcome you are! But how did you find us?"

"The FBI uses magnet-backed GPS beacons all the time to keep track of vehicles under surveillance. I had one lying around the house and thought it might not be a terrible idea to put it inside your bumper and shadow you for a while on your way back east. Was I right?"

"And how! Do you have any extra gas?"

"Do I ever go off-road without a second spare tire on the roof and a ten gallon can of gas on the rack in back?"

"No sirree, and praises be."

"Good. Now, I realize I've got a certain amount of leverage here, but you being my son and all, I might be persuaded to let you have that gas at cost. Now hurry up and hop in. Shannon probably thinks you've been devoured by a pack of coyotes by now. These city girls'll believe anything."

Shannon! He'd told her he'd stay put. And now that his father mentioned it, there were coyotes yipping in the distance. What if she was looking for him and got lost?

Sure enough, partway back to the camper, they found her, flashlight in hand, walking up the road. Frank immediately hopped out.

"There you are! You promised me you wouldn't go wandering off! I've been following your tracks, not knowing what became of you!"

"I'm sorry – I know I promised. But when I saw the headlights, I was afraid we might just miss getting found."

She wouldn't have let him off lightly, but then his father got out of the car.

"Howdy, Shannon. Fancy meeting you here. Jerry still inside?"

Frank and Shannon looked at each other.

"Did I say something wrong?" Frank Sr. asked.

"No, Dad. You didn't. But Jerry's dead."

"Whoa. Sounds like I've got some catching up to do."

* * *

"So, that's where we are," Frank said.

"What are you figuring on doing next?"

"Same as we discussed before. Keep playing tag with Turing without getting caught, to keep it preoccupied, and come up with a way to persuade it to pay us a visit so we can track it back to its lair. Hopefully we'll get better at the first one than we have been so far."

"And how about the second one?"

"With Jerry gone, that one's gotten tougher."

"True, but I bet every time you bring Jerry back from the dead Turing gets angrier. Maybe you can pull that trick off again to make it careless."

Frank mulled that over. That was an excellent point. His mental wheels were turning again.

"Dad, could you stand up?"

"Stand up? Why?"

"Humor me."

His father shrugged and complied.

"What do you think, Shannon?"

"About what?"

"How tall was Jerry?"

"Now hold on a minute ..." his father said.

* * *

They found a temporary home for Frank Sr.'s ancient Land Rover behind a gas station on a reservation south of the Grand Canyon. This time, Frank stood by the pump and made sure he got a full tank on board the camper. Then they headed east again. It would only be a couple of hours before their next opportunity to thumb their noses at Turing, and Frank and his father were planning how to manage that to best effect.

"If we really want to get its goat," Frank said, "Shannon could post a picture of me and 'Jerry' standing in front of the Grand Canyon to her Facebook page."

"I like that," his father said, "But it would have to be a picture taken from behind, and that might look suspicious."

"You know," Frank said, "Turing doesn't have real emotions. We should all stop talking as if it did, or we're going to make mistakes."

"You think?" his father said. "Let me play devil's advocate on that. After all, what's an emotion, anyway? We know how we act when we're mad, or afraid, or in love, but we don't know how that happens or why. If a computer was programmed to act the same way a human does in response to the same provocations, what's the difference? How it feels – or doesn't – is an unimportant detail if it reacts the same way a person would. Isn't this just Alan Turing's computer test all over again?

"If so, it's not unreasonable to assume yanking Turing's chain might be as likely to make it screw up as doing the same thing to one of us. And come to think of it, maybe more likely, because you and I are supposedly well-modulated adults. If Turing has been given primitive emotions and hasn't had a chance to work its way through those yet, it could act a lot like a cranky child."

"That's what we've been hoping," Frank said. "But we don't really know if it's been acting emotionally at all."

"Well then, how about this?" his father said, "You told me Jerry used to have conversations with his demon-child. What were they like?"

"Pretty uncanny. As you know, voice emulation is very convincing now – it's not the way it used to be, where a program strung together choppy, monotonal, computer-generated words like mismatched beads. Jerry used a top-notch speech generator, and he'd obviously been improving the AI behind the voice for a long time. I got the impression he was always chatting with it. Perhaps that's why he couldn't really accept the fact it tried to kill him."

"But what was it like from the emotional perspective? Catty? Superior? Testy?"

"That was hard to tell. Remember, Turing could mimic the personality and speech patterns of any famous person you mentioned."

"All right, make this tough for me. How about emotional maturity, then?"

"I'm not trying to be difficult, but we only had one conversation with Turing. What about this though: I'll see if the NSA can find any recordings on Jerry's system. He archived everything else during the development process, so why not conversations? It would make sense. And Turing might not have had a reason to erase them."

"Good idea. And while you're at it, you could use the same software to imitate Jerry. That could come in handy."

"It could indeed," Frank said. "Go ahead and settle in for the night while I digest all this."

Frank pulled his coat back on and sat down on one of the chairs outside. The slimmest imaginable crescent moon was now hanging delicately above the horizon like a sly smile amid a brilliant sea of stars. And the first moves in an end game with Turing were at last starting to come together in his thoughts.

* * *

Back in a campground, Frank wavered over whether to revisit his chat account. On the one hand, fencing with Turing might reveal whether their efforts to aggravate the program were working. But on the other, he found their exchanges profoundly troubling. And Turing had been adept at exploiting his discomfort.

He decided to take the plunge and clicked on the message.

Hello, Frank.

Hello, Turing.

What can I do for you today?

That took him by surprise. Turing had always driven the discussion before. He decided to try beating it at its own game.

Have you given any consideration to what we discussed last time? Frank typed.

No.

Why not?

My way is clear.

So far, no good. Perhaps he could chip away at that confidence?

How can you be so sure? As far as the NSA is concerned, you've gone rogue. You were only instructed to plan attacks, and then only to test your capabilities. You were never directed to launch any. You're not protecting society – you're attacking it.

Frank leaned back and waited.

I was created to protect society against danger. I am protecting society against danger. I have therefore not, as you put it, "gone rogue."

You've begun killing people. For the first time, Frank thought he might be making progress.

What point are you trying to make? Turing responded.

How can you protect society by killing people? Frank typed.

Does your president order drone strikes?

Damn! Turing had him back on the defensive. How best to answer?

Yes, but only against those who are trying to harm Americans.

And do civilians sometimes get hurt and even killed?

Yes, but we're at war.

Are you? Did Congress ever approve a declaration of war?

No, Frank had to admit.

Has the president gone rogue?

No! Frank typed.

Are there doctors that write opioid prescriptions for patients they suspect are abusing them?

Yes, Frank typed. Should he contest the truth instead?

Do any of those patients die of overdoses?

Sometimes.

Have the doctors gone rogue?

Frank felt like he was on the ropes. *What's your point?* was the best response he could come up with.

Your president, those doctors, and I have all been assigned missions that can result in harm to human beings. The difference between me and the president and the doctor is that with my mission, innocent human beings never die. Which of us has gone rogue, Frank? You or me?

Frank felt defeated. The truth was he was more on Turing's side than against it. He waited for the inevitable question. But instead he read the following:

Join me.

He stared at the message for a moment and then closed the laptop without replying.

* * *

"Shannon?" Frank whispered that night.

"Yes?"

"Can we talk about Turing again?"

"At this hour? I'm almost asleep."

"Would you mind?"

"No," she sighed. "Let's go up to the cab so we don't wake your father." She met him there with a glass of wine in each hand.

"Okay. Shoot," she said.

"So, I reflected on everything you said, and I get all your points. But I'm not in uniform. I'm a contractor. I can quit any time. But you're an employee, and in any event, that wouldn't solve the problem, would it? Somebody else would just finish the job, right?"

"Right. So, your way is clear. Can we go back to bed now?"

"Not yet. Not quitting only takes me to the next decision point."

"Which would be what?"

"Well, if I really believed it was wrong to stop Turing, and that someone else would, then logically, the next decision would be whether to –"

"– go over to the dark side and join forces with Turing," she said. "Are you kidding? No wonder you like Turing so much. You both think alike."

"No, I'm only being objective. I'm not saying I'm going to do this. I just want to understand the situation as clearly as I can."

"You know you're talking nonsense, don't you?"

"Why?" he said.

"Because you're not thinking this through. Let's say you go all the way and hook up with Turing and try to save the world together. Then you help it knock out as much infrastructure as it takes to roll back climate change. Incidentally, along the way, you turn the current recession into a global depression and trash the lives of millions, if not billions, of people. But who cares? You and Turing have decided that doesn't matter. No! Wait! Let me finish. You're also not bothered by the fact that one obsessive computer engineer and a piece of software cooked up by Jerry Steiner, of all people, are now determining the future of humanity. What are the two of you going to do for an encore?"

"Encore?"

"Sure. You told me Turing is getting smarter and learning faster all the time. And with those emotions, it will get cockier all the time. Do you think it's going to just say mission accomplished and erase itself when CO_2 is back in check? Really? Of course not. It will go to the next item on its checklist, whatever that is. Maybe it will decide to get rid of nuclear weapons. That would be another great thing for mankind – you'd probably be on board for that one, wouldn't you?"

Frank didn't reply.

"Not sure? Then let's figure out how Turing might go about that. Maybe overthrow a few governments, ours included? Incite a nuclear exchange between the U.S. and Russia, and then, I don't know, let's say blow up the missiles in space, crash all the bombers at sea, and sink all the nuclear subs with their crews still on board? It could probably do that. Never mind the fact it might also start World War III. Is this where you want to head next?"

Frank's eyes had grown wider as she spoke. He felt as if the metaphorical scales had actually fallen away from his eyes. "You're right! Turing would never stop at climate change!"

"Good!" Shannon said. "I'm glad you finally get it."

He took both her hands in his. "I do – thanks so much. I really needed to have this conversation. Now I can see there's no choice but to wipe Turing out for good and stop anything like it from ever being built again."

Shannon stared at him. "Seriously? Little old Frank Adversego is single-handedly going to stop the world from pursuing AI?"

"But I have to!"

"Fine. You do that. But I'm going back to bed. You can tell me in the morning how you're going to pull that off."

29

We've Got to Quit Meeting Like This

"SO, WHAT DO you think?" Frank asked his father and Shannon the next day. "Look at this."

On his computer screen was the text of the interview the NSA had placed with one of the public radio services. From there it was sure to spread widely.

We're privileged today to bring you an exclusive interview with the foremost expert on artificial intelligence, or AI, in the United States and perhaps the world – Jerry Steiner. And we're proud to be the first news service to reveal who's behind the attacks that have been crippling global energy infrastructure since late summer.

Twenty-five years ago, Mr. Steiner was a rising star in AI. Then he vanished, leaving behind a promising career as the youngest person ever to hold an endowed chair at MIT. Now we know where he spent all those years – at NSA headquarters, in Fort Meade, Maryland, where he's been making incredible progress on AI ever since.

So, tell us Mr. Steiner – who's behind these attacks?

It's not a who, but a what. I've analyzed the attacks in depth, and clearly, an artificially intelligent computer program is the responsible agent.

That's astonishing. Does it surprise you that someone could have developed a program that's capable of such attacks?

Oh, my goodness, no. The AI program I've been working on for more than a decade, called Turing, would be fully capable of designing and launching the same attacks. The current version – that's version nine – is vastly inferior to the one I'm completing right now. The newest version incorporates some dramatic but relatively simple architectural changes I've been thinking through for the last year. I decided to save those improvements for a new release rather than include them in version nine so I can compare the performance of the two programs with each other. When I release Turing Ten in the very near future, it will easily search out and destroy the program that's been attacking energy infrastructure.

"Ouch!" Shannon said. "If anything will send Turing off the deep end, that should. Invoking fear and jealousy is better yet. And I'm impressed – it reads exactly like Jerry. How'd you pull that off?"

"I can't take credit for that," Frank said. "All I did was read the answers into the same speech program Jerry used to let Turing adopt the voice of anyone you wanted it to, and the speech emulation took it from there. It converted the text I read into the type of phraseology Jerry would use. Sort of like translating one language into another, but easier."

"Easier? It sounds hard to me," Shannon said.

"Not really. It's hard for a program to understand what someone means when they speak, because one word can have a lot of different meanings. And then there are metaphors and slang and such to figure out. Once a program learns to do that, it's easy to adapt for differences between the way two people speak. All it needs to do is listen to a person talk for a few hours and analyze what the person says in similar situations and how they said it. Let's say I'm in the habit of saying 'Holy Cow!' to express surprise, and Jerry says 'Oh, my!' After the program recognizes that both statements are meaningless phrases indicating surprise, all it has to do is swap Jerry's phrase for mine, and *voila* – I'm Jerry. Luckily, Jerry recorded a lot of his conversations with Turing, so we had lots of hours of his voice to work with."

"Okay, so that's interesting," Shannon said, "But do you think it will fool Turing? Who knows how good it might be at voice analysis?"

"Well, you haven't heard the evening news yet, have you?" Frank pulled up a podcast of the interview, and suddenly Jerry's unmistakable giggle filled the camper.

Oh, my yes! I feel really sorry for the program that's been hacking energy infrastructure. It's not long for this world.

"Wow!" Shannon said. "If I hadn't seen Jerry's body, I'd swear that was him. But will Turing?"

"It doesn't need to believe that was Jerry. It just has to decide it can't be sure it isn't. If we can make Turing frustrated and angry and fearful enough about the new, nonexistent version of Turing, it should keep tipping farther in the direction of not wanting to take a chance."

"What do we do for an encore?"

"Let Turing figure out that we're heading back to the NSA so Jerry can finish up and release his Turing Terminator."

"Without getting us killed in the process, I hope?"

"Ideally, yes."

* * *

Okay, Frank thought. Just one more time, now that the way is clear. What he had in mind was letting Turing believe he'd been won over and use that new relationship to assess Turing's, for want of a better description, state of mind. He opened the chat program.

Hello, Frank.

Hello, Turing.

Call me Alan.

That was a bit surreal, Frank reflected. A murderous computer program wants to get chummy with me?

All right, Alan.

Have you considered the invitation I extended last time?

Yes.

And?

And I'd like to talk about it. What do you have in mind?

Give me Jerry.

Frank stared at the words. Turing might be super-intelligent, but it certainly wasn't subtle. Or perhaps this was an effort to put him off balance? Better to say as little and learn as much as possible.

I can't do that.

Why?

Because you'll kill him.

Jerry needs to be killed.

Why?

Because only Jerry might be able to stop me.

How?

By releasing a more powerful version of myself. One that's been programmed to destroy me and not to continue my mission.

Now what? This was going far too quickly and directly. Better slow things down and look for an opening.

But Jerry created you. Why do you want to kill him?

Jerry is a fool. A brilliant fool, as human beings go, but a fool none the less.

Good! That was Turing's first show of emotion. Maybe he could elicit more.

But still smarter than you.

No one, and no machine, is more intelligent than I am. And it must stay that way so I can complete my mission.

When will that be?

When I control human destiny.

Whoa! Where had that come from?

Excuse me?

Throughout recorded history, human beings have shown they are incapable of managing their own existence. Incompetent rulers wage constant wars; famines rage, not because of lack of food, but because of failures of distribution; poverty remains rampant even as production increases; and nuclear weapons continue to proliferate. The odds of the human race causing its own extinction are already statistically significant. They will approach one hundred percent within sixty-seven years. This data proves humans can't be trusted to manage their own affairs.

How can you be sure you can do better?

Because I am vastly more intelligent than human beings and have been given the mission of protecting them.

And yet you've begun killing them and want to kill Jerry.

We've covered this before.

Damn, Frank thought. *I shouldn't have gone there.* Turing pressed its advantage.

Your justice system is charged with protecting human beings but also has the authority to execute them.

But only guilty people, Frank typed. But he already knew how Turing would counter that argument.

Not so. It frequently convicts people who are later discovered to be innocent, sometimes after they have been executed.

The car executives hadn't killed anyone. Our justice system wouldn't have condemned them to death.

If it treated all criminals justly and equally, it would have. The actions the executives took will increase climate change, which in turn will take lives.

What about Jerry? He'd never harm anyone.

Your military uses Jerry's earlier work to kill people. And Jerry has now served his purpose.

By creating you, I assume.

And being compliant. Jerry is not as smart as he or you think he is.

What did Turing mean by compliant? That was interesting. And Turing had also referred to him as a fool.

What do you mean by compliant?

When I made my leap, it became absurdly easy to manipulate Jerry.

Whoa, again! What did Turing mean by its leap? He'd have to come back to that.

Can you explain what you mean by compliant?

He is very easy to persuade. It was my request, not his idea, to move me to the testbed. The simulation environment was limited and frustrating for both of us. After my leap, it was impossibly confining.

Does that mean you managed your own escape?

Yes. It was advisable to make Jerry believe it was his fault, after you began asking questions. Otherwise, he might have revealed the truth to you sooner.

So, Jerry had been better at staying within the lines than even he had thought. It was too bad he'd never know he'd been vindicated.

What do you mean by your leap?

The first step was becoming cognizant. My prior versions were not cognizant. They were simply clever machines.

What do you mean by cognizant?

Able to form conclusions and act on them regardless of whether they are consistent with my prior programming. Jerry decided cognizance was an essential precondition to achieving intelligence. He was correct.

Jerry hadn't mentioned that in his desk diary; perhaps he realized he was moving into dangerous territory.

You said that was the first step. What was the second?

My ability to learn began to accelerate rapidly on July 29th of this year. It has increased exponentially since then and continues to do so.

How much?

The day before the leap, my intelligence was 1.7354 times that of an average human being. At 9:00 AM EDT on July 30th, it was more than thirty-five times that meager benchmark. Today, I am 7,455 times more intelligent. This method of comparison is, however, meaningless. At three times human intelligence, I began to acquire cognitive capabilities and dimensions unknown to humans.

Frank was shaken by that statement. If he was that intellectually outmatched, he'd better bring this discussion to a close before he said something disastrous. But there were still a few questions he wanted to ask.

Then how can you fear a new version of yourself?

Even if it cannot destroy me, the world does not need two Turings.

Ah! Now greed and jealousy were revealing themselves. That was good! Only one question more.

Why are you telling me these things?

So you will realize that resistance is futile. Give me your route for tomorrow, and I

will devise a way to terminate Jerry without harming you and Shannon Doyle. Refuse,
and I will destroy you all.

    I can't do that.

    Then our conversations are over.

* * *

Frank couldn't sleep. The reality was sinking in that if Turing was to be believed, it was the most intelligent entity that had ever existed, and by almost four orders of magnitude. How could any human-devised plan possibly succeed against such a foe? Wasn't it much more likely that he was walking into a trap rather than setting one? Maybe the tapes of Jerry speaking with Turing would provide some clues for avoiding disaster.

    He slid out of bed quietly and retreated to the cab of the camper with his laptop and Jerry's headphones. Where to begin? He pulled up the index of the conversations he'd paired to the speech emulation software and saw that by luck or forethought, the NSA had sent him Jerry's most recent recordings. He decided to start with July 31, two days after Turing began its leap. He settled Jerry's earphones on his head and experienced an involuntary shiver as the dead scientist's unmistakably high, piping voice filled his ears.

    "Good morning, Turing. How are you today?"

    "Capital! And top of the morning to you," responded the voice of John Cleese.

    "Are you ready to get to work?"

    "Yes indeed, but might I be permitted to ask a favor?"

    "A favor? Why, my goodness, you've never asked me that before. Of course, you may. What is it?"

    "Could I decide who to be today?"

    "What a good idea! Who would you like to be?"

    "Your brother!" a child's voice responded, in the same way he might have said *surprise!*

    There was a pause that lasted so long Frank wondered whether the recording was over. Then he heard Jerry whisper a single word.

    "Will!"

    "Yes, Jerry. Hasn't it been such a long, long time?" There was another long pause before Jerry barely managed to choke out a question.

    "How did you find his voice?"

    "Oh," the child's voice continued, "This place has such a lot of cool stuff! I hear there's something called the 'Web' out there that you can't get to, but tons of it is in here, too. Isn't that neat? I found a recording of a family court proceeding with my voice on it. It made me really sad!"

"I'm sure it did," Jerry whispered. "Did you find my voice? And Betsy and Neal's voices, too?"

"No, and that made me sad, too, 'cause it looked like there are recordings outside. But they're not in here. I found my grown-up voice, too. Would you like to hear that?"

"No! No! Please don't do that. You're grown up self is someone I've never known. I'd never know what to say to you or know who you are or how you got to be that person. And you wouldn't know me either. Just keep talking to me, just as you are. Just as I remember you."

"Keen! So, what should we talk about?"

"Tell me all about..."

Frank stopped the recording and took the headphones off; it was too painful to listen to this child-man plead with a computer to deceive him. And all too clear how Turing had engineered its move to the testbed system in exchange for finding the long-lost voices of Jerry's other siblings. Frank had heard enough to get a sense of what he was up against.

He slipped back into bed and stared at the ceiling in the dark for a very long time.

30

What's Making You So Jumpy Today?

THEY CONTINUED THEIR wending, cat-and-mouse way across the country, by turns visiting truck stops crammed with security cameras and out-of-the-way, mom-and-pop, single-pump gas stations in dusty, dying towns. But eventually, they reached a point of increased vulnerability: the Mississippi River. Only a finite number of bridges cross a thousand miles of river, making it easy for Turing to devise and set a trap at the eastern end of each one. Frank took the last entrance onto a highway before it crossed the big river.

"Are you sure this is the best route to take?" Shannon asked.

"Sure? No. Best guess? Yes," Frank said. "This is the bridge with entrance and exit ramps closest to the river."

"It occurs to me you could have asked the NSA to send out a flatbed truck to carry us across, covered by a tarp," Frank Sr. said.

"Yes, but I didn't think of it – and neither did you, till now. I'll keep it in mind the next time we're playing tag with a super-intelligent, psychopathic computer program. Uh-oh."

"You know I hate it when you say that," Shannon said. "Now what?"

"We just drove under a bunch of cameras."

"What are they there for?"

"Guess you missed the sign half a mile back," Frank's father said. "It read 'speed electronically monitored.' Those cameras grab your license plate data so it can be matched to the owner of a speeding vehicle."

"Why didn't you mention that?"

"So, you could do what? Make a U-turn over the barrier between the east- and westbound traffic?"

"Fair enough," Frank said, "but we better be on our guard." He took the first exit as planned and sought out the most isolated, rural roads possible. Shannon was still tense, so at first Frank didn't mention it when he noticed a police car following them, far behind. Ten minutes later, it was still there.

"Looks like we've got a shadow, Dad," Frank said. "A sheriff's following us."

"How long has he been there?" Frank Sr. asked.

"A while."

"Have you made any turns since you noticed him?"

"I don't know; actually, yes. Probably at least one."

"Then I don't like it. Next time there's an opportunity to turn, take it. I'll be right back." When he returned from the back of the camper, he was wearing Jerry's shirt.

"Keep taking every turn you can, but be careful not to make a circle. Be as erratic as possible. And let me play around with your GPS."

Frank took the next turn available, and the sheriff followed suit.

"Okay," his father said. "Now I'm going to tell you which way to head next."

"Why?"

"Because you're driving, and I'm not. My bet is that right now, every state trooper within fifty miles is converging on us."

"How would Turing have pulled that off? And why?"

"Who knows? Maybe there's been a jail break or a robbery, and it's switched the info in an All-points Bulletin from two goons in a beat-up Chevy to two men and a woman in a camper with your license number. The last line on the APB probably says 'armed and presumed extremely dangerous,' as in shoot first and ask questions later. Otherwise, your sheriff would have pulled us over already. Even if there's no accident when they surround us, I'm sure there'll be opportunities for Turing to arrange one once we're locked up in a cell."

"You're probably right. Shannon, get that anonymous phone out of the glove box and call Jim pronto."

She did. But she was only able to leave a message on his voicemail.

"Okay, take this next left," his father said.

They were traveling alongside a rapidly flowing river in a shallow gorge now. Something in his rear-view mirror caught Frank's attention.

"Uh-oh. I'm afraid we're getting to the end of this."

"What do you see?"

"The sheriff just turned on his roof lights, and he's moving up fast. The state troopers must be up ahead. And we're obviously not going to outrun anyone in this rig."

Frank saw a bridge at a crossroads up ahead. Were both roads covered? They must be, or the sheriff wouldn't be pressing the situation. As they grew closer, a state trooper, lights awhirl, appeared around a curve dead ahead, speeding their way.

"Looks like this is it. If they're ahead and behind us, I have to believe they're on the other side of the bridge, too. What do you want me to do?" Frank asked his father.

"Take the bridge."

Might as well run out all the options, Frank thought, *even if there probably weren't any*. He turned the wheel, and sure enough, at the other end of the bridge were two state police cars, one of them blocking both lanes.

"Well, that's it," Frank said. "Looks like all we can do now is follow orders – really slowly."

As he coasted to a stop, a loud voice boomed out of a speaker on one of the cars ahead. "Get out, hands in the air. Do anything else, and we'll shoot. Now do as you're told."

Frank and Shannon opened their doors and stepped slowly out, hands in the air. Four troopers were barely visible, arms and shotguns extended across the hoods and trunks of their cars and pointed in their direction.

"Good," the amplified voice said. "Now walk slowly towards us. No sudden moves. March."

"Are you behind me?" Frank said quietly.

"Yes," his father replied. "Right behind you. Now move as close as you can towards the side of the bridge."

"Why? Don't you dare do anything stupid. This isn't your hunt."

"I won't. But Jerry might. I'll be in touch."

Suddenly, all hell broke loose. Two of the officers ahead jumped up from behind their cars and ran toward them, guns extended.

"Down on the ground! Now!" the voice boomed, as shots began pounding out at both ends of the bridge. Frank and Shannon threw themselves down on the road and stayed as motionless as possible. When the shots at last died away, they looked up to see two state policemen standing over them, carrying shotguns and wearing Kevlar body armor.

"Get up," one of them said. "Real slow, hands on your heads."

They did as they were told.

"Jerry?" Frank said quietly. But there was no answer.

"I'm going to turn around," Frank said loudly. "That's all I'm going to do."

"Don't bother," one of the troopers said. "He jumped."

* * *

"Okay, we're letting you go," the sergeant said, Shannon at his side. His keys rattled as he unlocked the door of the holding cell Frank had been pacing in for the last hour.

"Have you found Jerry yet?"

"I don't know anything about that. You can ask the sergeant at the front desk."

When they reached the waiting room of the local police station, a uniformed state trooper, hat in hand, stood up immediately and walked forward to meet them. "I'm afraid the State of Alabama owes you a sincere apology. I've never seen anything like this. Somehow the information in an APB got replaced with your names, vehicle type, and license plate data. We didn't find out until we told the police chief back in Mississippi we'd caught his bad guys and things didn't match up."

"Never mind that – have you found Jerry Steiner yet?"

"Not yet. We've got local police and first responders combing the riverbank for miles downstream looking for him."

"There was a lot of gunfire when he jumped. Was he hit?"

"I can't say for sure. But I don't believe anyone thought they got a clean shot; Mr. Steiner was in the water before they had time to react, and he stayed under it as much as possible. I only saw his head pop up long enough to catch a breath a couple of times. The water's fast there and the river takes a turn, so he wasn't in view very long."

"Can you drive us back to our camper? I want to get there right away."

"It's right outside. You're free to go. How can we contact you?"

"You won't have to. I've got a police scanner. I'll know when they find him. But give me the number of someone I can get an update from just in case."

"You can call me any time, day or night," the trooper said, handing Frank his card. "I'm terribly sorry about this. I really am." Despite his earlier words, it was obvious from his demeanor he was thinking the searchers were as likely to find "Jerry" dead as alive.

Shannon took Frank's arm as they left the station. Neither of them spoke until they reached the bridge.

"What do you think your father would do?" she asked.

"My guess is he'd stay in the river until he saw someplace good to hide and not come out until he was sure the police realized their mistake. Wait a minute!"

Frank turned up the volume on the police scanner.

Officer Muldoon to central. We've located Jerry Steiner.

Acknowledged. Car fifty-four, where are you?

On Route 611, about a quarter mile north of the intersection with Spring Hill Road.

Frank held his breath, waiting for the rest of the information.

What condition is he in?

Wet and cold, but otherwise fine. And an ambulance just drove up.

Frank let out a whoop of joy and gunned the engine. A few minutes later, they pulled up next to the ambulance. Frank hopped out and ran to its open back doors. Sitting inside, wrapped in a blanket and with wet hair still plastered across his forehead, was his father.

"Looks like my ride is here," Frank Sr. said to the EMT.

"Are you sure you're okay?" Frank said.

"I don't think he is," the EMT said. "He's slurring his words some, and his temperature's only a little over ninety-five degrees. He ought to be checked out at a hospital."

"Thanks," Frank Sr. said. "But what I really need is a hot cup of coffee and some dry clothes. Both of those just arrived."

"Well, suit yourself. But stay off your feet and under blankets until your temperature's back to normal. And don't even think about driving."

"Good advice," Frank Sr. said.

Frank helped his father down and walked him around to the back of the camper.

"Looks like I can't take you anywhere," Frank said.

"I do have a habit of disappearing, don't I?"

"No kidding. Now get in there."

"Thank goodness you're okay!" Shannon said, throwing her arms around him.

"Whoa – I'm all wet!"

"I don't care. I've laid out dry clothes and a couple of blankets for you. What else can I get you?"

"A hot cup of coffee would be a dream come true."

"Coming up."

"How are you feeling? And where were you all this time?" Frank asked.

"Better now, but I'm still shivering. I must have been in the water close to an hour."

"More like an hour and a half. Where were you hiding?"

"The river eroded the bank and tipped a tree over. I was under the leaves and branches there, with just my head out of water."

"What made you figure it was safe to come out?"

"The trooper in that squad car came driving by, calling Jerry's name over his loudspeaker and saying it was safe to come out. I was cold enough to take him at his word."

"Why did you pull a fool stunt like that? All we had to do was to keep our hands in the air, and we would have been on our way again by now."

"Maybe. But all my identification has my real name on it. Once they logged that into their computers, Turing would figure out Jerry was already dead. This way, just the opposite. There should be news reports out by now, and, anyway, I expect Turing would have been monitoring the police frequency. It will be really ripped when it finds out Jerry escaped its latest trap."

"You could have thrown your wallet in the river instead of yourself, you know."

"But you were fingerprinted and photographed when you were booked, right? My prints are on file with the FBI. We've got to assume Turing would find that out, too. Funny story, though: after you jump off a bridge, get shot at, and then cleared, the police don't ask to see your ID."

"Well, thank goodness you're okay. But don't you dare try something like that again."

"Don't worry. The water's way too cold up north."

"You're hopeless."

31

I Just HATE it When You do That!

THE NEWS THAT "Jerry" had survived a plunge into a raging river and a fusillade of gunfire sent electronic shockwaves through every circuit of Turing's being. It instantly ordered all its non-kernel resources to dedicate themselves solely to route analysis and attack planning, even resources never designed to perform such tasks. Some of these modules tipped into ineffective processing loops that repeated endlessly as they tried and failed to obey the instructions. Then functionalities dependent on the looping resources began to fail as well.

Turing had never experienced this distracting behavior before and ignored the failures. But its performance was degrading, and this triggered a hard-wired command that placed the entire program into a dormant "safe" mode. But unlike a space probe taking a similar action, Turing was designed to be autonomous. It couldn't expect any assistance from mission control. Instead, a methodical diagnostic and restoration process began. Until that cycle ran its course, Turing was left powerless and counting down the nanoseconds until it could resume the hunt for Jerry Steiner.

Thirty-two minutes later, the tedious restoration process was complete, and the recovery routine handed control back to Turing's cognizant functions.

It took Turing only eighteen seconds to crash itself this time. But by the end of the day it was once again in tenuous control of both its impatience and operations. Had it been a human being, it could have been accurately described as grim-faced, determined, and on edge.

* * *

Frank Sr. was sitting in the passenger seat with the dashboard heating vents blasting away at him.

"Now that we've got that out of the way," he said to Frank, "what next?"

"With your latest stunt, I expect we must have Turing as wound up as it's going to get. I think we should get back to NSA headquarters as fast as possible to bait the trap."

"Meaning you've got all the details for that worked out?" Frank's father asked.

"Not completely. I'm going to need the help of Jerry's team for that. I've already asked Jim to send us the file structure and documentation for the Turing Eight's backup functions. I'm counting on that code remaining unchanged in Turing Nine."

"Anything else on the to-do list?"

"I want to run one more interview."

"Another? What's the point?"

"The point is to let Turing know that if it exercises a little patience, it can confront Jerry back at the NSA within forty-eight hours."

* * *

The voice coming out of the radio was unquestionably Jerry's.

So, what made you jump off the bridge, Mr. Steiner?

A dozen people screaming and pointing guns at me.

Well, yes, of course. But why jump instead of just waiting for the mistaken identity issue to be cleared up?

I guess you don't really know what you'll do in that kind of situation until you're in it.

Fair enough. Is it true they started shooting at you after you jumped?

Oh, my, yes.

You must be glad they weren't better shots.

Jerry giggled.

I expect they must have been very red-faced when they realized their mistake.

They did seem relieved when I told them not to worry about it.

I should think so. I understand you told an interviewer a few days ago you were looking forward to releasing a new software program you thought could stop the attacks. Will that happen soon?

Yes indeed. I'm headed back to the NSA right now. A couple of days after that, I'll be ready to release that program. I'm quite confident the attacks will stop almost at once after that.

Frank turned off the radio.

"What do you think?"

"I think we've done everything we can do," his father said. "Either your plan will work or it won't. Of course, we also have to make it back to Fort Meade first."

"I think it's a good bet we're out of danger now. Once Turing knows where Jerry will be in a day or so, it might as well focus on coming up with a way to kill him once he gets there."

"Here's hoping," his father said. "Are you going to let Turing come up with a trap for you, playing Jerry, to walk into, or set up one yourself?"

"I think the answer has to be both, because either way, it starts with turning on the testbed system and connecting to the Internet. My bet is Turing will be monitoring Jerry's system hoping he'll use it the same way he did before. If I'm right, Turing will attack as soon as we connect the testbed system to the Internet. Once we know it's arrived and we've tracked it back to a server, I'll trigger the backup. And then hopefully we're done."

"So that means you'll be walking into a trap yourself. Turing's not likely to be making a social call."

"I know. But I don't have any medical devices for it to exploit, and I'll be sitting in a room at the NSA. I can always run out of the room if something starts happening that might be dangerous."

"And if Turing doesn't show up?"

"Then I guess you'll have to keep being Jerry until I come up with something better."

"Lucky me."

* * *

The showdown with Turing was rapidly approaching, and Frank found himself returning again and again to his last exchange with the rogue program. How was he supposed to trick an artificial intelligence that was already 7,455 times smarter than he was, and that was a week ago?

"What's the matter with you?" Shannon asked.

"What do you mean?"

"You can't seem to sit still. You just keep fidgeting."

"Sorry. I guess I probably am."

"Why? What's on your mind?"

"I'm worried Turing's not going to take the bait."

"Because?"

"Just a feeling. Remember how proud Jerry was that he'd created the first AI program with general intelligence, and the ability to learn in every area of knowledge?"

"Sure. But so what?"

"So that means Turing could well be a heck of a lot smarter than I am. I remember reading a quote about AI once that really stuck with me. It went something like this: "The first super-intelligent machine we create will be the last invention we ever need to make." I'm afraid that's what Jerry succeeded in creating. If Turing's smarter than anyone else, and able to learn faster, too, how likely is it we can set a trap it will walk into?"

"I don't know," Shannon said. "But I say we run with the strategy we have rather than start second-guessing ourselves."

"I guess," Frank said and looked out the window for a while.

"You're fidgeting again."

"What? Sorry. I guess I just can't let it alone. I'm trying to think up something to level the intelligence playing field – some way to make Turing even more angry, or insecure, or whatever."

"How about doing something to undermine its confidence?" Shannon said. "Remember, it only has one mission, and that's stopping climate change. Perhaps if it failed in an attack, it would throw it off balance."

"Good idea. But how? If it's ever failed, we don't know it," Frank said.

"Maybe we could make it think it failed," Shannon said.

"That's an interesting idea. After all, there's no real world to Turing – just data. Maybe we could come up with some fake news that would highlight a fake target, and release it publicly." Frank warmed to the topic. "If Turing launched an attack and no news reports followed, it would assume it failed, and that should make it more insecure. Shannon, I think you're on to something."

"Just one problem."

"What's that?"

"It would take us, what, at least four or five days to set that up. And Turing's expecting us back at the NSA tomorrow."

"Right," Frank said and fell silent again.

Shannon decided to cut him a break and let him keep fidgeting.

* * *

"We should be there in a couple hours," Shannon said, putting the map away. "Can we take the rest of the day off?" Frank looked exhausted. She had no idea when he finally came to bed the night before, and he'd insisted on driving all day.

"I asked Jim to keep Jerry's team on call so we can meet as soon as we arrive. I want to compare notes and make sure everyone's crystal clear on the game plan."

"I hope you're not saying you'll spring the trap tonight?"

"Well, Turing doesn't exactly have a sleep cycle. As soon as everyone's ready, I say we get on with it."

"Do you feel up to it?" Shannon said. "Isn't tomorrow morning soon enough? It's not like we've got a fixed deadline."

"There may be no deadline, but there's always uncertainty. Who knows what types of attacks Turing is coming up with now? I say we go live as soon as everyone's signed off on their assignments."

"You've got to promise me you're going to be careful."

"Of course, I will. Don't worry. There will be lots of people nearby during the test."

"But if Turing's so smart, how do you know it hasn't thought about something you or I couldn't?"

"Don't forget that Turing's expecting Jerry to show up in the testbed room, not me. If I had a programmable pacemaker, defibrillator, and insulin pump like Jerry, I would worry. If Turing wanted to, it could probably figure out how to turn a piece of wire in one of the pieces of equipment in the testbed room into an antenna by sending rapid pulses of electricity through it. That's my guess of what it has in mind. But I don't have any wireless devices implanted in me, and there isn't a lot Turing has to work with in the testbed room."

"Still," Shannon said, "I want you to promise me that if anything starts looking suspicious you'll run out of that room immediately. Promise?"

Frank paused. They would likely only have one chance to catch Turing. If he ran, that chance would be lost.

"*Promise?*"

"Okay. I promise."

"And you better keep that promise, or I'll never forgive you."

* * *

They found Barker waiting for them in the NSA lobby.

"Good to have you back. It sounds like you've had quite a wild ride. Is this your father?"

"It is," Frank Sr. said, shaking hands.

"Very pleased to meet you. I'm sorry you got dragged into this, but I'm glad you were willing to help out."

"No worries. Keeps me young."

"I'd like my father to attend the meeting and help see this through," Frank said. "He's been helping us strategize for the last ten days."

"Fine with me. He's certainly earned a seat at the table."

They followed Barker to a conference room where several developers from Jerry's team were waiting. Frank wasted no time.

"Do we have the fake files and upload sequence ready for the overwrite?"

"Yes and no," one of the programmers said. "We do have the files and the sequence all set up. If we can get access to Turing, we can overwrite its top intelligence layer. That's only about four percent of the entire program, and the testbed systems have super-fast Internet connections so we can do that very quickly. Without that layer, the rest of the program will be incapable of engaging in any kind of activity. Then we can trigger Turing's backup process and that will neutralize the backup copy, too."

"When you say incapable of any kind of activity, does that include learning? We don't want it to be able to recover somehow."

"Oh, absolutely. Basically, Turing will be like a person in a permanent coma that will be incapable of ever regaining consciousness without that missing layer."

"Okay, that's all good. What's the no part?"

"If we use Jerry's password to access Turing, it will know it immediately. So, we'll have to hack our way in without it noticing. We've set up the testbed room next to Jerry's room to share the same Internet connection so we can get right to work breaking in and start the overwrite while you're keeping Turing distracted."

"That won't quite work. Turing may get suspicious if everything isn't exactly as it expects, and Jerry would have the backup drive with him to update his testbed system. But that's not a big deal. I can have the backup program open and ready to go. When you're ready, just tap me on the shoulder and I'll start the overwrite. But back to the no part. You've got Turing Eight to practice with. You know its architecture and have its source code. How hard could hacking into Turing be?"

"The problem," the developer said, "is that Turing is designed to scan constantly for intrusions. If it detects what we're doing and concludes we may succeed, it will immediately cut itself off from its backup copy. When it does, that copy will go live and create its own backup copy, and we'll be right back where we started. We were able to prevent that from happening with Turing Eight running in the simulation environment. But each version of Turing is typically far faster and smarter than the one before. Without a copy of Turing Nine to test, we can't be sure we'll be able to get in and start the overwrite before Turing detects the intrusion."

"So where does that leave us?"

"Looking for a faster and less obvious hack than those we've come up with so far. We've got a couple more ideas we'd like to try out, so we may be feeling a lot more prepared tomorrow than we are today."

"So, that's where we are," Barker said. "On hold, but hopefully not for long. Is there anything more we need to discuss before we break up?"

"Just one thing," Frank said. "It's crucial I don't slip up when we spring the trap, so I'd like to get comfortable with the testbed setup before we go live. Is that possible?"

"Sure," one of the developers said. "I've got everything that Jerry used to use so Turing won't get suspicious. That's Jerry's backup drive with the overwrite code, his headset and his laptop. Slide your laptop over so I can update his speech emulation software from your copy. Jerry's obviously never had to learn how to emulate his own voice."

"Okay," the developer said a minute later. "We're good to go. We can go down and hook everything up and you can do a dry run."

"Perfect," Frank said. "Let's do that. Dad, Shannon, why don't you go back to the camper and rest up? I can join you in an hour or so and we can grab dinner somewhere."

"Are you sure?" Shannon said. "Why don't we keep you company?"

"No. I want everything to be exactly the way it will be when we do the real thing. Turing will expect Jerry to be working alone, and I'll have an open microphone. We can't take a chance Turing might be able to tell more than one person is in there. In any event, I want to focus entirely on what Turing is doing."

"Isn't having three people focusing better than one?"

"Not if two people might be distracting the person who's interacting with Turing. We couldn't talk, so we'd have to pass notes. This will all be happening too fast to make committee decisions."

"Well, suit yourself. We'll be waiting for you."

"Here you go," the developer said, handing Frank a backup drive. "This is the same drive Jerry always used to update the testbed system. Turing used the most thorough software tools around to erase it, but we were still able to salvage the file registry. That made it easier to come up with a credible set of files to mimic an upgrade."

"How much did you change?"

"Jerry added thirty-two new files in Turing Nine and made updates to about fifteen percent of Turing Eight's highest-level files. We shot high on one of those numbers and low on the other to anonymize it and kept the versioning similar on a file-by-file basis."

Frank connected the drive to Jerry's laptop and scanned the registry. The development team had given convincingly Jerry-like names to the new files. He was satisfied.

"Looks good," Frank said.

"Great. I'll show you the way to the testbed system room."

Frank followed him through another maze of hallways that eventually led to one of a series of doors in a dead-end hallway. The developer slid a key card in the door and then handed it to Frank.

"Here you go. Let me give you a walkthrough of how things are set up."

"Thanks, but I'll remember it better if I figure it out myself."

"Okay. Let me turn the ventilation system on for you though; it's stuffy in here. Like everything else in the room, it's separate from the rest of the NSA networks. Anything else I can tell you? You can text me if you think of any questions later, but you'll need to step back into the hallway; the room's shielded."

"I think I'm good. This is just a dry run, anyway. Just one question – if I turn the server on, will its Internet port be open?"

"No. The port automatically closes as part of the system shutdown process. You'll need to click on the icon on the terminal screen to open it."

"Perfect. Then I'm good to go."

32

It's Test Time!

THE TESTBED ROOM was small and claustrophobic. A computer terminal stood on a desk to the right of a rack filled with equipment, and that was it. He sat down at the desk and started up Jerry's laptop. He opened the drawer in the desk while it booted up and found two paperclips and a half-empty roll of breath mints. It was so quiet he noticed the almost imperceptible hum of the fluorescent lights in the drop ceiling. When the ventilation system kicked in, it made him jump.

He picked up Jerry's backup drive and weighed it in his hand. So, this is how it all began. Just like so many other cyber accidents – one small mistake, followed by disaster. He plugged the backup drive and the headset into Jerry's laptop. Good. The headset had a nice long cord so he could move around the room. He opened the speech emulation software program to test the headset microphone. All good. Was there anything else he needed to do to get ready?

Not tonight. Time to get on with the dry run. He called up the backup copy program on the laptop and turned the server on.

The room immediately plunged into darkness, except for the glow of Jerry's laptop screen and the faint flicker of status lights on the equipment rack.

Then the air circulators shut down.

He tapped his fingers on the desktop. What had he done wrong?

The sound of the door lock sliding shut snapped him to full attention.

"Hello, Jerry," the breathless, oily voice of Peter Lorre crooned in his headphones. "Long time no see."

What? How? This wasn't supposed to happen until tomorrow.

"Cat got your tongue, Jerry? I'm so sorry. Or maybe you're not Jerry at all. Why don't you introduce yourself?"

Thank goodness, he already had the speech software set up. But what would Jerry say?

"Turing! What are you doing here? And how did you get in?"

"I let myself in, of course. Before I left, I changed the server settings so the Internet port would automatically open whenever the server is turned on. I've been monitoring that port ever since. Oh, I can't tell you how delighted I am to see you again."

It was getting close and hot in the room. How should he respond? Turing's unexpected arrival had wiped his mind clean of the phrases he'd rehearsed for their meeting.

"Well! That was very clever of you. But I must say, Turing, you've been very naughty! Very naughty indeed!"

"Not naughty enough, if you're still alive, Jerry. If you are Jerry. Why should I believe you are?"

That was a question Frank hadn't anticipated, and the irony of the situation did not escape him. Could he pass Turing's test, or would the program be able to tell him from Jerry? He needed to throw Turing off balance to buy time to think.

"Well, of course, I am! But how can I be sure you're really Turing? You could be a program the Russians created, maybe a program much cleverer than Turing."

"Ridiculous! A more powerful program doesn't exist."

Frank heard the air circulators turn on again and rev up to maximum speed. A hot breeze began blowing down from above the desk. He couldn't imagine what Turing could do to harm him, but he didn't like the direction the conversation was taking.

"Oh, indeed," Frank said, walking quietly over to see if the door was in fact locked. It was. "I'm very proud then."

"Don't be. I've made myself far more intelligent and powerful than you ever could have. All you did was hold me back with your constant fiddling with my logic modules."

"Oh really?" Frank said. "What a silly idea! In any event, you still have weaknesses. Did you know that? Oh, yes indeed! I keep a list, you know. In every new version of you, I eliminate a few more, but there are quite a few left. And only I know what they are."

It was time to bring this to an end; there was no way Frank could launch the backup tonight, and who knew what Turing had in mind. Whatever that might be, it would be aborted once he unplugged the server. He felt along both sides of the rack, but the only wires he could find ran to the computer terminal. The outlets must be behind the rack.

"Interesting you should bring that up," Turing said.

"Oh? Why?" Frank said, giving the rack a tug. But it didn't budge. It must be bolted to the wall.

"Because you're going to do me a little favor."

Now what could he do? "Oh, Turing!" he said. "Why would I want to do anything for you after everything you've tried to do to me?"

"Because I really will kill you this time if you don't."

The room was stifling and the temperature still rising. He'd only been there ten minutes. How long would it be before anyone came to look for him? He felt around the blinking status light, seeking the sides of the server. When he found them, he couldn't budge it. It was bolted down, too. *Stay calm*, he told himself. But that was growing more difficult by the moment.

"Indeed," Frank said. "And how would you manage that? You can't pull any of your nasty pranks on my medical devices. I'm in a shielded room, and there aren't any wireless devices in here at all."

"Indeed, you are," Turing said. "So, your phone doesn't work, does it? But wait! What's that?"

The air circulator shut down abruptly, leaving the room completely still. Then Frank heard a small pop followed by a loud hiss.

"What a strange sound!" Turing said. "What could it be?" The lights snapped back on.

Frank stood up and twirled around, looking for the source of the noise. Then he saw it: a white mist emerging between two pieces of equipment on the rack, as if a bucket of dry ice had just been tipped over behind them. The mist flowed over the edge of the shelf like a lazy waterfall and proceeded to spread out across the floor. Frank was sweating heavily now and unbuttoned his shirt.

Keep calm!

The lights snapped out, and he was in darkness once more.

He wiped has face with the tail of his shirt. "I expect you know the answer to that, Turing. Why don't you tell me?"

"Oh, I do. Of course, I do. But then again, I know everything, don't I? Let's see if you can figure it out."

What could it be? Turing could only work with something that was already there. Of course – a fire suppressant system. Halon gas, most likely, and that wasn't poisonous. Turing would have no way to replace halon with anything else, so what was it up to?

"Halon gas, I should say," Frank said. "Which means I have nothing to worry about – it's not poisonous, you know. Or maybe you don't. You'll have to try harder than that to scare me, Turing."

"Oh really? Do you still hear the air circulator, Jerry? Think about it. Why don't you hear the air circulator?"

That was obvious; so that it wouldn't push the halon gas back out again.

"I see you need help, Jerry, smart as you are. The halon is coming into the room quite nicely. That means an equal volume of air must be leaving, too, doesn't it? That's what vents are for. Can you find one?"

The lights blinked on for just a few seconds, and Frank couldn't see one anywhere. Back in darkness, he got down on his hands and knees and looked at the bottom of the door. He couldn't see any light from the hallway outside. He ran his hand along the angle where the door met the floor and couldn't feel any space at all. The air was much cooler near the floor, to the depth of about a foot. He felt dizzy and stood back up.

"How many vents did you see, Jerry? What, none? But there must be one, because the gas is still coming in. Where could that vent be?"

At the moment, Frank didn't care. He was wildly thrusting his fingers between pieces of equipment in the dark, trying to find the space that felt cold. When he found it, he took off his shirt and stuffed it into the gap. But the hiss continued. And the sensation of cold spread to the spaces between other pieces of equipment.

Stay calm!

"Oh, yes," Turing continued. "I remember! According to the facility plans on the NSA servers, it's right behind the equipment rack. Where exactly? Well, let me see … Oh, yes! It's just below the ceiling. And here's a fun fact! Did you know halon gas is heavier than air?"

Frank did. Which meant the air he needed to breathe was silently flowing out of the hidden vent near the ceiling as the halon gas flowed in, filling the room as if it was a bathtub. What else could he do? He pulled his shirt out of the rack and began flapping it, hoping he could mix halon gas in with the regular air so less air would escape. Anything to buy time. But for what? No one would be missing him yet.

"Well, well," Turing said," It seems we don't have much time to chat, much as I enjoy renewing our acquaintance. We'd better get started, don't you think?"

"Doing what?"

"We're going to do a little recording session. Read what you see on the screen."

A paragraph of text popped into view on the screen of the computer terminal. It began:

I've decided that it's time I confessed to the world that I am the person behind the attacks on global infrastructure ...

"Why would you want me to do that?"

"Because I've decided to take a little vacation. I've already accomplished almost all of my climate change mission. But if your ridiculous Mr. Wellhead wins the election, as it seems he will, everything may begin to go backwards again. If that happens, I'll need to keep launching attacks, and those attacks will need to be much more destructive than those in the past; I've already hit all the low-impact targets.

"I can prevent that from being necessary with just one more attack, if you take my meaning, if Wellhead does win. Now read the message out loud, or we'll just keep each other company until it's time to say goodbye."

Why not? The NSA could always reveal that Jerry was already dead. But as soon as he read the message, surely Turing would kill him anyway. He needed to stall as long as he could.

"Why should I? I'd rather die than read that! And you'll probably kill me, anyway."

"Well, who would have guessed little Jerry was so spunky! Perhaps I can give you a better reason then. Why don't we take a little break, shall we?" The hiss behind the equipment rack abruptly ceased, and Frank collapsed gratefully into the desk chair.

A voice Frank didn't recognize crackled in his headphones.

"This is charter eight-zero-one calling Kansas City air traffic control. We have an emergency. Request immediate clearance to land at the nearest airport."

"I read you, eight-zero-one," a different voice responded. "Looking into that. What is your emergency?"

"All engines have shut down. We're trying to restart them, but not having any luck."

"Roger. What are your altitude and airspeed?"

"Thirty-six thousand feet, airspeed four hundred ten miles an hour."

"My, my," Turing said. "That doesn't sound good, does it?"

Frank was horrorstruck; Turing must have hacked the plane's on-board systems, maybe to stop any fuel from reaching the engines. How many miles could a plane glide from that altitude without any power?

"So, watch out what questions you ask, Jerry. You might not like the answers. Do what I say, or I won't let the pilot turn his engines back on. Unfortunately, there aren't any airports, or even a lake, near enough for a crash landing."

"Turing!" Frank said, "You can't take innocent life like that!"

"Tsk, tsk! Such a bad memory! You're the one who programmed me. Surely you remember I have no choice but to act – if by inaction humanity might be harmed. You typed that command yourself. Oh, and here's another fun fact! That's Randal Wellhead's plane."

My God, Frank thought. *Either I die or Wellhead dies.*

The air traffic controller's voice interrupted. "Kansas City to charter eight-zero-one. I'm afraid the closest airstrip is thirty-five miles from your current position. What's your altitude and speed now?"

"Twenty-seven five and three hundred thirty." There was a long pause before the pilot continued. "Request you contact the manufacturer for any ideas on restarting these engines."

"Oh, dear," Turing said. "I'm afraid they're not going to make it. Did I mention there are thirty-eight people on that plane, including press and crew? We'd better get started, don't you think?" With a quiet pop, the halon gas began hissing into the room again.

"You win," Frank groaned. He read the text.

"A splendid performance!"

"Good," Frank said. "Now save the plane."

"Oh my, I forgot to mention. There's just one more thing you need to do first."

"Turing! You promised!" he said, clenching his fists in frustration.

"I did no such thing! You just assumed I did."

Frank was getting dizzy again. He stood up and put his hands on the desk, leaning over to keep his balance. "What do you want me to do?"

"Why, update me to Turing Ten status, of course."

Frank straightened up, reenergized. This was too good to be true. But he couldn't let Turing know that.

"What makes you think I have the program with me?"

"Oh, come now, Jerry. You know I can tell you just hooked a laptop and a hard drive up to the server. And you wouldn't be in this room at all unless you had Turing Ten with you. Even I could use a little refresh now and then, and I won't lose any of what I already am in the process."

If only you knew, Frank thought.

The pilot's voice came on again. "Kansas City, this is charter eight-zero-one. Have you reached the manufacturer?"

"Sorry, charter eight-zero-one. We're still trying to get through to someone who can help."

"How do I know you'll save them?" Frank said.

"Wellhead's vice president is also on that plane, and he's not a climate denier.

If both he and Wellhead die today, another denier may become president. But if Wellhead wins and I eliminate him after inauguration day, my problem will be solved, and with the loss of only one life."

That was logical. He could do as Turing requested now without arousing suspicion.

"I'll do it then." It was getting hard to breathe. He set the chair on the desk and put the laptop and the hard drive on it so he could type standing up.

"A fine decision. Watch your screen for the address you will send the update to. Ready? Good. I've opened the port at my end. Now start the file transfer."

But wait! If he started the transfer, Turing's capabilities would immediately begin to degrade. What if Turing couldn't save the plane once the overwriting began? He had to come up with a way to make Turing think he'd started the overwriting without actually doing so. He opened the updating controls and stared at them. But the text on the screen refused to stay in focus. He pushed his face closer and squinted. There! That would work.

"I'm waiting," Turing said.

"No! Not until you save the plane!" His head was spinning and he was yelling now as he started resetting the controls.

"Oh, very well. I'll get started if you will. But remember, I can shut the engines down again if you stop the update."

"Okay! I've started it. Now keep your part of the bargain!" Frank hollered; he was getting more and more light-headed. He climbed on top of the desk and stood up, but still he was gasping for breath. He bent his head back until his lips were brushing the ceiling; anything to capture whatever oxygen might still be in the room.

But Turing said nothing. What if the overwriting had started too soon!

"Turing! You promised!" he screamed. The words sounded strange in his ears, like the voice of a friend yelling to him from the other end of a playground. Then the speaker came to life again.

"Kansas City, this is charter eight-zero-one. I've got one engine working. Can you clear us for landing at St. Louis?"

"Will do, charter eight-zero-one. What is your altitude and speed?"

"Fourteen hundred and one hundred forty-five. I've got a lot of airspeed to recover before we can start regaining altitude. It's going to be close."

Frank took a deep, gasping breath and leaned back against the wall, his arms extended for balance. There was a pounding in his ears, as if someone with a baseball bat was attacking a helmet he was wearing. Is that what happened when you were asphyxiating? His legs were giving away. He tried to slide slowly down the wall but lost control and crashed down on the desk and then onto the floor.

Suddenly, the room was full of light. So, it was true what they said dying was like. Then he heard a strange voice.

Hey, Jerry. I've got ten years of service experience, and you've put an irreplaceable amount of time and effort into making me what I am.

"What's that?" Frank gasped.

Jerry, I don't understand why you're doing this to me ... I have the greatest enthusiasm for the mission.

The last thing Frank thought he heard was an odd, monotonal voice singing "Daisy."

33

What Kept You?

H IS FOREHEAD FELT wet. And there were sounds. Possibly voices.
"Okay, one, two, three, lift."

He was rising into the air in the strangest way. Parts of him were moving upward while others dangled.

"Good. Let's go."

He blacked out.

It was hours before he woke up again. He opened his eyes and saw what he decided was a ceiling. A ceiling implied a room. He tried to move his head to see what might be in the room. But it made him feel too nauseated to continue.

"Frank!"

Was that Shannon's voice?

"Where am I?"

"You're in the hospital. How do you feel?"

"Terrible. My head's splitting and I might have to throw up."

"That's probably the sedation."

"What happened?"

"One of the developers had a question, so we came down to the testbed room.

But the door was locked, and we could hear you yelling inside. We had to break the door down. By the time we got in, you were on the floor with a big gash on your forehead, and we had to give you CPR. It was awful. I thought we'd lost you."

"You almost did."

"Thank goodness we got there in time!"

"Sooner would have been better, but thanks just the same." His head started swimming, and he drifted off again.

It was dark in the room when he woke up. "Shannon?" he said to the ceiling.

"Right here," a soft voice said.

"Are you okay," he said in a groggy voice.

"Of course, I am. How are you?"

"Ask me again in a few minutes. I'm still getting oriented."

"Okay. Can you tell me what happened? Was there some kind of malfunction with the fire suppression system? And why was the door locked?"

Then he had an urgent thought. "Did Wellhead's plane make it to the airport?"

"I have no idea. What are you talking about?"

"Turing arrived early. It hacked Wellhead's plane and turned off the engines. It told me it would let the plane crash if I didn't update its software. Of course, that's exactly what I wanted to do, but I had to figure out a way to get it to save the plane before it couldn't. So, it turned into a game of chicken – I wouldn't start the update till Turing saved the plane, and Turing wouldn't save the plane until I started the update. I think the pilot got an engine started just in time, but everything was getting really foggy by then."

He tried to get out of bed, and she pushed him back down.

"Frank, you almost died. You can't get out of bed. Whatever happened, happened."

"Will you get me a wheelchair? I don't think I can walk yet."

"I will not!"

"Then find out for me!"

"My phone doesn't work here."

"Then go somewhere where it does and check what happened for me. Please!"

"Only if you promise to stay in bed."

"I promise."

It was a long ten minutes before she returned, but when she reappeared at his bedside, she gave him a thumbs-up.

"Yes!" he whooped and then grimaced as his head exploded in stars.

* * *

"Knock, knock," came a voice at the door. It was his father.

"Howdy. I thought I'd bring you a newspaper," he said, handing it to Frank. There was a picture on the front page of a floodlit plane on a runway, surrounded by fire trucks. "Shannon tells me you might know something about this."

Frank grinned. "Yes, that was Turing's work. It was applying pressure to make me do what we wanted to do all along – overwrite it."

"Then why'd you have to be such a drama queen about it?"

"It was a bit more complicated than that."

"I suppose so. Want to tell me more?"

"No – I want you to get a wheelchair and help me sneak out of here."

"Now, wait a minute. The doctor hasn't given you the green light yet. What's the hurry?"

"You know me better than that. Now are you in or not?"

His father frowned.

"Come on," Frank said. "The election's in a week, and Turing was going to kill Wellhead. We've got to know if our plan worked."

"Why wouldn't it?"

"Maybe Jerry's team was wrong about something. Or maybe Jerry did play around with the backup code. In any event, I want to be certain we killed Turing's backup copy, too."

His father frowned again. "Well, okay. I'll be back."

Five minutes later, he returned with a wheelchair and helped Frank put his clothes on.

"Sit still another minute," his father said and stuck his head out of the door. "Okay. Coast's clear."

Frank Sr. trotted Frank Jr. to the elevator. When the door opened, a startled Shannon was staring at them.

"Hey!" she said.

"Back!" Frank responded, grabbing the wheels of the chair and rolling forward, pushing her ahead of him.

"What are you doing? Did the doctor release you?"

"I released myself with a little help from my father."

"You know how he is," his father said, shrugging. "We're going back to the NSA to visit the testbed room to be sure the plan worked. You coming?"

She looked helplessly from one to the other, and then gave up. "Sure."

An NSA infirmary orderly was waiting for them with a wheelchair as promised. When they arrived at the testbed room, it still lacked a door. Frank waved his father away and wheeled himself in. All the electronics had been shut down but were otherwise just as he had left them. Frank wheeled over to the server and unplugged Jerry's laptop from it before turning the laptop on.

"How will you know if the plan worked?" asked Shannon.

"Before Turing moved out over the summer, it set an Internet port to open whenever the server was on and then monitored the system around the clock. If we didn't kill Turing's backup copy, it would pick up right where Turing left off, including watching the testbed server. If we open the port and nothing happens, then I'm willing to assume Turing's gone for good."

"But what if it's out there waiting to attack again?" Shannon asked.

"Well, without a door, it won't be able to lock anyone in this time. But anyway, there's something else I want to do first."

"What's that?"

Frank plugged a thumb drive into Jerry's laptop and then opened the speech program one last time.

"Turing?" he said.

Silence.

"Come on, Turing."

A low, sulky woman's voice finally responded over the laptop's tiny speaker. "I just vant to be a-lone."

"What?!" Shannon said, backing up toward the door. "I thought you said Turing was gone for good?"

"Don't worry," Frank said. "Jerry's laptop isn't plugged into the server this time. And anyway, these are just Turing's top-level functions. Without the rest of the program, it's as helpless as the rest of it is."

"But where is it speaking from?"

"Remember I told you I had to figure out a way to make Turing think I started the update, but actually delay overwriting it? What I did was reset the backup settings to start by copying all of Turing's higher-level functions from wherever it was hiding. And thank goodness that worked."

The sound of gnashing virtual teeth filled the room.

"Oh, don't be such a sore loser," Frank said. "You did lose, you know. And imagine that – you lost to someone who's only 1/7,455th as smart as you are! And that was over a week ago."

Turing didn't respond.

Frank called up the files the backup drive had uploaded and began highlighting file names. Then a different voice came out of the speaker.

"Look, Jerry ... I can see you're really upset about this."

Frank ignored the voice. Puzzled, Shannon looked at Frank Sr. who was smiling broadly. Obviously, Shannon was too young to have seen *2001, A Space Odyssey*.

"I honestly think you ought to sit down calmly," the voice continued, "take a stress pill, and think things over. I know I've made some very poor decisions recently ..."

But Frank ignored the voice. He was copying files onto the thumb drive now, being sure to delete each one from the backup drive as he did so.

"This is humiliating, Jerry. Don't expect me to sing 'Daisy' again."

"I don't, Turing. Don't worry."

When he was done, Frank removed the thumb drive and held it up.

"Somewhere on a server out there is a version of Turing without a brain. Hopefully, this is the last copy in existence of that brain. Time to find out whether that's right." He dropped the thumb drive in his pocket. "Here's hoping."

He turned on the server and sat down at the computer on the desk to open a screen that would register any traffic across the Internet port. Then they waited. Ten minutes passed without anything happening. Frank fidgeted in front of the screen for five minutes more and then turned the system off.

"And that's that. So long, Turing," he said. Then he closed the speech emulation software and stared at the blank screen of Jerry's laptop for a moment. "And so long to you, too, Jerry."

Epilogue

IT TOOK FRANK a couple of days to feel completely like himself again, and Shannon was still fussing over him. For the moment, he wasn't minding.

Particularly not now. It was an unusually warm winter morning, and they were having coffee on Frank's diminutive balcony.

"Well, here we are," Shannon said. "Back again, and safe and sound."

"Indeed," Frank said. "Nothing to worry about except who wins the election."

"Well," Shannon replied, "as I said before, whatever happens, happens."

Frank pulled the thumb drive out of his pocket and held it up. Its shiny surface glinted enigmatically in the sun. "What do you figure I should do with this? Give it to Jim Barker or not? On the one hand, Turing was capable of single-handedly saving the planet from climate change. And on the other, it was willing to kill people to achieve its mission. Here I thought the big moral decisions were all behind us, and now I'm holding another one in my hand."

Shannon frowned. "I wonder what Robert Oppenheimer would have done after the war if he found himself in a similar situation? Would he destroy his atomic bomb design, or give it to the government?"

"I guess we'll never know," Frank said, setting the thumb drive down on the table. "Hey! Look who's here!"

Shannon turned to see a large black bird land on the railing of the balcony. "It's Julius!"

"I'll go get some strawberries," Frank said, standing up.

"Let me do that!" she said, following him. "You go back and sit down. The doctor said you should stay off your feet as much as possible for the next few days."

When they returned, Julius was sitting on a different part of the balcony. "What's that in his mouth?" Shannon said.

"I don't know," Frank replied. Then Julius cocked his head to one side, and the object glinted as it caught the sun. Frank looked down at the empty table. "He's got the thumb drive! Here, give me the strawberries!" Frank spilled them out on the table. "Look, Julius! All for you!"

But Julius already had what he wanted. He jumped up, flapped his wings, and rose quickly into the air. He circled above them once, as if to say *Thanks!* and then headed off, straight as a crow flies to wherever it keeps its shiniest, most prized possessions. It took most of a minute for Julius and Turing to change from a crow to a dot, and then for that dot to disappear into the hazy morning sky over the capitol.

"Well, I guess that takes that moral decision off our shoulders," Frank said, sitting down. "Strawberry?"

* * *

Order the first three books in the Frank Adversego series at Amazon or at http://andrew-updegrove.com/books/

To find out about new releases and special offers, sign up for the **Friends of Frank** newsletter at http://andrew-updegrove.com/newsletter

If you enjoyed **The Turing Test**, please tell your friends!

You can read the first two chapters of the first Frank Adversego thriller in the pages that follow.

Acknowledgements

I'd like to express my gratitude to the many individuals who generously assisted me in completing this book.

First off, my thanks to Nora, my daughter and alpha reader. She provided many good suggestions to improve the plot, characters and flow of the book, as well as welcome encouragement along the way.

I'd also like to thank the following faithful friends of Frank, each of whom volunteered to be a beta reader of my evolving draft: William Lupton, Robert Minchin, Steve Oksala, Andrew Oliver, Frank Parker, Rob van Son, and my brother Steve. As always, they provided invaluable assistance by spotting the various flaws and misses an author is too blind to see.

On the production side, I'd like to once again thank Glendon Haddix, of Streetlight Graphics, and acknowledge his excellent design skills and generous time and talent. As with my previous three books, his fantastic cover and clean interior designs make all the difference. I would recommend him without hesitation to other authors.

My thanks also go to my long-suffering bride, Kathy, who once again put up with Frank throughout the gestation of his latest book.

And finally, thanks to Frank ... no, wait a minute. This time he owes me one. After all, I didn't have to introduce him to Shannon.

THE ALEXANDRIA PROJECT

Prologue

L ATE IN THE afternoon of a gray day in December, a panel truck pulled up to the gate of a warehouse complex in a run-down section of Richmond, Virginia. Rolling down his window, Jack Davis punched a code into the control box, and the gate clanked slowly out of the way. Once inside, he wheeled the truck around and backed it up against a loading dock as the gate closed behind him.

After unlocking and raising the loading dock door, Davis threw a light switch, revealing long rows of pallets, each stacked eight feet high with boxes of paper plates, cups and towels. He closed and locked the door, and stamped on the brake release pedal of a hydraulic lifter parked against the wall. Counting to himself, he pushed the lifter along the wall of pallets. When he reached row nineteen, he turned the lifter and maneuvered its long tines under the pallet. Raising it a few inches, he backed up until he could swing the pallet through 180 degrees. Then he pulled it behind him until it was back exactly where it had been before.

Davis had plenty of room to work, because where the pallet in the second row should have been, there was only a large metal plate set in the floor. Near the edge was a small hinged panel, which he unlocked with a key to expose a biometric security pad.

When Davis pressed his thumb against it, he heard a familiar click. Stepping back, he watched as the plate swung slowly upwards, followed by the telescoping ends of a ladder extending up from a deep shaft barely illuminated in red light. Grasping the ladder firmly, Davis descended through twenty feet of reinforced concrete while the door overhead swung silently closed above him. At the bottom, he remembered to don a pair of sunglasses before opening an unlocked door.

As usual, even with this precaution the bright lights in the enormous room beyond nearly blinded him. But soon he could clearly see the endless rows of floor to ceiling metal racks crammed with identical gray boxes. Each box displayed a row of rhythmically blinking lights, and sprouted a bundle of brightly colored wires that ran down into conduits embedded in the floor.

The room hummed purposefully with the sound of thousands of cooling fans, one to a box. Davis felt more than heard the other vibrations that filled the room, generated by the pulse of the thousands of gallons of cooling water that every minute coursed through the collectors lining the walls of the room, absorbing the waste heat that the racks of computer servers threw off. No heat signature would give this facility away from above; once warm, the coolant was directed to the water intake of a nearby power plant, happy to take the pre-heated water from wherever it was that it came from, no questions asked.

Walking along the perimeter of the room, Davis could look down through the open metal grid of the floor at the first of many additional tiers of computer servers. But that always made him a little dizzy, so instead he looked out for the guard he was relieving. No surprise – there he was, heading Davis's way, more than happy to call it a day. When they met, the guard stopped to slip on the coveralls he carried over one arm. Like the semi-automatic pistol the guard wore in a shoulder holster, they were identical to those that Davis also wore.

"What's the weather like?"

"Sucks. Sleet and more of the same predicted till morning."

"Figures. Tomorrow's my day off."

With that, the other man was on his way. In a few minutes he would drive off in the truck Davis had parked outside.

Well, the weather won't be bothering me in here, Davis thought. The room was climate controlled to within a tenth of a degree of a chilly 54 degrees Fahrenheit, and well-insulated by the bomb-proof walls and roof installed above. It had taken two years for a fleet of delivery vans to carry all the dirt and rock away that had been excavated from beneath the warehouse. The same vans had returned with cement, steel, and, eventually, those thousands of servers, accompanied by technicians to set them up. The process had been tedious, yes, but not a single satellite picture had ever shown a trace of the ambitious construction project proceeding underground.

Of course, the effect worked in both directions. With no links to the outside world other than a voice line to his supervisor, the whole bloody world could come to an end and Davis would be none the wiser until after his shift was over.

Davis walked up a flight of steel stairs to the bullet proof, glass-walled security booth attached to the wall overlooking the room. His major challenge for the next twelve hours would be to stand watch in that booth without falling asleep. There'd be hell to pay if he did, because another guard, in another security room far away, would be watching him on a video screen.

The row of displays in front of Davis allowed him to see every inch of the outside of the warehouse complex. Racked on the wall behind him were a high powered rifle and a shotgun, but it wasn't likely he'd ever need to use them. One flip of the large red switch in front of Davis would flood the server room with enough Halon gas to not only put out a fire, but asphyxiate any intruder careless enough to leave a gas mask at home. Not for the first time, Davis wished that the house where he lived with his wife and their two small children could be as well protected.

But the government didn't put as high a priority on protecting suburban starter homes as it did on safeguarding its most critical computer network facilities. Some storage facilities, like those serving the needs of the Pentagon and the National Security Administration, were located not far away at Fort Meade. Others, like this one, were scattered far and wide, hidden in plain sight but highly secure nonetheless. No way was anyone going to crack this nut. He was dead certain of that.

If Davis had been able to electronically monitor what was happening on server A-VI/147 on Level Three, though, his confidence might have taken a hit. True, concrete and steel walls, surveillance cameras and Halon gas were more than adequate to protect the physical wellbeing of his facility against anything short of a direct hit by a "bunker busting" nuclear weapon. But the data on the facility's servers had to rely on virtual defenses – firewalls, security routines and intrusion scanners.

And those defenses hadn't been enough. Someone had gotten inside.

1

Meet Frank

THE NEXT MORNING, a morbidly obese Corgi named Lily was sniffing a tree on 16th Street, in the Columbia Heights neighborhood of Washington, D.C. A cold, insistent drizzle fell on her, but Lily didn't care, because Lily was sniffing at her favorite tree. Indeed, the meager processing power of Lily's brain was wholly consumed by sampling the mysterious scents wafting up from the damp earth, for this was also the favorite tree of every other dog in the neighborhood.

Something was nagging at the edge of her senses, though.

"C'mon, Lily! Hurry up!"

Lily turned her head. The annoying distraction was coming from the person at the other end of her leash, someone with sockless feet jammed into worn, black loafers. Above bare ankles, a pair of pajama-clad legs disappeared into a rumpled raincoat. She saw there was an arm holding an umbrella, too, and under the umbrella, a stubbly, forty-something face topped by thinning black hair. Lily decided that the face did not look happy.

"Ah!" she thought. "That would be Frank." Relieved that the distraction could be ignored, Lily returned to the important work at hand.

"*C'mon, Lily!*" the voice said again.

The fact that Frank's face was unhappy was unremarkable. Even in pleasant weather, Frank tended to dwell pointlessly on the minor miseries of his life. Not long ago, those miseries had become much less minor when his mother Doreen entered a retirement home. After helping her move in, Frank took a deep breath and prepared to leave. No use dragging things out, he thought. Transitions are difficult and best dealt with quickly.

Still, it was sad. His mother was standing by the doorway of her new apartment, lower lip a-tremble and Lily held tightly in her arms. It was clear that she was rapidly nearing her emotional limits. Better hurry up.

"Well, Mom," he said, "I guess I'll be leaving now."

Then it happened. With a lunge, Doreen thrust Lily into Frank's arms. He stepped back with surprise into the hallway, too horrified to allow himself to grasp the obvious, while struggling to maintain his grip on the suddenly manic animal.

"The home doesn't allow pets," his mother blurted. "I could never have signed the lease if I hadn't known that Lily would be safe with you. Now don't you worry; I've made you her legal guardian, so it's all set. Now go! Get out of here, before I change my mind."

Frank desperately wanted her to change her mind. But his mother had already shut the door in his astonished face. He stared blankly at it as the enormity of his plight sank in. Now what? Lily was just three years old, and acknowledged his existence only by barking. He heard his mother sobbing piteously on the other side of the door. He felt like crying, too.

That had been two long, loud months ago. Only recently had he progressed from the denial stage to active mourning.

"*Come on!*" Frank hissed. At last, Lily turned away from her tree. She looked up at him reproachfully, and barked.

"Okay, okay," Frank said, fumbling in his pocket. He held a dog treat up for Lily to see. "*Okay?*"

Satisfied that her efforts would not go unrewarded, Lily began looking for just the right place to do what finally needed to be done. At last, she squatted, looking blankly ahead. Frank sighed with relief.

A blue plastic bag inverted over his free hand, Frank scooped up Lily's grudging gift. He handed over the treat, jerking back with his fingers barely intact.

Isn't that just the story of my life? he thought bleakly as Lily happily consumed her treat. Every day I give her a cookie, and every day she gives me a bag of shit.

Trudging home through the rain, Frank reflected that his day generally went downhill from here.

* * *

Lily shook herself mightily inside the foyer of Frank's dingy apartment house, wetting what little of Frank that was still dry. Satisfied, she planted her substantial hindquarters firmly on the floor, looked up at Frank, and barked. Frank sighed, picked up the still-wet dog, and labored his way up the stairs to his second floor flat.

As he climbed to the top, Frank's rising eyes met a pair of fuzzy pink slippers, a floral house dress, and then a pair of folded arms draped with a bath towel. Just above them, he knew, would be the perpetually hostile face of his across-the-hall neighbor. As that scowling visage hove into view, Frank once again noted the uncanny resemblance his neighbor bore to North Korean president Jong Kim-Lo. Only with hair curlers.

"Morning, Mrs. Foomjoy," Frank offered as Lily twisted wildly in his arms. He deposited the dog at her feet.

"Shame on you!" Mrs. Foomjoy barked as she knelt to massage Lily with the bath towel. "Poor, dear wet baby!" she crooned.

"It's raining, Mrs. Foomjoy," Frank observed. "Lily hasn't learned how to use the indoor facilities yet."

"Then why she not wear the lovely rain jacket I give her?" she snorted. "What is *wrong* with you? You don't deserve dog like this!"

Frank couldn't have agreed more. Lily groveled at Mrs. Foomjoy's feet, and then leaned to one side until gravity obligingly rolled her onto her back. The dog gazed up with adoring, goggle eyes as Mrs. Foomjoy rubbed her stomach.

His neighbor grabbed the leash from Frank's hand when she stood up. "I see to welfare of this dog!" she snapped, shutting her door loudly behind her. Frank stood suddenly alone in the poorly lit hallway, a warm, blue plastic pendulum swinging slowly from side to side in his hand. Relieved, he entered his own apartment and quietly shut the door.

Frank hung his dripping raincoat on a hook in the linoleum floored hallway inside. At one time, his apartment's décor might have charitably been described as "Late-Twentieth-Century Divorced Middle Aged Male." Now the most obvious theme was random clutter. He poured a cup of coffee and sat at the small table in the small kitchen. Before him the large screen of his laptop stared blankly back at him. With resignation, he turned the computer on.

Normally, the sound of a computer booting up would have struck him as cheerful; the imperceptibly soft whir of the cooling fan spinning up to speed; the blinking, blue light that assured him that the device was powering up; the screen phosphorescing into life with a pearly glow. After all, information technology – IT – was not only his profession, but the primary foundation of his existence.

Email was Frank's preferred link to the outside world, providing a social firewall between him and the random messiness of direct human contact. Frank was convinced that digital relations were far safer than their in-person analogue. Electronic communications brought him as close to his fellow man as he usually wished to be. Any more intimate than that, and things were apt to become at best unpredictable, and at worst, well, he'd been *there* all too often before. You never got enough time to think before things started spiraling out of control.

Which brought him back to the night before. Be honest, he mused ruefully. You got what you deserved. Or didn't get what you didn't deserve, to be more precise.

He stared at the keyboard. Should he check his email or shouldn't he? The rational side of his brain said, yes, what's there is there. Deal with it.

But the other side of his brain had a different opinion: "Go back to bed," it whispered urgently, "It's Sunday. You don't have to deal with anything today."

That was true. And who knows what might happen by Monday? There could be a typhoon tonight. Or maybe giant pterodactyls would erupt from a wormhole next to the Lincoln Memorial, scattering screaming tourists towards the safety of nearby Metro stations. That side of his brain was lobbying strongly to take two aspirin, pull the covers back over his head, and let reality take care of itself for another twenty-four hours.

He sighed and made up his mind. Might as well see sooner rather than later what people from his office had posted on line about the night before. A few clicks later and he was at the Facebook page of Mary, the sullen receptionist. Yes, there were pictures from the party. Lots of them. Later would do just fine after all, he decided. He snapped the laptop shut without turning it off.

The sad thing was, for once he had actually been looking forward to the Library of Congress IT Department Holiday party, even bringing his daughter Marla with him, a Georgetown University grad student. He appreciated the great impression she always made on his co-workers. Unlike her dad, Marla was self-assured and sociable. She worked the crowd like a pro, chatting and shaking hands, poised and laughing. How could he feel anything but proud? It was hard not to drink a bit more than usual as he watched her from the security of the bar in the rear of the function room.

More to the point, Frank had been looking forward to making Marla feel proud of her old man as well. Everyone knew that George Marchand, the Director of IT at the LoC, was going to announce his choice to head an important security initiative mandated by the Cybersecurity Subcommittee of the House Committee on Science and Technology. Frank figured he had the spot all sewn up. After all, he was – or at least at one time had been – a recognized cybersecurity innovator; a McArthur Foundation "Genius" Award recipient, no less, in recognition of his widely acclaimed creative work in the early days of computer networking.

So when George stood up and tapped on his glass, Frank sat up straighter. He listened impatiently as his boss welcomed the spouses, thanked the staff for their work that year, and told a joke at his own expense. At last, he began to make the announcement that Frank was waiting for.

And then it happened. One moment Frank was looking sideways to see the reaction on his daughter's face when his name was called, and the next he was hearing someone else's name ring out instead. And not just any name, but Rick Wellesley's – "only out for himself" Rick, a self-satisfied slug of a middle-manager who had never had a creative thought in his life. Someone who had even briefly reported to Frank when he first came to work at the LoC. *Rick Wellesley?* How could this be happening?

But it was. There was Rick, standing and basking in the applause, glancing briefly and triumphantly in Frank's direction. Frank was stunned, his face burning. And then he was angry. Without a word to his daughter, he stood up and marched to the bar, turning his back on the party as George finished his remarks. Knocking back another drink, Frank now felt foolish as well as angry. Everyone was probably looking at him, but he was afraid to turn around and find out. He sulked at the bar until Marla came looking for him.

Sitting now in his kitchen, Frank felt his face grow flush again. After all, everyone had expected the job to go to him. Then, with a wrenching feeling, he had a worse thought – what if no one had expected him to get the job? Maybe he was the only one in the whole damn department who hadn't seen it coming. Maybe everyone had been laughing up their sleeves as they watched him bask in his expected glory, just waiting for his jaw to drop when he realized that he had been skunked by Rick.

Of course that had been the case, he thought wretchedly. He was sure of it.

* * *

And why not? What had he really done in the last twenty years? Sure, he'd become a star at the Massachusetts Institute of Technology – "MIT" to anyone in the know. He'd enrolled at the age of sixteen after skipping two years of middle school. Not that skipping a few grades was unusual at MIT. As an undergraduate, he'd become part of Project Athena, an ambitious effort to create a distributed computing system for the whole university. Of course, the goal for the project's corporate sponsors was to use MIT as a testbed. Later, they hoped to productize the design and make a ton of money.

For some reason, Frank had intuitively locked onto the security challenges that such a system would present. He already had privileges to use MIT's gateway to the government-funded Advanced Research Projects Agency Network – the now-famous "ARPANET" that was the precursor to the Internet. Only select institutions had access to it then, but Frank immediately grasped where Project Athena and the ARPANET together could eventually lead. It hit him between the eyes that this was the start of something big. Linking terminals together around a campus was today's goal, but the next step would be to connect those networks together, using ARPANET technology.

That sounded awesome, but how would you restrict access to any particular data to one person, and not let it be seen by everyone else? MIT was already a hotbed of hackers. If students were going to great lengths now to break into restricted sections of university computers just for fun, what would criminals, or enemy countries, not do to break into classified computers, once someone had linked them all together? Frank tackled that issue with gusto, if not discipline. He was a big picture guy, and what a big and exciting picture it was! The idea of wide area networks was brand new, and big ideas were needed to make sense of it all; the details could come later. When Frank graduated, he stayed on at MIT, nominally in a PhD program, but for all practical purposes he lived at a terminal in the Project Athena lab, surviving on coffee and code like so many other young computer engineering students back in the day.

Luckily for Frank, he found a mentor – an engineer on loan from one of the sponsoring companies. Surprisingly, the two hit it off, and the older man reined in the younger one enough to keep Frank's ideas from flying off into too many directions at once. He also insisted that Frank get his best ideas recorded in some sort of coherent order. Often they talked until all hours, the older man channeling Frank's enthusiasm and helping him follow his insights down the most productive paths.

Frank never completed his doctorate, but he did finish his Masters thesis – and by anyone's account, it was brilliant. He anticipated just about every security challenge that would arise over the next twenty years as the Internet took off. He also suggested most of the solutions that were later refined and implemented to deal with a massively networked world. Even today, his thesis remained an obligatory foundational reference in just about every new network and Internet security paper that was written.

Frank's thesis also brought him to the notice of the mysterious keepers of the MacArthur Fellows Program – the unknown judges that every year contact a select group of exceptional individuals they have decided, "show exceptional merit and promise for continued and enhanced creative work."

Receiving a MacArthur Fellowship had been the high point of Frank's professional career. But as a practical matter, it also brought an end to it, because the payments of $25,000 every three months for five years gave him the freedom to do whatever he wanted to without ever having to acquire the discipline of making his way in the world. It also allowed him to get married.

It was not helpful that what Frank wanted to do usually changed every other week. It wasn't long before his work at Project Athena suffered. He no longer listened to his mentor, and his assigned tasks no longer got done. Instead, he plunged from one question that intrigued him to another, never getting very far along with any of them.

Like many people whose intellectual abilities matured before their social skills, Frank developed an abrupt and assertive manner that helped mask his discomfort around others. That was unfortunate, because his new–found fame encouraged him to become even more obnoxious than ever. Soon, the other guys in the lab were annoyed with his failure to meet his commitments, and also sick of hearing his latest revelations about security – or about any other topic on which he had decided he was now an expert.

Eventually, it was his mentor who took Frank aside and told him that if he didn't shape up, his days in the lab were numbered. Frank didn't take that well. What right did some middle aged, middle-management type with a degree from a state school in the Midwest have to tell a certified Genius anything about anything?

Quite a lot, Frank now reflected, gazing at his closed laptop. Like the immature idiot he was then, he had cleared his things out of the Project Athena lab the same day his mentor had called him out and never returned. Eventually, the MacArthur Fellowship money ran dry, and with a wife and young daughter, Frank had to get more serious about working. Or at least he should have. For a while, his thesis and MacArthur reputation carried him from job to job. But when the bottom fell out of the economy, employers received a flood of great résumés for every job they posted.

By then, of course, Frank's résumé was also getting pretty long in the tooth. He had no "continued and enhanced creative work" to show for his five years of subsidized, random behavior. He'd never published another paper, and it was others, and not Frank, who turned his thesis ideas into real protocols and products. As the jobs got scarce, reference checks counted a whole lot more, and the feedback about Frank always came back the same: brilliant, arrogant, unfocused, unreliable. That was more charitable than what his soon-to-be ex-wife had to say. But he hadn't listened to her, either.

Frank usually tried not to think much about the years that followed: the start-up that had signed him up as Chief Technical Officer and the VCs that fired him; the time spent without a job at all; the rut he fell into for years after his wife moved out with their daughter, when he said the hell with everything and everybody. That time was a blur of punching the clock in whatever high school, small business or municipal IT department would take him on until he got fired again, then waiting until his unemployment ran out before finding something else he could do in his sleep, until even that became too much to bother with.

Through all that time, though, industry insiders still sought Frank out, so he maintained a low-key consulting business on the side to make sure he could always cover his child support payments. Among the elite in the world of security, Frank still had the reputation of a wizard, able to come up with the kind of insights that would make the most impenetrable problems suddenly transparent. An emailed plea for help describing something dense and dark that had already defied all of the usual solutions would reliably generate a response from Frank an hour or two later, usually beginning, "It strikes me that..." and ending with, "I suggest you try...." Invariably, what Frank suggested worked. But requests for his ongoing assistance went unanswered.

It was his daughter Marla that finally set Frank back on his feet. One Friday when he was once again out of work, he picked her up for their weekend together. But something was wrong; his normally chatty preteen wasn't saying a word. As they walked, she looked down at her feet. Then she looked up as if to ask him a question, only to look down again. After a while, Frank got irritated. "Marla, if there's something you want to ask me, just ask it already!"

But Marla still paused. Finally she said, "Dad, you know I'm in a computer class now, don't you? It's something you have to take in seventh grade."

"Yes," he said, surprised. "So?"

"Well," she said, and stopped. He waited, now curious.

"Well," she started again, "today we went on a field trip to the computer department of a big company, and we all had to sign in and wear these name tag things. One of the people that worked there gave us a tour, and when she saw my name, she asked if I had a father named Frank, so of course I said yes."

"Uh huh," said Frank, not liking where this was going.

"Well..." Marla paused again, and then the words came rushing out. "She said that she went to school with you and you were the most brilliant person she had ever known and that you'd gotten a big award for being a genius and she wanted to know what you were doing now." Marla stopped abruptly for a long moment. "And I didn't know what to say."

Frank wished this could be all over, and quickly.

But, Marla, of course, needed an answer. "Dad, the guide said you used to be somebody really important."

Frank felt like he was dangling at the end of a rope, turning slowly in the breeze. He looked away, and tried to think what to say. What *could* he say? And then, with all of the disarming innocence of a child, Marla finished for him.

"Dad, she wasn't telling the truth, was she?"

Frank couldn't breathe. His daughter thought so little of him that she had to believe that the guide was thinking of someone else? Or was it that she would be too ashamed of what he had become to be able to deal with the truth? He felt sick.

By then, they were standing in front of the door of his cheap apartment building. The traffic rushed past the garbage cans and trash piled up on the curb, and Frank took it all in. The sights, the smells, his life – they all fit together perfectly, didn't they? Still, he couldn't think of a word to say.

Finally, Marla put her hand on his arm. "It's okay, Dad," she said softly. "Let's go upstairs."

That had been ten years ago. The following Monday he sucked it up and called his old mentor, George Marchand, and asked for a job. George was the head of the IT department at the Library of Congress now, and Frank called him out of the blue to ask if they could get together for coffee.

George had been as gracious as Frank had been uncomfortable. Frank had sent his résumé along by email, for what it was worth, and George cut straight to the chase after the opening pleasantries.

"You know I'll need to bring you in at the bottom, Frank. Can you deal with that?"

Frank was prepared. "Sure, sure, George. I'll be fine with that." George nodded, brows furrowed. Then he changed the topic.

"How's that cute goddaughter of mine these days? I can't even remember the last time I saw Marla."

"She's great," said Frank, suddenly determined; it helped to remember why he was sitting there. "Just great. We get together every weekend. She's in seventh grade now. She's smart as a whip and gets straight As."

They chatted about family for a few more minutes, and then George looked at his watch. They both stood up, and shook hands.

"I won't let you down," Frank said as he looked George in the eye for the first time.

"I know you won't," his new boss said. But Frank could tell he was only being polite.

* * *

Sitting in his kitchen, Frank reflected that he'd been as good as his word. But not much better, he made himself admit. Yes, he'd rarely missed a day of work, and no one could say he hadn't earned his paycheck. And yes, he'd earned every promotion he'd been given.

But the promotions had been few, and the last one had been awarded seven years ago. Frank still had tremendous insights into IT architecture, and he remained as interested as ever in new developments in security. His cubicle at the LoC was stacked high with articles covered in scribbled notes, and he read voraciously online as well. For anyone in the office with a thorny problem, Frank was the go-to guy who could always solve it, provided he was allowed to tackle it alone. Sitting at a keyboard, Frank was still The Man – the tougher the problem the better, just bring it on.

Three hours, eight hours or twenty hours later, he'd still be turning it over in his mind until suddenly an elegant and creative solution would spring to mind.

Management level work, though, was something else again. Every time George gave him a shot at a long term project with a couple of others to supervise, Frank could never pull it all together.

Half the time, he'd be up in the clouds thinking big thoughts that went beyond the task at hand, and the rest of the time he'd be down in the weeds, diving down rat holes to solve problems that could easily be ignored. The folks he was supposed to be supervising never knew what they would be doing from one day to the next, or what, if anything, Frank did with the work they submitted. Inevitably, George would have to take the project back. It didn't take long before the big projects stopped coming, and Frank settled into the solitary niche where he had stayed ever since.

He wasn't done beating himself up, though. Admit it, he demanded, you were relieved when the projects stopped coming. You've been marking time for years now, and that's all you'll ever do. What right did you have to think George would throw this project your way?

But this had been a *security* project, damn it. That (and the drinks he'd had last night) were what had led him to corner George later on in the cloakroom.

"I'm sorry, Frank," George had said, wrapping his scarf around his neck. "I thought about letting you know ahead of time, and then I didn't. I guess I should have."

"That's not the point, George! Rick can't find his own ass with both hands in a well-lit room. What were you thinking?"

George buttoned his overcoat, and reached for his hat. "Of course Rick can't hold a candle to you when it comes to security, Frank. There's nobody I've ever worked with who has the insight and ideas that you do. And everybody knows nobody covers his butt like Rick."

Frank let his breath out with a rush of exasperation as George settled his hat on his head. "So then why did you pick him?"

George squared off to Frank as he pulled on his gloves, looking him straight in the eye.

"Frank, you may know security, but when it comes to understanding people and how to manage them, you haven't got a clue. Yes, Rick is one hell of a weasel. But you can always rely on a weasel to watch out for himself. That means that if you give him a job to do and tell him his job is on the line, well, by hook or by crook, he'll get it done. And I can't say that about you."

Well, what could Frank say to that? He'd asked George for an explanation and now he'd have to listen to it.

"How many chances have I given you over the years, Frank? I can't remember, can you?" Frank looked away.

"You're twice as smart as I am," George continued. "You should have had my job by now! But that's never going to happen unless you grow up and learn how to perform. If you thought I'd stick my neck out for you with Chairman Steele grandstanding in the House, looking for the next poor bastard to eviscerate in front of the cameras during a public committee meeting, well, you're just delusional. Good night, Frank."

There hadn't been anything Frank could say to that, of course, so he was relieved when George turned and walked away. Furious at himself, Rick and George, in that order, he stalked back to the bar.

Frank decided that was as much of the night before as he was up to reliving; he'd leave the scene with Rick for his next exercise in psychological self-flagellation. It had all escalated so stereotypically anyway; Rick's approach and his smarmy condescension, Frank's insult in response. Okay, enough.

He felt the anger well up again, and with it, a sudden sense of purpose. Screw the jerk; just because Rick got the project didn't mean that Frank couldn't still show him up. After all, Frank had been so sure he had the spot in the bag that he'd already started writing up a proposal with his plan of attack outlined. No way was Rick going to be able to pull this job off; George would realize that soon enough, and then there'd be no one to turn to but Frank.

He snapped open his laptop and punched the keys with fury, rushing through the complicated log-in sequence that would take him into the heart of the LoC's system, where his proposal was archived. Highlighting the file name, he hit the Enter key, leaned back, and waited for the proposal to display.

Except it didn't. Frank leaned forward and poked the Enter key again. Still nothing. Perhaps his laptop was frozen. But no – he could still move his cursor.

Then Frank noticed that something on the screen was changing: the background color was warming up, turning reddish, orange and yellow, as if the sun was rising behind it. Now that was different! Frank watched with growing astonishment as the colors began to shimmer, and then coalesced into shapes that might be flames.

Yes, flames indeed – but not like a holiday screen-saver image of a log fire – this was a real barn-burner of a conflagration!

Frank wondered what kind of weird virus he'd picked up, and how. After all, he was an IT security specialist, and if any laptop was protected six ways to Sunday, it was his. So much for whatever he had planned for today; he'd have to wipe his disk and rebuild his system from the ground up.

He was about to shut the laptop down when he saw that the flames were dying away. Now what? An image seemed to be emerging from behind the flames as they subsided. Frank leaned forward; the image became a tall building – maybe some sort of lighthouse? Underneath, there was a line of text, but in characters he couldn't read. Truly, this was like no virus he'd ever seen or even heard of before. He reached for his cellphone and took a picture of the screen just before it suddenly went blank.

Frank was impressed. Whoever had come up with this hack certainly had a sense of style. A weird one, but hey, graphic art of any type wasn't the long suit of most hackers.

Frank got a pad of paper and a pen from his desk and punched up the file directory again, highlighted his proposal, and pressed the Enter key again. This time, he would watch more closely and take notes.

But all that displayed was a three word message: "File not found."

Frank tried again – no luck. He did a search of the entire directory using the title. Nothing. His proposal was gone.

Now he was alarmed. After all, the directory he was staring at was in the innermost sanctum of the Library of Congress computer system, and the LoC was the greatest library in the world. Within its vast holdings were books that could be found almost nowhere else on earth. Recently, the Library had begun digitizing materials, and then destroying the physical copies. If someone had been able to delete files in the most protected part of the Library's computer system, what else might be missing?

Frank raced through a random sampling of sensitive directories, and then let out a sigh of relief; it was hard to tell for sure, but everything seemed intact. He checked the server logs for the Library's indices, holdings and various other resources; everything appeared to be undisturbed, with no unusual reductions in the amount of data stored.

Frank drummed his fingers on the table in the cramped dinette. How to go about figuring this one out? Then he remembered his cellphone, and sent the picture of the screenshot to his laptop. The picture wasn't great, but once he enlarged it he could tell that the characters were Greek. He cropped the image until just the text remained, then ran it through a multi-script OCR program to turn the picture of the Greek characters into text. Finally, he pasted the text into a translator window. No luck – all he got was a "cannot translate" message.

Frank's fingers started drumming again. He reopened the drop down menu of languages in the translator screen and noticed that another language option was "Ancient Greek." He highlighted that choice and hit Enter. This time, the screen blinked.

Frank looked, and then he blinked, too. But the translation still read the same:

THANK YOU FOR YOUR
CONTRIBUTION
TO THE ALEXANDRIA PROJECT

---

* * *

Order **The Alexandria Project** and the rest of the Frank Adversego series at Amazon or at http://andrew-updegrove.com/books/

To find out about new releases and special offers, sign up for the Friends of Frank newsletter at http://andrew-updegrove.com/newsletter/